# ROOMS FOR VANISHING

# ROOMS
# FOR
# VANISHING

*- A Novel -*

## Stuart Nadler

**DUTTON**

**DUTTON**

An imprint of Penguin Random House LLC
1745 Broadway, New York, NY 10019
penguinrandomhouse.com

DUTTON and the D colophon are registered trademarks of
Penguin Random House LLC.

Book design by Kristin del Rosario

LIBRARY OF CONGRESS CATALOGING-IN-PUBLICATION DATA
Names: Nadler, Stuart, author.
Title: Rooms for vanishing: a novel / Stuart Nadler.
Description: First edition. | New York : Dutton, 2025.
Identifiers: LCCN 2024036906 (print) | LCCN 2024036907 (ebook) |
ISBN 9780593475461 (hardcover) | ISBN 9780593475478 (ebook)
Subjects: LCGFT: Novels.
Classification: LCC PS3614.A385 R66 2025 (print) | LCC PS3614.A385 (ebook) |
DDC 813/.6—dc23/eng/20240816
LC record available at https://lccn.loc.gov/2024036906
LC ebook record available at https://lccn.loc.gov/2024036907

International edition ISBN: 9798217046331

Printed in the United States of America

1st Printing

Title-page art: background © simplf / shutterstock

The authorized representative in the EU for product safety and compliance is
Penguin Random House Ireland, Morrison Chambers, 32 Nassau Street,
Dublin D02 YH68, Ireland, https://eu-contact.penguin.ie.

*For Shamis*

# CONTENTS

# ROOMS FOR VANISHING

# Kindertotenlieder

LONDON, 1979

# SONJA

Oh, I had tried to reach her before. That was never the problem. I was always trying to reach her, to talk with her, to be nearer to her, to experience her visitations more completely, but when I grew close, which I often did, she wasn't there. If anyone ever bothered to ask me what happened then in the darkness as I lay waiting for my child to come home, to return to me, to appear to me as she had in life, I would have told that person the truth, which is that she goes away, she goes, she goes.

As she should have. I never expected otherwise. Not really.

THE truth was that she had been going from the moment she was first here with me. When she was born, she was calm, like a woman in middle age having already been told the terrible news: this is life, beware, no one gets out unscathed. On the morning of her ninth birthday I found her outside in the sun speaking aloud to someone who wasn't there, and when she came inside finally, after an hour of this, she told me it was my mother she was speaking to, my first mother, shot dead beside a train in a forest nine hundred and ninety miles northwest of my house in London, and that my mother had been asking after my well-being, that she had come to talk after all this time among the dead, and my daughter told my mother that she was looking after me, but not for long, others would have to do it soon because she was going too, she said, just like everyone else had. We have no power to stop this rushing off into other heavens, do we?

LATER, I had to ask Anya, did she say anything else, did my mother tell you anything more? This was near Paris, in the small house we went to, a place I could not afford, a place I detested. The old wisdom says that when a child dies, the child dies having known everything, having received all knowledge. During those final months, someone said this to me. It was the case then that people very frequently pulled me aside into strange corners to tell me ghastly things like this. And it was also the case that I found myself asking ghastly things of my child.

For instance, this question, which I asked in the back garden, while bees hovered. They were bees that Anya understood somehow would not sting her but would only sting me. Part of this new wisdom was to understand the amount of suffering a mother had to endure. Did she say anything else, I asked again, and Anya looked to me and said, what was her name, and I said, my mother's name was Fania, and she said, this is a very pretty name Fania, and I said, I remember almost nothing about her but the name, and she said, this is something your mother told me, and I asked her to repeat this, and she said, your mother says you probably remember nothing, that she is a shadow to you.

The opposite of reason is not always the same as a lie: doctors had given Anya medicine, and the medicine was making her hallucinate, and the combination of the medicine and the hallucinations was making her talk about my dead mother. This is what Franz was always reminding me, that the drugs had powerful consequences, but I hated Franz very much then, and I did not care for the truth.

Everyone after all was dying everywhere and I was not dying anywhere but there in the garden, in the city's heat. I dressed as if I were mourning months before I needed to, and I never stopped.

There are separate rooms, Anya said, when I pressed her to describe how it was she got to talk to my mother. Separate rooms, like separate trains. I am on one side of the wall, you are on the other side of the wall. I am on one train, you are on the other train. What don't you get, Mama? Separate rooms, separate trains.

The day before, Anya and I had played hide-and-seek, and when she could not find me, when she grew too tired to keep looking, I said, I am on one side of the wall, you are on the other side of the wall.

Move through the wall, Anya had said. Move through the wall, Mama.

And I told her: It doesn't work that way.

Close your eyes, she said, and move through the wall, Mama. Just try. It's not that hard. Fania does it all the time.

She goes, she goes, she goes.

THE last trace of living I saw in her, we were holding her, passing her between us as if this was what she needed, what was prescribed to her by doctors, to be moved between her parents, shared in love, offered our silent benedictions, when in fact it was us who needed the holy intercession. A mirror of her birth, all of us in this room holding her. In the moments immediately after, we were visited by a profound quiet, an absence of all sound, and I am sure this was the noise of her passing over.

Are you in there, Franz asked her at some point, or have you gone already? We were young. It was late, and July. She had come as a surprise. We were students. Very much unprepared to become parents. After it was over—really over—he stood over her body. I do not believe it, he said. I refuse to believe any of this is possible.

ALL of this is embarrassing to admit. All this business of anticipating the dead, putting one's ear against a wall and expecting voices. I was always in the process of embarrassing myself, or revealing to myself some new territory of embarrassment that I had not yet discovered. It was, others had told me, a problem of sensitivity, a problem of the times, a consequence of my personal history. I go back to these moments, if only to remind myself of what happened and what did not.

And what happened was this: my husband had gone missing. It had been days. Two days, three days; I had not slept, and it had become difficult to judge the time. He was a conductor of an orchestra here in London. Not one of the very famous ones, or even one of the very good ones, but one successful enough that he occasionally appeared on television looking appropriately bewildered, or in the pages of the various newspapers whose readers cared about the obsolete arts. He'd been at the concert hall the last I knew. It had been an ordinary evening. He'd left before supper, as always, already in his dress slacks. A car came to retrieve him. Near eight, I listened to him on the radio, which was something I used to like to do.

Our last moments together were rushed. I took him by the shoulders. We'd suffered an unsettling encounter recently and I thought he might want me to come with him, if only to try to forget about it all for a few hours. This encounter was all we'd talked about lately. But I am getting ahead of myself.

He didn't want me to come. You'll hate it, he said, meaning the concert, the music he was conducting, the graveyard air of the concert hall.

That last day, Franz seemed taller, I thought. He was always physically very lovely, even when he was young and stupid. You have been good to me, he said. Well, you are very easy to please, I told him, I can always tell when you are unhappy.

I thought I was telling the truth when I said this. I'd always believed I knew him better than I did.

He put his hands against my cheeks and kissed me and then he was gone.

When he did not return by his normal time that night, I figured it was because there was some official dinner or event I had forgotten about. It was autumn, the beginning of the season, and this was not uncommon. I'd long stopped paying close attention to the endless cycle of benefactors and begging that attended his job. When he was not there in the morning, I thought I must have slept through his arrival and his leaving, his coming and going.

By that afternoon, it was obvious something terrible had happened. His assistant, Jonathan, called to ask whether I had seen him. He had not come to work. The players were waiting. We think maybe he's confused his schedule, Jonathan said. Maybe he thinks we are meeting in Fulham, he told me, which was where the orchestra occasionally rehearsed, but we went to Fulham and we couldn't find him. He has not been himself lately, Jonathan admitted, which hurt me to hear. I'd thought Franz would have been able to hide himself from his colleagues.

Do you have any idea of what might have happened, or where he might be? Jonathan asked.

I was in our kitchen. This was Stamford Hill, Dunsmure Road, a Tuesday morning in October. Out the back window children were playing a game in which one of them was a monster and the others were competing to tame the monster. Each of them got to take turns being the tamer and then the untamed. For years, they had played this identical game every morning, even as they aged. It fascinated me how badly each of them wanted to be the wild creature, the one the others had to struggle to contain.

Across the line Jonathan was telling me that they'd sent someone around in a car in Knightsbridge hoping to find him on the street, or maybe in Hyde Park. This same car had already searched Westminster and Chelsea and Kensington. If I heard anything, he said, would I ring them as soon as possible? We're all very worried, he said. For good measure, he repeated himself. Very worried. Many of his belongings are still here, Jonathan wanted me to know. His coat, for example. And his shoes. I'm looking right at them, he said. He left them on his desk. He's even left his wallet behind. It's right here in my hand. It doesn't seem good, he said.

By then, I had stopped listening. On our kitchen table, I'd found what Franz had left me. It was a photograph of a woman standing in the center of a church. She was maybe eighteen years old. There was nothing else. No farewell note. No explanation. This was his farewell: this picture, which would come to mean so much. He was gone. I almost said this to Jonathan, as a way to tell him don't bother looking any further. Or better yet, to say the truth:

I'll have to go. I'll have to go get him myself.

IT was Franz's idea to go to Paris at the end, which is another way of saying that it was a terrible idea. Perhaps also: the beginning of my hating him very deeply, and simultaneously needing him as much, the combination of which eventually became ruinous and dejecting. Like all good poisons, one doesn't recognize the poisoning until far too late. A doctor at Gustave Roussy had promised a treatment unavailable to British doctors. I did not want to go. I did not believe in the doctor. I did not believe that the promise was real. I had no interest in traveling to France. We could not afford any of the treatment, nor could we afford the travel, or the house in Neuilly-sur-Seine with the garden where we ended up living. Franz had convinced me we were doing the right thing by trying the doctor there. England had failed us and here is hope, he said. Here is a possibility. Here is a chance at another life, he said. Among the very stupid things he said then, it is perhaps worthwhile to point out that this sentence did not alarm me when I heard it.

Franz did a great deal of convincing then. Or to put it better: I made a long series of mistakes in allowing him to convince me of anything. He convinced me to come with him, to stay there for the weeks it took to exhaust all hope, and after she died there, he convinced me to bury her not far away, in Bagneux, in a perfectly pleasant graveyard in a place an entire life away from my life. Yes, it was a far distance, Franz said, a terribly far distance from the two of us, but it was important I remember that when the Messiah arrived, and the prophet Elijah blew his shofar, all the mountains on earth would split in two and the dead would be returned to earth.

On her deathbed, Anya reached up at one point to be lifted into the air so that she could see the flowers in our garden. She believed in some way she had planted the garden herself, although this was, for countless reasons, impossible, not least among them that we had been there only a month, and that for quite a long time she had not been strong enough to walk. At all hours, birds descended in the yard to roost in the branches of the apple trees. It was Franz who told me once that a common mist crow, such as the kind we used to see in the trees in London, and which, on occasion, descended there in the backyard, with light on the hood of their heads as if they, too, were pilgrims, could not only remember the face of someone who wanted to attack them, but would transmit the memory of this face to their offspring, and that this offspring would do the same, onward into time, forward into history.

If only Jews knew to do this, I remember him saying.

I'd like to believe that this bit about the crows was true, just as I would like to believe everything that Franz ever told me was true, such as the reason for our moving Anya to this place, and the reason we left her there. When he told me about the prophet Elijah, and the imminence of the Messiah, I exploded in rage.

Although the greatest rage I reserved for my own sense of submission. We went. I went. Franz went. Anya went. And only two of us returned.

THE day we buried her, I began to hallucinate in the heat, and I became convinced, after weeks of sleeplessness and grief-induced catatonia, that those around me that morning—all of them players in various orchestras Franz had conducted, variously insufferable Englishmen and -women, a good deal of them religious afflicted, not one of them a friend of mine—were members of my family, long-dead ancestors, the grandmother of my grandmother, for instance, everyone delivered from wherever it was they had been living all this time, on whatever near-earth, to stand beside me, to offer ancient solidarities I did not understand. This was ten years ago now, and I have retained no real memory of the service, or of the ride back that afternoon to our rented home, nor do I remember anything of the train we took back to England later that week, under passports that still felt to me like a kind of false identity: me in the picture, but a different me, a sister I had never met, a version of my lost mother beaming back at me. What I do remember, and continued to re-member long after we returned, was the feeling of everyone around me that day, so many of my mothers, and my grandmothers, the chorus of their crying married to my crying, my baby in the earth just as their baby was in the earth, a part of them in the earth just as a part of me was in the earth. And I remember waking my first morning in London, in the house where Anya had lived all her life, and discovering a letter folded neatly on my nightstand written very obviously by Franz, in which he pretended he was one of these same ancestors, writing to assure me of the comforts of perpetual life or some other rank idiocy. *Dear Sonja,* his letter began, *I write to you from the world to come.* He thought somehow that this might make me feel better. He was always confusing the bottomlessness of mourning for something larger and more foolish.

That first morning back home, I rose and burned his letter in the kitchen sink with a cigarette lighter while he watched from steps away, eating his breakfast.

If you ever do this again, I said, I will burn you down.

He tried to play it off, or to play the fool, and so I took his newspaper and burned it.

I repeated myself: I will burn you down.

This was the atmosphere into which I returned home: Franz was the sensible and generous one, and I was the one lighting our life on fire. I would think of this later, after Franz began to come apart into pieces.

JONATHAN arrived late in the morning. He came in a hired car, wearing camel hair, appearing unwashed, briefly discussing the possibility of morning cocktails to fortify our courage. Don't worry at all, he was telling me, do not worry one bit, even though it was obvious he was the one worrying. I had known Jonathan since he was a boy brought to the orchestra by his mother, a woman generally mystified by her child's affection for all this music of the dead empire, and for his wild desire to be close to people who shared this affection. When he was younger, and we were all younger, we used to joke that he was our first child, such was his attachment to Franz—a joke that made his actual mother hate us deeply, even as it thrilled Jonathan. He was in his twenties now. His mother had moved with her sister to a house in the north, and when she came back to London, she made a point to let us know that she felt revulsion toward us, and that we had ruined her son, that before our arrival in his life he had been a normal boy, a football fan, a lover of rock music, a devotee of various television programmes, and look at him now, she said to me once, look at him suffering over the whims of a subpar conductor, delivering coffee, pressing slacks, yammering on about dead Austrians. What sort of life is this?

I had to agree. What sort of life indeed.

Jonathan wanted to know if he could look around the house. Could he inspect our car, he asked, even though we didn't use the car anymore. Both of us were awful drivers. We'd bought it mainly to make our daily trips to hospital more manageable, and when we were finished with hospital, we were, it turned out, finished with the car. When I told him all of this, we were standing in the front room, near the piano, which was another object neither of us ever used anymore, not since Anya, and this was when Jonathan asked whether I thought Franz might have died. I've been having awful thoughts about him, he said.

This makes two of us, I said.

Don't joke, he said.

He's not dead, I told Jonathan.

Do you know this for sure? he asked. It seems like the news can't be good.

I feel confident that he hasn't died, I said. Trust me. If he wandered off somewhere to die, he'd have issued me an invitation to watch.

Is that supposed to be funny? he asked. Should I be laughing right now?

Jonathan had lived a cosseted life. A life without any personal loss. What this meant was that any hint of darkness getting close opened something enormous and threatening in him. He thought of it sometimes as a noise, this feeling, something coming out of the walls and promising to grab hold of him. He'd said this to me once. I feel it rushing toward me sometimes, he said, and when I asked what he did when he felt this, he told me he sometimes closed his eyes, or he turned on music very loudly, the most beautiful music he could think of, and eventually everything brightened again.

He went to inspect the piano. I'd let it fall out of tune. I liked it better this way, I said. He plunked a few very bright notes and winced at the way it sounded, and also at the thick layer of dust that we had allowed to settle atop its lid. I had started to think of the dust like the curtains of ash that fall on villages wiped out entirely by volcanic eruptions. I had begun to think of our whole house in this way, in fact, as a tomb for something better, something more vital, some collection of oddities and arcana that an enterprising future civilization would thrill to unearth.

Jonathan wanted to know if Franz had also been acting strange at home. Because at the office, he said, he's been very odd. When I asked whether he could describe this oddness, Jonathan fell quiet and began, I think, to cry. He turned around toward the window, where the children were playing on Dunsmure Road, pretending to be wolves, howling at the traffic. He had his eyes closed. No, I told him. Please don't do this. Please don't cry in my home. Not for Franz.

I thought to tell him the truth, but the truth, at least as I understood it then, was absurd. And telling anyone an absurd truth had always seemed to me a way of doubling the absurdity. What could I tell him? That my husband had come apart into pieces of himself? That he had begun to see the world as a baby does, as an unreal tapestry of images that threatened to vanish if one looked away? Yes, he was acting strange at home. Obviously, he was acting strange. So was I. How does anyone really ever act normal?

We moved into the kitchen. I think I offered to make him tea. I think also that we began to drink quite heavily. He really was a sweet boy. A terrible musician, even worse than me—which is saying quite a lot—but a sweet boy nonetheless. He had been good to Franz, even when Franz did not deserve it. I told him this. His mother was right. He could have been a good dentist. His teeth were especially well cared for.

Behind us, in a drawer, was the photo of the woman in the church. I could have very easily taken it out and explained that this was all Franz had left behind, but saying it out loud would have shamed me. An entire life together and this was all he'd left for me. Instead, I hugged Jonathan. I should say here that I had lived thirty-five years as a British woman, and before that, five years as an

Austrian, and I did not hug, not ever, especially not people to whom I was not related. Problematically, my hugging him seemed to make Jonathan want to reassess this issue of our relations.

You know, I consider you two my parents, he said. If something terrible happened, I'd grieve you both like my own mother.

But you have parents, I told him. You have a mother.

Not really, he said. Not in any real way.

Yes, you do, I said. Don't be an idiot.

WHAT Anya said of my mother: You probably remember nothing.

Put the photographs of a thousand strangers before me and, yes, I would not be able to tell which was my mother, this is true. What I held, I held uncertainly. For instance, I remembered only a piece of our last conversation. I had, I liked to think, a memory of the skin on her hands being quite rough. I had also a half-constructed idea of the sound of her voice, but that was likely unreal, likely the product of my having spent too much time leaning my ear against the wall of whatever earth lay beside our earth, which was where Anya had said my mother lived now, in separate rooms, this was where I might find her walking and talking and singing and breathing and cursing all these different futures. At least this is what Anya would have had me believe.

Franz, it turned out, was not the only person to spend so much time building a series of imaginary futures. When I did this, when I pressed my ear against the wall of this other room, I had the thought that everyone else was doing this too, that my mother and my father were pushing their own ears against the walls of the dead, that they were listening for whatever heartbeat travels by way of the living, and I thought, maybe, maybe, it was possible Moses was doing this too, maybe they were all writing to me as I am writing to them: sweet Moses; how would he ever even remember us?

I'D come to London at five. This was on a train from Vienna filled with other children. A great deal of my memory begins with this train. My mother did not come to see me go. She remained at home with Moses. Instead, my father took me. We went in the morning, and an hour later, two hours later, one whole life later, he picked me up by the elbows and put me and my doll through the open maw.

My last memory of Papa: Do not speak to anyone, he says, do not fall asleep, do not under any circumstances say anything in Yiddish, remember what happened to your cousins, give no one your memories, read your children poetry before bed, take care to hold your breath over bridges, remember what happened to your aunts, beware of poisoned water, take care to put your family photographs at the bottom of your suitcase if in the future you have to flee, remember what happened to your grandfather and his sisters, take care to pray but only when you are alone and only when you cross borders, find me when you can, remember me, remember your mother, remember your brother, Moses, may our memories bless you into a million futures.

At the other end of the train, I was retrieved by a man called Alfred Smithson and his wife, Sydney, in whose house in Finchley I lived until I turned seventeen. My bedroom was on the top storey, in an attic room, beneath a rooflight that offered views of Alpine cloud formations, migratory bird paths, children's kites tangled in the thicket of the plane trees that Alfred had planted. The night I came to live with them, Alfred told me it was good to have a room where one could see a way out. In case you are wondering, this window faces south, he told me that first night, which was his way of telling me that it did not face east to Vienna, where he thought I might find myself looking for people. Das ist nicht ost, he said, in bad German. This way is south, he kept saying, this is not east, this is not east, this is not east. If you look out there thinking you are looking home, you'll be looking to the Mediterranean, to Greece, to India, to the South Pole where the penguins live, where everything is ice. You understand, right? You understand what I'm saying, don't you?

I did, of course, even though he was speaking to me as if I had never heard the sound of a human voice before. But was I really looking?

WHAT official information I had I gathered in pieces. For instance, that they were dead. When I was twelve years old, a woman at the War Office told me this in perfect Oxford English, which made it seem like I'd heard it by way of the BBC. And how much more official does news get than that? They are dead. How else to say it? This is what the woman said to me. Dead, she said. Toten, she said, as if in German it would make better sense. Although, in German, the word she used means *kill*, not *dead*.

I leaned forward across the counter to hear her say it again. And to see if this was true even of my brother. He was a baby, I said. Him too?

This is what I'm trying to tell you, she said. They are all dead, dear. Start the story wherever you want, the ending will always be the same.

I asked her to say it again, and she said it louder. Tot. Tot. Tot. The story is the same backwards and forwards, love.

I went to the War Office because a friend had told me I could go there, to the building in Whitehall, and wait in line and fill out a form with the names of my parents and siblings and that the clerks there would give me whatever information was available. We were on a bus headed to our piano lessons when my friend said this to me, and for years afterward I imagined this was where my family was living, where they were waiting for me to come get them. They were all on the other side of the building's large windows, I thought, overlooking the statue of Spencer Compton, eighth Duke of Devonshire, a bearded bronzed man in a cape. When I finally went, I skipped school to go. I had memorized the train line. I filled out the form. I spent hours on a wooden bench waiting for my name to be called. Outside, the new birch trees had gone bare. This building was bombed once, someone told me. Did you know that? Bombed by aeroplane. Elsewhere, a girl walked by pushing a doll in a toy pram. Here we are in the War Office, she sang, here we are, child, in the War Office, here we are, little baby, in the big War Office, and she looked straight to me and asked, do you want to hug my baby doll?

A memory returned: on the train from Vienna, a girl traveling with us became very sick and eventually died somewhere outside Saint-Denis. I remember we were in Saint-Denis because medics came on board and they had to take the girl away, and in my confusion I thought this was her name, Denise. She was not yet dead, but quite ill, and crying for her mama. I felt terrible to see this, she was very small, her lips and mouth had become a bright red from her illness, and as the medics took her off the train, I gave her my doll to have. I had just been given this doll by my own mother. On the train, I talked to it endlessly. When the medics were taking the girl away, I remember saying to the girl, you can talk to it, she will keep your secrets.

In return for giving away my doll, one of our minders on the train gave me a blank journal to have. Not exactly a fair exchange, but the counselor told me I could put my own secrets into it. I would like to think that I knew already that I would never become the sort of woman who wrote in a diary. A secret always needs a strange ear, or else the secret loses its power and it dies. The page is no substitute. Instead, what I did was write out the names of my family, all of them, Arnold and Fania and Moses, as if they were not Papa and Mama and baby brother, but as if they were business acquaintances of mine.

When I went to the War Office for my family, this is what I brought with me, this empty book. All that time, and I'd put nothing in it but these names, and when I left that day I put into it the piece of paper I was given, onto which a clerk had written that my family was dead, all of them were, Moses was dead and Papa was dead and Mama was dead.

How else to say it: start the story wherever you want, the ending will always be the same.

Do you understand? the clerk asked.

I don't know if I do, I said.

She said it again. Tot, tot, tot.

Do you understand? the clerk asked.

I'm still not sure I do, I said. My brother, I said, he was very small.

I could come back, the clerk told me, a week later, a month later, a year later, and I could receive the official report, which would include, she told me, all the extant information available to the Crown. I can't remember precisely what she said after this, or when exactly I returned. Perhaps Spencer Compton, the eighth Duke of Devonshire, remembers exactly when I went again to get the information: deportation records; transport routes; the names of the officials in charge; the exact date Mama was killed; the exact hour in summer Papa was killed; the exact moment Moses was killed. I also received a mimeographed attestation submitted to the incipient Israeli government by a former neighbour of ours in which I learned that the soldier who took my family was a nineteen-year-old with red hair and a port-wine stain on his face, and this man was incensed apparently by the fact that one of the stairs in our house was broken. *I heard this man through the walls of our apartment*, the neighbour wrote.

This odd piece of information, left among all the bones.

*I heard him through the walls of our apartment.* Different rooms, different trains.

Whenever it was I returned, I left all this on the desk in the War

Office—the official documents, the death records, the attestation from my neighbour.

When I turned to leave, the same clerk bellowed after me.

You've left your book! she yelled. You've left your book and your information!

The clerk was holding it in the air. How are you going to remember all this? she asked.

FRANZ had vanished, but it was also impossible for him to get far from me.

At the end of a long day of looking, I did find him. Or a version of him, at least. On a small television in his personal office in Knightsbridge I found him flickering on-screen. He was playing a familiar piece, precious music, our daughter's favorite piece of music. At one point, my own favorite piece of music. A piece I associated with my deep past and also the more approachable past, the past I felt at times I might be able to reach out and hold the way one holds any ordinary object—a plain soupspoon, a page of newsprint, a child's shoe. I would tell you what it was, but it is not important. Also, the knowledge is mine. I cannot give you everything.

A small message flashed across the bottom left of the screen to tell me that this performance had been recorded a week earlier. I knew this already. I'd been in the audience. And so I knew what was going to happen. As the piece began to swell, the camera found him coming apart. Soon, he'd start to weep. Lately, this was something that had begun to happen to him.

I did not want to keep watching, but I figured maybe there might be something here to help me. For instance, as the camera came closer, his eyes met the lens, met my eyes. Where are you? he mouthed in German. Where are you?

And in response, I found myself yelling aloud, I'm here. Right here. I'm here. Come find me.

It is important to know that I had only ever been apart from Franz for brief moments. Less than a week combined since we had met as teenagers. I had calculated this once and had come to think that the number was six: before this, I had only been away from Franz six days. A tiny number, obviously, but also, six days was the length of time it took for God to make the world. A number of almost immeasurable briefness, but enough to make another world entirely. Franz had been away from me, of course. There is a difference. He was always leaving, always traveling somewhere to audition some new player, always in rehearsals, only to reappear on the radio, or, as it happened, on public broadcast, in a performance from which I could not detach myself. But I almost never went anywhere. I was always at home, at a permanent remove. The world was not my world, I had decided. It was only mine where I could make it—in our house, at our window, in front of our stereo, with my eyes closed at night, praying for a visitation.

And yet here he was, in this stale office, miles from me and also, somehow, right beside me, with a cigarette lit, his sweat in the room, his breath, the weight of him shifting behind me, saying to me, oh, Sonja, look at this ridiculous man on the television waving his arms around like a lunatic, do you see that man in his tuxedo about to weep like a child, where did he come from, what happened to the old me? He was, in this way, so close I could sense his body coming and going, and, some months after this, ultimately leaving me altogether. What I want to say is that I had been near him, with him, around him, attached to him, for so long that even in our separation, I found his shadow cast on the walls of my future.

Jonathan came to find me. He had a copy of the same photograph of the woman in the church. I got this in the mail today, he said. He asked the obvious questions: Do you know what this is? What am I supposed to do with this? Also, he wanted to know why I had changed my clothing and why I was wearing all black. What did I know that I wasn't telling him? Had I heard something? Is he dead?

And I said what I thought was the truth: I can't say. I had the urge then to run home. It was late. The weather was warm enough. Also, I think I had seen on the television some part of the dark past threatening to swallow me.

There is a word for a woman who loses her husband, a word for a woman who loses her mind, her reputation, a word for a woman who loses her money or her employment, but there is no word for a woman who loses her child. This is what I thought as I rushed home. Tell me the word. Maybe if I had the word I would know what to do.

Death is running, I heard a woman say to her child as I rushed past them. Death is running.

WHEN I was a girl my mother used to tell me about a woman who, in the moments before her death, came loose from the soil and was able to travel over the landscape of her life as a bird, in preparation for a second life in a world above our world. In the story the woman becomes so consumed with flying over her life that she ends up spending eternity like this, suspended atop a reproduction of the world. After I left my mother and came to England, I used to think of this story constantly. Would it be better to live on the ground, or to live in the air as someone who never aged, who would never die, but who had the ability to supervise the wreckage of her past from a great height?

We were outside in our garden when I told Franz this story about the woman for the first time. This was two years ago. It was summer. The sun was out and on his back and shoulders, and we had citronella lit in the grass to annoy the bugs, and he had music playing from the open window. I remember the details of this afternoon with Franz because it was the very last normal moment. When I was finished, he grinned at me. As a man, Franz was limited to only three distinct smiles—boasting, lusting, and mocking. And this was the mocking smile.

Tell me, I asked, what did I do?

You've told me this story before, he said, the one with the woman flying over her life, and I asked him when I'd done this, and he said, oh, a number of times, and I said, tell me one time in my whole life when you heard this story, and he said, once a week in Paris you'd drink all the liquor we had and you'd tell me this, sometimes more than once a week, only ever before falling asleep or losing consciousness or telling me how much you hated the music I made and about how much Bach hated the Jews and how much Chopin hated the Jews and how much Tchaikovsky hated the Jews, et cetera, et cetera, and how you wished I had become an optometrist because at least then we might have a reasonable life together.

It turned out he loved this story of mine. Lately, he said, he'd been thinking of this story a good deal, thinking of it every day even, this story in fact came to him in the mornings while the orchestra was tuning, and sometimes still a second time during the evening while Jonathan drove him home, he couldn't get it out of his head, he told me, even when he tried, this notion of lingering atop one's life, it was like someone was whispering it to him, like Anya was rushing up to him from her hiding place and telling it to him fresh and new.

And when he said this, I sat forward, and I asked him, did you say Anya's hiding place? He whispered to me in a dark and conspiratorial fashion, as if I were a dummy: Yes, he said, you heard me right, her hiding place. And although I knew I shouldn't have kept poking at this, I did. Does Anya come out of this hiding place often? I asked, and he sat forward and smiled. All the time, he said, and when I asked whether he saw her when she came out of hiding, he paused and said, you don't want to really talk about this, do you?

I asked him, when you say that she does this all the time, do you mean she is actually, physically doing this?

Yes, he said.

In the flesh? I asked.

Yes, he said. The real Anya.

And I asked him, are you sure you're not just talking about the usual stupidity—the whole dumb vocabulary of spiritual derangement: ghosts and spirits and dybbuks and sheydim and all of that embarrassing emotional adolescence? He smiled and said, I am talking about the actual Anya. And a real hiding place.

Oh, Franz, I said.

It's somewhere nearby, he said. Somewhere in West Sussex, in Horsham, maybe, I'm not sure.

You're serious, I said.

It's wonderful news, isn't it?

How drunk are you?

But she's making her way toward us, he said, and I had the thought that we should leave a map. Or that we should leave signs for her. I wouldn't want her to come for us and not be able to find the way! Do you think she's able to carry all her belongings with her? Her dollies and her storybooks and such? Her blankets and her toy elephants and her favorite music box? Do you think she needs a suitcase?

Franz, I said, do you hear yourself?

You should be quite a bit happier at the news, he said.

Out in the garden, Franz glowed full of life. He lay back in his reclining chair and beamed at me: the dumbest smile that stabbed at the heart. I wanted to say something good and wise, something that would eradicate the deep idiocy of what he'd just said to me, but in the moment I could not think of anything except to tell him the truth, which was that she was gone, we'd lost her, she had died, she is dead, Anya is not living anymore, Anya was sick and then she was not sick any longer because medicine could not cure her. This is the story, I said. It does not continue. There is, in our case, a real ending. She is nowhere. She is not coming to you. She is not hiding. She is nowhere, I said. She is nowhere, nowhere, nowhere!

In the garden, Franz grabbed my arm and kissed it. A cold kiss, as if he himself were already a ghost. Don't worry, he said, don't worry at all, Sonja. You'll understand eventually. I promise you.

I LEFT him that night. I went on foot, committed to never going back. Crossing through the city, I must have seemed, to everyone who saw me, like a phantom, talking aloud to myself, cursing my husband and his ugly mind. I found myself later that evening, after hours of walking, standing inside Victoria station, where the trains were running east. I had fifty pounds in my pockets, enough to get me away from England, to deposit me somewhere new, to make of the rest of my life a picture unencumbered by ghosts, by foolish men, by a life of music that offered me no pleasure.

At the ticket window I bought a trip to Vienna. Even in the moment, this choice of destination seemed deplorable and ridiculous. But there it was, available for me, and I took it. I had not been back since. I had not been within five hundred kilometers of the city since. I could have gone anywhere that evening. Tickets remained available for Denmark, for Holland, for Turkey. I could have gone to Heathrow and flown to California, to the spot in the canyons on the West Side of Los Angeles where I'm writing this to you now, in a future far removed from all this ugliness, in a place where the sun promises to burn away all memory of the past.

But no—it was Vienna, large and frigid and music-haunted and blood-ruined Vienna, the Vienna filled with its dead Jews, the Vienna of my mother, whose last words to me returned while I waited for the train to arrive. Mother says come here. Mother says come here, baby, so I can see your wonderful face one more good time before the train takes you. Hold still, Mother says, I am making a picture of you. I am making a million pictures of you. I am letting the picture set. I am putting that picture in my mind so it stays. Come here and stay here a million years, Mother says. I know already what is going to happen, I tell her. I have memorized the map. I know the name of the king. I know the names of the cities through which I will pass: Brussels, Lille, Calais. Mother buttons me into a black raincoat, and over that raincoat, a white wool parka she has saved somehow for this exact purpose—to swaddle me into the next world. To pass between one life and the next, I need two coats. We practice words in English, we say good afternoon, we say this is a beautiful place, we say this is a magnificent home, thank you for the food, we say I am happy to be here with you. Even if it is not true, we say it. In our final minutes Mother gives me a doll to hold while aboard the train.

Our last conversation: A doll is better than nothing, talk to it, Sonja, talk to it and tell it everything, so that when you lose it eventually, it will find its way back to me and I will know everything of your life.

How simple it would have been to leave that night while my husband was still obviously mad. When the train came, however, I did not leave. Or maybe it's better to say I couldn't. At the moment the conductor asked me to climb on board, I backed away.

Don't you have a ticket? he asked. I see it in your hand. It's right there. Time to get on board.

I've changed my mind, I said.

Are you sure? We're leaving. We're leaving this moment.

I'm sure, I think I said. Or maybe I said nothing and the train moved slowly away from me.

You'll be sorry! the conductor said. Vienna is a great city! You'd have loved it!

I T was late by then, past midnight, past the point at which the Tube might get me home. The streets outside Victoria had emptied. I had spent all my money on the ticket I did not use, which meant that I'd have to walk all the way home, through Covent Garden and Islington, more than seven miles, something that would have taken me hours on foot. By then, the temperature had dropped. The weather had worsened. In stories like this, the weather always grows worse.

Outside the station I found a bank of telephone boxes and had the thought that I could call someone to help, but as I stood there with the receiver in my hand it occurred to me that I knew no one to call. Where were my friends? Where was the rest of my family? After Anya died, I receded from everyone I knew. Suddenly, I had become the shadow. Franz was the only person left.

As it happened, he found me not long after. He'd driven in search of me in a panic. I'd learn this later. What I knew in the moment was the relief on his face when he pulled our car onto the Euston Road and saw me at the phone bank.

You're here, he said. You're here, you're here, you're here.

I had the phone in my hand still, gripping so hard that I felt blood rushing to my fingers.

Are you all finished with running off? he asked.

When I didn't answer immediately, he opened the door to my

side of the car. Its heat leaked out onto the pavement in waves, and in that heat the familiar scent of our house.

Are you all finished with this? he asked again, and when I said nothing, he nudged his chin toward the car. How about you come home? he said. How about that? How about you come home and we stop talking about all this sadness? How about that?

THE third night Franz was missing, I found him once more on television. It was the same performance from the night before, although I had arrived at the programme at a different point, earlier, this time in the first movement, and he had not yet begun to come apart into pieces.

I had spent all that day walking and looking for him and intentionally making myself lost. I had wandered into neighbourhoods without a map, languishing, for instance, in the Tottenham Marshes until the light changed above me and I began to feel afraid. I had practical reasons for doing this. For one, I believed the more I walked, the better chance it was that I'd find him. Or, likewise, that someone would come to find me. Either Franz himself or one of his players, a man with a violin, would come running for me, a man with a flute or a tuba, Jonathan would come across Stamford Hill surrounded by rabbis and wise men and they would tell me what had happened, that they had found him, he was fine, he was looking for me all the time I was looking for him, we had been going in circles, they would say, he'd been maybe at Paddington all this time waiting for me while I was here in the park waiting for him, we were each coming apart into a thousand pieces searching for one another. This was how I spent the third day without him.

At home that night, on the television, Franz was talking to me again. Where are you, he was saying, where are you, where did you go?

A memory: at some point before we leave for California, Anya is listening to this piece of music on our stereo, and it is still possible for her to dance, and it is likely the beginning of summer, because I remember the windows being open, and the onrush of wind across Abney Park not far away, and because she is so young her idea of dancing is merely to spin, not even to twirl, but to spin, the act of someone who understands that the way to transport one's self, to leave the body, is to first disfigure one's sense of the world, just as the mystics do, by way of rocking, spinning, by attempting levitations, breaking herself into pieces and then surging herself into a world where the physical falls away and is replaced by everything else. Visitor—this is what Franz called her that day. He meant it, I think, because she seemed in that moment like she had been born to the wrong parents. I understood her differently. She would be here with us briefly, I think he meant, and then onward.

This is what I thought I saw him saying to me as the orchestra played: visitor. The word in German is Besucher: a small compression of the lips, and then a slow stream of air, as if you are kissing someone. Then the lips parting in an opening just the right size for a life to pass through.

All of us, it turned out, were splitting into pieces.

As he cracked, I anticipated the camera's movements. For example, the slow push into his face as the music swelled. This close to him, I could feel him once again breathing beside me. At a quiet section in the score, the television showed the audience, and there, in the middle of everyone, I found myself. I was wearing the same clothing I always wore to see Franz, a bright and vivid blue dress he always disliked. Again the message appeared briefly on the television to tell me when this had been recorded—*14 February 1979*, it said, *London, Royal Albert Hall*, which was yesterday's date. Of course, I thought, I had read this wrong, I had confused days, superimposed one past for another.

I pulled close to the screen. I was alone in my house, watching, waiting once again to appear to myself. I imagine the camera operator must have known to find me, that I was the wife of the conductor who was falling apart so visibly onstage. When he began to cry, the camera pushed into him very fast, an effect that brought him rushing toward the screen, rushing to me, while everything else—the crowd, the orchestra and their instruments—fell away one by one off the edge of the frame. There I was again, in this same dress, this same necklace, and the camera was, in this same way, zooming in to me, except that I saw that it was not me at all, but instead a woman who looked a good deal like me. The camera did not leave her, this woman, this person in my clothes and my jewelry and my seat, this new version of me.

Of course he would like her, I thought, this new woman, this new me, this other me. She was me without a memory of being me.

THE end for us came when my mother died. This was my second mother, Sydney. She had been living in a care home in Ombersley. My brother Teddy called to tell me the news. I had not talked to him in twenty years, not for birthdays or for holidays or for the deaths of other family members. At gunpoint, I was sure he would deny we were related. Imprisoned by foreign enemies, he would probably deny we had ever even lived in the same house. Because of all this, the conversation the day she died was suitably painful and brief. Mother has passed, he said. Maybe he said it differently. Maybe he said *my* mother has passed. We were all there, he said, by which he meant he and my cousins and maybe even Alfred, who was both my father and not my father. He put the emphasis on *all of us*, meaning not you, meaning we intentionally did not let you know. The funeral is Tuesday, he said. We're thinking you may want to be there. This was the totality of the call.

At the church, none of them spoke to me. The only mention of my name came in a eulogy delivered by a woman whom I did not know, and who made a vague mention of my mother's momentary interest in the fate of Jewish refugees. The woman, it turned out, had my name wrong. She called me Mona. As in: When Sydney adopted Mona during the war we all went to work getting the house ready for a baby to arrive. We brought tiny baby clothing and stuffed animals! You should have seen all of us when the child arrived and she was not a baby at all! You should have heard the way Sydney complained! I expected a baby! An infant! Instead, I have an actual German in my house, speaking German, looking German, speaking in full sentences, asking after her mother and father! What is the exchange policy, she kept crying! Someone please send help! I don't speak any German! What will people think with the enemy in the house!

All this met with clamorous laughter in the church, especially from Teddy, who sat two rows ahead of me. Clamorous laughter in a church is a terrifying sound. The cavernous ceilings are designed to trap an organ's thunder and make it tremble overhead, as a reminder of God's power and, consequentially, your lack of power. I shrank backwards in my seat. This was when Franz leaned over to check on me. He was whispering, I think, saying something in German, but I wasn't listening.

We left together. I suppose people thought I was overcome with emotion, which was not untrue. It was summer. Our car's air conditioner was broken, and in the immediate moments after leaving my mother's funeral we found ourselves slick with sweat. Franz tore away his jacket. I had a preposterous shawl on and I tore that away and left it in the grass where they ended up burying Teddy's mother. We thought maybe we would go to the beach, to a friend's house in Eastbourne. Or that we would go back to London and drink ourselves into a state where this last hour had not ever happened.

On the M40, however, Franz mentioned that colleagues of his were performing at Glyndebourne. When he said it, I moaned in the car. Let's not, I said. Let's toss me off Waterloo Bridge instead. But of course, we went; when the music called, he ran to it, and when he ran, I was often pulled behind in his wake.

And so this is where we went, and where, some hours later, we suffered the unsettling encounter I mentioned earlier. A man in a blue jacket stood in the grass waving at me, calling my name, Sonja! Sonja!, and then calling Franz's name over and over. The man had a tumbler of gin in his hand. Where is she? the man yelled. Where is your child? Where is that wonderful child of yours?

THE man was Lionel Feldman. A middling doctor with a reputation for charm. The story was this: Feldman had been Anya's physician. By the time we'd brought her to his office, she had already lost the use of her left hand and her arm, and then eventually the entire left side of her body from her ear to her toes. He had thought it was something more benign than what it ended up being, which was a way of dying, and although I came to understand that there was nothing I could have done, or for that matter that Feldman could have done, Franz saw it differently. To him it was Feldman's fault that we'd had to go to Paris to find a doctor to repair his work, and it was Feldman's fault that Anya was gone, which somehow made it Feldman's fault that Anya was in the dirt awaiting the moment when the Messiah was supposed to return, and it was likely his fault that Franz had lost himself in a child's idea of ghostliness, and to see him here, looking healthy and humming "Sì, Mi Chiamano Mimì," made Franz temporarily murderous.

You'll need to hold my drink, he told me, and when I asked him why, he said, it would be difficult to strangle Feldman with one hand. By then, Feldman had begun to make his way across the lawn. His arms were out in a joyful premature embrace. He was shouting our names: Franz and Sonja! Franz and Sonja! A part of me was happy to hear someone use my real name that day. At least I wasn't Mona. Franz meanwhile had put his drink on the ground. Don't be a moron, I said to him in German. Suddenly, this was how we spoke to one another, in this language we had each pretended not to know any longer.

I had a speech I used to give. All mothers like me have this speech. It had been years since I'd used it. There was always someone who had not heard the news, and who'd ask the usual questions, the friendly inquiries after one's child, and I'd have to tell them the truth, and also have to do so without making the person to whom I was speaking feel horrible for asking, or having not already heard, or for not sending along a typical note of sympathy. Even for someone like Feldman, someone who probably already knew, I still had to tell him, or find the shortest and easiest words to let it be known that he should turn around and forget he'd ever seen us here.

As Feldman got closer, though, he made a show of looking around and made a visor out of his free hand in order to shield the sun.

Where is she? he asked again. Where is she?

Who are you talking about? I asked.

Anya, he said. Where's your little Anya? I just saw her last week in Tottenham, he said. In a shopwindow. She looked terrific! Absolutely terrific. I was so happy to see this. I have to tell you! So happy! Honestly, he said, I was elated at how well she looked. Elated for you both. Medicine is a wonder! Isn't it? A wonder!

A pall fell across Franz and me. If two people can simultaneously experience a shared form of nausea and bloodlust and also the derangement of impossible hope, Franz and I did in that moment. Feldman was smiling and was about to say something else when a woman from across the grass called for him. The weather was threatening. I think this was what Feldman said to me when he left. Shelf clouds overhead—the sort of weather where one understands what the end of the world will look like.

Feldman was grinning wildly. The smile of a lifesaver. I'll have to call on you sometime, he said as he left. Maybe we can all meet up in Kensington for a good dinner. You call me at the office, he said. Okay? You promise?

Both Franz and I watched him go, an old foolish man in an old tuxedo and a half-drunk tumbler of gin. When we were alone together in the field, I grabbed Franz by the elbow.

He doesn't know what he's talking about, I said. Look at me, I told him. Look at me. He doesn't know what he's saying.

But Franz was already elsewhere.

Look at the two of us, I might have said. Dressed for a funeral. Standing in a wet field, half-drunk, tempted by impossibilities while instruments tuned far off. Look at the two of us. Do you see us? Do you?

FOR a long time, I've heard trains running at night near my house in California, which is where I'm writing this to you, whoever you are. This is near Los Angeles, west of the city, in the canyons. I hear the noise sometimes in my sleep and for years it's gone on like this, in the same way: a sound grows near but it never arrives. Not long ago, however, the sound began to change. Or I changed with it. Now I hear not only the cars approaching, but an operator's voice in German, always in German, telling me that there is bad weather ahead, snow on the tracks, ice in the mountains. Also, small mundane details: Someone has left behind a blue raincoat. Is it yours? Ask an agent, the voice says, and we will bring it to you. Eventually, images begin to emerge, sometimes in the yard, other times over the canyon. Madness, no?

When I first moved to California, I hesitated to furnish this house. In the house I shared with Franz, it had remained, day after long day, always, Europe. On our stereos, our televisions, in our kitchens, in every shade of light, we existed as we had before. Or maybe I should say that we had existed in some fashion resembling how we had imagined we might have lived before, in the old life, a life which, week by week, we felt receding from us, altered imperceptibly, or covered over by ghosts. It had taken years, but we had built a facsimile of life, a manufactured version of existence, in which we were, I sometimes felt, reduced in size, as were the walls of our house, our gardens, the food we grew.

The first days in a new place have always existed for me in a version of reality that feels inexact, proximal, a room away from earth.

I'd been in Los Angeles six months before my first earthquake. I was alone in the house, in bed. I was forty-seven years old. Everything came off the shelves, as one imagines it does in a powerful quake, and I felt, from my bed, the moorings of the house straining, a large wave rising, as if the ocean had crested the mountains. Outside I heard a neighbour cry out. A clock on my mantel—the beginnings of a new life—toppled and broke. But for me it was the most natural feeling. Yes, something is beneath me, has always been beneath me, tilting the ground, opening up and closing. Yes, the earth is trying to swallow me whole. When has it not?

Afterward, I spent hours reassembling what had broken. It is a small place, painted gray, built by hand by the man and woman from whom I bought it, partially hidden from the road. In the mornings, there is a brittle light, and in the evening that light grows thick enough sometimes I think I can hold it. I have allowed myself the possibility that this is the last home I will live in. Forgive me for purchasing some degree of America's great export, which is its militant adherence to historical amnesia. Among the objects broken by the quake was this small clock Jonathan sent me after I moved. It had split into two pieces, cleaved along the noon meridian, although it had never worked, not even when it was new.

That night, after the earthquake, the train came again, this time bearing music. I went outside to meet it, and when I did, the door opened for me. Inside was Anya—the same version of Anya I knew last. Nine years old, her hair piled up on her head. She wanted to know where I'd been. I've been trying to get to you, she said. Where have you been, Mama? Why haven't you been trying to get to me?

THE fourth night without him, Jonathan called me at home. He was in Franz's office. There is something here you'll want to see, he said.

It was late by then and Knightsbridge was stubbornly, annoyingly pretty. I could never understand how Franz felt like he belonged in this neighbourhood, filled with its international hotel chains and awful restaurants and commercial appendages of the royal family. I always felt like a tourist here. Or I feared that strangers could perceive the true version of me, the version only my personal mirrors revealed: my funeral skin, my graveyard hair, this old voice of mine that was neither here nor anywhere.

In the office, there was music going on the hi-fi. I would tell you all about it, but it would bore you, all of it would, even the beautiful parts. The piece is about a river, and the river is a metaphor, but even the metaphor is boring. I know this. Beauty very easily turns boring. I was always trying to tell Franz this.

Jonathan took me into a library room. This was where they kept the scores for the music they played. It was a large room filled on all sides with tall cabinets and filing drawers. He'd opened everything for me.

Go look, he said. Look anywhere. Look in any drawer or cabinet.

And when I did, I must have made a noise. Inside, all the scores were gone. Instead, I found piles of copies of the picture Franz had left in our house—the woman standing in the center of a church.

How many are there? I asked.

Maybe a thousand, he said. They're everywhere. They are all the same.

I splayed some out in front of me, this same face multiplied over and over into a crowd.

Who is this supposed to be? he asked.

Please get rid of these, I told him. Any way you can. Burn them if you have to.

I've tried, he said. I keep finding them and tearing them up. But they're everywhere, he said. They're everywhere. He left them everywhere.

EARLY the next morning, I went to see Lionel Feldman at his office on Exhibition Road. I had not called ahead the way I should have, and because of this I found myself waiting for the better part of an afternoon in this same room where I had often waited with Anya. As far as rooms like this went—rooms in which one waits patiently to die, or in which one accompanies someone else who is waiting patiently to die—it was a lovely room. A bank of windows revealed the red drum of the Royal College of Music. Someone had hung perfectly anodyne landscapes on the interior walls, pictures of alfalfa fields and inert tractors and Hereford cattle and poppies caught in mid-sway. Perhaps it was this same someone who had painted the rest of the place pink, or rose, or blush, a calming color, the color of blood diluted by water, the color of healthfulness, the color of living. I had said this to Anya once, talking about the shade of pink in this room, and said it as if I had just thought of it. Anya said, every time we are here, you say this. Every single time.

This was always happening then, this endless repetition of myself. Who better to alert me to it than this person I had made, this halved and improved repetition of me. The truth was that her illness had exploded my understanding of time as a progression of constant intervals, in which the next minute was always the same distance away as the previous minute, and also it had undone the juvenile notion that these passing minutes were capable of healing me, or forestalling the moment I dreaded.

Feldman was a specialist of the brain and an author of a well-regarded book that reflected what he had come to understand of its

interior geography, its networks and electricities. It was a book I had
stayed awake to read in the weeks after Anya died. He had dedicated
it to patients of his who had not lived, a lovely and personal touch.
Before we saw him again recently, I had often imagined him alone
in a room not unlike this room, writing at night from a place of
great uselessness and grief, another person trying fruitlessly to place
their ear against the walls of the world.

I thought of this when I came to finally sit in Feldman's office.
Pinned to the walls behind him were photographs of recuperated
patients, a new development, he told me, a testament to the massive
shift in novel therapies available to treat the sick. He attempted to
explain to me the basis of these therapies, but I could not follow
him. It was clear I'd found him in terrific spirits, just as I had recently at Glyndebourne. Here he was, with his foot in the door of
death. He was in such a good way that when I told him the truth,
which was that he could not have seen Anya in a shopwindow in
Tottenham because Anya was not alive, that she had not been alive
for many years, it took him several minutes to register the truth,
long minutes in which I reconsidered the limits of my capacity for
violence: his smile matched the smiles on the faces of the pictures
behind him.

What do you mean she is not alive? he asked.

I mean that she is not alive, I said.

Say it again, he said.

Tot, tot, tot.

This cannot be, he said.

You're not the only one who's said that to me, I said. My husband, for instance.

Yes, he said. Of course.

I felt I needed to come, I said.

I understand, he said.

I felt I needed to come in order to ask who you saw, exactly, I said. Who did you see in that window? Who was it?

He had no answer. He tried to answer, but he couldn't. All Feldman could do was lean over his desk and tell me that Franz had come earlier that week and asked all these same questions. He'd come twice, in fact, although when Franz came he hadn't said that Anya was dead, only that she was away somewhere else.

Somewhere else? I asked.

I thought he meant she was away at school, he said.

I had to close my eyes at the thought. And when I did this, Feldman attempted to hold my hands, maybe to comfort me.

All Franz wanted to know, Feldman said, was which shopwindow. That's all he kept asking. Which shopwindow? Which shopwindow in Tottenham?

And what did you tell him? I asked. What did you say?

WHEN Jonathan drove me home that night, the neighbours were celebrating. They had the lights on bright in every window. The brightness was beautiful, but also extreme, especially beside my house, which was so immaculately dark I worried that my house had begun to vanish along with Franz. It was a Jewish holiday, Jonathan explained, as if I should know. We ought to talk to them, he said, because we'll need to make preparations, we'll need to make sure we do everything appropriately, exactly what he would want, what music he'd have wanted us to play, for instance, what sort of service we'll require. I knew without him saying it outright: he was planning for Franz's funeral.

Inside, I thought for a moment I could sense him in the house. His footsteps or his humming to himself or his cologne. It was a game we used to play. Close your eyes and tell me how near I am to you. I was always very bad at this. I sensed everything when nothing was near me, or I sensed something profound and everyone was gone. In the kitchen, I called his name. I went to the wall of our bedroom and I called his name. I went into the back garden, where the neighbours were celebrating. What Franz told me once was that when one is waiting desperately for someone to appear to them from a crowd, or from across a telephone wire, what one is really waiting for is to jump from one skin to another. We were on a train when he said this, and I remembered him changing his shirt as our car passed through a forest, and seeing his body beneath the harsh overhead lamps, and noticing that I could see the skin over his heart moving with his blood-beat, the way one sees it in a hummingbird.

The only place I could reliably find him was on the television. When he came to me on-screen, he had already come undone, and he had turned around to face the audience and had begun to try to conduct the crowd. I should not have watched. It was the same broadcast as before. I stayed watching long enough that I appeared on the screen, as I knew I would. However, when my moment came, the image was different.

A young woman sat beside me. At home, I called for Jonathan to come. On-screen the young woman beside me put her hand on my hand. This young woman said something that I had no trouble making out. She said, Mama, calm yourself. Mama, you are on the television. Mama, we're both on the television, collect yourself.

At some point Jonathan came to find me. By then, I was on my knees at the glass. He was holding a stack of the photographs. Maybe he was the one to say it: that the woman on the screen was the woman in the photograph, and that both of them were supposed to be Anya. This was something I already knew. I had begun talking to the screen in German so that he would not understand. Perhaps this is why I felt I could say what I wanted to say in my own language, which is that I knew she was a fake. You are a forgery, I said, you are not my daughter, and also I wanted to say that I missed her very badly, that I had many holes within me now that she was gone.

Where did you go, I was saying, where did you go?

Behind me, in the house, the neighbours were singing so loud, their voices bled into the room. Or their voices came into my house and got stuck there between the walls.

The woman on-screen who was supposed to be me said something to her daughter just then, although both of them had turned away and the camera could not catch it. It seemed important that I hear what they were saying. I thought maybe I was wrong, that she was the real version and I was the false version. Otherwise, what could account for her being there with her daughter and her husband and my being here alone in the dark?

Eventually, the camera found me again in the audience and it held me so long I became old and beautiful and I found I knew the person looking back me, and for this, and for nothing else over the course of these next days and months, I began to cry. I had become my mother, I thought. For once, she had turned old. She leaned forward, closer to the lens, grabbed Anya, looked close, looked across the city, looked from the street into my house, through my television to see me in darkness, and like in my mother's story, they were talking to me, can you hear us, they were saying, can you hear, which I could not, because I was rising up and up and up over my life.

# Hiding Places

MONTREAL, 1966

# FANIA

H E wants to know where I've lived, and I tell him.

"First," I say, "the forest."

"Fantastic," he says. "A woman of the forest!"

"More specifically, my grandmother's house," I say. "The back door opened to the woods. In retrospect, it was nothing. Barely anything. Four walls. One roof. Not even a real floor. This was when I was an infant. Is this at all interesting to you?"

"A baby of the forest, then," he says.

"I remember very little."

"Which forest?"

"Who knows," I say. "One forest is the same as all forests."

"I agree," he says, not for the first time.

"A place in which people are hiding."

"Yes," he says.

"Also, animal eyes from behind trees. Or a river rushing somewhere that one cannot see. Also: moss on the trees. Also: the sound of birds, owls, forest cats. Also: the site of various massacres, stakes in the earth, handmade memorials. At night, women arriving from somewhere in order to cry alone. What else can I say? It was the forest."

"My forest is the same as your forest," he says.

"All forests are this forest," I say.

"Then where?" he asks.

"First, Vienna."

"Ah," he says, "grand, beautiful Vienna."

"You have been?" I ask.

"Of course not," he says. "Vienna is filled with Austrians."

"You think you can joke about this?" I ask.

"You are right. This is a bad joke. Beneath my capabilities as a joke maker."

"What I remember I remember badly," I say. "Not the memory but the memory of the memory."

"It is the same for me. Very difficult to trust this feeling."

"We came, I think, by horse. As if we were eighteenth-century peasants. Although I do not know if this is true. My mother told me. Or, since I can barely remember my mother, maybe it is that she told me this in a dream and I have understood it as fact since then," I say. "This is a way to tell you not to trust this."

"I want to hear everything," he says.

"I rode in the back with her. My mama. Her name was Stisie. She was not even seventeen years old. A child, basically. When I remember her, I remember her in the long, flowing jackets she wore when she was older. Not as she was when I was young and she was young, but the Viennese version of her, which was, I understand now, a pretend version of my mother. Or I went with my father. Perhaps they were both with me. I do not know. I wish I did know. We arrived in the city at night, and at once we were surrounded by automobile traffic, hundreds of automobiles on the Ringstraße. Before this I had seen automobiles, of course, we weren't that primitive, but they only came one at a time, a loud noise on the road, the rich man from the village, we could hear the car coming in the forest for a minute before we saw it, which made us run out from our house, always running to the road, where we could see the automobile passing us in the distance, a tiny speck of nothing, thinking the driver would throw us candy or throw us coins, and now here we were, on a highway of cars, and our old horse spooked, our village horse who knew only the stables and the forest and carrots from our palm, she became frightened, we could not console her, she began to buck and tug and attempt to take us back. Look, my father said, or my mother said, she wants to go back home."

"Animals know before we know," he says. "Like in stories of typhoons. You see the snakes rush out of the sea, it is time for you to run for your life."

"When I am faced with a typhoon, Hermann, I will remember this."

"It will certainly come in helpful," he says.

"From there," I say, "prison."

"Yes," he says.

"Many prisons, in fact," I say. "This is the word I choose to use. Prison is a better word."

"It is the same for me," he says.

"Apparently I committed many serious crimes."

"I am also, apparently, a serious criminal."

"After that," I say, "some other place that is hard to name."

"Not a real place," he says. "But also, a place that is very real."

"Yes," I say.

"Just out of reach at all times."

"If my story is the same as your story," I ask, "then why do you want to hear it so badly?"

"How else will I know you if I don't hear this?"

"After prison, a DP camp," I say. "How is that to hear?"

"DP camp," he says.

"This is a camp for displaced persons," I say.

"Displaced person. Such interesting words they choose," he says. "Displaced. As if you are water from a teacup."

"Spilled water from a teacup," I say.

"Spilled water," he says. "Not you, Fania." He goes to take my hand, take my fingers, but stops just short of me. "Never you, Fania."

He likes to repeat what I say. In this way, he is learning English. My English is better than his. Not that this is any great achievement.

But this is why I have been paired with him, with Hermann Pressler, a man about my age, an auto mechanic by trade, newly arrived in the country. The program is explicit. Six months of biweekly conversations, after which, evidently, some fluency will settle in. After this, another pairing, another man or woman like Hermann Pressler, stinking of whatever indignation has befallen them: engine oil, fish eggs, scrapyard cologne. They will, he and I, or she and I, endeavor just to talk, a continual conversation in coffee shops, cafeterias, Automats, always at uncomfortable hours, the under-daylight of Montreal before work hours, empty late nights, a not-so-sly way of forcing conversation between people who cannot make conversation.

When I arrived, years ago, I was on the other end, repeating words, making notes. For me, it was always dessert with an elderly woman named Beatrice, a woman who had lived in London, had fallen in love with a man in Berlin who sold musical instruments, and who, in the end, became stuck. Most days, Beatrice told me, I am convinced I am dead, and that I've in fact *been* dead a very long while, which makes this, if I'm being dreadfully honest, a very odd form of the afterlife, speaking with you in this weird snowy place.

When I squint, he is Arnold. Or maybe, when I squint, Montreal is Vienna, and everyone becomes Arnold.

"For a year I lived in this place," I say.

"Not a good place?" he asks.

"Of course not a good place. This is a question an idiot asks."

"I never told you I wasn't an idiot."

"A better place than prison."

"Every place is better than prison," he says.

"But a terrible place anyway."

"Where?"

"Who knows. Germany, I think. It could have been Czechoslovakia."

"You don't know?"

"Who wants to know?"

"I do. I want to know everything about you, Fania."

"I never asked," I say. "Or maybe I did ask, and they told me, they said: You are here, in such-and-such a place, which is, normally, a beautiful place, a place with great history and many fabulous palaces and castles, and a lineage of great holy men and kings that our schoolchildren have memorized for generations, and maybe one day, I am driven in a car to the edge of such a place and I see how beautiful it is, maybe with mountains and streams, which show the reflection of the mountains, and the reflection of the streams, and also the reflection of our reflection, in which I can see myself, with some American soldier to my side, maybe telling me, look at you still alive in the world, Fania, look at all this world you get to enjoy now, and maybe I am unconvinced by such talk, maybe I am instead sickened by such talk here beside the stream looking at the reflection of myself, which may as well have been a reflection of nothing at all. So I don't ask the name of the place. And if they told it to me, I forgot it, as one forgets something in a hotel room after a trip, something they might want to go back to retrieve."

"But you did not go back for it."

"I did not go back for it, no."

I squint again. Outside, there is snow, always snow, months and months of snow, and in this way, it is not so different here than before.

"Americans told me the same thing," he says. "They say to me: Hermann, buck up. Whatever that means. They said to me that I should be happy I am here, look at the beautiful sky, how big it is, how much sky there is to live beneath, buck up, kid, buck up, as if I am at a bad party, as if I had not just watched world come apart."

"*The* world come apart," I say.

"What?"

"It's *the* world come apart. You left out a word."

"What would I do without you, Fania? Without you everything good would be left out."

"Every day in that place," I say, meaning the DP camp, "there are small pieces of bread. There are also large idiot men telling us not to eat too much, that our stomachs will explode. What I would have given for my stomach to explode. Then, American boy rabbis, coming to minister to us, to tell us we were not forgotten, that there is wonder in the world that awaits us, and when we ask where, where is this wonder you speak of, he has difficulty naming any real place, because he is a child, he is a little boy rabbi, and he cannot name any real place, not America certainly, not England, nowhere. Again, he is so young that he is basically a little child dressed up in rabbi's clothing, and he says to me, don't worry, Fania, there are many other wonderful nations of the globe, and there, in those other places, you will find wonder."

"Wonder," says Hermann.

"This is the word, yes. Wonder. Just you wait, I was told. Wonder awaits you."

"Has it come?"

"The wonder?"

"Yes, the wonder. Are you experiencing the wonder, Fania?"

"Not unless this is what they meant. Lunch with you, Hermann. My strange job. Strange Canadian cake in this cafeteria. This seems to be the extent of my life."

"We can always go to a nicer place."

"With what money?" I ask.

"Give me a moment. I will go outside and rob a rich man. Then we will have money."

"You will go outside and freeze to death before you find a rich man in this neighborhood."

"Then, from the camp, where? Where did you go next?"

"Then, Vienna."

"Ah, grand, beautiful Vienna," he says.

"Have you been since I asked you last?"

"I am not that much of an idiot."

"You say you are not an idiot, but you wear the face of an idiot."

"My mother gave me this face," he says.

"Your mother must have been very tired. After birthing you, she reached for a good face and found this one instead."

"Perilous ground you tread, Fania."

"Vienna for two months," I say. "Winter months. Not unlike winter here."

"For what purpose?" he asks.

"Stupid question," I say.

"Of course," he says.

"My husband," I say. "My babies."

"I see."

"You see nothing," I tell him.

"I meant to say that I gather what you are trying to tell me," he says.

"I had some ideas of what I wanted to do in Vienna, but they were children's ideas, they were bad ideas maybe, and instead I did nothing. I walked. I hurt my feet walking. I walked so much I became sick on the street. I vomited many times on many exquisite buildings. I am at this point captured on camera one day by a man with a movie camera. I don't see him until it's too late. He thinks I am worth putting on film, and when I try to ask him not to shoot me, not to capture me being sick, he runs away, and for many years afterward I am convinced he is lurking behind me, around corners, photographing every part of me so that all this will become a movie one day."

"A good movie?" he asks.

"I am here with you, Hermann, in the always-winter, required only to speak English or French. Do you think it is a good movie?"

"You saw nothing else in Vienna?"

"I saw lots. Many bones of my life, for example."

"Your house?"

"Occupied by cretins," I say.

"Describe, please."

"One day, I followed the Hausfrau as she did her daily errands. Ordinary errands. Bread at the bakery. A bottle of beer. Laundry. And then, an hour in a shop fingering the dresses."

"A perfect place to murder her," he says. "While standing in the department store handling fine dresses."

"And I recognize that she is wearing my clothing. A green dress. A particularly lovely green dress I had received as a gift from my sister. My favorite dress. We are about the same size, me and this woman. I follow her for an hour or so and eventually I see that in addition to having on my dress, and my shoes, that she is wearing jewelry Arnold gave to me on my wedding day. A small ring, which I wore on this finger," I say, holding up my left hand, my second finger, "but which she, because her hands are larger, wears on her pinky."

"And who is Arnold?" he asks.

"My husband."

"And he is gone?"

"My husband is gone."

"But this woman with the large hands, she has belongings your husband gave you."

"She does."

"Do you murder this person?" he asks me. "Tell me you murder this woman with the large hands."

"Oh, I thought of it."

"Who wouldn't think of it?"

"In my dreams I am a champion murderer."

"As am I."

"I can throw an axe from Dubrovnik to Prague and hit a man between the eyes."

"I collect all the bullets fired from all the guns and make them into an arrowhead of birds flying overhead in search of every one of my enemies."

"But I did not murder anyone."

"Of course not. How could Fania murder anyone? Look at you. Sweet angel of youth, Fania."

"All my life people are putting axes in the brains of people. So I think to myself, Fania, how about no more murdering for now? How about you become a normal woman who has passions and enjoyments and who does not put any axes into anyone?"

"What did you do then in Vienna for those two months?" he asks.

"I vomited on it," I say.

"Really?"

"I walked in circles. If you were in Vienna then—"

"I would not go. For all the riches in the world, I would not go. Even if every woman on the street was you, Fania, I would still not go."

"These are fine and sentimental words, Hermann, but—"

"—and I would never go back, not ever, not anywhere near that place, because look at where we are, look how we have been sitting here in this place all this time without being bothered, and after this I'll go home and no one will bother me there, and I'll wake tomorrow and no one will bother me there and on and on until I die and this seems to me like heaven. The real heaven. I have no need for the world to come. This is the world to come: a mediocre cafeteria in Montreal eating this strange hard bread. A cold apartment into which no trouble comes. This is why I am glad to hear you were sick all over that place."

"Will you let me finish?"

"I am sorry, Fania. A thousand times I am sorry for interrupting."

"We are supposed to be learning English. But I will gladly teach you how not to be an asshole."

"Teach me," he says. "Please, teach me."

"Lesson number one?"

"Yes, Fania?"

"Don't be an asshole."

"I am failing this lesson, you are saying?"

"You are intermittently failing, yes."

"Intermittently," he says.

"In and out," I say.

"I am, in and out, an asshole, you are saying," he says, which makes me laugh.

"Hermann, you are doing fine."

"Fine for an asshole," he says.

"Would you like to hear the rest of the story, Hermann?"

"Please, Fania. Finish telling me about Vienna."

"If you had been there, Hermann, which I know you would not have been, but if you had ended up there as I did, you would have seen me walking around in circles and circles of those circles, and then wider circles surrounding those smaller circles looking for anyone I knew."

"Describe them for me," he says. "Anyone. All of them." Then, perhaps recognizing I might not be able to do this, he relents. "Or whoever you think you can maybe describe."

"I would rather not," I say.

"Whatever you like, Fania."

"Thank you, Hermann."

"This is what life will be like with Hermann," he says. "Always whatever you like."

"If 'always' means life in this cafeteria."

"This is a good cafeteria. Best cafeteria in Montreal."

"This place also promises wonder." I point at an advertisement for cake and bread. "The cake is full of wonder. The coffee is full of wonder. This place also, I think, does not issue passports in or out."

"Fania make funny joke!"

"I have been in this cafeteria for many decades, it seems," I say.

"You just arrived. Ten minutes ago. I see you come in from down the street looking like beautiful queen. The queen of Canada."

"Ten minutes. Or a decade. What is the difference in Montreal? It is always winter."

"Give me a second," he says. "I will go book us a trip on a first-class steamer. To all the wonderful places. To Tahiti."

"On what steamer?"

He reaches out and waves his hand over my eyes in such a way that I know to close them.

"Here," he says. "Your eyes are closed. As are Hermann's eyes. This is our steamship. Feel the water, will you? Do you feel the tide coming? Can you smell the sea?"

I open my eyes while his are still closed. He is in a suit, always in a suit, the same suit, the color of chestnuts. I have not seen his apartment, but I suspect he lives in the YMHA. Most of the men in the program live in the YMHA. His hair is swept back into waves, the first wave shorter than the second, which is shorter than the third; his head is a weather pattern.

"You are a sweet man, Hermann," I say.

"I tell you this all the time! That Hermann is a sweet man!"

"It is true occasionally," I say.

"When I am young I am a sweet man. Everyone say this."

"Where were you young, exactly?" I ask.

"My face," he says. "On my face I was young. Before, it was a good face. Face of a movie star!"

"Not where on your body," I say. "Where in the world? What city? Where were you young?"

"Oh," he says. "I thought I told you."

"Not yet," I say. "Not in all our conversations."

"In Vienna, of course," he says. "I told you this. I must have. Didn't I tell you this? I come from Vienna. Just like you, Fania."

HERMANN does not ask me about how I came to live and not die, not ever; no man like Hermann would ever ask a question like this. The foolishness of it would overwhelm both of us, but in the event he does, I know what I will say. That seven things had to happen for me to live. First, quiet. Second, the opposite of quiet. Third, hunger. Fourth, the boy rabbis of America feeding me small pieces of bread. Fifth, the opposite of prayer. Sixth, murder. That is: the murder of my family, the murder of my husband and the murder of my son and the murder of my daughter and, as a consequence, the murder spree I dream of as retaliation. Seventh, luck.

Some mornings, while I am on the train from Plateau-Mont-Royal to the hotel on Sherbrooke Street, I think that maybe there are in fact eight things, eight being the number of miracles, the days of creation plus one, the number of nights the oil lasted in the remains of the temple. And that is this: the hotel. This is what has saved me, what has actually saved me, the hotel, the blue room beside the soaking pool, the dim lights above my worktable, the shimmer of chlorinated water against the white ceiling, and the subtle wafting of bleach, the quavering music piped into the room from some other faraway place. Or it is this: the array of creams on the counter behind me about which I have somehow become an expert, eucalyptus to open the soul, peppermint to make the hairline tingle, bergamot to remind a man of his mother.

Beneath me on the table this morning, a businessman complains of pain in his sides. He has come, I know, from elsewhere, with the smell of elsewhere on his body, from California I think he has said, and like all my patients he stands before me in almost nothing, pointing at the place where the pain has come. I have no training, but nevertheless, here I am, in a dimly lit room on the bottom floor of the Hotel Sherbrooke, my hands full with a cream that smells of pine, a smell that is said to induce calm, to aide in the retention of memory, and which, suitably, reminds me of my grandmother's kitchen in Dubno, a house I can conjure only in parts, and where, I am sure, in the evenings, there were pine needles boiling in water on the stove.

Here, the man says, reaching behind to touch a sore spot, a place of tenderness, and with a quick motion I am upon it with my hands, and then when my hands are no match for the trauma in this man's skin, in his muscles, I attack with my elbows, all my weight, up on my toes, pressing deep into the buildup within this patient of mine. And then, as if obliterated by munitions, it is gone, I have won, the man settles beneath me, the man nearly melts, I can feel it, I hear it in his breathing, a quick calmness, a slackening. The men who arrive here do so from elsewhere, arrive desperate for help, in agony, trapped amid the desperation of great pain, which is in itself a country composed of nothing but loneliness. The pain, they tell me, I can't believe the extent of this pain, I am in a meeting with my colleagues and the pain blinds me, I am on the phone with the lawyers, the board of directors, my children, I am swimming in the St. Lawrence River and it severs my senses, when it arrives I can't hear anything, the rooms go dark because of this pain. If the pain vanishes for even a moment, I can think of nothing else but how much time I have until the pain returns. Pain, they tell me, is an echo without end. Please do something, they tell me.

One can tell a great deal in the skin. Anxiety reveals itself between the shoulder blades, depression at the base of the neck. Problems with romance, I believe, express themselves in the feet. Fear of death, the jaw. A longing for someone, someplace, some vanished scent from the person who slept beside you for years, who lay dreaming where you lay dreaming, this reveals itself in the hands, especially in the meat of the thumb, where I can, if I press just slightly in the right spot, with the appropriate level of force, put a patient in mind of the past, of a room, for instance, that has been exploded, or incinerated by bombs, or raided by soldiers, but here, with my hands pushing, the room builds itself in the mind from out of nowhere, in black and white first, as in the movies my father loved, then walls going up one after the other, then a chandelier, its teardrops broken by children, paintings of one's grandparents long ruined by water, but made clear again here, and hung perfectly in the mind, in this basement, in Montreal, beneath my hands. Nonsense, I know. All this is nonsense. Then again, who really cares what is nonsense now and what is not. We are living in the absence of the world and nonsense is fine. Patient after patient enters this room to tell me of their injuries. It is a small room, the size of a sleeping car on a train. I lived for years in rooms smaller than this. When the session is up, they rise newborn, slick with peppermint, with bergamot, free of pain, wearing nothing, or wearing only slim underpants, some of them plainly aroused, and they tell me how I have helped them. You don't understand, the man from California says, I am always in pain, every minute I am suffering, in my sleep I am in pain, you don't understand, he says again, you don't get it. And I say, smiling, always with the stupid smile I am commanded to wear, no, you are right, I do not understand, I do not know, I cannot know, I can never understand.

Which is partly true: I knew nothing when I started. I did not know, for instance, that when a muscle is emptied of trauma, the body will go loose for an instant before the trauma finds a home somewhere else, in another limb, that trauma always rushes back, that it travels faster than any force in the universe. I did not know, either, that if I massage the tissue in between a man's ribs, that he, whoever he might be, is likely to crack open and wail like an infant. I certainly did not know that by pushing with all my strength into a man's armpit, he will tell me anything—all his crimes, his worst sins, his most hidden regrets.

What would my mother think of this life, in this far-flung place, this frigid life, this deranged future, this arctic snow-heaven, which involves the sight of men like this, men in their colorful underpants, having confused the relief of pain with the onrush of eroticism, doused with oil like they are salad anchovies, standing in a tiny room, just the two of us, everyone speaking in this ridiculous language. My mother, gone now two lifetimes, two of me, my mother so far away now from the Montreal of 1966 that she has become in my mind an artifact of ancient history no different than that of Tutankhamen. The last I saw of her she was in her own mother's house in Dubno, on Grodski Street, my grandmother's house, moss on the roof, chickens strung up, a feather singed by the fire. Arnold and I had traveled to see her. When we were leaving, I stopped for a moment to regard her from the doorway. For a few minutes, I was able to watch her without her knowing. Or maybe, I think sometimes, my mother did know, and this was her last gift, to allow me simply to look, to take this final image of her, back in her family house, the house of her own mother, pine boiling on the stove. Arnold waited behind in the street.

We are leaving, I said, we have to go back, I told my mother. She who could not abide Vienna, who had gone back home the day after I was married to Arnold. She had never adjusted to the city, could never lose the village in her, could never pretend to be who she was supposed to be, a generic Viennese woman, content over hot chocolate in a café near the Prater. Everything for her was an echo of home, a place she missed—this tiny village, the river Ikva, which curled in a half circle near the old castle, ravens in the alders, the mud-rutted highway, the ancient superstitions, which told her that there were dybbuks in the forest. If you are going, don't go through the forest, she told me, go on the road, there are terrible things in that forest. I told her she was mistaking fiction for life. The forest is nice, Mama, I said, it is fine, I happen to like the forest. It is so green there, I told her, you should go someday, go for a short walk in the middle of the day and look up when the sun is coming down and you will see the deepest green. She smiled at me. The patient smile of an exhausted mother. Please, she said, do not go through the forest.

Before I left, I tried once more to get her to come with me. What would I do in that terrible city? my mother asked. Would I stand around on a street corner selling fruit? Look at me. And I did. I looked. My mother, an old woman that day, but not even forty-five. Dark-haired when she was young, an impossible beauty, the source of so many poems. My father had told me this when I was young. Every boy in Dubno had written a poem about her. She was the Helen of Troy of Dubno. She could have launched a war, I'm telling you, said my father, she was that amazing, that beautiful. I tried again, a last time. I'll buy you a train ticket. Come, Mama, come. You can live in our house. You don't have to sell anything. I'll bring you the fruit. Just come. I will take care of you. Bad things will happen if you stay, I said, to which my mother, knowing every-thing as mothers do, had said simply, then let the bad things happen where I live, where in my heart I have always lived. My mother kissed me on my forehead, between my eyes.

You come back, my mother said.

Last words. Last words.

And then she returned to what she'd been doing at the stove.

I wonder some nights what my mother did in that place. What remains is only this: the sight of my mother in her old home in a village, which was, not even three years later, emptied out person by person, everyone taken into the forest my mother had always feared, the forest where I had played as a girl, a gorgeous place, overhung with the deepest green, a kind of green I have yet to encounter in this second life of mine, and where, one by one, the Jews of the village were shot, put into the earth unmourned, my childhood friends, their parents, their babies, everyone, every single person, including my sweet mother, Stisie, who all her life knew something about that forest, who felt it, who smelled the darkness before the darkness arrived.

A new man waits outside my room. He comes in hobbled. The pain, he says, you can't understand. The pills have stopped working. Everything, he says, is on fire. You just can't know, he says, how it feels inside me.

Ten a day, ten men, a minyan of injured travelers, all with the smell of elsewhere on their bodies. Come, I tell them, get on the table, show me where the pain begins, point if you can, tell me all about it.

BACK in the cafeteria, Hermann asks the same question. "I need to know everything. Give me," he says, "the history of Fania."

"The history of Fania," I say, "is short."

"This cannot be," he says. "Not Fania. Impossible."

"You see something in me that is not there," I say.

"In Hermann's mind, Fania is a giant."

"Like I said. This is a delusion. I am, by every measure, something small."

"Explain the delusion," he says.

"I am a hotel worker. This is all. A masseuse. Nothing more. A lady with an accent."

"Very much like the exiled empress being forced into labor," he says, speaking of the former empress Zita, whom both of us have seen gleaming back at us from a photograph in yesterday's *Gazette*, standing in front of her castle in Switzerland. "If this was the truth, if you told Hermann this was so, that in your steamer you had a crown, I would understand this as the truth."

"Lord. The things you say."

"Tell it to me brief," he says.

"You want brief, how's this? Life before, life during, life after," I say. "That's it. That's all I have."

"There is more than this," he says.

"Birth, escape, life, escape, prison, escape, hunger, escape, then Canada."

"O Canada," he begins to sing.

About our language lessons: even now, I suffer every moment as an act of continuous translation, from German to English, from English to French, a process of immense slowness, gradations of comprehension, time drawn out to its maximum thinness, a process I have been told will end when the brain rewires itself, learns the language the way a baby does, as a process of immersion, a word I know only in English, a word I associate with being caught within tides, feet deep in water.

I know this from having watched my daughter, Sonja, the quick accumulation of knowledge from one day to the next, a matter, I thought then, of geography, a rumbling within her, and then, at once, knowledge, a crack in the earth of her, speech, the names for her emotions: consciousness. Not Moses, though, Baby Moses, my small heartbeat come to life, Moses, whose whole life was nothing but his being immersed in me, immersed in my breathing, never far from that drumming of mine, a fact that comforts me on nights when there is no comfort. That all his life he had known almost only one thing, which was the sound of his mother. He was pried from me. At six months old my son was pried from my hands while I stood. Two men took my son, Moses, from me. Maybe you know this already, whoever you are. Maybe there is no need to write it out in such explicit terms. This is what comes to me at night. An image that requires no translation, this one moment, the prying loose, as one pries loose with a hammer a rotten floorboard in a home. Someone had been the hammer, a man behind a leather glove, and we were the nails, put down in the earth as firmly as anyone else, but taken up, torn, pulled, tossed, melted down, blown back into the air as vapor.

"I came to Canada by myself," I say. "I came by myself because everyone else was dead."

"As did I," he says. "Everyone else was also dead."

"Only time on an airplane in my life."

"I have never flown," he says.

"I had thought that from my seat I might be able to see something wonderful."

"Such as what, Fania?"

"I thought, here I am on my way to my second life, flying over the last life, surely there will be some great remainder of myself to see."

"No such view?"

"Middle seat," I say.

"Of course."

"Beside me, a woman is looking at pictures of Jerusalem for many hours, the same pictures of holy places, stones kissed by God, ancient rock walls that are the site of miracles, and I wanted to say, look where you are, you are halfway to the moon, what other miracle do you need!"

"Before this I was in Jerusalem," he says.

"You did not stay?" I ask.

"When I arrive," he says, "everyone is bombing everyone. Everything is put on fire everywhere. And this is just the first day. Every day afterward it is this same story. People are furious. People wail in the street. People arguing with their various gods. A man one day, he says to me, what a miracle that you are here! Can't you feel the miracle, and I am feeling like a crazy man. So I go out on my motorcycle."

"Motorcycle?" I ask.

"Oh yes, when Hermann is young, Hermann has a motorcycle."

"Is that so?"

"Two motorcycles, actually. One motorcycle for weekdays. One motorcycle for the Sabbath."

"You had a Sabbath motorcycle?"

"What? God does not deserve a good motorcycle?" he asks.

"Which was the nicer motorcycle?" I ask. "The one for you or the one for God?"

"The one for me, obviously."

"God probably already has all the motorcycles he needs."

"This is what I tell myself," he says.

"Describe this motorcycle for me," I say.

"If Fania likes motorcycles so much," he says, "I can go get you a motorcycle."

"It's not that," I say. "It's that they're so dangerous."

"But what is not dangerous, Fania? You are eating cake from a vending machine. You think that is not dangerous?"

"Being imprisoned is not enough for you? You have to ride a motorcycle?"

"Very funny," he says. "Also, very inappropriate. Joking about this. How dare you, Fania."

"Finish the story," I say, smiling. "You are driving your motorcycle. And then what? Finish. Please. And then what?"

"Oh, Hermann tries very hard to solve Middle East peace. And then very quickly I am asked to leave the country."

"Describe this trouble for me."

"I go out on my motorcycle somewhere where I am not supposed to go, a place we are forbidden contact, or something else which is stupid, but I go there anyway, so close, ten minutes, over hills, across many important and holy boundaries about which I am ignorant. I cannot be told what not to do anymore, I think, no one on earth is my jailer, I recognize no such stupidity, and apparently in the process I commit terrible and grave sins."

"Oh yes?"

"Oh yes. I meet many people and they are suffering, the suffering is terrible, their homes are on fire, their trees are on fire, the walls of their houses are on fire, and I give them the key to my house, I say come with me, come back to my house. I have rooms for you, I tell them, but they want their own house, they have their own key."

"Of course," I say.

"Very long story short, Hermann is given ticket to Canada."

"You have been here that long?" I ask. "And you are only now learning English?"

"Oh no," he says. "I traded in my ticket to Canada for a new motorcycle."

"Of course," I say.

"And I drove around for a very long time."

"How long?"

"I should not say."

"Tell me," I say.

"Many years, let's say." He has turned red. "The actual number is not important."

"I want a real number. How long did you drive around on your motorcycle?"

"Maybe the number is eighteen years," he says.

"Maybe?"

"Perhaps," he says. "Maybe."

"Off and on?"

"If by off and on you mean to say morning to night, then yes, off and on."

"You drove a motorcycle for eighteen years."

"You make this sound like it is an unreasonable number of years to drive a motorcycle continuously," he says, smiling.

I think about this.

"I did not want to stop," he says, very quietly. "Stopping seemed potentially dangerous."

"Where does one go on a motorcycle that does not stop for eighteen years?"

"Anywhere you could think."

"Russia?"

"Briefly, yes."

"Only briefly?"

"There are many forests in Russia, Fania."

"Afghanistan?"

"For months," he says.

"South America?" I ask.

"All over."

"Greece?" I ask.

"Oh, for a very long time. Greece is very lovely. Would you like me to take you to Greece?"

"And how did you sleep?"

"With great discomfort," he says.

"On your motorcycle?"

"It was stopped," he says. "Most of the time, at least."

"And you did what in these places?" I ask. "In South America and Afghanistan and Greece?"

He is probably my age, although it is difficult to tell with men like him. What is clear to me is that he both does and does not want to tell me this, that he cannot tell the story but must tell the story, that for all this time he has likely been trapped in this space, between wanting and not wanting. With every new song on the jukebox, a glister of recognition shows itself in him. An echo of another place, a different iteration of him, the resurfacing of memory, a momentary burst of transportation from here to there, wherever that is.

Hermann leans over, comes closer, brings himself nearly to my ear. "On a normal day, Fania, I would drive, morning to night to morning again, and I would try while driving to reconstruct in my head every day of my old life. You are laughing," he says, which is true, "but I am telling you the honest story. For instance, I would think of an important day. A particular birthday. Or the day on which I went to school for the first time. Or a day on which someone I loved was buried. Or, for example, my bar mitzvah, which was in the big synagogue in the Eighth, the Neudeggergasse, and afterward, the dinner we had at a restaurant near the park, where, I remember, my mother took me aside into a private room to give me advice. I would do this. Think into this, think about this, think over this. And I would go through it minute by minute, trying to find the memory, make it real again. I would drive around and remember my way through this day in very close detail. For instance, this day with my mother is important because I cannot remember what she told me. I have, at this point, reconstructed every conversation we ever had, my mother and I, and I can, if I want, play them back to myself in my head, as if they are on a recording somewhere inside of me. But not this conversation. I had thought my father would give me the advice. I had been to other bar mitzvah celebrations and this was what was done, this bestowing of advice between fathers and sons. But for me, it was my mother. I should have known it would be my mother. What advice did my father ever have to give me? Sometimes I think that inside his head there was nothing but the sound of bees buzzing. Not so with my mother. She was a powerful woman, a towering figure of my life, a surgeon, the only woman surgeon I had ever heard of then. Hearts, organs, bones. She could operate on anything. Even an engine. I learned the rhythm of the human body from her. I learned how to operate a tourniquet. How to pack a lost finger in ice. How to know when a person was close to death. How to tell when someone had been poisoned. How to fix an engine with a stocking. Things a boy should not know, but things she had the good sense to teach me. She would arrive home in the evening smelling of lemon soap. And juniper. And also, I knew, of blood, although I did not know then what this smelled like. At my bar mitzvah she brought me into a room near the dining room, and outside there was, I remember, ice in the trees."

He pauses for a long moment. The cafeteria is, around us, completely empty.

"And this is it," he says. "The memory ends. The night ends."

"No more?" I ask.

"This is the sort of thing I would think about on my motorcycle. Why is there nothing but blackness at the end of this day? I see my mother's mouth moving, I see the room we are in, a big room with gray curtains, I see the people around me, my family, all of them are no longer, I can smell the buttered rolls, the clear broth in white bowls, I can feel the crunch of the bone in the meat put on my plate, I can see the building we are in, the park around it, the trees encased in ice, the entire city at once, with steam rising, and higher up, backing away, as if I am floating, Fania, as if I am on top of my own life so that now I can see the whole country itself, I can see all of it, but for my mother there are no words, no sound, everything lost, everything gone. I would drive through this day from morning until night to morning again. I would do this all day for many days straight until I thought I had lived it over fully, that I had appreciated it, maybe, in a way I hadn't before. And then, of course, after time, it's as if I have had my bar mitzvah a hundred times over, all across the world, in the desert of North Africa, in Buenos Aires near the sea, in Greece, in the west of the United States where the land is like the surface of Mars. I have this day again with my mother and my father."

I am struck by this. As struck by this as by anything any person has said to me while living on this continent. And it comes here, of all places, in this awful cafeteria. I have begun to cry without recognizing it. We are alone, thank the Lord, me and this man who I have known only five weeks. He is someone I might have passed on a street when I was young, or sat beside on a crowded bus on the Ringstraße, or seen, perhaps, in the Tiergarten, mooning over the polar bears. And in this way, perhaps, it is not too much to say I know him, and have known him all this time, that these evenings together are not evenings with a stranger, but with an old acquaintance, some relationship severed abruptly by time and begun again here, beneath this harsh lighting, amid the forever-winter of Montreal.

"I am always doing this," says Hermann. "Making beautiful women weep at the sight of me. It is a terrible curse to possess this kind of fantastic beauty."

This makes me smile. Yet it is true that he has made me cry.

"It began to become a problem. Here is Hermann, devastatingly good-looking, driving God's motorcycle, arriving in town from far away, having suffered gravely, wearing the face of a harmed man, in possession of many stories, most of them tragic, eager to talk, to learn the language, so that I might tell them out loud. This is how one begins to become a human again, after all."

"By making people cry?"

"By telling the story," he says.

"Driving a motorcycle every day for eighteen years wasn't effective?"

"When you drive a motorcycle that much, Fania, you are always driving a motorcycle, whether you are or whether you are not. This is what I learned about driving that long. Does that make sense?"

"I don't know, Hermann. Does it make sense? I don't think it does. I have no idea anymore."

The idea of these conversations is the byproduct of a local resettlement committee, a group, as far as I have heard, that consists of ten women, all of them living in the wealthiest parts of this city. A group for the well-being of people like them, run by the untouched, the warm, the safely kept. A program to teach English and French, to reestablish community, to help, in their words, smooth away trauma. Hermann had introduced himself by way of a card in the mail, a small yellow postcard. My first personal mail on this side of the earth. *Come meet, come eat,* he had written in English. And then, in German: *I am new to Montreal: not even one year. I am not the best human being who ever lived, and I have, even still, great difficulty expressing myself in English as I would like, but I am decent company. Also,* he had written, in English, *I am alone.*

I am tired and what I say next I say in German, and dutifully, he waves his hands to stop me. This is the rule, that we speak only English, or that we speak only French. According to the literature of the resettlement experts, this will help acclimate us. Learn the language of today, I have been told. What I say is that I'm tired. And what I mean by saying this, that I am tired, is that I am exhausted by the way these stories end. Eventually, badly. Always, badly. Everybody goes looking for their loves, their babies, and nobody ever finds anybody. Every story ends the same way.

"I thought, certainly, when I grew older," he says, "I would forget. I thought—a gigantic trauma plus old age plus eighteen years of continuously driving on a motorcycle—this would do it, this would equal at least some forgetting. But then, Hermann wakes at night, having remembered. And then, you know, there is terror. Not eating. Not sleeping. Hearing voices. The sensing of ghosts."

"When I came here first, I had many bad days," I say.

"How many bad days?" he asks.

"All of them," I say.

"And in these bad days, what happens?"

"Like moon phases," I say. "In which I am full, not full, pregnant with hope, or with hope carved out of me. Or I am sleeping."

"Yes," he says.

"And in sleeping, dreaming."

"Yes," he says.

"And in dreaming, suffering visitations of old faces."

"Yes," he says.

"My babies' faces. My son. Moses, especially. His face."

"Not the Moses on the mountaintop," he says, which makes me smile.

"My baby Moses," I say. "Forever baby. Always baby."

"Always and baby," he says. "These are two good words, which when put together become two awful words."

"Yes," I say. "The most awful."

"And then what?" he asks.

"Losing."

"Of course," he says.

"And hearing him at night crying for me."

"Crying from where?" he asks.

"From just beyond the wall of my apartment, just beyond the bedpost, the street and weather. Here he is, on one side of the wall, but I can't move through walls to get to him. You know what I'm telling you, don't you? Do you understand?"

"Yes," he says.

"For all my life, these noises."

"I understand," he says.

"Right now. Right now, these noises."

"The thing about motorcycles," Hermann says, "is that they are very, very loud."

THERE is more to say. For instance, the facts: that they are all dead. Our program wants us to say this part aloud, even though I believe that I should not have to do so. This is obvious. This part of the story is obvious. Only people on the outside would think otherwise. Here I am, in this snow-city, frozen down to the blood vessels, and the truth is obvious, the truth is on me, on my graveyard skin. They are dead. Sonja dead on a train, Arnold dead in a forest, Moses dead after being pried from my hands as I stood.

My small Moses. Sweet-smelling Moses. Six months of life and that is it. Born, I think sometimes, to accompany me to the end of life, as Virgil accompanies Dante. All that way, from Vienna to the darkness, and he did not cry. I think sometimes that he knew, that the old life was in him still, the remainder of who he had been before, in another version of the past, and this allowed him to know what I did not know. This, I know, is more nonsense, but what penalty should exist for nonsense now that the world is no longer? After all, nonsense seems sensible to me in ways that I could have never expected in Vienna, in our old living room, beside my piano, my radio, my wool blanket, my teacup, my portrait of Grandmother.

I had the thought when I was liberated that all of them had been liberated as well, Arnold certainly, he had lived, Arnold had survived, Arnold had not been shot dead as I had been told, I knew it, he was somewhere else, a mile away, a country away, but he had lived, and so had Sonja, somehow she had arrived in England on the train we put her on, she was alive, she had made it in one piece and had not, as the letters told us, perished on the journey. And my baby

Moses, although he had been torn from me, and although everyone knew what happened to infants torn away like this, he was, I knew, liberated just the same.

I walked for a month through Poland, warm and wrecked Poland, and on that first day I understood the truth of it, that everyone had been survived into different futures and that I would never see any of them again. I could sense this. I would hear them in their separate rooms, within their separate lives, but I would not be able to cross over to meet them. I would feel the vibrations of their voices in these rooms, and hear the songs they sang, gather word of their days, hear the news of these other futures, but still, it was impossible to get to them. A barrier had gone up between me and my babies, between me and Sonja and me and Moses, through which I could feel them moving, as I had when they were inside me. Some mornings I found it possible to press my hand against my body and to feel them this way, to feel them far away, but these feelings were both temporary and permanent, like storm wind, like lunar tide, like madness. And what I knew was this: they were there, and I was here, and there was no door, no entry, no dream, in which one was let through. Where they lived, they might be writing, just as I am writing. There was only this: talking and breathing and waiting and breaking mirrors and walking beneath ladders and tempting all the dumb wisdoms. Knee-deep in the warm mud of the bloodlands and I knew this to be true. An instance of motherly intuition and future seeking. I could not cross over.

"I would like to tell you about him," I say. "About Moses. And my daughter, Sonja. I would like to do this."

"Not necessary," he says, which is another way of him saying that he knows the story already, and a way of him extending to me the kindness of not having to say more.

What I would say is this: We were taken in the morning. They sent only one man to take us. I had seen him before. He had red hair

and a distinctive red mark on his face. He spit on my child. He put
out three of Arnold's teeth with the end of his pistol. He berated me
about the state of my home. Maybe you want to bring your jewelry,
the man said to me, your diamonds, your best gold earrings. It was
only the three of us in the house, Arnold and Moses and me. Sonja
was already gone. We had already put her on a train to England, and
she had not lived, she had died somewhere between here and there,
"taken ill," the official letter said, whatever that meant, we were
never able to find out, how can a five-year-old girl possibly die on a
train in a country like England, this is what I was thinking when
the man came to take us, this impossibility, that I had given away
my daughter to a train and the train had killed her somehow, I
was thinking this when Arnold's teeth were on the floor, when they
put us on the cattle train, which was in itself a form of death. We
took turns holding Moses. He did not cry. I told him not to, and
he did not. A million years he aged on that train, and I was carrying the grown man Moses, and not the baby Moses, and I told him,
do not cry, and he did not. A million years he aged on that train,
and he was old like the prophet and I was a child and Arnold was a
child.

The last I saw of Arnold he was being walked away from me.
You know the rest, whoever you are. To say it aloud is a profanity;
this much is already a profanity. A bullet in the belly, a bullet in the
cheek, a bullet between his gray eyes, a thousand bullets for every
thousand strands of his black hair, poison made for insects inhaled
deep in the lungs. Then Moses was taken from my hands. Two men
came. Let me help you, one of them said, and he took Moses. Let
me help you, let me help you, let me help you. This is what they said.

I would like to tell Hermann some of this. I search for the words,
I am always searching for the words, but the continuous act of translation fails me. This only happens when I am exhausted, after my
shifts, when my hands hurt. I wish I had the words for what the pain

in my hands is like, this deep, gnawing ache, which radiates in my sleep and becomes something else within the logic of dreams. A monster growing off the bones of my wrist. Someone with the face of everyone I have been missing. When I offer the words for this in German, Hermann again waves away my sentences, as if, once leaving my mouth, they have become physical objects aloft between us, like birds one can warn off. The rules are the rules, I know.

"That day on the motorcycle, after the bombings, after I traded in my ticket to Canada," Hermann says, "I eventually went to the sea, the Dead Sea, which is not a sea but instead what happens when a sea is almost gone, and there are many people standing there on the ledge watching something that is not there, captivated in a trance, seeing and not seeing. When I got there, I went in, step by step. The water is hot there, the water hurts it is so full of salt, and I begin to float. The sea is so confused because it is dying that it does not know to sink you, and so I float. And around me everyone is laughing. It is a tacky place, actually, a terrible place, but I am here. This is the strangest thing. All the laughter around me. That we should laugh at the idea of experiencing this feeling of death. Or this defiance of death. I stopped to watch this. All of us in the water, dripping with mud, laughing at this place where the two worlds converge, floating and rising, swimming and drowning, living and dying."

Outside, streetcars pass. Women with my mother's walk. Streetlights holding white fire. I see myself in the dark mirror of my coffee cup. Still here, still here, still here.

"What are you thinking?" he asks. "What is in your head?"

Hermann waits for me to say something. Maybe, I will think later, this is when everything changed.

"I was thinking about your English, Hermann. It's getting really good. You made almost no mistakes tonight."

He waves away the compliment but seems to know that I've wanted to say more. "I have the very best teacher," he says.

THE following morning a woman arrives for an appointment with me at the hotel. At once, I see that the woman is me. She is Fania just as I am Fania. Or some version of me, let loose from wherever we are kept when we are not inside our bodies.

The woman does not seem to understand, as I do, that she has come face-to-face with someone with her same body. She is in a rush, this version of me, delivered from the outside world, smelling of coconut, her skin quite obviously better than mine, her hair pulled back behind her head and tied up with a painted silk ribbon that I could not afford. The woman makes a sign with her hands to say she does not know English—the universal sign of confusion, her hands turned up as if testing for rain. I try in French, je pense qu'il y a eu une erreur, surely there has been an error. These are the only words that come to me at first, the only explanation. An error has occurred. Some mistake in the larger order of worlds. Otherwise, I feel terror. What else to feel but the bone-quake of terror.

The woman has her hotel key in her hand, and as she stands in my room, she twirls it anxiously around her finger. She eyes me and sees something in me that I do not know exists, some sign. Then she begins to speak in German. In unmistakable Wienerisch. She is suffering, she explains. A continuous burst of pain has been punishing her left side. Sleep is impossible.

"I am left awake nightly in a state of prolonged agony. I have come here on business and everyone in this city says that you are the very best pain artist," she says. "It has become so bad that my husband does not know what to do with me."

I pretend not to have heard this. I ask the woman to repeat herself. My husband. Mein Ehemann. The woman takes a loose strand of hair from her face. "The pain has become so extreme that my husband claims he is in pain as well." I feel the floor give way. This woman wears my wedding ring. A curled ribbon of silver, with one emerald stone, the emerald of the Danube in my memory. Arnold gave me this ring. I was seventeen years old. I had it for nine years before it was taken. This woman's ring is older, worn. With marks on the silver. Age on the stone.

"Your husband," I say.

"He is upstairs," she says. "In our room. Awaiting my old body, free from pain. But he is always awaiting my body. This way or that."

The woman laughs. It is my laugh. Or a version of my old laughter. Hoarse, riven by cigarette smoke. Her voice is an accent I have lost.

"Upstairs," I say. "Your husband is upstairs. Upstairs here."

"He would come for an appointment as well, but he is too modest. Certainly too modest to be touched by a stranger."

But I am not a stranger, I want to say.

"The air travel was grueling," the woman says. "It made matters worse."

"You have traveled from Germany?" I ask.

"Vienna, of course." The woman smiles. My smile. My old Wienerisch. "But you know this already," she says. "Of course you know this."

So she knows, I think. The woman takes her robe off and climbs onto the table, lies flat. She is me and not me. She bears none of the marks of my adult life. Nothing of my encasement, my removal, my having tried to hold on to everything. Instead, there is the pearl-hued half-moon behind my knee left over from a fall in the Tiergarten. And a gash the size of a small coin given to me by the hard rusted edge of a fence post in Dubno. Scars of my childhood, on her body and my body. But nothing of Canada, the life here, my hands on the bodies of so many men, nine years of nothing but men, so many of them so similar to one another that I have come to believe that they are all the same man, with the same body, that pushing my palm into the shoulder of one man should affect all of them at once. In this way, perhaps, I am reaching through to touch Arnold.

I put my hand on this woman expecting to feel something. Instead, there is nothing. The past leaves marks, Arnold had said when we were young, when I was distraught to have to leave our apartment in the Eighteenth for the ghetto, which is when I last wore this ring.

Or this: the past comes walking back in, a rich Viennese woman, suffering from pain and sleeplessness.

"Tell me about your husband," I manage to say.

"My husband," the other Fania says. "What is there to say? A husband is a vessel of complaints. Eventually, if we are lucky, a husband becomes a different version of you, one that you feel happy to see smiling at you at the end of the day."

"But," I say, "your husband: Is he kind?"

"Oh, of course. I would never do with an unkind man. Neither would you. I know this. I can tell."

"And is he well?" I ask. I would say that I feel that I have cracked in two by this point, but that has already happened without me knowing.

The other Fania meets my eyes with a measure of pity. A way of considering the loneliness of others.

"He is perfect," the other me says, in very bad English. "Arnold is always perfect for me."

Something horrible has happened: I have lost my mind. Across the hall, my colleague Danilo is still with a client. He is tall, delicate, formerly beautiful, a dancer from Belgrade, smuggled here in a packing container. All across the Atlantic, packed inside a metal coffin punched with air holes, with barely enough room to move, he had continued to dance, doing this for so long that he eventually forgot where he was, thinking that if he moved, continued to dance, he would not die, that he would be delivered alive, delivered twice in one life. He will understand me. What I need to do is to knock on his door, to bring him in here so that he can assure me of what I know to be true, that I am asleep still in my bed on Le Plateau four kilometers from here, and that this is a dream. That I am warm beneath my bedcovers still, in my efficiency apartment, overhung with greenery, behind four dead bolts, and that none of this, none of it all, is happening.

On my first day, Danilo had given me a warning. You are working with people in pain, and people in pain exist in two places at once: within the pain, which is an endless place, a place of incomprehensible depth, and they are also in a place where the pain has vanished, a future place. It was my job, he told me, to bring them from one to the other, from a place that lasts forever into a place that does not exist at all.

"The pain," the other Fania says, "is like an electrical wire laid down within me, severed by an axe, shooting sparks. My husband," she says, "he believes that I am imagining all this. That I am actually fine inside. That the pain is more mental than anything. My daughter tends to agree with him. Sonja always agrees with her papa. This stays the same, even into adulthood."

"Sonja," I say, my breath blood-punched out of me.

"My daughter," the woman says. "Her name is Sonja. She is a musicologist. Too smart for us. Lost in the notes, always. Away, always, always, her ear pressed to a speaker."

"A music—" I cannot say the word.

Instead, I exit the room. Or better said: I escape. On the way out, I take the woman's hotel key. Left on the countertop, a key like any other key, and I swipe it cleanly. Upstairs, I rush past the reception desk to the elevators. In the nine years I've worked here, I have never been upstairs to see where the guests live, nor have I been in this elevator, which is glass, and which rises now in a murmur over my new city, mist hung, snow covered, white from edge to edge. This is as high, I think, as I have ever been. From this height, inside this private capsule, the city is so small, able to be cupped in my palms, like each of my children were at their birth.

At the door, I knock, wait not even a moment, and go inside.

"Arnold," I yell into the empty room. "Arnold! Arnold!"

THE next time I see Hermann in the cafeteria, days later, I tell him I am coming apart.

He puts his hands on my shoulders. This is the very first time we have touched.

"You seem to be existing in one place," he says, and although I suspect he means that I seem to be in one piece, I do not ask, nor do I correct his small error, as is my responsibility to him.

I have been walking. At night, in circles, across Montreal, through snow, on foot, walking. Hour after hour of this, in search of some explanation for what has happened. After my shift I go, go for so long that going after work turns into going before work. This is how long I have been walking. It is November, already dark, already frigid. From the edge of the basin near the frozen fountain in the Parc La Fontaine I understand that I have somehow become split, a version of me on earth in two futures. Here I am, on the edge of this piece of manufactured parkland, amid the zoo stink of the nearby elephant enclosure.

And here I am, also, quite obviously, somewhere else, wherever the other version of me has gone. This other version who has managed to hold on to her husband still, and also her daughter. Sonja the musicologist. All this time I have been walking I have said these words to myself. Sonja the musicologist. Whatever it means to be a musicologist I need to know. Give me the directions, and I will drive there. If I need to live inside the music, I will shrink myself to the size of a sixteenth note and I will crawl inside the score.

This is the other future where Sonja is living, in the world of music, wherever that is. I walk in my uniform, the same uniform I have worn to meet Hermann, the red smock, the hospital scrub bottoms, the hotel-issue clogs. All night, into morning, as I walk, and as the city both sleeps and comes again to rise, my hands ache. I have walked without washing away the oil, the eucalyptus, the camphor, the arnica, the birch root cream, the residue of so many bodies on my skin, pushed beneath my fingernails, buried into me. I walk until I find myself somewhere on the city's north side, deep in the middle of the night. Once there, I am struck by something about my displacement: that this other Fania did not mention anything about Moses. Suddenly, alone on the corner of a street I have never seen before, never once stood on, I collapse into grief over the fate of my baby, Moses. Gone in my life, gone in every other life.

Hermann has come dressed in better clothes. This is the only time I have ever seen him in something other than his normal uniform. He has come instead wearing an argyle sweater, pressed trousers the color of cooked chestnuts, buckskin loafers stained wet at the toe from the weather. When I ask why he has come in such fancy clothing, given our history of meeting one another in various states of dishevelment, and given the weather, the atmosphere, the snow, our shared darkness, our having ended up here speaking like this, he blushes.

"Let's talk first," he says. "Then you'll find out."

We are seated at our usual table, beneath the mouth of the exhaust system, out of which blow warm streams of heat, and beside the window, where along the strip of the Avenue Trans Island the snow has swept up against the glass in wind-feathered hills that have frozen solid.

I explain what has happened, and do so in a language that still feels like an invention of mine, a secret argot I've acquired from a best friend I can no longer find. I tell Hermann in the simplest terms. That a woman came to see me, and that this woman was, in every way, very obviously me, and that this other version of me had come to Montreal with her husband. My husband who was shot in the forest a thousand times is here with this other me. And most importantly, distressingly, unforgettably, this woman spoke of her daughter, who is obviously my daughter. She is a musicologist, I tell him. "I don't know what this is, a musicologist, but my daughter, wherever she is living, this is what she is doing, whatever that means, this is who she is." The important point, I tell Hermann, is that she lives, she lives, my daughter lives.

His first reaction is grief. "This makes me very sad to hear," he tells me. "When you are grieving," he says, "I am grieving." However, his second reaction to my telling him this—to my telling him that I have seen myself out in the world, dispossessed of my own body, living a life of apparent free will—is not to believe me. Across the table, Hermann is unfailingly polite, but the message is unmistakable. Either I am delirious, or I am a storyteller.

"This sounds like the ravings of a madwoman. I know. I think so too. But I have not been able to get myself to sleep, Hermann. Not since it happened."

"Because of this? Whatever it was? Two of you in the world and you can't sleep? This is all? This is the extent of your problem? We should all be so lucky. Two of Fania. This is Hermann's dream."

"I have been looking for her," I say.

"The other you? The one that does not exist?"

"Says you."

"And if you find her again, what will happen? You think that you can have all that she has? A husband again? A daughter who studies music and who answers the telephone when you call?"

This, of course, is exactly what I want. The telephone, especially.

Perhaps this wish of mine is visible in a way anyone can notice. That I have had a telephone installed in my small apartment for this very purpose, for the making of calls one could not connect or answer. A small red telephone, like the one rumored to exist on the desk of the American president, through which he is purported to be able to summon the detonation of worlds, to throw us all into these different futures of mine. For months I have sat up at night at the edge of my bed to talk to my family, to Sonja especially. This is my worst secret, my deep shame, these conversations, this indulgence in the impossible. A sign, I suspect, that long before this moment in the hotel with my double, I had already lost my mind. Or a version of religion, manufactured especially for my hands. There is always a moment on this phone when the imaginary operator asks to whom I'd like the call connected. And my answer is always Sonja. If I say Arnold, which on occasion I have, he will tell me of his day at work, where he exists, it seems, forever in the same office that was his father's office, a high perch in a factory that manufactured linens. And if I say Moses—sweet Moses—there is nothing to hear but his infant cooing, his rustling in the bassinet, his quick baby breaths, which come across the line in bursts, inhaled from some far place, and exhaled into my ear as if he were still in my arms. Or else there is an adult man living somewhere I have never been, having been raised by someone else, another woman, and he has no memory of me. And so there is Sonja, who has gone on with her life, who has always gone on, and who is now, evidently, a musicologist, lost in the puzzle of the notes.

We had, Arnold and I, given her away for safekeeping, as one puts away important documents into a bank vault. She was to go to England for the duration of the war, and then come back to us. An impossible idea to reconsider, this giving away a child as willingly as one gives away a sweater to charity. Like severing my feet with an axe. We had given her a doll to talk to, a doll she had named after me: a small toy named Fania. Two months later, we received corre-spondence informing us Sonja had in fact taken ill. These words, *taken ill*, have always brought to mind all the taking a child does. A taking of love, a taking with her small hands your hands, a taking after you, taking after Papa, taking off running into the garden in chase of the dogs, taking up the piano so that she might play for you when you are old and you need music in your life, a taking of your old jewelry, a taking of your magic and beauty and youth, a taking, eventually, of everything. But not taking ill. Not these words, which have yet to make sense, twenty-eight years after the fact. Sonja would be thirty-three years old today. The age at which I boarded a boat in Trieste, where, amid the heat, the palm sway, the stink of the sea, I wandered down a gangplank in hope of something I could not name. That something, I think now, was what I saw the other day, a version of myself untroubled by calamity, not yet swallowed up, a glimpse of a life where I have not been talking into a telephone late at night, this dummy conveyance through which no one, not yet, has ever spoken back to me.

I have found myself continually circling back to the zoo in the park, where the elephants stand languidly near fake banyan trees to regard me dolefully, and where I struggle to consider whether these animals, who as a species mourn their dead with songs, who bury their kin, whether they also imagine themselves on earth in two places, once maybe at the spot where they were captured, on what-ever lush heat-stroked savannah they lived last, and also here, in this always-winter, this white everything of Montreal.

I'm telling this to Hermann when he brings me a mug of warm cinnamon tea into which he has slipped a stick of rock candy that he has found somewhere, or that he has unwrapped from his pocket for this very moment. "To help it steep," he says. "Also, we are grown and there is no one to tell us not to eat as much candy as we want." This is his way of telling me to stop thinking of such impossibilities.

When he sits, he is quiet for a long time, too long, past the point where it is comfortable, and he is, I think to myself, quite obviously a beautiful man. Or more accurately, it is clear that he must have been a very beautiful young man. He has something in his face that Arnold had, a certain shyness, a lack of cruelty. He is nervous. Eventually, too late, I see this, the extent of his nervousness. He takes a square napkin from the table, folds it, turns it into an elephant for me, his tusk raised, like your zoo friends, he tells me, and he pushes it across the table to me, where I take it, keep it forever, have it beside me now many years later, many lifetimes into the future where today I find myself writing to you, and he tells me that he was once startled awake by elephants running toward him from across a hill, a mother and a child he thinks, this was in eastern Africa, that he wishes he could buy for me a trip to see it for myself, but that he has no money to do such a thing, that the rock candy itself nearly bankrupted him, and that also the elephants have become nearly extinct because so many men like him want to buy the women in their lives a nice trip like that.

"And I am the woman in your life," I say.

"Quite obviously," he says. "You are the only person I know in this whole city. My only friend."

"I think the same is true for me," I say.

"But I have not been entirely truthful with you, Fania," he says.

What I expect him to say is that he has not needed my help to learn English. That he has been pretending since the first moment. That we are long past the point where I ought to have figured this out and ended the lessons altogether and moved on to the next person lost without language in this cold city. I expect him to say that he has known English all this time, that he has been speaking it longer than I have, that he was speaking it, in fact, in childhood, that his father was a man from the north of Chicago who found his way to Vienna to study painting, and that in their home in the Leopoldstadt of the 1920s he was known to recite Francis Feeble's line from *Henry IV* that *a man can die but once. We owe God a death*—all of which he would confess to me later. But I am getting ahead of myself.

"I told you I would not go back to Vienna," he says.

"Not for all the money in the world, I thought."

"Not for money. Certainly not for money. For other things, yes. For my children, of course. For my wife, yes. For my old apartment, where I had my books, my dog, my warm blankets, my collection of records, photographs of my friends. For that, yes. For money? Not for money. Money is the last thing I would go for."

"So you did go back to Vienna? This is what you were not honest about?"

"I wanted to. I tried to go so many times. When I was driving all that time," Hermann tells me, "I kept circling home. Getting closer and closer, but I could never get myself to go back."

He takes a pencil from the pocket of his jacket and on the paper place mat between us he draws an astonishingly accurate map of Europe, replete with its fresh occupation of the cities I remember visiting as a girl—Leipzig, Dresden, Potsdam. "I'd often found myself driving someplace unexpected. Turkey, let's say. I'd find myself there, driving in big circles from Ankara to Izmir, where I would try to relax on the patio of a big international hotel, where all the beautiful and rich people were imbibing powerful and blinding alcoholic cocktails. But I couldn't relax. So I'd get back on my motorcycle and I'd go, say, to Antalya, where I would try to relax once again, in full view of the Mediterranean, which is a deep blue, a mirror of the sky, the blue of every blue on earth gathered up for this one afternoon, and there, across the water, I'd imagine my wife and my children were somewhere in Jaffa on a beach much like my beach, looking out at me just as I am looking out at them. A fiction, of course. My wife never saw the ocean. Her name was Elma. She spent her entire life in Vienna. She had many thoughts of the ocean, though. What it would smell like, how she would dress for it when she saw it finally. How she would approach the water. Timidly, she decided. Because it would be cold. And carefully, because one never knows how deep the water runs, how strong the tide pulls. My children obsessed over the ocean as well. My son, Viktor, he slept with a conch shell he had been given as a gift. He would hold it up for me to ask if the sound was true. I had never seen the ocean either, although I suppose I must have told him I had. A fatherly lie. Is this what it sounds like? he asked. And I would put it to my ear and say, yes, exactly, this is what a shell is, a piece of the sea one can take away and keep forever. When we go together, I told him, you can take a piece of it away for yourself to remember the day, and the shell will sound forever like the sound of the sea on the day you were there. What did I know? I thought this was how the ocean worked. Our last night together, packed into the small apartment we had been moved to, in a room with a dozen other people, I saw my son had taken this shell with him. Of all his belongings, his treasures, this was what he had taken. It helped to calm him. He was my oldest. In my last real memory of my son, a memory I have lived back a thousand times, so many times I can step into it now if I want, he is holding this shell to his ear as he falls asleep. My sweet boy. The last night he slept as a human."

He speaks quietly. As if talking in his sleep.

"And so, when I'd find myself on the ocean in Antalya, I'd think of this, and think that it must be so that Viktor is out there on the beach of Haifa, of Jaffa, what world takes a boy like Viktor, who once played the piano on the radio, who at the end of the earth takes a seashell with him. And so I have the impulse to go find him. This is why I tried Jerusalem. Because one day on the beach in Turkey, I thought I saw him across the water from me. It shames me to say this aloud, Fania. Do not judge me. But I had been standing on the shore, looking out, and I swear, I saw him looking back at me. Foolish, I know; crazy, I know. And of course, in Haifa, in Jaffa, in Eilat, I searched and could not find him. But then, on the beach in Eilat, looking across the Red Sea to Aqaba, I see him again, my boy with his shell, standing and listening, and so I drive there. I take my motorcycle through the wadis where I wouldn't find him. I drive for days and find myself near the Strait of Hormuz, in Musandam, looking out at Oman, a shimmer, a mirage, maybe nothing, maybe everything. And on like this, for eighteen years, chasing this picture, which always appears to me from across the water. If you were to draw my path"—which he does for me on the map between us, a circle of stitches around the heart—"you would see that I had suspended myself in orbit around Vienna."

When he is finished, he repeats himself: "I have not been truthful with you." I tell him that I don't understand what he is saying to me, and he says in German that he hasn't come to Montreal because he enjoys Canada so much, or because he has a particular inclination for snow and frigid temperatures and sterile cafeterias.

This is all he says, just this sentence about why he hasn't come to Montreal, nothing more on this subject for as long as we know each other, which is a period of many years.

"So will you tell me why you've come dressed like this?" I ask.

He has been waiting for me to ask. He leans back in his chair. "Dressed like how?"

I suppress a smile. "Would you like me to tell you that you look nice?"

"Not if it's a lie," he says.

"You are impossible," I say.

"Very possible," he says. He pinches himself. "In the flesh. Both possible. And actual."

"Then what?" I say. "The sweater. The comb through your hair. The cologne."

"Green Water it is called. As if this is what one wants to smell like. Green water."

"So you are merely fishing for compliments."

"I would not need to go to such extreme lengths, Fania," he says. "Your being with me here once a week is compliment enough. Rather, I have a surprise for you. Come outside."

We leave through the back door. The weather is brutal. What he has brought for me is parked in front of a bright pharmacy window. It is blue, sleek, old, but will run for as long as I need it to. "I have put it together for you," he says, showing me the motorcycle he has fixed for me to drive. He has made the assumption that while I would not readily accept a motorcycle, that escaping death once, as I've put it, is once too many, that I would accept a motorcycle made especially for me. He has affixed two wheels onto the back. "So you do not fall," he says. Like a child's bicycle. He shows me the seat. "There is, as well," he says, "the matter of space. Enough room for me. Enough room for both of us."

Because I don't know what to say, I tell him that his lesson is overdue. That the committee will want to hear about our progress.

"Our lesson," he says.

"Our English lesson," I say.

"Of course. The lesson. I must learn my English."

"Which is why we are here together."

"Yes," he says. "This is the only reason we are here together."

"The only reason."

At this, his accent thickens. "For the learning of the language of English," he says. "Hermann has difficulties. Needs teacher."

"Yes," I say, smiling. "You certainly do."

And would you believe me, reader, whoever you are, wherever you are reading this, that back inside at our table, Hermann's paper elephant began to rise between us, that alone in this dark and frigid all-night cafeteria, a folded elephant made of paper began to run circles around us?

T HERE is one more thing:

The next morning, she returns.

My body, my hair, the scent of what had been my favorite perfume, my wedding ring, my old accent, my old laugh, stories of my daughter, my husband, my apartment, which this woman speaks of with relish, a sanctuary she calls it. She possesses details of my home that I have forgotten. A quality of sunlight in the back, for instance, during the morning hours, when one feels the heat of summer through the windows. Also, a loose slat on the staircase that leads from the kitchen to the bedroom, which is still bothering her, still bothering my husband. Does she or does she not know that when I was taken, when she was taken, the agent who removed us, who pulled us down this staircase by our hair, berated us for having allowed such a hazard in the house? What is the fucking problem with you Jews that you cannot have a functioning fucking staircase? Too miserly to fix it? Too busy destroying Vienna with your sickness and your profiteering and your bloodletting to keep a functioning staircase? He had come to rob us of our remaining food, had come near midnight to steal our butter, which he swiped from our icebox with his hand, to steal our ration tickets, which he put into the fire. He grabbed me by the shoulder and asked, where do you want to go, where on earth would you like me to have you sent, take your pick, it's your lucky day, he said, and for whatever reason, I chose New York, a fantasy place. He was the one who took my ring, this ring, which I can see now, into which this whole room is reflected.

"This staircase," I say to this woman, "this sounds very problematic."

"A small blemish," she says, "in an otherwise lovely home. If you are ever in Vienna, you need to come visit. You just need to come. I will show you the city, show you what is important, necessary, life-giving."

She tells me about how tired she is. "I have been all over Montreal," she says, "searching for the perfect gift."

When I ask for whom she is shopping, she tells me it is for her granddaughter. "Anya," she says, a name I repeat then, a name I will repeat until I am elderly, a name I am sure I will repeat into the void.

"Just born," the woman tells me. "I have a photograph in my purse, which is across the room. We were there when she was born," she says. "There is nothing like it. Nothing on earth, anywhere on earth, when you hear that first cry."

"Your granddaughter," I say.

"A miracle," she says.

"Every new child is a miracle," I say.

At this, I think of Hermann, who will, when I tell him this, assure me that none of it can be true, that there is only this, the real, the press of my skin to this woman's skin, which is still electric with pain, she says, still alive with tension, preventing her from sleep. "The pain has made me delirious," she tells me. "I am seeing things that are not there, people who are not there, seeing double," she tells me. "Do you know this feeling," she asks, "do you?"

She has allowed herself onto my table without my telling her. A peeve of mine. This is my dominion, I want to say. The sole place on earth in which the rules are mine, the time is mine, what happens to your body is dictated by me. But here I am, we are, she is, putting herself before me, describing once again the extent of her pain, and as she does, a light brightens in me, Hermann's voice enters, and I am struck by a moment of clarity. This woman is not a version of myself at all, but instead the woman who has taken my place. The hausfrau I'd tracked those first weeks back in Vienna, alive in the house where I was alive. I take the ring from her hand. I do this while saying that she cannot have any jewelry on for the treatment. I'll have to take this, I say, in an English I know she does not understand. In the light, I see that the ring is not my ring, it could not be, the probability of it is too slim; the chances, the chances, no chance. With it in my hand, however, the ring has replaced my ring. Whatever I remember of the way my ring looked, it is gone. This is the way memory works. What has existed before is replaced, filmed over.

"Your daughter," I say. "What was her name again? Sonja, was it?"

"Sophia," she says.

"Yesterday you said it was Sonja. A musicologist, you said."

"Her name is Sophia. She is a scientist."

"Yesterday you said she was a musicologist."

"I don't even know what a musicologist is," she says, in German, this whole time, the German of my childhood. "I think you're mistaking me for someone else."

"And your husband," I say. "His name is Arnold?"

"Alexander," she says.

"Not Arnold."

"Who is Arnold?" she asks.

"Arnold is my husband."

"Your husband is not my husband," she says.

"Yesterday you said he was Arnold."

"And yesterday you ran out of here like a mad person," she says. She wiggles on the table. "I am paying for this time," she says. "Like I paid for yesterday's time."

"Do you have a son?" I ask.

"I don't want to talk about my son."

"What happened to your son?"

"We can begin the massage now," she says.

"Was your son taken?"

"Was *your* son taken?" she asks.

"What is the address of the home where you live?"

"I am in great pain," she says.

"As am I."

"Can we begin the treatment?"

"What street do you live on?"

"Can we please?"

"Is it the Herminengasse?"

"Why do you know so much about me?"

"Tell me the number."

"Can we begin please?"

"Is it eleven?" I ask.

"You should stop," she says.

"Why is that?"

"Because you already know the answers," she says.

"And how do you know what I know?"

Finally, she gets off the table and holds the base of her spine as she straightens. A memory returns. This woman fingering the dresses in the Neumann Department Store. This woman in the kitchen window holding a mug of tea, steam rising, staring out impassively at the ruins. I remember the rules: they are out there, Arnold and Sonja and Moses, and even though they are in other rooms, on other trains, beyond me, and even though I can hear their stories, told to me in their clear voices, on and on into their other futures, they are not here.

"Hausfrau," I say.

"Well, what are we to do?" she says, standing before me without her clothes. "What are you going to do with me now that you have me?"

# Blue Cities

NEW YORK, 2000

# MOSES

IF anyone ever asks, if anyone is interested, and if I live long enough, I'd like to convey to my grandson something about the expression he gave me when we met. An expression of recognition, but also delight, as if he wanted me to know that he'd just made the most amazing trip. He was hours old. Take a seat for a second, Eli seemed to tell me, get comfortable, pay attention for a moment, Grandpa Moses, oh do I have a story to tell you. Are you listening? Are you listening, Grandpa Moses? You would not believe what I've just seen!

Maybe he knew already that I was headed to the place he had just arrived from. If not right away, then at least soon, or soon enough, at some point, who knows, in the future, in the near forever, in my sleep on some warm night not so far from now, in dreams, in flight, in some last vestige of everyday love I might be lucky enough to receive at this late hour.

Hours before my grandson was born I stood alone with his father's mother, his grandmother Žofie, in the empty hospital chapel, a small room with a view onto the linden trees in Central Park. For a short moment in another life, on what had long seemed to me like another earth, Žofie and I had lived together while we were students in Prague, a place where we were very much in love, and where, on nights when the government cut the power, we drew plans for our future into notebooks we hid under the floorboards. These plans looked in some way not entirely different from the scene one might have encountered if one were to have walked into the chapel that morning to find us as we were, with our heads pressed together, her hand clasped around mine. We were not praying. Or maybe we were. It occurs to me that I have gone this long without really ever having learned how to pray correctly, or what it feels like to ask something serious of the world without any real hope for an answer. I felt then, with our heads pressed together, that time had fallen away and that the baby we were awaiting was our baby, rather than the baby of our children, and that the intervening thirty-three years had not gone by, that we were still the same two people in our same apartment in Josefov, where she used to sing to me, old songs she had learned from her mother, Czech folk songs, in a voice I knew was not good, a voice she loved because it was so bad, and which I can still hear if I try.

Outside in the park a neighborhood prayer group was attempting to levitate a woman. This was midmorning, mid-July, the middle of the beginning for Eli, and the middle of the end for me. This group had been out most of the morning, harassing passersby into letting them try to do this to them, to try to float them. They were often outside the hospital then, searching for vulnerable people, sick people, people for whom help would not arrive. In certain patients, it was something, I understood, that was not very difficult to discern. Are you well, they asked, do you have a moment, can we help, are you comfortable in your body, are you willing to be let loose from it for a moment, it will only take five minutes of your time, it will not hurt, just come with us, come right here into the park, lie down in the grass, for five dollars we'll levitate you six inches, for twenty dollars we'll levitate you six feet, we are friendly, we will not hurt you, let us pray over your body, close your eyes, there you go, close your eyes, tell us when you feel the spirit within you, just say the words. In the center of the group, a woman, about as old as my daughter was then, lay on her back, very firmly on the ground. From where we were, stories up in the sky, we could see her expression, which was one of amusement, but one also of hopeful expectation. Žofie shook her head at this, and in a quiet Czech she knew I understood still, even if I pretended not to, she muttered that they were crazy, and that moreover everyone in here with us was also crazy, her foolish children, my foolish children, all of whom were spoiled beyond comprehension, and that the hospital staff was crazy, the nurses certainly, the doctors especially. How hard is it, she asked, to deliver a child in the twenty-first century? And in a place like this! A palace! Room after room lined with computers! With robots! What a deranged future! Do they know where I delivered my children? In what conditions?

When we were younger, I watched her run for her life outside the central train station as troops opened fire. I was supposed to run behind her, alongside her, but I did not. Everyone around her was taken down, friends of ours, her included. I would not see her for twenty years, until she and her son appeared on my doorstep in New

York. I had thought, very reasonably, that she had been killed. I had seen it happen. A bullet hit her in the leg. I saw her grab for it. Then, right in front of me, she died, or I thought she died.

Outside the hospital, everyone had collectively fallen onto their backs into the grass, the entire prayer group, so that they might all be levitated. Or maybe they had fallen into the grass to rest from all the difficult work of failing to levitate. I watched one woman, maybe my age, who wore an expression I recognized as bliss, but also of surrender, an expression of asking to be taken, lifted up, kept there forever, held above everyone in some state between the life of the body and the life of the spirit.

"Look at that," I said, moved by what I was watching. "Look how happy she is."

Žofie turned to me. "You have always been vulnerable to idiocy," she said. "It's your great failing in life."

"Is that why I was vulnerable to you?" I asked. I was trying to make a joke.

Behind us, in a waiting room, our collected families, more than a dozen of us. Out of nothing: this. Somehow: miracles out of miracles.

"Yes, it is," she said, softly. "Of course."

THIS was Mount Sinai Hospital. Everywhere I went in those two days we spent waiting for Eli to come, people wanted to joke with me about this. Do you feel at home, Moses? Has the face of God appeared to you in the guise of a vending machine? Have you heard revelations in the hum of the air-conditioning systems? Do you have a moment, Moses, to talk to me about your experience with the pharaoh? Have you received any news you would like to tell us? Any additional laws and testaments that God wants us to know about? Did you really split the sea, or was the tide just very, very low?

It likely did not help that I had a cane with me during those days, one I did not want, but which my son-in-law insisted I carry, and which, while I walked, I liked to hoist above me, as if in anticipation of my flock. Who knows why I did this? Maybe when one lives as long as I have with this name, hoisting a cane into the air is something that comes naturally. And it likely did not strike others as normal that I was so constantly muttering to myself, lost in my own head. What would you do, waylaid in a building like the one where we'd found ourselves, within a wing of the future we had not yet encountered, worried about our only children and our first grandchild?

In my defense, we were on a high floor, the twentieth floor, a genuine peak, with views out across Randall's Island and the Throgs Neck into Long Island Sound, where there were boats coming and going, jet wake threaded through the atmosphere, a boy flying a kite alongside his father, and during the night before Eli came, I did find myself at the window trying to see what could not be seen, which was to say the life I would have spent with Žofie had I run and somehow had the Soviets not fired their weapons, or the life of my friends who were running beside Žofie that day outside the train station. Friends like Ambrož, whose poems he'd sewn into the lining of his pants, poems not about the government, which he would have surely felt the need to hide, but poems instead about beauty and desire, a poem, for example, about a painting he had seen once of a seascape, an ordinary seascape. I had thought for many years about this poem. If one was to get close to the painting, wrote Ambrož, one could see that there was trash across the beach instead of sand. In the poem, he tells the reader how deeply he has loved this painting, how he lingered before it for hours, just as one always hopes in a museum to find a painting that is already, in some way, painted within one's self. To find a painting like this in the world is to suffer a sense of recognition, an echo of one's self in art. When, in the poem, Ambrož leaves the museum, it's because his lover, after hours, has come to find him. What could you still be looking for in this picture? he asks. At home that night, Ambrož is struck by something important. He cannot remember who painted the picture. All those hours, and he either did not look to see, or did not care enough to remember. The next morning, after he wakes, he rushes back to the museum with a camera. He will capture it, he thinks, so that he will have it with him whenever he needs to remember the experience of finding a part of himself outside himself. Except the painting is not there. Not in the place he stood yesterday, not in the room adjacent to the place where he stood yesterday, not in the gallery beside this gallery, not on the floor above this floor. It was here, he tells a docent, an elderly man, who says, son, I have been in this room since before the war, and this painting you speak of has never existed. Who, in any case, would ever paint a picture like the one you are speaking of? Day after day, Ambrož returns to the gallery, to the room where he spent so much time that first day. He returns believing he will find the painting that captivated him, that the picture will reappear, until he begins, in his way, to see it everywhere, on walls where there are no paintings, on top of other paintings, in the hallway between galleries, in the Pleiades, in between the eyes of a lover who begs him to forget what has happened, to forgo this confusion, this belief in an image he has seen but which no one can verify has ever existed.

That day outside the train station, we were all gathered together in a group, huddled in a circle. We were supposed to break off all at once, and run, each of us in a different direction across the pair of tanks the Soviets had installed outside the train station they had occupied. Our idea was to reclaim the building, the trains, the transportation lines, the way in and out, the freedom of travel. From there, we would regain the city, then the country. We believed this. One of our friends was the daughter of an important city official whose voice we often heard on the radio, making certain demands of our inner lives, and she was, because of this, very nervous to be among our group, and when we broke apart to run, she did not, just as I did not, a decision I made in the moment, not before, certainly not in the hours I spent that morning writing a note to my mother, a note that looks something not unlike what I am writing here, and in which I was sure of my death. After the gunfire, my friend looked to me, and touched my hand, and said, Moses, go, Moses, run, and as she said this, she had already begun to run like the others, a decision she had likely felt was impossible before, but now that we had all been murdered was not so impossible after all, and so she began to sprint, straight ahead into the square toward the row of tanks, and upon the tanks, clusters of soldiers all much younger than us, toward the front door of the train station. Within moments she, too, was murdered.

In the photograph that was published of this day, a photograph that ran in all the newspapers, and that was issued days later by the propaganda office, the bodies of my friends were in the road, but I was not. I had been erased. In the middle of the square was my friend whose father was an important man on the radio, a friend who in her last moments begged me to do something I did not. Beside her lay Ambrož, whose poems pressed against his skin and nowhere else on earth. And there, very clearly, was Žofie, on her side, with her eyes closed, as if sleeping in our bed miles from this spot, on the second floor of an old building, in an apartment that had our secret plans for the future buried under the floorboards, and which often smelled of cooking apples, and where we had hung, on the wall beside the back windows, photographs of our parents, photographs I was never able to claim, not mine or hers, because neither of us ever went back after that morning.

Where, though, was I? For days afterward, I roamed the city searching for different versions of this picture in the newspaper, hoping to find myself, as I knew I had been, standing against the exterior wall of a café, poised to run into the station, dressed as we all were in a white shirt and a pair of white pants. We had anticipated blood, had chosen clothing to accentuate it, had planned to have our corpses photographed.

But I was nowhere. All of this presented an alternative explanation for my behavior: I did not run because I was not there. I must have collected dozens of versions of that morning, every picture made of the moment, pictures in which I had been removed by way of a process that must have been painstaking, men and women with magnifying glasses, with tweezers, small scissors, men and women sitting in offices not far from where I was sitting days later, hunting for proof of myself. I was searching in all those different copies for mistakes, for a hint of me, an inch of my skin left hovering, my neck, say, or my fingers, reemerging from the other world. Instead of me, there was a wall, a normal wall, no trace of anything amiss.

I was there, I told a friend once, months later, sitting in an apartment not far from the train station. I had the picture, the spot, the normal wall to which I was pointing, drawing an outline of myself. Imagine me here, I said. Imagine me in this place as I know I was. My friend held the picture to her face. But you were not there. But I was, I said. But you were not. But I was, I said again. What don't you understand? my friend asked. You were not at the train station. Someone, somewhere, has seen to it that this is the case. That is the official designation—you were not where you thought you were, or even where you knew yourself to be. Maybe they were ashamed they did not kill you. Maybe they are planning on coming to kill you later. Either way, this is a gift from the people who can see everything. A gift you should accept. She gave me back the picture. What do you see now? she asked. This is a question I have been asking for years. Because, she said, all I see is a wall, bricks, white paint, nothing, which means that all that was there that day was nothing, and all there ever will be of you and your friends is nothing.

It seems possible even as I write this to convince myself of this truth, that on the day my life was to end, I was instead picked up out of history and replaced with nothing, with a wall between myself and my life, a wall I would never cross or break or rest against, just as I remembered resting that day, with all our friends, with my grandson's grandmother, in the moment before we were all killed and not killed, drinking lemon tea, listening to Billie Holiday singing "They Can't Take That Away from Me," a voice from a world none of them would ever visit.

DURING the night, a nurse came to find us in the waiting area. We thought Eli was here, that the hour had come. However, it was going to be hours more, the nurse told us. "If I were you," she said, "I would go home, get some sleep, take a long, hot shower. Come back in the morning. There's traffic on the runway, if you get what I'm saying, and the flight is going to be delayed," she said. Then she laughed to herself.

Beside me, Žofie began to curse in Czech. "Who is this person with these terrible jokes? What kind of person says that a woman struggling in labor is like an airplane with engine trouble? What sort of terrible human makes a joke like this? Why are we surrounded by so many imbeciles!" Žofie grabbed my arm. "I should have died in the street thirty years ago, so that I wouldn't have to live into a future in which this woman, with her horrible jokes, also lives!"

I smiled at the nurse. "My old friend here, she wants me to tell you that she is grateful for all your hard work, and for the good care you're giving to our grandchild."

"Oh, that's lovely," said the nurse. "Tell her that you're very welcome."

"Could you also tell her," said Žofie, "that I have been shot at by men on tanks, many men, with very large guns, and that being shot pales in comparison to the torture she is inflicting on me."

"Also," I told the nurse, "my good friend here wants me to tell you that she appreciates your kindness, and your constant updates on Martha's progress. It's very difficult waiting all this time, as you can imagine, and we are understandably worried and anxious."

"Well," said the nurse, "your daughter is doing her best, and your grandchild is on the way. I promise. A beautiful grandchild. You will see."

Žofie stood slowly. There was a bullet still in her knee. If you were to put your hand there and pull taut the skin, you could see it in its entirety, a small missile, deflected in midair, she had always thought, by the wind of other bullets, and caught there, suspended in between pieces of her. Over the years, her kneecap grew around it, covered it up to cloak it, she told me once, just as history grows around every new wave of children born in the hospital like this, unaware that there are bullets hidden in plain sight, in walls, beneath their feet, in the knees of their grandmothers.

"Build me a hospital waiting room with a cocktail bar and I will be a happy woman," said Žofie, holding on to me for balance, speaking in an English accented by way of Czech boarding schools, then Alsace, then Barcelona, then Tangier, certain apartments near the port, bedrooms in which she lingered over American newspapers, reading to herself aloud at night in the immediate aftermath of her needing to leave Prague, beside windows where she wrote letters to everyone who did not survive, to our friend Ambrož, to our friend whose father was on the radio, letters the censors ensured she would not send, but which, years later, she would deliver back to Prague to bury in the earth of each of the homes of their mothers. She tended to her knee with balms she made herself in the kitchen of her apartment in Tangier, a place where, not long after being shot in the square outside the train station, she met Amado, a student, a maker of poems, reportedly a wonderfully good singer, someone I have seen only from a photograph hanging on the wall above her son's nightstand, a young man at a microphone caught in a moment of rapture, his mouth open to sing. By the time Žofie showed up at my door in New York with her son, Felix, in the summer of 1988, Amado was gone, taken in circumstances I was to understand would be familiar to me if I were to have heard them, which, for many years, I did not.

When we left the hospital that evening, Amado was on Žofie's mind. We walked south along the park for a long time and then we crossed through it and went to sit in the plaza at Lincoln Center, where we could hear through the open stage doors the sound of the musicians playing. A cheap way to hear a good concert, the only way I was able to do so when I was younger, new to America. It was Mozart's Requiem, near the end, the Lacrimosa, music of the end, the last music of Mozart's life.

Unable to forget the moment of his final hours, Žofie told me, Mozart's sister-in-law wrote her memories of his death some thirty-five years after the fact, in which she recounted that the last thing Mozart did in life was to try to mouth the sound of the timpani in his Requiem; I can still hear it now, she wrote.

"He liked to play this for me," Žofie said, speaking of Amado. We were on a low stone wall outside the auditorium. It was a warm evening, and there was wind from the river in the plaza, and I had bought us pastries to eat and wine to drink. "When Felix was born," Žofie told me, "we had an apartment on a hill in the medina, near the Hotel El Minzah, where I was married in the courtyard beneath a chuppah my sister-in-law stitched for us, and at night when the baby was fussy, he would often play this softly on the stereo, the Requiem, and he would take Felix's hand and let him hear the vibrations from the speaker as the record turned. This is Mozart, he would say to him. His face appears to me now as he's doing this, standing in our old apartment with orange carpet, in which I felt my life starting all over again. My Amado, at twenty-four years old, with white hair at his temple already. Say it with me, Amado would tell Felix. *Most—art.* In his accent, this was how it sounded, but I could not disagree with the new pronunciation. Mind you, Felix is a baby. *Most—art*. Brand-new to earth. Barely able to focus his eyes on anything. *Most—art*. And here is my husband, my very young and very sweet and foolish husband, to whom nothing bad has ever happened, carrying our son to his breast, trying to get him to say *Mozart* before he says *Mama*. He was convinced he was going to be able to program Felix from the start, to indoctrinate him, to give him the language of great culture as one gives a child the language of their mother. Which was fine, I suppose," said Žofie. "Would I have chosen the music from a funeral service for my little baby? And this funeral service, in particular? Could I even consider this as great culture any longer?

"By that point, Moses, I'd had enough of Germany and Austria, of Germans and Austrians, of the music of Germany and Austria, of anything that reminded me of my girlhood, of the old dead world and all their holy musical saints. I could not resist hearing footsteps in the prettiest melodies. Military melodies, marching tunes, martial music, the music of industrial murder, the harmony of gunfire, the counterpoint of doors being blasted off their hinges. And besides, I have often found that for people like Amado who love this music so, for whom music like this is their passion, that they possess a precise relationship to their own tragedy. Once a month, Amado would wake me to say that he felt he was going to die soon. He was always relaying this information to me with exact specificity, and with a sense of calm I found eerie and very cruel. As in: Žofie, wake up, Žofie, habib albi, love of my heart, meine schöne Braut, are you awake, I have news, I am dying, it is true, the angel Azrael has come, I am almost dead, in fact, your sweet Adonis of a husband is practically a dead man and very soon you will be a widow. I have detected a lump, he sometimes told me, which means I very likely have a tumor, a tumor on my spine, a tumor in my nerves, a tumor in my blood, which means I am not long for you, for our life together, for our boy. Or: Yesterday in the souk a woman looked at me in such a way as to tell me that I had darkness growing within me, which means, of course, a tumor, a swell, an artery about to explode.

"How, Moses, could I take a man like this seriously? I tell you, in the moments after I was married, when we were in the yichud room still, I said this to him, I said straight to his face that I did not believe I could ever take him seriously, not in sickness or in health, not when he was always carrying on the way he was, whining about himself. After all, I had a bullet in me! I had been shot! A foreign government had tried to murder me! A man on a tank had opened fire on me and he had succeeded in striking the target! So you have a stomachache, Amado? Big deal! Try having a bullet in your knee for years! Try feeling *that* every time you try to climb a staircase! Try dreaming for years that this bullet might explode within you at any moment! Try that! And you are the one who is dying? Try having your infant play with the missile-shaped lump in your knee! And there are, as you might know, Moses, many, many staircases in Tangier. A whole city of steps. An entire life of climbing up to heaven and down to earth.

"And so what happens then, Moses? I believed, as you would, that I had married a man suffering from a fear of the world, a disfigured sense of reality, like my father, like you used to be, like all our old friends used to be. This sense of doom only hit him in the morning. At night, he was a normal man, my normal Amado, clarity had found him. When he was gone from me, however, I understood that I was the one who had been wrong. I should have taken him more seriously, protected him better, wrapped him up in thicker blankets, in better armor. I should have known that when he was carrying Felix to his breast, one ear to the world, one ear to his heart, that he was marrying the music of the world to the music of his heartbeat. In this way, whenever he heard this music, Felix would always be able to feel his father's presence in the world.

"I should have taken up witchcraft," she said finally. "I should have practiced whatever our mothers used to practice when they wanted to prevent the world from doing what they knew it would do."

Žofie put her hand on my hand. "I think he knew deep down what would happen to him," she said. "Just as Ambrož did."

THIS was the first time she had ever mentioned Ambrož to me. When I came back to Prague for the first time, she told me, I saw him in a pizzeria, mixing dough with his hands, the same age as I had last known him. It stopped my blood to see him again. The next day, however, I saw him standing outside the president's residence at the castle, taking photographs as a tourist, and I saw him, she told me, I saw our sweet Ambrož riding a bicycle on Zborovská Street, and I saw him behind the desk of the hotel where I had chosen to stay, a very fancy hotel, because of course, I was by now a wealthy American professor, a master of the literature of various Romance languages, and I was, of course, a Jewess, a word I was called for the first time in decades while on that trip, in a restaurant not far from where I was shot, by a small elderly man who understood my presence in his city—this is what he said, *my* city—as a sign that the bugs were back, the infestation had begun again, the way one moans at the sight of ants on the windowsill.

"Do you remember him?" she asked me. "Our friend the poet? Ambrož?"

By now the Lacrimosa had ended, and we were listening to the parts of the Requiem that Mozart did not compose, the parts finished by his friends and rivals, on account of his wife, Costanze, who needed the money to survive, who walked Vienna in the winter of her husband's death with the manuscript under her arm, knocking on doors, asking those she knew to imagine it as her husband would have. Just pretend you are Mozart, I suppose Costanze must have told these people, just imagine you are him, my husband, just be Mozart for a minute, channel him, sit at the keyboard and put yourself in the mind of my Mozart.

"I used to think of him quite often," Žofie said, speaking of Ambrož, "especially the way he was in those final months, in the spring, before the tanks arrived. He had fallen in love for the first time. Do you remember, Moses? It was someone he met at the museum, if I remember correctly, and he was amazed, Ambrož was, by the shock of love, by his own capacity for it, and I remember one night, when we were outside, walking along the river, he was wearing a new jacket, which his boyfriend had managed to have smuggled from the West, from London, I think it was, and he said to me that being in love felt to him as if he had recently acquired an echo of the world, that before this he had understood his loneliness as a form of silence, something he had grown used to as one does with the quiet of the countryside, a version of earth that he understood as home. But now the noise had been let in, the windows open to the city street, and with it came a sense of reciprocation that he could only understand then as echo. All these sounds I have been putting out into the world, he told me, all these thoughts that have escaped into silence ever since my childhood, they have finally come back to me. That day on the Vltava," said Žofie, "he told me that if there were an Olympic event for love, Czechoslovakia might be wise to make him a team member, this was how good he was at it, at love.

"I had laughed at him, Moses, and I said that everyone feels this way in love, that love offers a vision of one's best image of themselves, and I probably sounded very condescending, and very rude about his discovery, and I have often regretted taking this tone with him, and I had very likely given him a bad definition of love, the definition of someone who had lost more than I had gained, but he was undeterred. You think I am being foolish, he said, but it's true, I'm excellent at love, I don't know how anyone could be any better at it than I am. I am the very best at love there has ever been."

WHEN I went back to Prague for the first time," Žofie told me, "I did so because I thought I might move Felix home with me. Already, we could not speak the way I wanted to. His Czech was terrible, is terrible, will always be terrible. Years of my talking to him, reading to him, paying for lessons, imploring him, guilting him, telling him that he would never really know his mother if he did not succeed in learning my language, explaining to him eventually that when I am dead my ghost will come back to him one day and she will only speak Czech and nothing else, but still, nothing from my son, garbles only, noise, awful noise. He has none of his father's Arabic either, no Ladino, no Spanish. His German sounds to me like someone being strangled. There are parrots living somewhere in the South of France that are more capable of carrying on in French than my son. It seems obvious to say that he has, of course, no Hungarian, no Russian, no Hebrew. So we were left with English, which feels to me like the language of a television commercial, of someone trying to sell me soap, someone telling me that I am not clean enough, too dirty for polite society, or it reminds me of various political functionaries at the lectern in the United Nations delivering stern remarks about nuclear arms, doing so in English, because English is the language of warnings, collective anxiety, missile trajectories, red lines. I did not want to always talk to my son like this. Because I was now a wealthy Jewess, I could have the fanciest apartment in Prague, the houses in Staré Město I had always envied as a girl, a palace practically. A playwright had been made president! How bad could it be? But Ambrož was everywhere I went. Not anyone else. Not you, Moses, although I looked for you in every room I entered, and I felt the possibility very strongly that you were only minutes away from me wherever I went, that you might turn the corner at any moment as I was turning a corner, the version of you I had woken up beside on the last morning of our life. Instead of you, or Valerie, or Tomas, or Claude, or Theodora, or anyone, it was Ambrož, only him, everywhere, in every place, waiting for me at the table I had reserved, standing in the hallway of the room I had rented. And do you know what he was saying to me, wherever I went, wherever I took Felix? Do you, Moses?"

The concert hall began to empty just then. Swarms entered the plaza. "Night after night in every city of the world," said Žofie, "Mozart dies onstage, his deathbed is resurrected from time, pushed out onstage for us to watch, and if you close your eyes—Amado believed this very seriously—you might find him somewhere within you, *Most-art*, and people pay money to see this, to be in the room alongside his death. When you think of it, his death has been playing to sold seats for hundreds of years. This is not an unamazing fact to consider," she said.

Žofie asked me to get her on her feet, and when I did, she said to me, "I will go home now." This meant, I knew, that she wanted me to ride in the taxi back to her apartment. She did not like to be alone if she could prevent it. She did not like entering a dark apartment by herself. She also did not like to spend the final hours of the day in silence. I understood this without needing to ask. She lived close by, north and then west, along the river, in a large space paid for by the university, at which she was now an important dean, a queen of the humanities, prized for her mediation skills, but also her ability to read in whatever language was necessary.

"You know what is not lovely?" she asked. "Having to supervise several scholars of the humanities. This is not unlike having to oversee a party meeting of a small, occupied Soviet satellite. A great deal of coded language, many men in terrible brown clothing, some obvious amount of quiet fear over the fashion of one's ideas. What Kissinger said about academics is not untrue," she told me, although I did not know what Kissinger had said. "Generally, I find that people at the school listen to me, and when they don't listen to me, for whatever reason, because they are petulant children, or because they see me as a startled little woman with a funny accent, or because they suspect that I know that their ideas are indeed insipid and worthy of shame, I show them the bullet in my knee. I do it at least once a year. I lift my skirt hem to show them the small missile in my body, and tell them how I lay in the square outside the train station for twenty hours when I was young pretending to be dead and how I had a white bedsheet put over me, the white sheet of death, and that when this happened, I really did believe for some time, for hours, that I had died, and that death was very different than I had imagined, that it was a good deal like life, just with less movement, and with a great deal of pain in my knee. And if this happens, say, when we are discussing budget allocation, or which wretchedly mediocre visitors they want to come, or which professor gets which office, this is usually when I talk about the death sheet, Moses, and when I do this, they shut up and let me tell them what to do."

In her apartment, she made us tea from a new electric kettle. "I have only the fanciest consumer goods now," she said, marveling at the kettle, which bore no buttons, and resembled, I thought, the early space capsules of the Apollo program, forever on the launchpad, occasionally dispensing steam, always awaiting takeoff. "It knows my fingerprints," she said, showing off how it worked. "The old agitator in me suspects that the kettle manufacturer is probably doing something unsavory with all this information, storing my fingerprints in some large database so that soon, eventually, inevitably, I will be framed for some terrible crime, hauled before a judge, asked where I was on such a date, shown photographs in which I am holding a murder weapon. But," she said, "I am tired of being para-noid of everything. And besides, this kettle boils water very, very fast, so fast that if I were to somehow discover time travel, Moses, this is what I would travel back with, to show my great-grandmother in Novograd-Volhynia, a woman who likely spent most of her life peering into pots, cauldrons, vats, waiting for life to boil. Imagine that life, and tell me we have not discovered magic here in this life!"

We were in her living room, thirty stories up. On every wall there were windows, opening to every side of Manhattan, but mostly, as it turns out, opening to water, which I suppose I under-stood, having lived in the city now thirty years, but having lost the sense at some point that I was on an island. Žofie was reclining in a chair over the Hudson, where there were barges floating by below her, and where, in New Jersey, we could see dogs, or the shadows of dogs, or maybe just the idea of dogs, running alongside the river.

"The curtains are electronic as well. Look," she said, moving the curtains up and down by way of another button: like magic. "My bed is also electronic. It moves when I want it to move, lifts my head up so that I can read more easily, lowers my feet in the morning, does everything but rock me like an infant. There is a speaker in my pillow, Moses, and it plays whatever I want as I go to sleep, whatever I want."

She picked up a small remote control and pushed a button and a television screen rose out from the mantel. "Look at this," she said, showing off now. "I don't care what anyone says," Žofie told me, "I love the future. I love American excess. I am a terrific capitalist, it turns out. I welcome the robots. How could they possibly be any worse than the people? Look at this life! I have a bed that moves and shades that close themselves and a movie theater in my living room. When I was young, my mother told me that if I ever came home to find the furniture moving on its own, then I needed to rush out and find the rabbi, because the house had been occupied, spirits were at work, and you know, Moses, this is what I'm choosing to believe, that yes, I have a remote control that makes my curtains go up and down, but also, yes, that spirits are at work, that my family is here with me, all our old friends, Mama and Papa, and I've just asked them to tend to the curtains, and that they are here with me, taking care of me."

Maybe it's necessary to say that by now we were drunk, potentially very drunk, maybe even blindingly drunk. Yes, on the day before my grandson was born, his old grandparents, who in another life lived together in love, were drunk together once more: wine in the plaza outside Lincoln Center, more wine on the walk back, Becherovka in tall clear glasses while standing at Žofie's windows, several hundred feet in the air, safe from harm, watching the tourist helicopters chuffing over the water.

Eventually, a call came from the hospital. Our hopes rose. More runway trouble, the nurse explained. Traffic has waylaid our best plans. We are hoping, she explained further, to get the traffic cops out and to clear the runway.

As she listened beside me, Žofie's disgust mounted. "They are quite stubbornly committed to these metaphors," she said. Each of us took turns talking to our children. First, Žofie put Felix on the speaker. He sounded dreamy, enraptured, heart-captured by fatherhood already. When we spoke to my daughter, Martha, she sounded, it must be said, like a frustrated passenger, awake on a plane long past the point when it was supposed to have landed, glaring impassively out a dark window at a landscape that refused to change. "When will it end, Papa?" She was speaking in German, a language she used only when she wanted others not to understand her. She had disavowed the epidural, wanted to feel everything, but now, twenty-four hours into the labor, she had begun to doubt her promise to herself. Because it had taken so long to deliver the child, she had become a spectacle in the obstetrics wing. This was a teaching hospital, affiliated with a medical school, and doctors had asked her whether she might want to contribute to the cause of science, to the collective welfare of all future mothers, by having the students gather to watch.

"The room," she told me, still in German, "is packed to capacity. All these strangers, all these young students, gawking at me and shaking their heads and making worried notes on their clipboard. One by one, they are filing by to diagram my cervix. I can't take it anymore, make the boy come out, make it end."

When the conversation ended, Žofie could tell I was worried. "Listen, Moses," she said. "I gave birth in a bathtub in a room with intermittent electricity. I'm fairly sure that the doctor was eleven years old." She shrugged. "Was it wonderful? No. Did it hurt more than being shot? A good deal more so, yes. At one point, did the little boy doctor suggest I might run around in a circle to help dislodge my child? Yes, in fact, this did happen. And you know: everything ended up fine. So there is nothing to be concerned with."

"My daughter was raised here," I said. "With every available luxury. She's made with American material. Material which is not as durable."

"I've been to your apartment, Moses. Calling your home luxurious is an insult to capitalism."

I had moved across the room to look east, at the consecutive string of bridges spanning the river, one of which was the bridge that delivered me to Manhattan for the first time. My first apartment was not far from here, a kind of kingdom compared to my life in Prague, three peaceful rooms in a building I had no trouble making out from the window of an airplane. And also—windows onto the park, and windows onto the wide swath of a street full with gingko and elm, as well as windows that opened at night into the apartments of my neighbors, Broadway dancers in their old age, whom I'd found some nights clutching one another, their furniture pushed away, reworking the old steps, both of them spinning and spinning.

"Do you know something," Žofie said then. "I have no pictures of you." She was on the couch, her shoes off. She had lit a cigarette. The shoulder of her cardigan had slipped, and her bare shoulder was out in the room. She said it again: "I have no pictures of you as a young person, Moses, no pictures of when I loved you, nothing at all. All I have is this," she said, dragging a finger in the air up and down over me, pointing at me in a way that made me laugh. "Not that this is very terrible," she said, "but it is not the original you, before everything, the first you. What happened to the first you?"

On a low bookcase was the photograph that had run in the newspapers across Europe, of all of us in the street, everyone but me. I did not understand why she would have this, but I also understood why she would never want to be without it. I brought the picture to her. You do have a picture of me, I explained. I traced myself against the blank white wall.

"Here I am," I said, "right here, just as you left me, just as your memory imagines me to be."

"This is not the same," she said, and she put her hand to my face. "You are an old man now, Moses."

"Younger than you," I said, which was true.

"You are a grandfather," she said.

"Not yet, my dear. Not yet."

THE first time I saw Žofie again, she had shown up at my door here in Manhattan with her boy, Felix, beside her. She did not believe I was real. She had been awake for two days by that point, and I had taken her into my apartment, set her down in a chair in my small kitchen, where, in a corner, my daughter and her son met for the first time. You are not him, Žofie had said to me, convinced then, as she was now, that there were people on earth whose bodies were not unlike the bodies of others, that there were only a certain number of possible iterations, a finite number of available models, like an automobile in a showroom, each with some small, nearly undetectable difference, and that if one traveled long enough, one could encounter the face of their friend, the hand of their grandmother, a hand they had felt once but then had lost, something they had known from childhood, could trace from memory, could identify in darkness. I was one of those people, she believed, a version of myself from the past, but altered in a way I had not been aware of. I resembled him, she said that night, meaning me, my old self. I had given her tea to drink, and hot chicken broth, and a poppy-seed roll, and fruit, so much fruit, a plate of cut bananas, melon, dates. I can get you whatever food you want, however much of it you want, I said. Eat, eat, eat, I told her, and I told Felix, both of whom were too skinny, and I worried neither of them had eaten in a very long time. In response, she put her thumb against the concavity of my wrist, where my pulse lived, and after listening, feeling for a moment, she met my eyes and told me that the resemblance was good, but that I was not him exactly, not the Moses she had lost, that she had traveled a good and long way and not slept in many days, but that she had made a mistake.

Whenever I thought of this day—the day she returned, and how I had pulled out the sofa bed in my small living room and let her sleep while I took Felix into the kitchen to make him a second lunch and then a third lunch, and how, even later, I lay awake weeping over her return from the dead—I thought of Ambrož again.

"What did Ambrož say to you?" I had put the photograph of the day we were killed and not killed back on the shelf. "When you saw him again."

"Excuse me?"

"Earlier, outside, you said that when you went back to Prague for the first time, he was everywhere."

"Yes," she said. "Everywhere I went he was there."

"And he was saying something to you. What did he say?"

"Oh," she said. She closed her eyes. "You don't want to know."

"I do, though."

"It will upset you."

"I don't think it will."

"It's quite sad, Moses."

"That's okay," I said. "I can handle it."

"You have never been as tough as you think."

The phone rang again. We jumped. "This must be it," Žofie said, but it was only Felix calling again, frantic, searching for his mother, suddenly terrified anew that something had happened to her, that she had wandered off somewhere, that she had been taken. Now he was the one who had gone without sleep. He had forgotten that he'd just called us. No, sweetheart, Žofie was saying in an English that did not sound like the language of war or advertising. "I am here, don't worry, I am here, we just spoke five minutes ago, I love you, the doctors sent us home, they made us go, but I am so excited for you and for what is about to happen to you. Please go get some rest," she said. "Get some sleep." She took the phone into her bedroom and closed the door behind her. Through the wall, I could hear her laughing. "Who would ever take me," she cried. "I am unbelievably fierce. Even more fierce than you could ever imagine."

WHEN I left Žofie's that night, I walked home along the water in the dark. On one side was the river, men on boats, bargemen coasting into port, their legs fluttering out over the dark water. On the other was the highway, shadows beneath dome lights rushing out and leaving, and then a solitary man, standing in the road at the traffic light on Ninety-Sixth Street selling flowers, holding a sign that read SOMEONE, SOMEWHERE, DESERVES AN APOLOGY FROM YOU.

Žofie did end up telling me what Ambrož said to her. As I made my way home that night, I thought of this. What Ambrož told her was that he wanted to move to America. Would she take care of him? Would she teach him English? She had a way with languages, he knew, an ability to learn quickly, to communicate no matter where she lived. One hears this sort of news in the afterlife, he told her. As it turns out, this is a good deal of what the afterlife is, he apparently said, news from home, an everlasting dispatch from a world where events occur to a world where everything has already happened. Would she show him New York? If she was amenable, he could meet her there. He was able to travel, to go anywhere on the planet he wanted. There were ways of getting places quickly, and without much trouble, but the dead, he told her, need a companion, just as the living do, this is the only way to move from space to space, and his lover, the man from the museum, he would not do it, his lover could not believe that he was real when he visited him. When he found him at night on empty street corners, when he put his hand to his cheek during the night, in the same bed where they had slept, when he whispered his name, came to him in dreams, approached him in the darkness, his lover considered Ambrož a haunting. Would she take him to the ocean, he wanted to know. He had never seen the ocean, never heard it, never felt it against his feet. Could she do this? Would she take care of him? Please say yes, he said. Please say yes.

BLOCKS from my apartment, I saw her in the window of an all-night coffee shop. She was, I was sure, the woman who had that morning lay in the center of the circle of prayers while everyone around her tried to get her to levitate. It was very late, or very early, or it was the moment when these are the same. I stopped when I saw her. She was alone at the table, an uneaten meal pushed to the side. She was ill. It was not difficult to tell this. She had the cutlery laid out before her, a fork, a knife, a spoon, and she was hovering her hands over everything, trying, it was obvious, to get it all to float.

I debated going inside to talk to her, to tell her I had seen her earlier, that I had seen her while the others tried to levitate her, and to ask whether it had worked, but I decided against doing so, because, let's be honest, a man like me, at this point in my life, with my cane, my beard, my general state of being in those weeks, a man like me coming to your table to ask how it felt to be risen—who wants this in their life? Just as I decided this, she arranged her spoon on the table, concentrated on it as one would on a difficult problem in a schoolbook, and then, with her eyes closed, everything began to rise into the air, the spoon, the dinner plate, the fork and water glass, the paper place mat beneath it all, everything went up into the air. I swear to you that this happened. Six inches, eight inches, everything.

Or maybe, who knows, I imagined this, I don't know, I was sleepless, exhausted, dream filled, confused by old love, tired of my body, in need of fresh air. In other words, I was elated. It was an ordinary Thursday in summer. A world without a grandchild, and now, a world in which my grandchild was almost here. What miracles!

"A bad trick," came a voice from behind me.

When I turned, I found a young man in a long black coat, his hair swept behind him. I knew straightaway. He had changed. Or my memory of him had changed. He was smaller; there was less of him. A certain angularity where, before, there had been roundness, smoothness, a sense of openness. A new pair of eyes, I thought. It was certainly possible.

"I shouldn't do it," he said, "but sometimes it's hard to resist."

He smiled, walked around me in a circle, walked right to the window where the woman was sitting, and where, now that she had opened her eyes, everything was resting again flat on the table. "Levitation," he said to me in Czech. "Is this what modern medicine has become? Our dreams of the future and *this* is what you have allowed to happen, Moses? Crazy people stalking the sick and promising them *levitation?*"

He walked back to me and turned so that we were standing side by side. He bore no reflection.

"Ambrož," I said.

He put his finger to his lips—a new finger, I thought, new lips. "Not so loud, my friend." He kissed my cheek hello. "Who knows who is listening and who is not listening." He kissed my other cheek. "You thought the secret police in Prague were bad."

"It's you," I said.

"Not entirely," he said, smiling.

"But I would know you anywhere," I told him.

He came close. "Most of it is me, Moses. Some of it I've had to piece together. Gather up. Accumulate for myself." He touched his stomach. "For instance," he said, lifting his shirt. "This is new." He smiled with pride. "You can touch it if you want. The smoothest, newest stomach there ever was on earth. One doesn't want gunshots in the afterlife, you see. The holes negatively affect one's aerodynamics. And being dead, one figures out quickly, is all about aerodynamics." Before me, he rose inches off the ground and then came back down. "You see, my friend, it's difficult to fly when there are holes all over you. You could say I made myself all over again."

It was dark, and there was, high above us, a towering streetlamp that glowed onto the sidewalk, creating the effect of a mirror in the window of the coffee shop, a mirror that showed me, alone at night, in my drab raincoat, talking to someone who wasn't there. Beside me on the street, there was nothing of my old friend, only taxis passing behind him, or through where I knew him to be standing. The geometry of the evening loomed in place of his ghost. Around us were the square apartment towers, the steel-hinged hypotenuse of fire escapes, the remainders of puddles, which were mirrors themselves, into which the electricity of the city appeared distinctly, but which, from my vantage, appeared to me as lakes do from airplanes, already in the process of drying up and vanishing.

I swept my hand out in front of me, expecting for it to pass through Ambrož, as hands in the movies often pass through the bodies of ghosts. Instead, I hit him, flat across his new stomach.

"I don't believe it," I said.

He took my hand. Put it firmly against his shoulders, his face, his hair. He smiled, then began to laugh, an ancient sound, unburied music.

BECAUSE the dead do not tire, we did not stop walking. For hours we walked. It was night, the long summer, and we crossed Manhattan twice, west to east, and then back. When we passed through Central Park, which felt tonight like the wilderness, I was put in mind of a campsite in Karlovy Vary where I last remembered Ambrož truly alive, one month before the gunshots outside the train station, a younger Ambrož asleep in the hammock at dusk while Žofie and I watched from the deck of a cabin, or Ambrož writing the last poems of his life at a small desk beneath an oak tree, into which he had carved his name, these same poems he would later sew into the lining of the pants he wore on the morning he was murdered. This was a memory, which returned to me uninvited, out of nowhere, reconstructed, very possibly invented. Did we ever visit this campsite? Was it true that I had watched him write? And where were those poems? In what building in Prague, in what basement furnace, were these burned? Out of which city chimney did the rest of him vanish?

There were rules, of course, rules for what he could say to me, and where we could go, rules, for instance, that he understood implicitly, even if, as he told me, walking much later that night along the East River, no one ever emerged to tell him. We were, at this moment, far south, in dark stretches of the city that were foreign to me, that felt to me like a city in a country I had never visited. "It's as if," he said, "the knowledge exploded within me." He was speaking of death, or what comes after. "This is the only way I can describe it," he told me. We were between bridges, beneath highway overpasses, below an always-rush of traffic noise, under an ocean it seemed like. "Waking in my new body felt to me like an explosion," said Ambrož. "This is because of what happened to me. But maybe if one loses their life in another way, in sleep, for instance, the knowledge arrives in a different way, like the way it feels when one wakes from a deep sleep and remembers, sometime later, the dream as a flash of daylight, or a burst of clarity. With gunfire, though, it came like a burst of noise. All at once, I knew. I awoke as a dead man and I knew immediately everything there was about what it meant to be dead, just as I had known on earth that I knew almost nothing about what it meant to be alive."

"But you are back," I said.

"I was homesick," he said.

These words struck me. Here we were, walking, my old friend and I, in a Manhattan that seemed, at this moment, to be a series of cities built without borders, lapped at by river water so that it had left all of us floating. Maybe it struck me because I had, all at once, felt home returning to me.

Ambrož could tell what I was thinking. Every thought was a thought he could read. A fact of the afterlife, I assumed. He could sense, for instance, my worry that he was not real, that I had dreamed him into being. He could sense, too, my anxiety about my daughter, my great desire to hold my grandson in my arms, to sing to him. A new generation is a miracle upon miracles. For a Jewish child: even better. He knew, for instance, that I had lost most of my memories of him, even the lines of his poems, which I had tried, with great effort, to keep with me. He knew, as well, that what I remembered most was the end of him, the first gunshot, which tore through his stomach. As we walked, often in silence, he would reach out to put his hand on my arm as if to say that I had no reason to worry about my daughter, or the hospital. Or, having caught me thinking of how much he must miss the world, he would tell me, Moses, you are quite close, you think like a dead man, you will make a great ghost one day. He would tell me this even though I had not said anything out loud to him.

Later, he warned me: "Beware of thinking anything too personal around me, or creating an image in your mind that you would otherwise wish to keep private. For instance," he said, "it might behoove you to stop thinking about the way Žofie crossed her legs on her sofa earlier. Or the way she ran her fingernails along the skin of her neck while feeling hot outside Lincoln Center. Or the exact words she used to express her desire to have an old photograph of you.

"Not that I mind being privy to such human feelings," he said. "After all this time, it's quite refreshing. A different sort of homesickness."

At one point he bent down to the river and put his hands into the water and took it to his mouth, a mouth that both did exist and did not, hands that met the water without a reflection, but that, even still, caused ripples to form. When he took his handful of river water to his mouth, the water disappeared.

"Ghosts will do this," he said to me, "rearrange the world, and also take something vital from it.

"It's amazing that the dead have not taken all the water from the earth already. It's all anyone talks about in the afterlife," he told me. "Water, sea, ocean, lake, pond, puddle, rain. At the beach, everyone is always staring off into the sea. All our attention in life is pulled to the water, the horizon, the vanishing point. Even in the desert, people can sense where the sea once rushed, and even there, they will gather on a hilltop to stare. Everywhere on earth I have seen this. Do you know why this is?"

When I didn't answer, he answered for me.

"It's the only place on earth where the living can sense the rest of us looking back, watching, waiting to see if you will ever notice us out there." He seemed to me to take a breath; an impossibility. "You look because we are out there, too, looking just the same."

FOR months, I used to return to the train station. In the first hours a memorial grew. Students had put down white flowers, placards onto which they had written protest slogans in a language they knew the Soviets could not read. In the evenings, musicians arrived to play the songs of the mourners, improvised requiems, the Holy Kaddish, songs I could hear blocks away, in the apartment where I had gone into temporary hiding. Those nights I did so little, dreamed nothing, ate nothing, heard nothing. I might as well have been as dead as Žofie and Ambrož. All of this was happening not far from the Jubilee Synagogue, built over the ground of the ancient ghetto, cleansed on account of what the old authorities deemed issues of sanitation, meaning, of course, too many Jews in one place, too many Jews in close proximity to too many Christians, too many Jews obstructing the return of the Messiah, too many Jews in this city for too long. The Jubilee: the same building to which my mother sometimes took me as a boy—a long drive from home—so that we could sit in the pews beneath the filigree, my mother, who knew, as I suppose I knew somehow, that all the stolen belongings of Prague's Jews had been brought here, their candlesticks melted down into bullets, their menorahs refashioned into medallions for good killers, their silver baby rattles bought in celebration of a blessing taken and given away to the children of murderers. For nights, crowds continued to gather in the Vrchlického Gardens. Against the wall where I had been erased, someone had drawn an outline of a person, maybe me, but also maybe anyone, and inside this outline, which was done with red paint, they had written in English the words *We are watch-*

*ing you*, an invocation to those with the guns, Muscovite boys, Leningrad boys, boys from the beaches in Crimea where once, when I was young, I had seen jellyfish swarming below me in the Black Sea. *We are watching you*: a way of saying that we had eyes on them just as they, for so long, had trained their eyes on us, had made us feel as if a great single eye existed in every corner, tracking us, taking notes, powerful enough to know our most silent transgressions. When the outline was erased, someone drew it again. When the warnings were painted over, new warnings went up over the fresh paint. When the Soviets came and destroyed the instruments of the musicians, beat the musicians with the cracked bellies of their cellos, new instruments emerged, new players, new songs. This did not last long. When people brought pictures of the dead and laid them on the pavement and held funeral services for them, for Žofie, for Ambrož, for me, the tanks grew closer, sometimes only by inches, but in cases like this, inches are miles. Eventually, the crowds were scattered, the pictures confiscated, Žofie was murdered in death as she had been in life. Better to erase the memory, to keep the street clean.

By winter we were, once again, policed by outsiders. Young boys on tanks, clean-shaven, always cleanly shaven; the face of mid-century evil, I discovered, was a cleanly shaven face. Everywhere, a silence had come. It was not that the people had disappeared, that everyone had been vanished as my friends had been. The streets were as crowded as always, but everywhere, in every neighborhood, people went about their lives in complete silence. Families walking with one another did so without speaking. A mother trying to corral her toddler did so with whispers. Even the dogs seemed to understand that the consequences for any loud disturbance were dire. There were, as someone whispered to me one night, microphones everywhere, microphones in the walls, in the lamps, in the bricks on the Charles Bridge, microphones in the lapping waves of the Vltava.

Where Žofie had lain, fruit vendors stood. And where Ambrož had lain, the ground had been scrubbed clean. And where I had stood, or not stood, there was nothing, just whiteness.

I began to visit the station because I was mourning Žofie. We had lived together three years. I thought that I might find what I was searching for outside the station. Some part of her, hint of her, whisper or scent of her. I could not go back home. We had left our life in our apartment in Josefov as if we would return. We were young and foolish and thought we would not be killed, how could we ever be killed, how would our government countenance our being shot at from atop tanks, especially us, the fruit of the country, the promise of the postwar years, the infants in the prams the country had been so proud to herald. We had left food in the small icebox, wine on the table, books open on the nightstand, a pen against a notepad with a letter half-finished. She'd been reading the complete works of Shakespeare in English. On our last night together she had read to me from bed as Hamlet's father returns to implore him to vengeance. *But that I am forbid to tell the secrets of my prison house*, he says, *I could a tale unfold whose lightest word would harrow up thy soul, freeze thy young blood*. I knew barely any English then, only the lyrics to songs that came across the radio from London during rainstorms. She may as well have been reading to me the instruction manual for a box of radio parts, but I swear, I understood what she was saying. Her heart beat against the skin of my back so loudly that it became my heartbeat.

I had been told that our apartment had been raided, boxes carried out, everything inside erased just as we had been, her complete works of Shakespeare, our corked wine, our student paintings, our blue jeans, our canned vegetables, our radio, our smuggled Miles Davis records, the photograph books in which Žofie had kept two pairs of pictures of her parents, the only pictures on earth that remained of these people, the first picture taken in their childhood, knee socks, freckles, cropped hair across the brow, Nuremberg shop-windows in which their parents could be seen holding the camera; the other pair taken the week before they were shot dead in the street outside the Vrchlického Gardens not far from where I found myself standing one morning, determined to leave Prague, to leave Czechoslovakia, to leave Middle Europe, to get as far as possible from the source of what I had come to understand was a form of collective madness that lived buried in the earth of this continent, beneath our feet, some rising swell of poison that threatened every three generations to swallow us whole. That first morning, this was all I had on my mind—leaving. I had wanted to go back to our apartment, to reenter my old life as if nothing had happened, to burst through time rearranged, rebuilt. I had the idea that she would be there. Even though I knew this was impossible, I thought it would be so. Even though I had seen her shot, had watched her die right before me, I believed she would be there on the sofa reading *Hamlet* as she had been weeks earlier. Come sit, I heard her say. Come listen to this, Moses. *'Tis now the very witching time of night.* Come and hear the rest of this play, Moses. I know you don't understand, but I think you will. I could use my house key, I told myself. The key would still work. The Soviets were too cheap to ever think of changing the locks. Instead, I went to the station.

I pretended to be a businessman. I wore an old suit I'd found in the borrowed apartment where I was living, carried a valise, acted as if I had important affairs to consider. I cut my hair in a way that aged me. I assumed the walk of a man who needed to go somewhere, my chin out, every step made with purpose. Daily, I passed through the square as if I were headed to some important room where I would sit in an important chair and discuss important events. A part of me believed that someone would eventually recognize me, capture me, that I would be taken as all my friends were taken, dragged before the new authorities, starved for weeks, made to confess every sin, each transgressive thought, that I would be erased from history, from life, from the memories of all who ever knew me, then, finally, ended with a bullet. Did I want this? I don't know that I did not. Every day I went, walking in and out of the station doors. Some days I went in circles like this, in one door, out the other door, over and over, entering and exiting, coming and going, day into night. What was I doing? In my head, I told myself I was practicing how I would leave. I had no money, no way of escaping, no place I knew to go. I desired peace, an absence of the memory of death, and where on earth was I to find this? Instead, I was rehearsing the steps to get there. I was both the departing and the arrived, a man in each crowd. Of those gathered to flee Prague that winter I recognized neighbors, schoolmates, future exiles, the faces of young men made prematurely homesick, men destined until they were old to complain in Czech on a park bench in a foreign city; I saw old faces from synagogue, a new group of Jews, the last group of European Jews, finally giving up after a thousand years.

At one point, I began to bring very small stones with me in my pocket, nine of them, one for each of my friends who had been taken, and as I passed through the square I shook them loose, which was the old tradition, stone leaving, grave building, monument making. When one is scattered across the face of the world, every space beneath every rock becomes a resting place.

After a month of this, the authorities caught wind of me. A constable hadn't seen me leaving the rocks—I had been too careful for this—but he had noticed all the tiny pebbles and he had noticed me and had the sense to put the two facts together. He was Russian, with bad Czech, awful Czech, a Czech more awful than my English when I first arrived here in New York.

"What are the purpose of these rocks?" an officer asked me.

I smiled a bad smile, the smile of a man without fear of a Russian occupier armed with a pistol. "What rocks do you speak of?" I asked.

"These rocks," he said, picking up stones from the plaza. "What are the purpose of the rocks?"

"What rocks?"

"What do you mean what rocks? These rocks!" He shook his hands at me and as he did some of the pebbles fell loose from his palm.

"I don't see any rocks," I said.

He picked one up. "This," he said.

"Oh. *Pebbles*," I said, speaking the word in Czech slowly. Oblázky.

"But why are there pebbles?" he asked.

"Are you asking me why there are pebbles in the world? Is this the question?"

He grew angry. "Tell me, what are the purpose of the pebbles?"

"You will have to find a geologist to tell you that," I said. I shrugged. "I don't know why the pebbles exist. There is probably a good answer, though."

"I am not asking about the why of pebbles," he said, in fine enough Czech, but in a Czech I pretended not to understand.

"I think there have always been pebbles here," I said. "Probably they were here before all of us were here."

"Not here," he said.

"Not just here," I said, "but everywhere. Probably on every inch of the earth you'll find pebbles like this."

He grew frustrated. He pointed, first at the ground, then at me. He tried English. "No you, no pebbles. You: pebbles. Why? What is the why of this?"

I told him that perhaps they were coming from the sky, the pebbles. That birds perhaps were dropping them. That this was a game they played, taking rocks from where they had been for so long, for thousands of years, breaking them in their jaws, taking the broken pieces, breaking them into even smaller pieces, taking the even smaller pieces and breaking them further. Not unlike the Soviet Union, I said. When I said this, he was looking up, and there were, at that moment, birds crossing overhead, pigeons loosed from the rafters of the station, rousted out of their nests by the vibrations of an arriving train.

"Why are there the pebbles?" he asked, again in English. "Tell me. Tell me please. I must know."

"The earth is made of rocks," I said.

He shook his head. "I need a better answer." He was very close to me, so close I could smell his breath.

"There are rocks because the earth is breaking apart," I said.

"The what?" He pushed me, two hands against my chest.

"We," I said, in an English I did not know I had. "We are breaking apart." I took the pebbles into my hands, my friends, nine of them, Žofie, Ambrož, everyone. "We, all of us, are breaking apart."

IN thinking about this, it seems to me that this conversation, which likely did not happen the way I have remembered it, and which likely did not happen the way I have told it to so many, including just now, was not unlike all the conversations I was having then, during my last year in Prague, my last year in Europe, this being the early winter of 1969, the year I returned to the city alive without my friends, a city that has always been old, was likely born old, and will likely seem just as old when and if Eli ever makes it there himself. Eventually when I left, I did so from this spot, where I had come and gone so often, where I had rehearsed the steps, waiting by tracks strewn with pebbles, surrounded by monuments, waiting as people often do in stations like this, craning their necks to see into the darkness, waiting for certain doors to open, certain paths to emerge, a way out, a seat in a bright, clean car headed to some glorious other future.

WE found ourselves hours after midnight in Brooklyn, near the sea, close enough that we could smell it. It must have become obvious to Ambrož that I had grown tired. We had made the trip on foot, over the East River, through the dark forest of Prospect Park, down Ocean Avenue, through Gravesend, until we reached Neptune Avenue, desolate at this hour, descended on by birds. He had led the way, had dictated all of this evening, just as he would dictate a hundred evenings after this one, and when it became obvious that night where we were headed, I remembered both what Žofie had told me, that Ambrož had become consumed with the sea, that he had asked her to take him there, that all his earthly life he had lived between water, in equidistance between the Baltic and Mediterranean, Szczecin and Venice. And I remembered what he had told me himself, that at the ocean one could sense the unseen, a thinning in the one-way mirror.

He asked whether I felt I needed to sleep, and when I said yes, of course yes, we've been walking for hours, my daughter is about to give birth, I am seeing ghosts, actual ghosts, speaking to them out loud, I have clearly lost my ever-loving mind, look at where we are, look how far from my apartment we are, obviously I am all by myself, in the midst of a serious madness, talking into the air, to no one, engaged by phantoms, in need of medication if not a bed, he asked me to close my eyes, to think of something that made me happy from my childhood—this was the only way, he said, to imagine childhood, to imagine your sweet mother—and when I said I could not, that I had not been able to picture my childhood for a very long time, that perhaps I had never been able to think of my childhood, he told me to try again, that he would help me—and when I did this, I felt Ambrož place his hand in the space between my eyes, where beneath the skin one senses how much blood it takes to power the human brain, the entire traffic system of blood and thought, and at once, I felt the exhaustion of the day leave me—the hospital, the drinking, the Requiem, the levitators. When I opened my eyes, we were, I promise you, feet from the sea, beneath a tattoo of the moon, and Ambrož was laughing. Another good trick, he said. I only know a handful. But this one is a good one. And then I watched him walk from the street into the sand and up to the water, where, for a moment, I lost sight of him in the mist and spray and the dark night. He left no footsteps. But from far away I heard the sound of him over the crash of the tide.

WHAT happened, he told me, was that Ivan began to make money. They had met, Ivan and Ambrož, in the museum, the Albertina, in view of Modigliani; later in front of Chaim Soutine. It was an exhibition on the art of the vanished Jew. Here were the faces of the artists, their personal effects, their hairbrushes, sketch pads, scraps of paper onto which they had written their mothers' addresses, the profiles of lovers written in candle smoke onto muslin, lists for groceries, small prayers. And most importantly their paintings, their mounds of clay, small mirrors of a world in which they had found themselves. Ambrož told me this later that night, from a bench overlooking the sea in Brighton Beach. I followed him from gallery to gallery, Ambrož admitted. Ivan was in black, entirely in black, trying, I thought that first day, to pass as a spirit.

"Within a month, I was living in his apartment. He was a textile artist: painted silk, hand done, largely at night, in secret. This was crucial, the secrecy. He worked in his father's factory, which manufactured dye, the exact dye that Ivan ferried out in small amounts, in special vials. He made scarves, mostly. Occasionally smaller pieces, handkerchiefs, for example. Or decorative inserts for gift boxes. A flash of color inside an eyeglass case. When the work escaped Prague and made its way to Paris, to London, it came advertised as art from the hands of occupied Europe. A certain person enjoyed the pornography of this. Ivan often imagined the parlor conversation out loud. Oh this, someone might say, fingering Ivan's work, this beautiful piece of silk? This was made by a poor, suffering man in Bohemia, living in hiding, beneath the Iron Curtain, the real curtain, made by a real victim, isn't that awful? He makes them in the darkness, these scarves, by candlelight. I've heard he weighs only forty-five kilos. That he has subsisted for years on scraps, bad bread, hand-brewed beer. And that if the ŠtB catches him or if the Soviets catch him he'll be sent to break rocks until he's an old man. The poor thing. But it *is* lovely, isn't it? Come feel it. Come put it between your fingers. Hold it to the light. Can you see the brush-strokes?

"I had never kissed another person," Ambrož told me. "Or, rather, no one had ever kissed me. A real kiss, I'm talking about. This fundamental element of love, affection, being human, this basic ingredient of sweetness, and until the last year of my life, I had never experienced it. Where would this have happened?" he asked. "In the street? In the museum where we had met? Tell me where," he asked of me. "I lived with my mother until I lived with Ivan. My mother who believed until I was gone that I would marry her best friend's daughter, Irena, a nice woman certainly, a pleasant person, a woman who went on to a fine career as a government minister, and whose watercolors are terrifically accomplished, but, Moses, she was someone who knew I could not love her, who saw through me in life as well as anyone ever did in death.

"Our apartment in Smíchov was a ruin of candle wax, canned food, records we played at the lowest volume. Scriabin, who was our favorite, and who could see music as color—we listened to him quite often. Our bed was the only piece of furniture worth anything. Elevated by wooden architecture, Ivan thought of it as a boat, a ship from today to tomorrow. His working space was nothing. Crates. Upturned boxes. When he worked, he made himself into a snail, everything curled over, his spine rounded into a shell, so that no one could see, no part of the world could interfere.

"When Ivan defected to Paris it was because someone had gotten ahold of one of the pieces. A scarf, I think it was, slung around the neck of a journalist. Someone in the offices of Agence France-Presse saw it and demanded one for herself. And a friend of that woman saw that scarf and asked for one for her mother. Letters began to arrive at the apartment written in code. *Another greeting from Paris*, the notes read, which meant one scarf. *Many happy greetings from Paris*, another might read, which meant five pieces, sent as quickly as possible. Eventually, it became clear that he would go. And if he was going to go, I needed to go. But it was not easy for me to get to Paris," Ambrož said. "For one, it was far away.

"Also, I was dead.

"The laws that govern the travel of the dead are such that I could not just go on board the train with him. Whoever it is that operates the ticket counter in the station of ghosts has long ago packed up, closed up, moved away forever. I told him this, pleaded with Ivan not to go. At this point, Ivan did not believe that I was there, that I was the source of the voice he heard in the morning. At night, he would return home from his job in the office of his father's company—this was his job, filing papers, adhering labels onto folders, affixing codes in a dossier that corresponded to the labels—and put himself to work, fold himself up, put the shell around himself. Already in those first months of 1969 he was preparing to go. He had long anticipated what would happen eventually, that someone, in someplace other than our city, would want from him what he could do, his abilities. He would take imaginary telephone calls from adoring customers. He would receive orders, large orders from pretend department stores. He would do this in French, at first, a language he did not know, but which he was trying to learn. And he would do this in English, or what he imagined was English. *Hello. Thank you. Yes. Paint. Pencil. Silk. Scarf. Neck. Dollar. Hollywood. John Kennedy. Rock and roll. Sure thing. Okey-dokey. Yes. Of course. No. Of course. Much monies. Of course. Very much monies. Okey-dokey. I will give you. I will promise you. I will make. I will give.*

*Good night. Goodbye. Once upon a time. Forever and ever and ever. I love you.* These were, I think, the only words he knew. And there I was, Moses, sitting in his apartment, our apartment, on the windowsill, amid his paintbrushes, his Hungarian turpentine, his many self-portraits, his books on Modigliani, his empty canisters of water, one of which had been my favorite drinking glass, a simple piece of white porcelain, aswirl now with red paint. Here I am, I was telling him. Here I am. Please look, Ivan. Here I am. What Abraham says to God in the moments before he is to sacrifice his son: Here I am.

"I was a houseplant. Another decoration. A bauble on the sill. An image in a picture frame that had gotten loose somehow. I would scream at him to see me. Look at me! Look over here! Tell me you don't see me, Ivan! After hours of this, I would break through to him. You are a phantom, he would say. I am not hearing this, not hearing you. This cannot be. Drunk, he would try to swipe his hands through me. Everyone always believes they can pass through the dead, which has never been the case. One always finds themselves hitting something, some limitation. And the fear one feels at this! The shiver that occurs! And for what? A reminder that you, too, will end up where I am?

"At night, while he lay in bed, I would tell him, don't go, I will not be able to go with you, don't go to Paris, to Hollywood, to Rome, to anywhere else but here. What will I do without you? Night after night of this, of me yelling, screaming into our apartment, Ivan at his desk, making the outline of an angel's wings onto a scarf destined for the neck of a wealthy Parisian woman. Or Ivan on the edge of our bed, massaging his sore feet. Or Ivan standing over the slow revolutions of a record as it played Bach, the music of church life, of his childhood, of the field beyond his boyhood home, of evenings with his mother while she played the violin to soothe him during the war. Or this: Ivan drawing on a sketch pad, sketching his dream life, a large apartment somewhere far away in which he was always alone, drawing windows onto a city life, small jewel boxes of light, in which there were always lovers, two people in silhouette, irrevocably kept from daylight. I don't know what I did to deserve to be haunted like this, he said one night, when he was lying in bed, and while I was lying beside him. The power was gone, and he had Sabbath candles lit everywhere. A fact of life then was that there were no Jews but that there were Jewish candles. Oh, Moses, all I wanted to do was to put my hand on his heart, to feel the sign of life. What one misses in death is the feel of earth—skin, hair, the pulse of blood. To exist as I exist now is to exist as wind exists, here, but also here inexactly, able to be blown apart. What does one do in this situation?" Ambrož asked me. "When you are trying to get across to someone who cannot hear you?

"He left a year after I was killed. Not long after you left, after everyone left. He packed his belongings in my suitcase. At the door, he said goodbye to me. I love you, he told me, but you are not real, and I need to be someplace where I can live in the present, among reality, with real people, real feelings, real voices. We were, at that moment, face-to-face, and he saw, I would like to believe, that I was indeed real, that he could, if he wanted to, reach out to feel me as I had wanted him to ever since I reappeared, that he could keep me around, keep me near him at all times, in every city, invisible to the world but visible to him. What is love if not that?

"I followed him to the station. Down the old avenues in the darkness. All the while he told me to go away. A boy talking to a pesky friend or a stray cat. Go, he told me, go somewhere, haunt another person. Still, I followed him, right up until the doors to his train closed, and the tracks were empty, and everywhere around me there was the smoke smell of the tracks having been heated. I should have known that when an angel leaves, there is always a bit of fire left over.

"At the station, I was left wandering. I found, then, that I could not leave. At every door, I was blocked. A rule of the life of the dead I suppose I had understood but had hoped would not apply to me. After all, what had I ever done wrong? For years it went like this. A hundred trains a day. Crowds of all manners. All the Soviet men coming and going, the East German men disembarking with their chins high."

When I ask what happened then, Ambrož tells me that he joined everyone else in the station, and when I asked whom he meant by everyone, he paused for a very long time. While I waited, some part of the tide shifted, some loose spray of waves beneath us at Brighton Beach came apart, and we were hit by the sea, and after this, finally, he said, quietly, "There are, as you might imagine, thousands of us there, people like me, perhaps more than thousands, all of us in suspension between sentences, waiting just as you are all waiting, gathered near the tracks, in the rafters, among the birds, leaning against walls, standing in lines that won't for thousands of years ever move, anticipating some direction, some ticket counter finally opening, watching the routine, which in a train station is an endless routine of embarking, disembarking, farewell, reunion.

"Imagine," he says, "a vivisection of the earth as it's cut away from Herculaneum, from Hissarlik, from the center of London, from old Kraków, Drohobycz, from our city, the new city built upon the old city, new earth atop the old earth, shards of pottery, upturned burial casings, one's horse laid to sleep for a thousand years until it is uncovered by mountain climbers in a future without horses, a woman's hand reaching out in an endless sleep, golden rings on every finger, the scrolls of the Holy Torah opened to a parashah that never changes. This is what the train station is like for those years I spend in it. There are those who arrived yesterday, from last month, from sixty years earlier, women who saw Napoléon climbing down from his horse at Trafalgar, and who can speak about the color of the sails on the boats of exile headed to Saint

Helena, where it is said he spent years looking at the ocean, trying to find a trace of home.

"A child arrives one day from the country, years after Ivan leaves, dressed in knee socks, thick eyeglasses, a hat which children have for hundreds of years worn in the fields of Bohemia, but which, after 1969, very quickly becomes unfashionable, and he is lost somehow from his parents, separated by a large group, and this child spends days wandering among us in a state of hysterics so pronounced that he begins to be able to see us clearly, to see me, to tell me that he needs my help, some crucial heavenly boundary has been breached and he tells me he is lost, he misses his parents, his mother especially, who had promised him a gift in this city, a stuffed animal, a particular bowl of cherry ice cream, and in this way I get to leave when he leaves. The door opens, and a flood of us are released. What do we sound like, I want to know. What does a charge of ghosts sound like at midnight in the Prague of the late twentieth century? At first, I don't know how much time has passed since Ivan's train left. Years, very clearly. Perhaps longer than years. At once, I am outside in the cool city evening, beneath the sky, the actual sky of the humans, among the actual people of earth, beside the actual Vltava, in which there are actual signs of life, plankton, trout wake, the reflection of starlings. We sit on the low-slung stone walls by the water, me and this boy and the others who have left with us. The city has been altered, obviously, but only in small ways. Prague can only ever be altered in small ways. Yes, where my father's Turkish bath stood, there is now a newer building, uglier, square, built in the Soviet style, which is to say, in no style at all. Yes, the automobiles are different, new lines, different curves, ideas of the future speeding on four wheels. Above us in the sky, airplanes describe the city, leave ribbons tied around us in vapor.

"The boy is found soon enough. Police have fanned out. When he is wrapped up in his mother's arms, news cameras are filming, and she asks him, his mother, how did you get here, how did you stay safe, and he tells her, in a clear voice, a voice of genuine calm and confidence, the ghosts took me here, the ghosts looked after me, a statement which, obviously, devastates his mother. The boy is looking right at me when he says this, a look of thanks, gratitude. He points at me, and I find myself smiling. We will never forget one another, he seems to be telling me, not ever.

"'Oh no,' the mother cries, nearly fainting, 'my son has lost his mind! He's seeing spirits! He has seen the face of death!'

"Not long after—or a very long time after, I have no idea, Moses, time confuses me, years speed away—I find Žofie on the street with her son. I understand at once that the boy is hers. A part of her, severed from her body, walking on his own. This confuses me at first, the boy. I did not know that the dead could have children. They are speaking in English, and although I can't understand what they are saying, I know that she is describing the city to him, pointing at various buildings, explaining, I imagine, that here is where I was a schoolgirl, where I learned mathematics, the warmth of this window light is where I felt most safe, where I was taught the distance between planets, where I imagined myself in a variety of futures, where I allowed my dreams to overtake me. Here is the apartment house where my father decided to stay after the war, I think she says, when she points out an otherwise ordinary set of steps. She sees me straightaway. Across the head of her boy, she sees me, and she appears both shocked and not shocked. Ghosts like me surround her. She has, I understand at once, continued to live, become a mother, moved away, escaped death, escaped Prague, wandered Tangier after dark in love, seen the muezzin eye to eye from atop a tower of books, struggled senseless in the heat of her bed with her sheets stuck to her slick skin dreaming of us, Moses, of you and me, and at times, dreaming that the bullet in her body would multiply into other bullets and scatter her in every country she has called home. And I can see into her thoughts the image of her clutching her infant to her body in the dark as if he were, like Ivan, a piece of heaven broken loose and given to her as a promise. In one moment, I understand all this. This is what a ghost gets in place of life. She has come back here with romantic notions, with the idea that she will encounter some sign to tell her that this is a good idea, to move home from America with her son, to give him some idea of Europe, a dose of the old culture. 'My friend!' I say. 'Žofie, my friend! You cannot imagine how good it is to see your face! I have been here in this city for so long, for longer than we were ever alive, and I have not in years, in decades, seen a familiar face, a face from my world of the living, not one!' At this, she places her body between me and him, between her boy and the dead.

"Do not touch my child with your finger, she tells me, although without words.

"'Don't be afraid,' I tell her. 'I can't hurt anyone. I'm barely here.' She pushes her son away. 'Go, Felix, go,' she says, 'run back to the hotel, go inside, close the doors, answer for no one but me.'

"A cry Jewish mothers have been making since the first sunset.

"Within moments, the boy is gone, and she is gone as well. She has fled. Without turning back to see me again, she has taken off in order not to see me.

"The rest I am not proud of, Moses. For days I followed her. Every young ghost, I suppose, goes through this. I haunted her. I appeared in her mirrors. Between walls. In steam, rainwater, river water, in restaurant walls, in the rafters of the old synagogues. I transposed myself on others so that I became inescapable. In every face she saw, there was my face, young still, trapped in time. I did this in every corner of the city, and when I did, I told her, I need your help, I need your help to take me to New York so that I can find Ivan. She ignored me at every turn. No person was ever better at ignoring the dead than Žofie. In the next world, she is famous already for this.

"Not until her last night in the city, Moses, when I found her alone by the Vltava, not far from your old apartment, did she speak to me. 'Fine,' she said. 'If this is what it takes, Ambrož, then fine, I will do whatever you want. Just please promise that you will stop with this,' she told me, 'stop haunting me, following me, torturing me with the past, this is why I am leaving, why I will never come back here, or to any of these places,' she said, meaning, I think, these cities in which we were children, Prague, Munich, Vienna, all of them are museums to history, monuments to misery, living tombs. 'So please,' she said, 'come with me if you need to, but stop haunting me, stop following me, I know what you are doing,' she said, and she touched me against my stomach, on the very spot where I had been killed on earth, and she said, plainly, 'Do you think you are the first ghost who has ever followed me? Do you think I am not practiced at this, that I have never been haunted like this before? When I was a little girl here my playmates were killed in a pit, they were shot in the face. My husband is gone. He was taken somewhere and never returned to me. This has been my life. Do you think I have not been living with one foot in your world ever since I was a child?'"

WHEN Ambrož was finished with all of this, it was close to morning. Soon, the sun would rise. I would be expected back at the hospital. As we sat, he began to roll the legs of his pants up above his knees, and there, against his skin, were his poems, small papers, folded into squares, dozens of them still stitched into the lining of the fabric. I understood at once that they had been there forever. Or, more accurately, since that morning in the Josefov when we sat, all of us, readying ourselves for the end. But also: forever. Carefully, he removed one for me, the smallest piece, a simple square, weathered by age.

"Here," he said, and when I asked what it was, this square lined with blue thread and the dust of the central train station, he said it was a poem he had written for my grandson. "I wrote it when I was young, in my apartment with Ivan. I knew that you and Žofie would have a grandchild. Everyone did," he said. "I don't know that everyone knew it would happen this way," he said with a laugh, "but when I wrote it I figured it would turn out to be true, and somehow it has, a small prophecy, made by accident."

I started to open it. How could I not, after so long. But he stopped me.

"The moment you open this, Moses, is the moment I have to go."

"This is how it works?" I asked.

"A strange rule, certainly," he said, "but a rule nevertheless. I can give you something physically, but then you lose me."

"Forever?" I asked.

He said yes.

I held it in my hand, this small square.

"Before you open it, though, I need you to do something for me," he said.

"What is it?"

"I need you to take me to Prague."

"Just a small favor," I said, joking.

"I would give you the money, but I am fairly certain my currency is not good any longer."

"You're done with America?"

"I am done, I think, entirely."

He told me that when he arrived in New York, he found Ivan in a bed at St. Vincent's Hospital, surrounded by orchids, friends, other lovers, newer versions of him, different models, always foreign, a Romanian Ambrož, a Hungarian Ambrož, several Serbian Ambrožes, all of them made with pieces of him, his slender frame, the bulb of his nose, his certain angularity, his innocence. Ivan was very ill. A slow and horrible process, doctors had told him. Tumors were appearing everywhere. On the skin. In the lung. Even still, he had the window open, a cigarette in his mouth. He was draped in clothing he had made, a silk gown onto which he had made a painting of a sky, but it was quite bad, this painting, the robe, the entire picture. He had lost himself. So much time had passed. "When he saw me," Ambrož said, "he knew he was almost dead. 'Ah!' Ivan said to me. 'Finally, you arrive.' He believed he was hallucinating. 'I have been waiting for you to show up.' But he saw me as I was, Moses. Which is to say, someone with wings.

"Ivan began to talk in that way people do when they have been separated for a long time, and he spoke about meeting me for the first time and how something about me reminded him of Chaim Soutine, whose paintings we had seen on the first day of our life together. He told me how Soutine had been a poor Jew from Smilovitz

living in Paris—imagine the trip in darkness by way of cabriolet—
in relative squalor, and one day a rich man from America came to
his studio, saw his work, recognized the genius at hand, and bought
everything in the room, every scrap, and in turn, made Soutine rich
and famous. And what does Soutine do at this point? He rushes out
onto the streets of Paris and hails himself a taxi and tells the driver
to take him to the sea. 'Take me to Nice,' he says. A trip of almost
a thousand kilometers.

"It was late when I showed myself to him," Ambrož said. "He
was alone. There was a great deal I could have said to him. A great
deal, in fact, I wanted and needed to say to him. Such as the real
reason Soutine wanted to go to the Mediterranean. The reason any
person wants desperately to go to the ocean. But instead, I told him
that he was mistaken. That we met first in front of a Modigliani
portrait of Jeanne Hébuterne. 'I introduced myself to you,' I told
him, 'but I think you were busy with the painting, or busy with
pretending to be busied with the painting. You were all in black.
You took yourself very seriously. I had come to Vienna hoping to
meet someone very much like you, and there you were, very obviously Czech, reeking of Prague. Later, after following you, we met
again in front of the Soutine painting. Finally, then, you noticed me.'

"'This sounds true,' Ivan said. 'I have always loved his paintings
of her.'

"'It sounds true because it is true,'" I said.

"Jeanne Hébuterne's parents would not let her marry Modigliani, Ivan told me. He had been gravely ill for a very long time. Tuberculosis. Coughing into cloth napkins. A feeling of a city being
built in his chest against his will, so much concrete, so much heavi-
ness. Nights filled with delirium. An inability to withstand daylight
or darkness. One can imagine the way the illness looked on him.
The coughing. The slow vanishing. Not unlike my last two years.
Jeanne Hébuterne was much younger than he. Nineteen when they

met. When he died, she was eight months pregnant with their second child. She was so distraught that her parents came to collect her. Days later, she threw herself from the window of her childhood bedroom. It took her parents a decade to decide to bury her beside him in Père Lachaise.

"Finally, Ivan put his hand to my face," Ambrož said.

"'What took you so long,' he asked me.

"'I was stuck,' I said.

"'Stuck where?'

"'Stuck in Prague.'

"'Which is the same as being stuck in time,' he said.

"'I was at the train station,' I said. 'I was waiting for a very long time for my train to come.'

"'Finally it came.'

"'It did,' I said.

"'And you are here.'

"'Here I am,' I said.

"Within days Ivan would be gone," Ambrož told me. Ivan knew this. He told Ambrož. "Don't worry, we'll be together soon. I am to be taken back to Prague by friends, and buried in the same cemetery as you, right beside you. I made money here. Too much of it. So much of it that I can die here in this futuristic place. I've taken care of all the arrangements. I bought the earth beside you," he told Ambrož. "This way, we will never be apart."

"I wanted to tell him not to do this," Ambrož told me, "to explain why his doing this would cause us to be apart, but he began to fall asleep. And anyway, how does one convey the logic of my world, which is a world of both endlessness and endless silence and a series of unbroken and endless rules, to a man like him, at the end, on the verge, constrained by the opposite, by endings, by the beeping noise of modern medicine, by the holy rule, which is the rule of life and also its opposite. He was, at this point, half machine—so many wires, noises, tubes, colors, displays showing various necessary functions that I did not understand. Funny that a man born in a city that never ages, he told me, should find himself here, in this state."

I held the folded square of paper that Ambrož had given me and we began to walk back to the hospital, up Neptune Avenue in the near morning, Ambrož and I, and I told him that I understood why he wanted me to take him back to Prague.

"Ivan is there," said Ambrož, "stuck there with no one, in a graveyard on the outskirts of the city, and I am here, and I do not know if I can withstand waiting until someone else comes by and happens to notice me hovering, pleading.

"So will you do it?" Ambrož asked me. "Will you?"

AND then, finally, there is Eli: rolled in cotton and wool, passed to me as babies have been passed to grandfathers since Isaac was to Abraham. Eli: a wild cry from the daylight, wearing the eyes of my mother born back into life once again. Eli: miracle of miracles, kadosh, kadosh, kadosh!

We had been in the waiting area, all of us, the entire family, never as large as it was that morning, seated by the enormous windows that overlook the park, where out amid the trees there were, as Žofie let me know, no more fools attempting to levitate themselves. And then three things happened. First there was Felix, whistling a conductor's whistle, stumbling toward us, love-drunk already by the thought of his son, pulled into the universe of fathers, which is a universe of love, of course, but more specifically, a universe of impossibility, a place where one is always trying to hold something that cannot be held, such as air or sound or love itself, and then second, we sat, Eli and I, beside the window, where out in the daylight, the reservoir was for a moment alive with light and bird shadow, none of which he could see at this point, not even hours old and here he was giving me the expression of a man on the verge of losing a memory, a man who knows eventually, minute by minute, that his knowledge of the past will peel away from him. Sit, I heard him telling me in that invisible language of family, sit down and hear what I have to say, but all around us there was the clatter that attends the newly born, and he began to cry, not because of what his mother or father thought, which was that he was tired, or hungry, or shocked at life, but because it was gone from him, the history of him and everything before him, and as he was taken away from me, he looked back with this look all of us share, the ashen look of having possessed something crucial and elemental and having had it vanish. It was right here, he was saying to me, it was right here in my thoughts, right here.

I suppose all this made me want to think about my own father, about whom I knew and remembered absolutely nothing at all, but then the third thing happened, which is that Žofie appeared with a small stereo that she had taken from home and put it beside Martha's bed, and while Martha slept, Žofie took Eli's small hand and put it to the base of the speaker. We thought for a long while about what to play, so that he would know us even when he did not know, just as your father had known his father, and probably onward, backwards, and when we did, when the first strains played, he quieted, and all of us, our family, we let the music play.

# Separate Rooms

## VIENNA, 2016

# ARNOLD

ALL of this starts at a dinner party to celebrate my birthday. It is a preposterous number, ninety-nine, a matter of science fiction, one year shy of truly unbelievable, a byproduct of medicine as much as it is a matter of luck—great luck, and also the luck of nightmares. At a certain point, one is always met by disbelief at this age, by a certain expression that is the opposite of rapture, especially from the young, to see if I am indeed real, or if, for some reason, it might be possible to pass through me as one imagines they might pass through a spirit.

The children of old friends organize the party. They call me Grandfather. Everyone does this. For a man with no living children, it seems I have become, impossibly, a grandfather to hundreds. We meet at a restaurant on the interior of the Stadtpark, near a window overlooking the snow-sealed sakura trees. This is where a stranger turns to me, a woman I have never seen before, a friend of one of the people who is my grandchild and also of course not my grandchild, and out of nowhere, and for no apparent reason, she changes my life. Within minutes of meeting her, everything, forever, is different.

The stranger is Franziska Bauer. She is a scientist at the Naturhistorisches, and when I ask about her expertise, she explains that she is the one who determines an image from the fossil records, the person who assigns color and shape and the pallor of skin to bones pulled out from the earth after millennia. I am the person, she tells me, who looks at the skeleton and sees not just the bones but the animal. A process, she says, of de-excavation, of assembling life from what she tells me is the great sleep of earth.

Ah! I say. You work in construction!

She, however, hears me wrong.

Resurrection? she asks. She appears to think very deeply about this, in a way that moves me. I suppose you could say that. I've never thought of it this way. I have not brought any creatures back to life, though.

Not yet, I say. It is a sentence that, a year later, after all this is over, and everything is irrevocably different, strikes me as a decent summation for what has happened to me.

Would you like to hear a story? she asks me.

This is how it starts.

SHE tells me about her mother, her first mother, whom she does not know.

I was given up for adoption, she explains.

We are, Franziska and I, alone at a table at the edge of a room, nearest to the window, nearest to the icy trees. She takes my hands while she talks. It must be, I think, that she knows already what this story will do to me, that it will bring me in the coming days to take leave of my life. Or perhaps it is because I appear to others to be a man in need of having my hand held.

What I knew about my birth parents, she says, I was told when I was very young. That they were, for instance, teenagers when I was born. That they were troubled people in no shape to raise a child. My eventual existence, I was told, was a cause for great alarm. They had, after all, no money, no consistent place of residence. Each of them, at various points, had been put out of their homes by their parents, as one might do to an animal not suited for domestication— like stories one hears about fools trying to raise alligators as pets. As a result, I was given all the regular pablum. You are better off here in your new life, I was told. Focus on your present situation, imagine life as a road that leads in only one direction, onward, forward, upward.

At eleven years old, she says, the adoption agency sends me a photograph of my father. In the picture he is standing on a street in a city somewhere that I have always understood for some reason to be Geneva. Maybe I was told this, maybe I invented it for myself. He has a bicycle beside him. His hair is messy, but in a way that

seems to have been cultivated to express a casual sense of both dis-
tress and deep soulfulness. He looks so young that it seems to me as
if he could be a schoolmate of mine, someone to whom I would have
wanted to confide my secrets. At fourteen years old, I receive the
name of my mother—June. This comes in an envelope one afternoon, a single sheet of paper with this information. And this is all I
have growing up. A photograph of one person and a name of another. And also the sensation of a doubling: my life as I am experiencing it, in a comfortable home in Salzburg, with all the requisite
consumer impulses, my Sony Walkman, my teenage sexual yearn-
ing for Simon Le Bon, my shameful hunger for American fast-food
hamburgers, the large suburban grocery stores where I wander after
school. And also, the life I was not living, with these people, with
June and her boyfriend from school, who lives in my mind perpetually standing beside his bicycle, no matter how I imagine him.
Every movement in my life is accompanied by the absence of movement in that other life. All the possibilities I am afforded in Salzburg, and then later in Heidelberg and Aachen and Oxford, are
doubled by their negative. These are parallel tracks as I understand
them, irreconcilable to me, but sometimes even now it occurs to me
that I might be able to, if I concentrate, experience myself in both
existences, the image and that image's reverse, my mother's daughter
and my other mother's daughter.

Franziska says that when she asks the adoption agency for details on her adoption she is told that she is disallowed by law to receive any identifying information unless she is able to get her
adopted mother to sign a form, and write a long affidavit attesting
in official language to her curiosity, my need for knowing, she says,
and the reason I desire the anonymity of my origins unanonymized,
all of which I cannot do, because when I am twenty, my adopted
mother dies very suddenly, a ruptured embolism, a personal explosion in her body that explodes also in my body. For years I have tried

to circumvent this rule, but they are Swiss, you know, and when they make rules about social opacity and the impenetrability of certain anonymous shields, they are quite serious, it turns out.

She explains the test. There is a fiberglass tube, a sealed box, a factory in Bangalore, autosomal sequencing, a mitochondrial investigation into her maternal line. After a few weeks, she says, I received by email a profile of my polyethnicity arrayed on a map, beamed to my laptop, the whole of me apportioned by a set of percentages that do not, for some reason, equal a hundred percent. Which confirms to me at least that some part of me is always somewhere else, outside of me. This is not uncommon in my line of work, though—to come upon a fossil of some disappeared species and to see that a crucial part of the reconstructed skeleton is absent—a wing, a tooth. A robber or bird or strong wind has taken just this curve of the rib. The map, I understood, maybe senselessly, is the negative version of me.

While around us the party continues, Franziska takes her laptop from her handbag and shows me.

The map exists in varying shades of blue: sea, sky, the luminescent blue my father used to stitch my teenage prayer shawl. Franziska's background splays across the European continent like a form of ribosome birdshot. This is me, she says, all these points. The points, she explains, are functions of time, not individual lives, an expression of migration and marriages, expressions of people swept up, forced into reinvention. As the technology determines it, I am, according to this, predominantly Irish, she says. Not Swiss.

Franziska shows me a photograph of a woman who is her, but older, a double of her but not a double. The woman in the picture is very obviously her mother. Importantly, she says, I discovered June, living in Galway, a mother to other children, my half siblings, a police sketch artist actually, which is not very different from what I do, assembling pictures out of the shadow of nothing. This single fact, she says, alters the idea I've carried with me all my life that one's interests and talents, such as they are, exist as the product of obsession and not genetics. Franziska pauses after saying this, which makes me understand that she means it to be an important statement, a reduction of this experience into the simplest language she can manage, but even still, it takes a moment for me to understand what she's saying.

Seeing that I am lost—ninety-nine years, I want to say; ninety-nine!—she tells me that these are popular ideas for someone like her, someone of her generation, someone who wants to distrust the logic of narrative explanations: everything is the product of her environment. I am me because of the world, not because of my mother. If one does not know their mother, the blankness of hereditary determinism becomes terrifying, she says, and I want to tell her, oh, Franziska, I have not been able to summon the image of my mama's face for close to eighty years; the idea of my ever having a mother seems at times like a folktale to me. I have always only existed like this, alone, on my own. But, she says, brightening, squeezing my hands gently, it turns out that my birth mother, June, had her DNA sequenced in the hope of discovering me, just as I have hoped to discover her. The parallel tracks, it turns out, are not so parallel. June messaged me via this website's system. Hi, the message said. It's me. The computer says we are related. Who are you? Are you possibly who I think you are?

All it took was this test, she says, and I found my mother.

I ask polite questions. I want to know, is this test expensive? And does it hurt? And where are the needles injected, and how large are they?

There is no pain, she tells me. And no needles. One just spits.

But how, I ask, does one assess your history without pain?

I HAVE come to the restaurant with my neighbor, Sandrine. She lives in the building across the street from my apartment. To the extent that I have any family anymore at all, there is Sandrine. She comes to fetch me at my table because there is a cake, and then, a last surprise, a photographer from the newspaper who snaps me looking appropriately overwhelmed, even as I try to convey in my expression a combination of resolve and dignified embarrassment and also anger that I am newsworthy. Later, the headline will feel both appropriate and vulgar: SURVIVOR KEEPS SURVIVING!

The restaurant is only a half mile from the apartment where I was born, close to the river, near the large weeping trees on the Ringstraße that I have loved all my life, and looking off in that direction I find myself aloft, no longer here in the restaurant with all these grandchildren who are not grandchildren, and this photographer who is speaking to me as if I am myself a fossil she has uncovered for Franziska's museum, but a fossil missing a curve of his rib, and I am back in the old house with Fania, and Moses is still here on the floor in front of us, playing on the red rug my mother has brought back from London, and we are sitting in the quiet, near the window watching the weather. Or it is the very end, and we are taking turns carrying the baby, and we have stuffed into our overcoats his blankets, his stuffed bear, a small book of pictures to soothe him, all this business of life and joy we were to have been dispossessed of, but which, for his sake, we have taken. We've buttered Moses up with cream, and he smells like talcum and linen, and like the daylight in the front room of a home I will not be allowed to enter, or within days, one it seems I will not be allowed to reconstruct in my memory.

This is where I go on the evening of my ninety-ninth birthday. The outside of me is in a bright restaurant in the park, encircled by false grandchildren, but the rest of me is gone. Into that other train, packed in such a way that no one could sit, where the light at the seal of the lock latch is the light of death. This is where I am in the middle of my ninety-ninth birthday party, in the Vienna of the future, in the tech-silver Vienna of 2016: the softness of the skin on Moses's cheek in his last hours is the softness of death. At the end, I feel a convergence of heartbeats between our bodies, and then, for a very long time, many years, nothing else. The men at the end of the ramp say that we will be reunited eventually, alles nacher, they say, everything after, olam ha-ba.

In the world to come, children are reborn with all the world's knowledge. In the world to come, fathers fall forward to wrap the old kingdom in their arms. In the world to come, the blessings of our memories are collected like kite string and let loose into the new sky. In the world to come, I put my hand through the walls that keep us apart to touch my family.

The last I saw my wife, we were being walked away from one another. The last I saw my son, he looked back from my wife's shoulder to find me. So this is death, I remember thinking, so this is the moment the world ends.

Does someone like me lose their memory in the world to come? Or is it held intact, delivered into amber? Because, here, it is all before me: I am in the train station with Sonja, and she is five years old. I walk her by hand from our house. I tell her of the sea. She will see fish, endless flatness. She will learn a new language. It is raining. I know almost nothing about England except the king. So I tell her, you will see the king. On the walk she hugs me. She does not want to let go of my hand. I thought you were the king, she says to me.

At the station I pry away every finger. You come too, she says. I wish I could, I say. She has taken her blond doll, whom she has named for her mother: Fania. Tell her everything, I say. When you are scared, tell her what scares you. She waves to me from the mouth of the train door. And she waves the doll's little hand. I saw her already talking into the doll's ear. This is the only picture left, the last picture.

In the restaurant, Sandrine knows I am thinking of this. Whenever I seem to go elsewhere, she suspects this is where I have gone. Two children given away to nothingness. What she does not know: a month after I gave Sonja away, a parcel arrived from Harwich. Sonja had taken ill on the journey. Those were the words, in English, in a grammar that defied me. The letter offered a preliminary diagnosis: scarlet fever. The doll was sent back. It lay there, inert in a cardboard coffin. I took its lack of motion for obstinacy. It would not tell me what it knew because I was not Sonja. This is the way a child's toy works. It has only one god on earth, one person who can make life. Inside, I know, it had all Sonja's secrets, all that frightened her. In the letter my name is wrong. It is a letter to Isaac, whoever that is, a different man, a man whose daughter had also been put on board, whose heart had also become ill at the separation.

Later, Sandrine will ask if she was right that I was thinking of this, and I will tell her that she was. What good is it anymore to lie? I am at times overcome when I am around her own young daughters, some of whom are as old as Sonja was, one of whom is the same age now as Moses was.

When dinner is finished, I want to walk. We live not far from the park. Ten minutes on foot. More, honestly, than I can manage without rest. It is a cool evening. Outside, there is chimney smoke. At all hours, if she needs to, Sandrine can see the lights of my study on, the outline of my armchair, the crown of my head encased almost always in headphones, through which, I think she knows, is the music of my youth. She comes to see me every evening before I go to bed, as if she is the parent and I am the child.

I have been thinking lately of Fania, I tell her. She was, I say, my wife. This is the first time, Sandrine tells me, that she has ever heard me say her name aloud. It would have been her one hundredth birthday last week, I tell her. She was older than me. A fact she found advantageous. In this way, she could always let me know what was coming. Which, I say, was not true in the end. Sandrine is watching me, I know, watching me regarding the empty park. What she does not understand, I cannot explain: that Fania is both old and young, always twenty-six, always here in Vienna, and she has also managed to affix herself in every room beside me, on every train, one moment away.

I am always talking to Fania, I say to Sandrine. The voice in my head is a voice directed to her, as if I am one part of a letter, and inside Fania, wherever she has gone, lies the other half. It is not so crazy to do this. It is just that there is a good deal to tell her about that she has missed. For instance, that the city sometimes can look exactly the same to me. It does not require a great deal of effort to see it as I saw it, say, on my wedding day, when my mother and father were with me, and my uncles and my aunts were with me, and all my many sisters were here. The buildings are the same buildings. The Schönbrunn Zoo is the same zoo where I took Sonja to see the polar bears in their tank. It does not seem that it should be this way. That I should be here still, and that all of this should be here as well, unaffected, with people still eating in restaurants. This seems violently strange to me, that all of us have not been turned to stone like the statues in this park, frozen in judgment.

As we walk, she stops me every few blocks to say that we have made a wrong turn, that we need to go in a different direction, that we are becoming lost. My memory is no longer good, she tells me, with such confidence, such authority. One's mind is on the inside, hidden from view. It is important, always, to remember this.

My oldest sister, I tell her, she had a fire in her apartment one day when I was young. Her husband was at work. The fire badly damaged the house, and she came that night to stay with my mother and father. Her husband, though, could not find her. And she could not find him. For hours we waited. My sister became distressed. Something terrible had happened. And so we went out to look for him at *her* house. Of course, at that moment, he had come to *our* house, to find us, to ring our doorbell for a long time. This went on for hours. Our circling one another. Just when we would give up hope, he would give up hope. He was a very big man. The largest Jew in the history of Jews, people always joked.

I saw him once, after everything, my brother in-law. He was the only other person I knew who lived, which did not surprise me, given his size. I had believed before that he was irreducible, that all of the misery would be nothing to him, that the cruelty was measured for men my size, not his, that even though I had wasted away he would not have, and that he would live. When I saw him again after, and he was intact, it confirmed for me that I had not lost all sense of life. He told me that he was going away, to Canada, to Montreal. Someone, he was afraid, was after him. Some particular soldier. He believed this man might come for him to settle some petty grievance, which may or may not have been the simple grievance of having lived. You might as well come too, he told me. He would pay, take me, set me up with a profession. Better to go than to wait here for it to come again, as it will, he said. It will, it will, it will.

That first year, a small group of people returned, sometimes only for days, these few people searching for one another, creating a perpetual circle of reunion and anticipation, and making out of this atmosphere so many circles and circles within circles, mothers in orbit, babies in orbit. I told my brother-in-law that I wanted to be in this place, which was my place, and which I believed still belonged to me, just in case, one never knows, anything at all can happen now, and he of course took great pity on me, it was not my place, he said, I did know what would happen, he said, nothing at all would happen, nobody is returning for you, and he told me I was a fool, and as he did this I reminded him of that night, of the fire, how we circled the city, our family, in search of one another, how we kept missing one another.

So I understand what that woman was talking about at dinner, I say, speaking of Franziska, what it is to live one life and have the sense that another life is occurring on a parallel plane: I exist with this idea. Me and a different me. Maybe at this point Sandrine realizes why I have walked her into a different neighborhood. I stop now and turn to a building with a red door. Maybe she knows this is my house, the house where I lived with Fania and Moses and Sonja, the house to which any one of them might return. For a while we stand here, and maybe Sandrine expects me to keep talking, to explain what perhaps she thinks I am thinking about—that this DNA test, which Franziska has promised to help me take, might restore something in me.

All I say instead is this: There is a man in this house who sleeps in the room I slept in, and who watches over his daughter in the room in which I watched over my daughter. Do you think he ever thinks of me and suspects that his life could be mine?

THE first letter arrives a month after I take the test. It is from a woman in Surrey, a retired ophthalmologist, writing, she says, from a room overlooking her garden.

My name is Vivian Silk, she begins.

*I was born Sonja Alterman in Vienna on 9 February 1933 in the maternity wing at Rothschild Hospital. I was adopted at five years old in Great Britain, having arrived by way of a Kindertransport arranged by the Central British Fund for German Jewry. My mother was Fania Reiter, born in May 1915 in Galicia. Like you I have had my DNA analyzed and it has come as a shock to see your name in the feed of my potential relatives. Your information matches the information I have regarding the identity of my father. You have his name, his date of birth. Your father's name is the name of my grandfather. I do not know if all this is true. Or if this is a mistake. If this is indeed true, and not a cruel error, I do not know if you are well. Or if your hearing from me will occasion good feelings or nightmares. I am, myself, an old woman, but not as old in my heart as I suspect my grandchildren think me to be. Could we meet? Would that be possible? I do not know what happened and why I was not told that you had lived and why we have been separated all this time. All I know is that I am here, and you are here, and that this seems to me a great miracle.*

*Love, V—*

NOT long after the first, a second letter. Like the first, it comes by way of email, and because I am more or less unused to the technology, I see these at once, one after the other.

*Dear A—*

*A memory came this morning. You have taken me to the zoo at the Tiergarten. I am young, four years old. There are polar bears in a glass pool, brother and sister you tell me, shipped from the north pole, a place I am not sure is real, but a place I associate nevertheless with elves, the dream life of my classmates. You hold me up, bring me to the glass, and at some point one of the bears shifts in the water so that we are facing him and he is facing us and at once the bear opens his mouth wide, with his enormous jawline full with sharp teeth, and I can feel you clutch my legs in fear.*

*Don't worry, you tell me, Papa has you. Don't worry. You are safe.*

*If you are well, A—, please write. This has all come as such a surprise.*

*Yours, V—*

I AM alone in my study when I get these notes, which begin to come eventually through the mail, overnighted on plain white stock. Somehow she has acquired my home address. Her handwriting is immaculate, the handwriting, Vivian says, of a woman raised in strict British boarding schools to believe in a connection between character and clarity. When I was young, she writes, I worked very hard to have perfect penmanship. I understand now that the closer my handwriting became to the ideal, the farther away my past seemed, and when this happened the more others around me saw me as British, as something other than what I felt, which was an imposter, a girl in another girl's clothes, speaking another girl's language. All my life I have felt pride at my handwriting, which is another way to say that I have been proud in my performing as British, but not now, writing to you. Writing to you, she says, I see it as a form of abandonment.

What do you think? she writes. Is the old part of me lost?

I collect these notes in a paper folder that I hide beneath my sofa, in case anyone comes looking. Not that anyone will. I live alone in this apartment, and it is, by any measure, too large for me, too full of air, an apartment better suited for a man who feels that his life has been a life of victory. How else am I to regard my bedroom windows, which offer a view, far off, of the Hofburg, a place my father took me once on his shoulders in order to show me an example of man's natural inclination toward immensity and also pomposity, often as a stand-in for religious feeling.

I spend most days here, in this study on the top floor of the house. I dreamed this place into being at my darkest, drew every room in my mind until I could live within it, just as I do now. A room where most of the ceiling has been cut away and replaced by glass. A way for me to see out and for only those in flight to see in. Airplanes, crows, all that finds itself in ascendancy. An old friend once mocked my doing this. Oh, you think because once you languished without light you must always have a way of looking out; call the doctors! Call the headshrinkers!

Nonetheless, there is this—my long afternoons, this translucence, endless gossamer jet wake, the lives of others caught in midair, and the changing light above this city, which is my city, where I was born, taken prisoner, the city I was delivered back into as if by shipwreck, and where I have become, improbably, an old man.

These letters terrify me. Quickly there are more than a dozen. There is no other emotion that strikes me as appropriate but terror. In the first days I think that surely I am dead already, and that this is how my experience of the afterlife has begun, with letters from Sonja, a lifetime's worth of absence. What other more perfect hell could the devil invent for me than to learn now, at ninety-nine, that Sonja is alive. And has been alive all this time. And that I have missed it.

From the first letter, I am sleepless. How can I sleep now when I know this has been the story of my life? That my Sonja is now Vivian, that she is British, vanished, turned from Alterman to Silk, replaced by a woman with handwriting like a machine, eighty-three years old. How is it that my daughter is so much older now than her mother?

She writes again. Letter number thirteen.

*Another memory.*

*You have taken me to see the Philharmonic. I am too small to be admitted, and so you cloak me in your overcoat, which*

*smells of pipe smoke, and of vanilla, and of the trees behind our*
*house, which I think are lindens. We rush inside in secret.*
*Because your coat is so long and I am so small we need to*
*coordinate our footsteps so that we do not trip. You have dressed*
*me as an elderly woman. I am a grandmother, you tell me. This*
*is why I am so small. The music is Mahler, the Ninth, where*
*the melody in the opening movement sinks down onto the*
*audience, down from nowhere, slipped loose from beneath the*
*buzz of life, or as I have begun to think of it after so many years*
*of playing this over and over, the music slips down from the*
*precipice of death. I have always associated this music, which is*
*the music of the poetry of dying, with you. My memory of that*
*night is of watching you watching the players, your face as it*
*shifted against the strings, a catch in your breath at the end as*
*the room grew quieter and quieter amid the dying away of the*
*tempo, your rough whiskers, and how you began to cry midway*
*through the final movement. Do you remember this? I was to go*
*onto the train in a week. I have managed to find the recording*
*of that night. The conductor is rushing. The final movement is*
*twice as fast as it should be. As if he knew that all of us needed*
*to hurry and leave. That a great end was approaching. Could I*
*send it to you? Or would that be too painful? I await your reply*
*to this, or to any of this.*

*Yours, V—*

The letters are in English, which I have to read slowly, to parse
as if I am reading an artifact of archeology, which in many ways I
believe I am. Every sentence of hers I repeat aloud, translate in my
head, then transcribe in German into a notebook. This takes time,
most of the hours of the afternoons, but time is all I have, time I
have discovered is, in fact, all that life amounts to—apportioned,

preempted, stolen, shared between one's children, cleaved from the heart.

In this room that I have made out of dreams, the face of the man who took me from my house comes to me out of the night. A small man, smaller than me, with red hair and a port-wine stain on his cheek, brandishing a pistol, he has come inside while we are eating our last dinner—a thumb of butter, a scavenged heel of old black bread, potatoes we have managed to borrow from somewhere, from the people who live beside the Metgers I think it is, Leopold and Willa Metger, their teenage son taken from their house the month before, the two of them dead before they could be taken, two drops of Veronal, the long sleep, the quiet sleep. When it comes to food, of which we have none, it is always this word, *borrow*, as if we will ever be able to return what we have been given. The man is knocking, yelling, and we are, on the other side, hiding toys our baby is likely not allowed to have, hiding a newspaper we are likely forbidden to read, and then, at once, he is inside. He has taken apart the lock on the outside door with one blow from a hammer. This face, which has been gone for me for decades, has returned alive. Bring one bag each, the man says. He hits me several times, a dozen times, and when I attempt to fight back he smacks me on the side of my cheek with his gun, puts the barrel into my mouth, makes me tell him the gun tastes good, all while the gun is in my mouth, something which makes speech impossible, a sin which occasions another beating. My teeth, I remember, are on the floor in front of me. It will be years before they are fixed. Maybe you want to bring your jewelry, he says to Fania, your diamonds, your best gold earrings. Where you're going you'll want to look nice. Fania does not move. He approaches her, puts his hands on her. If you could go one place on earth, the man asks, holding her, where would that be? Fania does not answer. She has a knife behind her. She had been chopping a potato for Moses. Where would you choose to go, the man asks again, this time with the gun pointed at her, then in her mouth. Again, this business with the sucking, does it taste good, does it, Jew, tell me how it tastes, you pig, you swine, you Jew pig, Judensau. And she says New York, says it twice, I would go to New York City. Words I never heard her say. For what reason, the man says, and Fania, not shaking, I have always remembered this, that she did not shake, she says I would go to New York because there I could be onstage and sing.

Something I never knew of you, Fania, this desire to sing!

The small man steps back to look at her, to measure her up, and then he says, you want to be onstage? This is what you want? To be onstage? So that we have to pay to see you? So that you get our money? So that you get more of what I work for? He steps closer and asks if she will send him tickets, will you, will you? He has her closer now. Will you? And what will you wear on this stage? Will you wear silk? Will you wear fishnet, lace, leather? She does not look at me. Nor does she look at Moses, who is not far away, watching everything. And when Fania says yes, of course, you will be on the very top of my list, Herr Officer, he claps his hands. Terrific, the small man says. We will send you to New York, then. I am here to make your dreams come true. How about that? Whoever said I could not be kind? New York City it is!

A spell has broken. The man backs up. We will be spared, I think. In my foolishness, I really think this. The man then sees Moses. Tiny Moses. In his chair, silent. He always knew to be silent. The soldier approaches Moses. A moment of humanity, I think. But then: he spits on him. Ridiculous that you have continued to multiply, he says. Ridiculous.

All of this returns.

As does an afternoon years later, in Miami, when I believe I have seen Fania near the beach on Collins Avenue, and I follow her for two miles north to Surfside, where she buys flowers in a shop near the water, and then goes into an apartment building near Bay Drive, where I watch her go inside, and where I see the lights go on inside an apartment on the fourth floor. And so for days I return to this building to wait for this woman who is obviously not Fania, I know this, or I think I do. In reality, she is a Lithuanian woman called Natasha who has Fania's hair and her way of walking and a certain way of wiggling her fingers when she is nervous that Fania also had, but she has nothing else.

There are others. A woman in Los Angeles whom I believe is my sister. A woman in New York working the counter at the Truman Hotel whom I believe is my aunt, aged twenty years, a woman with my aunt's voice, her round face, and everything else erased. Several people appear to me over the years across oceans, appearing alive on the horizon lines.

Natasha sees what I am getting at. I am not her, whoever she is. This is what Natasha says.

My lack of death is a mistake. Surely I have been forgotten by the god of my childhood, left here to age, passed over by all the various angels of death. In this way my first months back in Vienna return, when everything is destroyed, in ruins, when thousands of city roofs are caved in by bombs, aflame for weeks, when my neighbors with whom I studied in school and with whom I played football tell me of their suffering, their privation, you do not know what it has been like for us, they tell me, we were the first victims of the war, they say, the first true sufferers, look what has happened to us, they say, look at all this destruction, see all that we have lost. They tell me that it will take a generation to reconstruct our life. Think of it, they tell me. Think of it.

I AM lying on the sofa in my study, beneath glass, in utter safety, in the most immaculate silence and protection, under blankets, in a perfect quiet that can last for days, and I tell no one of the letters. Not that there is anyone to tell. Sandrine would not understand. A child born into real peace, what can Sandrine possibly know of this but the general outline, which is to say the outline of nothing, of emptiness, the outline of something that by definition can take no shape. She is too easily swayed by pity for me, upset by my visible frailty, how I can no longer manage a staircase, for instance. What words exist with which to say what needs to be said: that I have been rearranged by thirteen letters mailed by an eye doctor in England.

In my first email, I temper my enthusiasm. I am no fool. How do I know this is you? I write.

She responds within the hour. The instancy of the screen.

*The morning you went with me to the station in Vienna, you gave me a doll to carry. It was taken away from me before I reached England. A girl beside me had become very sick, either on the train or the boat, I cannot remember, a fever that spread to her chest, to her heart, and she began crying for home, for her mother, for her sisters, please take me back, let me be with them, she'd said, and the men on board came and saw I had a doll I was talking to, just as you told me to do, and they took my doll and gave it to her to comfort her. Somehow they thought she was me, and I was her. This is what happened. Do you remember this doll? Do you remember?*

IN the evening, I climb up into the attic. Something that Sandrine has disallowed me. To do this requires an extraordinary effort. First, a clearing away of large furniture. I hire boys from the neighborhood, pay them from my pension check. Then, a maneuvering up a narrow corridor, where a staircase pulls down from the ceiling. In my boyhood home, we had a staircase like this, and there, too, I was disallowed. My older sisters knew I wanted nothing more than to go there, for no other reason than that I had got it in my head that at the other end of the staircase was not our attic at all but some other place, someplace outside, away, beyond. And when I asked them, my sisters Zelda and Beylke, where it led, what it looked like, what it felt like to cross from someplace real to some other place, which was maybe less visible but no less real, they told me that for everyone the staircase is different. For me, Zelda said, I go to the ocean, to the Mediterranean, where it is warm, where the sky is endless, where I am delivered drinks on an enormous patio. And for me, Beylke said, I am in the front row of the best American movie theater, watching Rudolph Valentino in *Blood and Sand*, and at the end, Rudolph himself meets me outside the theater and drives me off in his Rolls-Royce. Where would you go, Arnold? they asked. Tell us where, and we will let you go up.

Now I have an answer. My attic is cold from a winter that has yet to come. Perhaps filled with last year's winter. Or filled with all the Vienna winters. It is a tiny space. Better suited for my boyhood. This is where I have kept the doll, in a box within another box, a coffin within a coffin, close enough to me all this time, but in a place reachable only in an emergency. Opening it is like opening the tomb of a pharaoh, thousands of years into a future they predicted would come, a future in which, even now, they are, as they might have expected, still heralded as kings. And there she is, looking at me so peacefully, a doll named for my young wife, still young just like Fania, a doll filled with last thoughts and worries. In my arms she regards me with the serenity of a real child just woken from sleep. I knew you would come, she seems to say to me. Alone in the darkness, I put her on the ground. Talk, I say. Tell me all the stories.

I START a letter to her but the letter is terrible. A preview of an obituary. How is it possible to write the story of a life and not see that one has been writing a death notice all along? For two days I suffer over the pages. A thousand beginnings. Her beginning, my beginning, everything interrupted.

Before I can finish, she sends me an email with a picture.

This is me, she writes. I have tried to pick a photograph that I think looks how I think I look. You know what I mean, I'm sure. Do you have a picture of you? she asks. Do you think I look like how you imagined? Do I look the same? Also: When can we meet? I can travel to you. I am retired. I can fly as early as tomorrow.

Who is this woman who stares back at me? A woman in a gray sweater, in a room flush with sunlight before a window, outside of which there is green and gray in equal measure, split between life and everything else. She is seated, turned sideways to the camera, having been caught by surprise. I search her face for Fania's face, for my face. I linger over the picture for hours. In the glare of the window there is the faint reflection of the photographer. A yellow blur. Who is this, I wonder, what family member, what loved one?

I tell her *come*, come immediately, and bring with you everything I have missed. What I don't say to her is come as the person I last knew you to be. Come as the five-year-old girl who believed I was king. Come in the year 1938. Come before all of us were vanished. Do not come as anyone else, I want to say, because I fear I cannot understand any person but that person, the version of you I had memorized. Come as the girl who had a name for the dark—

Albert, as in, I am not afraid of Albert any longer because I am big, I am five years old. Come as the girl who believed houseplants had souls. Come as that person who was the first person I loved totally, even more than your mother.

She responds with a travel itinerary.

*I will fly tomorrow evening, arriving around 21:00. I think it's better to see you in the morning, and for you to see me in the morning, and so I will take the train to the central station in the morning. Does that work? Expect me around 11:00. We can have breakfast. Or take a walk. You will know me by my blue overcoat, which is very blue, extremely blue, you cannot miss it. How will I know you?*

I write within the minute:

*I will be the old man beside the large newsstand on the platform. I will wear a red bow tie. I cannot believe this. It cannot be so.*

*Love, Your Father*

PERHAPS it is an axiom: it cannot be so and so it is not. I arrive that morning in my red bow tie and I wait for the eleven o'clock train, which arrives promptly on the hour, exactly, no later, no earlier. It arrives gliding. The noise of the trains of my youth has been replaced instead by the sound of phantoms—a sense of wind, and then the noise of so many footsteps. Although I am here, she is not. There is no woman in blue, no woman with the face of my daughter, Sonja, no one resembling the British eye doctor Vivian Silk, whose picture I hold alternately against my breast pocket, close to my heart, and also flat in my hands, measuring it against every debarking passenger. Other trains arrive. Eleven minutes later, twenty-three minutes later, all of them appearing noiselessly in the station at their expected times; reunions on the platform, but none for me.

Although this is a new building, filled with the flashing lights of the future, it is not really any different from the old building where I delivered her. This is the word I choose to believe is the best word, *deliver*, a process of moving from one state to another, delivery from doom to peace, quarry to liberation.

So I wait here in this place that is for me a place both of delivery and of disappearance, and no one arrives to find me, no woman in blue comes looking. I wait twelve hours. The first four hours of which I spend believing she will emerge at any moment. For the next eight, I believe she has died along the way, another casualty on these tracks. I have assured myself of this eventuality, that beyond the vanishing line of the EuroNight there is devastation, a billow of smoke that will announce itself eventually, blowing overhead to warn me: nothing comes back, everyone was scattered long ago, we are all with the wind. I have delivered her into death once, and now, nearly eighty years later, I have done it again.

At home a message is waiting.

Hello, she says. This is Vivian Silk calling.

For a long moment afterward, there is nothing.

Or, she says finally, I should say that this is your daughter calling. Sonja. Sonja Alterman.

Another pause.

There's been a small hiccup in my plans, she explains. Please understand that I am still coming.

This is the first time I hear her voice. Hers is the solid prim voice of England as I know it from media. The voice of the BBC, of Julie Andrews, Margaret Thatcher, somehow the voice of my child.

I will be there tomorrow, she says, at the same time, still in blue. Can you forgive me? she asks. Can you? I wish what happened did not happen and that I could have come to see you.

There is again a very long silence, nearly a minute. In the background, a hiss, which is maybe the recording, maybe the air between us suspended in the telephone wires like dust motes in brightness, maybe the sound of her home, a place that comes to me unbidden, risen like a memory I did not know I possessed—a red sofa, a window outside of which there is a silver oak, a coffee-colored tomcat bolting through high grass. Then, finally, her voice again: Okay, now. Good night, Daddy.

I don't sleep that night. For one, my heart has been sundered. *Good night, Daddy.* Sleep is a crime this late in life, a tax against what is left, a measure of theft against old age. That I should have to do it at all feels like indignation. Alone in Vienna, I play the tape over and over, for hours.

In the dark, all of Sonja's childhood returns to me. Her collection of small pinafores. The smell of her shampoo, which is the smell of apples. Also: a trip by car to see my mother at my boyhood home, my mother who will not let the girl go, who insists on having her portrait painted. Where is this painting now? On whose library wall is this picture of my little daughter? She detested sitting so long for the artist that we bribed her with sweets. Who gets to see this every day instead of me?

On my second day of waiting, still in my same suit and red bow tie, I am overcome by the rhythm of this place, the ordinary procession of this train station, every train station, the train station you know best, whoever you are, wherever you are reading this—its relentless schedule, armies of people moving in, moving out, the whole of this great building breathing around me. The thought comes that any train leaving here is the train on which I lost my life, gave my daughter away, arrived back home. It seems to me that I will die here. Where else, but on a train?

I remember that I was urged as a boy to understand the world as a series of revisions. My mother believed this to be so, that God was always in the process of making and unmaking the world, and our world, she wanted to believe, was a point in the process of creation and destruction and re-creation. We were to understand that what came next was a return of the light of creation, the resurrection around us of every city ever ruined or leveled or erased by war, a vanishing of suffering, the extinction of death. I remember that when she said this to me we were not far from here, in a café on Prinz-Eugen-Straße, across from the Belvedere, a café I had particularly liked, and I had asked her whether she would be angry at me if I decided I'd found all this talk of the after places to be foolish, the ideas of a lunatic. Because, I said, it's obvious that it's crazy. To which, smiling, she had said, it really doesn't matter what you or I think, Arnold. Either it will come or it will not. Like a train, she had said. Where are you? she asked me. Are you on the train or not? Where, Arnold, do you think you are?

Not a terrible question, Mama. But not really the sort of question one should ever make alone in a train station one has been standing in for two full days, in the same tired suit, in the same preposterous bright red bow tie. Especially when one is ninety-nine years old.

So here I am, waiting and waiting, and apparently, asking this big question to myself out loud. Where am I? Where am I? Wo bin ich? Where am I?

THE woman running the newsstand comes to help. Later, she will say that when she found me I'd been screaming this question into the station for hours and that everyone coming and going had either been too afraid to stop for me or too unwilling to engage with someone in such clear anguish. Her name is Leda. A student, she says. International relations. But also, she says, the violin, for when the degree in international relations does not work out. I must smile at the joke, because a wave of relief settles over her. You're in there after all, she says. She turns to a coworker. He's alive, she says. He's alive, she says again.

She has come from Germany, she says, Leipzig. *Turned up* are the words she uses, just as a set of keys is turned up after an afternoon lost. My whole childhood, she says, I felt the tug of this place, Vienna, which makes no sense, because my childhood was full of American television, American cinema, American pop music. One would think I would have rushed to Beverly Hills. Here I am, she says, opening her arms to the noise of the station.

A train station, she tells me later, is a very specific kind of hell, especially when everyone is going away and you are staying. Also, she says, once a month I'm witness to something awful. A child is fussing with his phone and walks mindlessly onto a departing train without his parents. Or the opposite happens, dazed parents thumbing at their screen walk dumbly onto a train headed to Frankfurt and their children are left behind. Inevitably, someone runs to me and asks what to do. And what can I do? I am just a woman at a newsstand. As if I have any answers for such tragedies? My child, people cry! What should I do? And I want to say—do you have a question about the violin? Or about the many treaties of Versailles? That, I can help you with. That, at least, I have some knowledge about. This? Tragedy? I'm helpless.

And then, some days there is a man like you, she says, screaming very, very serious questions into the station. Questions I would like answered myself. We debated fetching a holy person for you. Or a philosophy student from the university. Or one of the fortune-tellers down the road. Because you really seemed to want to know the answer.

She brings me a sandwich from a vending machine. It is made nearly entirely from shelf-stable chemicals, she says. Guaranteed to destroy your insides at the same time it makes you hungry for more. The first such sandwich I have eaten in all my life. Ninety-nine years of a life in which I managed not to eat a sandwich from a machine. She watches me eating. Are you okay? she asks. Do you feel yourself dying a little bit? To which, smiling, I tell her—it will take a whole lot more than a sandwich to kill me.

I saw you here yesterday, she says. And here you are again, in the same clothing, in the same spot, wearing your soul on the outside of your body. Who are you waiting for? What's on the other end of the train?

I tell her the beginning of the story, that I am waiting for a child I have not seen in many years, someone I managed to lose long ago. I want to tell her the story but cannot get past the very beginning— she was born near here, I say, not very far away at all, a ten-minute walk, it was snowing, her mother and I had gone to the café, the winter had assaulted us, we felt like chickens cooped up inside, but then the labor began and we thought the baby would be born in the street, she was born in February like I was, an Aquarius, doomed forever to carry the water of others. This is it, all I can say, all that is possible without speaking the impossible. So instead, I say this: She was lost for a very long time and she is now coming back on the eleven o'clock train, today, yesterday, tomorrow. A wall has gone up around my story. I exist within it, and everyone else remains outside. Anyway—everyone already knows this story, everyone has grown bored of it, distrusts it, says it is not true. I would like to tell her everything, certainly. Maybe she sees this. She is young, as young as Fania was. She has the brusque and wonderful and genuine impatience of real youth. She cannot hold her focus for more than a moment before it flies away. She brings me a chair. Sit, she tells me. Be at home, she says. We stay like this for a long time, Leda and I, as several more trains enter the station, leave the station. She does not ask any more questions, does not pry. This is unusual, I tell her, hours later.

There are doors, she tells me, and then there are locks. One needs to understand the difference.

Ahead of us, the last train arrives.

Maybe you can at least tell me what are we looking for, she says. This way I can help you.

Blue, I say. That's all I know. The color blue.

IN the evenings, at home, I return inevitably to Vivian's voice on my answering machine. An unscheduled interruption has intruded on her plans. A sudden minor emergency has prevented her from traveling. A problem with a tooth. A problem with a house cat. A problem with a window in her house. Poor weather has grounded the flights. A granddaughter has become ill. I cannot come today as I want to, she says in one message, in which she does not even bother with an excuse. These arrive always to my answering machine while I am out waiting for her to emerge from the train. They come always in her solid, steady voice, which I have come to regard as a source of corruption. Suddenly, I cannot connect the voice to the face. Instead, the voice on my machine, a voice that is always apologizing, belongs to the face of my tiny five-year-old daughter. When I see tiny Sonja at the train station clutching her doll, when I see her in the apartment dancing with Fania, when I see her on my shoulder at the zoo with the polar bears, the voice I hear in my head is the voice from my machine, the voice of an older British woman. Whatever my small Sonja's voice sounded like when it existed in this world, this is gone, another vanishing.

When I tell this to Leda, on day four, or day five, of waiting, she gives me the idea.

Stay home, she says. Wait for the call. In the event she arrives, I will phone for you.

I do as I'm told. Rather than go and wait, I remain in my study, with the plan that when Vivian Silk calls to tell me that she has not made it, I will pick up and speak to her. As easy as that: I will speak to Sonja again.

All afternoon I wait, lying on my sofa beneath the windows that open onto Vienna. My house sits beneath two intersecting flight paths: the transcontinental path used by the long-haul airliners, and the migratory path of common parkland birds. On more than one occasion while I wait on this sofa a bird has looked down at me at the same moment I have looked up. Or two jets have crossed at the same time, one coming, one going, each at a different height. Or a feather has been shed on the glass, more often than not white, or streaked with red, like an aviary version of the national flag. These are the sorts of common incidents when I was young I would have understood as augury, but now, given what I understand as the unrelenting cruelty of the everyday, I am no longer willing to entertain the idea of portents, good or bad.

I doze in and out of a dreamless sleep, until, finally, it is night, wine dark above me, and I am roused by the ringing telephone. I leap for it. As much as I can leap, I leap, the leaping of my boyhood, a wild, joyful leap, after which, clutching the phone against me, I say, in my best English, my heart leaping: Hello, daughter! Hello, daughter! There is nothing, however. Perhaps someone breathing on the other end for one moment. Perhaps not even that. Immediately after, the line goes dead.

Still, I speak. Sonja, I say. My child! How good to hear from you! When do you think you'll be coming? I've been waiting. For a very long time I've been waiting.

A MONTH I wait. Summer arrives. Birds nest above us in the rafters. Leda waits with me every day. With every woman who emerges in blue, she taps my hand. Her? she asks. But none, yet, are her.

In June, Leda's girlfriend arrives from Leipzig. Soon, she waits with us as well. She is Magda, until recently a docent in the butterfly room at the Natural History Museum. Not exactly an expert in Lepidoptera, she tells me, but I know more than I ought to know about butterflies. For instance, that butterflies taste the world through their feet. And that in ancient Egypt, it was understood that to be in the presence of a butterfly was to be in the presence of the soul of a warrior, reincarnated on earth with wings. She comes unannounced, running off the train. The distance from Leda, she explains to me some weeks later, had become too great to bear. One can only be away so long. Do you know what I mean? she asks me. Do you?

In August, Magda's brother comes. He is Simon, and he arrives carrying chocolates for me. He has heard that I am waiting and has brought me a gift. When I ask why he's really come to Vienna, he tells me, in private, that he has come because he misses his sister. Amid the noise of the station, I hear his story only in fragments. We are our only family, our parents are gone, a car accident on a busy highway, a terrific tragedy, great weeping at the graveside, stars thrown out of their galaxies by the force of great collisions are called orphan stars. Soon, he begins to wait as well.

In October, another arrival: Simon's girlfriend, Anna, to whom, in April, he proposes, right at the foot of Track 11, by the newsstand, which, by now, I have stood guard outside for close to two hundred days. Every morning, she reads aloud to us from the newspaper as we wait.

In November, Anna's sister Rebekah arrives, along with her husband, Lukas, and her two children. All of them stay. During the day, the children take it upon themselves to count every person who comes, and to categorize these people by the color they wear, and to put all this to paper, so that soon, we have a statistical basis from which to judge the probability of Sonja coming or not. A probability that verges, with every passing train, on zero.

By January, there are dozens of us. Rebekah's roommates from university arrive. Several of Simon's friends from university, their spouses, the parents of their spouses, the neighbors of these parents, the rabbis of these neighbors, congregants of these rabbis, and then photographers who document the congregants and the rabbis and the neighbors and the parents and the spouses and the brothers and everyone else who has decided to join me in waiting. Which is all we do.

My favorite: two violinists from Leda's conservatory come, and at night, when the station is quiet, they play at the mouth of the tracks, where the building both begins and ends. They play whatever I ask of them. Most nights it is Bach, the Partitas for Violin. Music I have known all my life, but have known, evidently, nothing about. These were composed in the year Bach's first wife died, Leda explains. You can hear it however you like, she says, but I hear it in this way, melody and the absence of melody, as a conversation between what is here and what is not.

Still, in the evenings, I return home to Vivian Silk apologizing. Every night, the same rhythm. Her clipped British voice, explaining away her absence. No matter how I plan it, I miss this call. When I plant someone in my house to pick it up, or two people, somehow the calls slip through. She is unreachable, Vivian Silk is, just as Sonja has been from the moment she boarded the train.

Back at the station, those in charge of the building regard us with a sense of amused detachment. Benches and cots are brought for us. If it is cold, blankets as well. If it is hot, we are given water. Twice a day, the authorities come to check on me. They worry, it seems, that the crowd is keeping me here. That I am being made to wait, to stare out into nothing. That I am a prisoner being held hostage. Twice a day they crouch beside me and speak slowly, as if by growing old I have also lost the ability to understand this language I have spoken all my life. Are you okay? they ask. Are you well? Can we bring you anything? To which, every day, whenever they ask, I say yes. Bring me back my child. Can you do that for me? Can you?

EVENTUALLY, it is February again, a year from the beginning of all this, a year from when I first heard that I could apprehend the story of my blood and have it unraveled and analyzed, a year in which I have stayed, largely, in this one spot, my eyes fixed on the same half circle of daylight and evening. I am weeks from turning one hundred, a number that as I approach it begins to accumulate a sense of cruelty. I count in terms of my children: one hundred Moseses; twenty Sonjas; four Fanias. All my life, I am either coming from February or leaving it, except for now, at the point that must be the end. I think this on the platform, awaiting the last train, surrounded by this new family: How else does my story end but waiting on a train?

Then, at the far end of the station one night, a burst of someone in blue. Leda is beside me. She sees her at the same moment I see her. Blue, she says. Around us, heads turn. Blue, everyone says. Soon, we are all chanting it. Blue, blue, blue.

From across the platform she is calling my name. Her blue is the immaculate and pure blue of clarity, the way a child imagines the ocean. From my position, she glows. The blue is inescapable and perfect. Arnold, she is saying, oh, Arnold, Arnold, how good to see you, and because I have stood here all this time, in this same spot, at the mouth of the outside world looking into nothing, I have a hard time understanding that the person calling my name is not the person I have been waiting for all this time.

She is the one who breaks the spell. It's me, she says. From your birthday party. Franziska from the museum. Franziska with the dinosaur bones. Franziska with the DNA test. She is both elated and miserable. She has just come from meeting her birth mother for the first time.

She explains this to me later over dinner at a restaurant not far from the station. I have recovered only slightly from the confusion. Beneath her blue coat is more blue. My mother, she says, asked that I come wearing blue so that she would recognize me. She said she would do the same, although she did not—she came in red, which angered me. My first emotion on seeing my mother was a flash of anger. Which was foolish, of course. She looks the way I look. Like an older sister of mine. We ran right into one another and it was like running into a mirror, but a mirror in which the future had been existing forever at a different speed. For me, the future was sped up. For her, the future was wound backwards. Also, when she grabbed hold of me, and hugged me, I realized that I had become so nervous I had stopped seeing in color.

She must have been very happy to see you, I say.

Oh yes, she was overcome. And I was overcome. Two people overcome in the middle of the train station in Berlin.

I was not prepared for it, Arnold, for our coming face-to-face. I thought I might have years before either of us had the courage to meet. But she asked to see me, and so I came. Of course I came.

They agreed on Berlin, Franziska tells me, because her birth mother had found a cheap ticket from Dublin. And because she wanted to meet, she said, on neutral territory. Not her home, not my home. This was only the second time in her life she'd flown. Both times for me, Franziska says. Her first time was to go to Geneva to give me away. She was seventeen at the time, Franziska says, suffering at home. What she wanted, apparently, was to have a rich baby, to put me in the arms of the richest people she could imagine, and when she imagined what that looked like, she thought of Geneva.

She could not say why. Although she thought that sometime before the adoption, when she was still pregnant, she had seen an advertisement in a magazine for an expensive Swiss watch, a woman beside what she assumed was Lake Geneva, her arm warm in the sun. The watch was something that cost more than all the houses in her village put together, and so this was how she took me here, how I ended up with this life.

They had a meal together, Franziska and her mother, and when it was over they went for a walk outside. It was cold that night. The part of the city where they walked was fashionable now, full of artists, inexpensive flats, Americans everywhere, but all of it felt to Franziska, she says, carefully staged, a corporatized homogenization, a Soviet nightmare of the future. They had little, almost nothing, to say to one another, it turns out. This is something her birth mother says out loud. Maybe you are nervous to see me, her mother says. None of this bothers Franziska.

I just want to lay eyes on you, to see that you are real. That's all I need.

At this, Franziska tells me, her birth mother touched her softly on the cheek. I thought it was a kind gesture, Franziska says to me, a motherly and kind gesture. Since this is, however, the last time Franziska will ever see her, this is the moment that lingers with her, this unnecessary but gentle gesture.

What happened next is this: her birth mother stopped suddenly and announced that she'd left her bag at the restaurant. It had her passport in it.

She told me, says Franziska, that there were photographs in the bag as well. Pictures of the two of us together. The only ones that exist. Just wait, she said, I'll be back, love, just one minute.

And then what happened? I ask.

She did not come back, Franziska says.

What do you mean she did not come back?

She left. Left me there. Left Berlin. Went home. She saw me, took stock, touched my cheek, and then fled.

Maybe there was a miscommunication, I say. Maybe you should still be waiting.

I stood for a long time on the boulevard, she says. Fifteen minutes passed. A crowded U-Bahn went by, with people standing inside, lit in green fluorescence like hothouse vegetables. There was a park bench nearby, behind which was a rhomboid square of dead grass and the remnants of maybe every lipstick-stained cigarette ever smoked in East Germany. I sat on the bench in the park. Another fifteen minutes passed. Eventually, a man came down the street. Are you Franziska Bauer? he asked me, and when I said yes, he said that he had been given a note to give to a woman wearing all blue standing at this exact spot. The note was from June.

Oh no, I say.

Yes, she says.

Just like that, I say again.

I'm not disappointed, she says.

Anyone would feel disappointed, I say.

She got to see me. I am not made-up. She is not made-up. Why be greedy in this situation?

Silence falls between us. Then Franziska takes the note from the pocket of her jacket and lays it out between us. It is a simple letter. Half apology, half rationalizing what she has done. *I am overwhelmed with grief,* her mother has written. *Both,* she writes, *to have done this to you the first time, and to have done this to you again.* She has dated the letter, and I am the one to notice that the date was weeks ago, even before the trip was suggested to Franziska. When I point her attention to this small fact, which she has not yet noticed, something escapes her. A moaning combination of mourning and confusion and the collection of years she has spent trying to draw the real image of herself.

She had this planned all this time, Franziska says. Then, looking up at me, she says it again, softly, almost whispering.

Eventually, Franziska walks me home. To do so, we need to pass the station. Outside, there is a small crowd. Among them, my gathered new family—the violinists, who serenade me jokingly, their friends who shout to me, several children who run beside me and call me Mr. Arnold in a flat, comic English. Also: the rabbis who smile from beneath their beards and who bow their heads, the photographers who take pictures as we go, and the station managers who emerge to greet me. Here I am, after all, with the woman in blue. For a moment, I am surrounded, shaking hands, smiling for someone's camera flash. Everywhere, I am waved at, sung to, treated well. Even though she is not the woman in blue we have been waiting for, she is good enough for now.

Franziska stops walking. What is all this? she asks. What's going on? Have you become famous? she wants to know.

A simple question. For the second time, everything is different.

ALL of this ends the following morning. My neighbor Sandrine comes to see me. Franziska has called her, and apparently, I need "looking in on." I have evidently lost some sense of what is real and what is imagined. In my study, Sandrine regards me as one regards the scene of a great crash. Where is the wreckage? she seems to be asking. She comes in, she surveys the room, she inspects me, she checks my skin, hair, fingernails, teeth—as if the problem, such as it is, has begun to exist on me and not in me. She asks plainly, what is going on, Arnold? Tell me the truth. I am your old friend. I am the person who checks on you. You held my children when they were babies. We are family. Let me know what is happening.

What is true is that I have, all year, lied to her about my whereabouts. Because she comes to visit only in the evenings, after she has put her children to sleep, she does not know that this is how I've been spending my days.

We go into my study, where the cold sun hangs undressed above the skylight, and where birds are roosting in the nearby lindens. She approaches the subject delicately.

I hear that Sonja has returned, she says. Have I heard correctly?

A blessing, I say, isn't it?

When is she coming to see you? Sandrine asks.

She arrives on the eleven o'clock train, I say.

And when is this train? Today, she asks, or is it tomorrow?

She says this with a smile.

I'm sure Franziska has made you concerned, I say.

Well, which is it, Arnold? Is it today or is it tomorrow?

She believes I am being defrauded. Or she believes someone is playing a cruel joke on me. Or she believes I have become in thrall to a fiction. Or she believes that in turning the age I am I have lost the capacity to tell the difference between what I hope to be true and what is in fact true. She takes my hand. She asks me, tell me, Arnold, have you been experiencing anything out of the ordinary these last months? Has anything unreal begun to occur to you? Have you been seeing things that other people do not see?

How else to say the impossible and indelicate truth: Sonja lives. She lives, she lives, she lives.

What I say is this: She is coming on a train.

And when does this train arrive?

Today, I say.

And by today you mean to say—

If not today, then tomorrow, I say.

And when you say tomorrow, you mean to say—

She is coming on a train, I say.

She presses her hand to my wrist. She is, it feels, both holding on to me and measuring my pulse. I feel distressingly small with her hand around me, a hand that is so much larger than my hand, and for an instant I am not here any longer, in my house, but blocks away, in my mother's house, and at once she turns before me from my pretend daughter to my real mother to my grandmother to my great-grandmother, may peace be with all of them, and I have, it seems, grown ever smaller, lost all signs of age, become young again, a boy once more—all this happens as she presses her hand against my wrist.

Outside, a church bell rings eleven times. I have forgotten the time. I have missed her, I say out loud. It's eleven, and I've missed her.

Arnold, Sandrine says, why don't we just stay in this room, in this nice room. Maybe Sonja will come from the train and visit you in this nice room.

But I've missed her!

Stay here for the day. Skip the station for once. Let's have time together, you and me.

When she says this, she sweeps her hand across my chest, as if she is anointing me, in much the same way that her children do sometimes, a way to test that I am real, that I am not just the living manifestation of the men like me they have studied in their history textbooks, the actual survivor, the last Jew left.

I have missed her, I say again. You've made me miss her. I know it.

I understand that you miss her, she says. I'm sorry it's happened this way.

The telephone rings. It's so quiet that Sandrine doesn't notice. I hurry to get it. It is Leda. She is shouting. Blue! she yells. Blue! Blue! The woman is here! she cries. Blue! Blue! She is waiting! Blue! She's come!

I am on the street at once. Sandrine rushes behind me. It has iced overnight. An enormous clean glaze over the city. The sort of weather that deserves skates. My first step sends me gliding, almost falling. In this, a memory returns from somewhere, from nowhere, from this last day here out of so many tens of thousands:

I have gone skating on the pond in the Stadtpark. See us if you can, see my family, my first family, out in moonlight, in hunger, in Vienna, in old clothing, in fear, in hell, or something close to hell, in disbelief, in search of passports, bread, tunnels, wings, cyanide and Veronal, in need of water, music, medicine, diapers, a place to hide, a secret room, a dark box impervious to time, see my family in the middle of a forbidden neighborhood that we know well, that we were married in, here we are, the Altermans on our last sun-filled day together, three and a decimal point we say sometimes, mother and father and baby and a child somewhere else, at the other end of a train, see my family, on iced ring roads, on last savings, on the last night of the old world, see my family, this one family, passing beneath the streetlamps on Seitenstettengasse, where the temple has been smashed, and where Fania is whispering to me and to Moses to hold on to one another, she is saying this out loud, I think this is it, hold on to him, she says to Moses, hold on to your father, you don't know what can happen to you, you don't know what's out there, just hold on, hold on, can you, she says, can you, just hold on, hold on to Papa, hold on, whatever you do, hold on, baby, hold on, baby, are you holding on, are you, are you?

Sandrine keeps a hand on my back. You will fall, she tells me, you cannot go this quickly. But I do. Somehow, I can go this quickly. I turn the corner and move nearly blind with impatience into the square at Judenplatz, past the statue of Gotthold Lessing, past the memorial to the killing, which is a tomb made of books, built to represent all the knowledge lost, a building I have never looked at closely, can never regard with anything but contempt, and in the process I rush eventually headlong into the crowds gathered outside the Stephansplatz, where the postmodern glass of the Haas-Haus has been jammed unwillingly up against the old cathedral. It's a place onto which I cannot help but superimpose my own narrative, a convergence of tenses, the future trying to swallow the past whole. Oh, Vienna! All the free days of my life I have spent in these few square miles.

As I grow closer, I feel my strength returning. At the station, I feel young again. My old body is gone and I am once more in the body of my youth, the body of the man who gave her away. The world to come is now the world of the present. In the world to come, fathers gather up in their arms all the wasted time. In the world to come, I take a seat on every train, I hear the music in every room. I take the steps down to the platform as if I am being pushed. I feel the need to run, and so I run. I jump from the last step. I land without pain.

Here, something is different. Everyone has gone. At the newsstand, my friends have left. Where are they? I ask out loud. Where are my friends? Where is this new family of mine? The person running the newsstand is a person I have never seen before, an older man with very little German. Where are they? I ask. Where did you take my friends? Where are Leda and Magda and Anna and Simon and Rebekah and Lukas, where are their brothers and their spouses, where are the parents of these spouses, the neighbors of these parents, the rabbis of these neighbors, the congregants of these rabbis, where are the photographers and the violinists?

A man is playing an accordion at the end of the platform. At once, the world has rushed back.

Come home, Sandrine says. Get some rest, Arnold. You're tired. You're seeing things. You've let a bad story grow in your head. Come home.

A train arrives on Track 11. A train from which Sonja has never emerged. Sandrine is holding my hand. Let's go home, she is saying. Let me take you back. Your apartment is waiting, she says. It is warm there, very comfortable. There, you can rest, look out the window, watch the airplanes, listen to your music, to whatever music you like, listen to it every day, all day. Come home, Arnold, she says.

Ahead, there are no women in blue. I peel away her fingers one by one. My big adventure, I tell her. And like that, I am gone, off onto the platform, into the breath of the train, warm now, steam on my skin, past the conductors in their red vestments, into the train, into a seat, into motion, out of the station, out of Vienna, away, away, away.

# Kindertotenlieder

VIENNA, 1979

# SONJA

My first moments back in Vienna I felt it necessary to remind myself of the obvious. I am here, this is me, and I am alive. It felt necessary to say this, especially in this place so interested in its dead.

A customs agent asked the obvious questions. What is your purpose in the country? Is it work or pleasure? Whom do you plan to see? Behind me, a long line of travelers queued for the same interrogation. I had arrived in the evening. Children lay asleep in the arms of their mothers. Beyond the platform, I saw a painting of a sun rising over an ocean, an advertisement to travel, but amid my exhaustion and the fear of everything that was to come, it was, I thought, a different sun, a different ocean. The agent had to ask me the questions again, this time in English. What is your purpose here in Vienna? Is it work or pleasure? Whom do you plan to see?

Out in the distance, the eye light of a cat crossed the tracks and blinked out into the dark. When you see that, Franz had always told me, what you are seeing is an omen, a sign from the kingdom of animals to the kingdom of humans. I am here, and I see you, I see you, I see you.

ALL of this was because of the picture of the woman in the church. It had hung first in the window of a shop not far from our house. This was where Feldman found Anya again, and where Franz must have found her as well. For all his faults, Franz was always someone who followed a doctor's orders. The woman was older and obviously she was not real, she was someone else entirely, another person's child, and yet here she was, and she was smiling his own smile back at him and once again she was here with him, she was back, she had never gone anywhere, we were the ones who had gone away, we were the ones who had left her.

At least this is how I imagined it happening.

No one has ever told me one way or the other what happened and what did not. Certainly not Franz, and not Dr. Lionel Feldman, and not the shop owner in Tottenham in whose window the picture hung. Of all the possible permutations of the truth, this is the option I consider the most plausible, the most realistic, even though it is the most ridiculous and the most upsetting: that Franz, having heard Lionel Feldman's claim that he'd seen our daughter alive in a shopwindow, pleaded with him to know exactly which window, which shop, which street, and having gathered all this information rushed there to confirm a part of himself we had both agreed needed to be kept hidden. Which is to say: keep hidden the version of yourself that has attached itself to childish outcomes; keep hidden the version of yourself that has refused the idea of death.

I WOULD like to think that as he stood in front of the window Franz suffered a moment of clear and rational thought. A thought that announced to him: This is not my child, my child is in the ground in France, in a part of the underworld only the Messiah knows, in the spot where the world will become new again; this woman in the window is a stranger. Perhaps he felt the critical choice ahead of him, which was a choice between reason and the opposite of reason. It must have been a difficult choice. Later, the man who owned the shop would tell me that Franz returned three times: twice at night, once at daybreak. I found him there each time, the man told me, and he would not respond to anything I said. I thought at first that he was deaf, the man told me, I thought he could not hear anything at all. Do you need help? the man was asking. But Franz, all this time, was smiling. Here is what you need to know, the shopkeeper told me: he was happy.

THIS was summer and we were both forty-six years old. The shopwindow belonged to a travel agency advertising journeys across the continent. A trip, for instance, to Trieste aboard a cruise liner that departed Corfu and languished in the Adriatic for five days. Or a trip to Florence, where one could be enlivened by the brushstrokes in Judith's hair as she beheads Holofernes.

The picture that Lionel Feldman saw, and which Franz took for himself, was an advertisement for Vienna. EXPERIENCE THE WONDER, it said. COME TO VIENNA. In the original picture, Anya stands beneath the painted roof of St. Stephen's Cathedral. She is photographed to appear small against the immensity of the church. In the version of the picture I ended up finding everywhere, she has been made larger, and the cathedral has fallen away. What I understood was that Franz had done this. He had manipulated the picture somehow. He had made the rest of the world fall away. And here she was, growing larger and larger and harder to ignore.

THE way I imagine it, Franz's reflection must have hung doubled in the window, so that when he saw her in the advertisement, he saw himself as well. This must not have felt altogether wrong, for he had her face, and she had his face. What I know for certain is that he stood in front of that window for so long that first night that I assumed he'd been held up at work, a fact that caused me to call on Jonathan to ask where he was, and for Jonathan to call me three separate times that evening to say that Franz must have been held up somewhere, that he must have become waylaid by something, which was not true, because he was there, in front of a travel agency on Clapton Common, staring at this woman who was very obviously my daughter and very obviously not my daughter.

When he went at daybreak, he must have wanted to see the picture in better light. It was not a good picture. Now that I have my own set of copies, I can tell you this. It renders Vienna incorrectly, as a temple city, a herculean gallery of the past, a tourist Valhalla of kitsch, God-kissed with white marble, a city-scaled explosion of white frippery, rather than the city of my parents, my father's linen shop, draft horses gathered on the Ringstraße, the prayer over the bread, the prayer over the wine, the prayer uttered over the Sabbath lights with eyes closed, whatever prayer exists to utter when your uncles are shot in the brains outside your childhood grammar school. This picture would likely entice no one to go to Vienna. Except for Franz.

THAT morning, he spent an hour in the waning light waiting for this image of Anya to reveal itself to be something other than what he thought it was, which was evidence that the past was wrong. Somehow, we had not left her in Paris, in that garden in Neuilly-sur-Seine, in that room in which she had hung trumpet flowers. Somehow, she had undone the casket lid, unburied the two meters of shoveled earth, walked off the grounds of the cemetery in bare feet as if the Messiah had come, the way all our dead are promised to. We had left her but she had gone on living. Anya was not in the ground; she was here in the picture. Somehow, she had found her way to Vienna, to my city.

LATER that same day Franz walked across Springfield Park before returning home. By now it was evening. Again, I am imagining all of this. Clearly, however, I am not wrong. By that point, everything would have been different. He had never walked this way before. The bats were out whipping blind at the night. Our house was partially hidden from view, here and not here, a house with three plane trees shading the front windows. One could walk and miss the house entirely. It was a place he dreamed about before we found it, which is always a sign that something is calling one to assign some meaning to it.

He could not tell me that any of this had happened. He could not tell me that while he knew all this time that the girl in the picture was not real, not the real Anya, he still kept it, he still spoke to it. Like a child with a doll, building stories out of the inanimate, he talked to it. Every day he talked to this picture and imagined a whole life in which the picture was real life and in which I existed on the exterior of that life. In which I, in fact, became the phantom, and he and Anya became real. Whole weeks passed in which the conversations he had with this girl, this woman, this other Anya, this photographic version of life, were the only real conversations he had. Of course he would come to Vienna. Phantoms are always drawn back to the source of life.

That night, before walking home, he must have stood outside the shop a final time. Eventually, the shop owner came outside to check on him again. If you're going to come every night to stare at this same picture, he said, why don't I give you a copy so you can have it. When you're ready, come back and I'll sell you a ticket so you can see the city for yourself.

I don't need to come back, he told the man. Give me the ticket now. I'm ready to leave.

I CARRIED all of this with me on the train. I had only three people to see in Vienna. The only three people I knew at all in the city. The first of these was Yasmin. She was a very old friend of mine. A particularly close friend of Franz's. Someone for whom I'd also once felt a great deal of deplorable and appalling jealousy. The jealousy was a stain on me, and I include it here only in the spirit of genuine honesty: it happened, I feel terribly about it, I can't change it, I may or may not have still harboured a hint of it. I had called before I went to Yasmin's house, which was situated on a street in Grinzing crowded with spruce, but when I arrived she appeared surprised to see me, so much so that it seemed in the hour that passed between my calling and my arriving via the U2 that she had forgotten we'd ever talked. This was not unusual. I was always passing by the lives of others, half-noticed, a breath of life one apparently had to focus to recognize.

As long as I'd known Yasmin she'd worn her hair tied behind her head with whatever objects she had at the ready, like a sharpened pencil, or even one of Franz's batons, which I once saw threaded against the back of her head in a galling display of casual intimacy that took me many months to erase from my memory, and which in the end reinforced for me the elemental ground rules of refinement. This is to say that there were some people who could seem elegant affixing their hair with, say, a single chopstick, or a slender water-color brush, and there were people like me, for whom the very basics of fundamental coordination and dexterity proved endlessly challenging. Which is why I likely ended up being such a poor musician, and why she, consequently, could make me believe in the flute as an object of real beauty. For instance, to hear her play was to hear someone strip the instrument of all its most cloying, court-maiden, tunic-wearing, frolicsome sheepherding qualities and to turn it instead into an object of mystery and breath. This is maybe a good descriptor for how I thought of her. She liked to dress in too many layers, as if I'd caught her in preparation for some great expedition, or some spiritual exercise that required too much silk, too many coiled pashminas flung gloriously and haphazardly around her neckline. And her breath: she seemed always to be exhaling, as if inside her lay a great unrelenting wellspring of pleasant weather.

When I found her that day, she was tending to a daughter I did not know she had. It had been that long since we'd spoken. The girl appeared to be seven years old, maybe older. And she, too, seemed impossibly refined, even this young. The girl greeted me first in French, and when I didn't answer right away, she tried again in Dutch, which was Yasmin's native language, and when I failed at that, too, she said hello in an exaggerated and loud and mordantly slow queenly English that she adorned with an unmistakable derision. I knew that Yasmin and Franz talked often, but either I had stopped asking after her or Franz had stopped telling me about her personal news, and I felt terrible to be standing there like I was, in the front room of her house—sun on the sand-jute rug, ice-hued orchids blooming on the mantel, jazz on the hi-fi—believing we were friends, and also needing her to tell me her child's name. It's Perla, she said. My grandmother's name. Also her grandmother's grandmother's name, she said. I am hoping she has some of their same spirit, she said, and when I asked what that meant, Yasmin said, in effect, that she hoped that her daughter would stay away from making music and stay away, too, from people who made music, or people who made paintings or theater or dances, or people who had paintings or plays or dances made about them, and would instead make something tangible of the world. Something to hold in one's hands. Something that does not go away so easily.

When she said this, her face changed, and I knew she was worried she'd said something wrong, that I might interpret all this to be about Anya, and she put her hand out to grab hold of mine, and she had many bracelets clung to her, far too many, although each one was very beautiful, many of them made of turquoise and silver, still more of them affixed with small jewels, and I said to her not to worry, not to worry.

What good would her worrying do any of us, I wanted to tell her. Engaging anyone about Anya, whether intentionally or in this case merely as a byproduct of someone's desire not to engage the subject intentionally, was to battle constantly the urge to say all manner of dreadful things aloud. Such as: Say anything else right now, anything at all, say something pleasant and you'll say the right thing, for all I want is a single human moment free from this.

WE went into another room, which was open and cool and insultingly gorgeous, and then into yet a third room, where Perla's paintings hung framed on the wall and where Bill Evans's piano was so vivid and clear I thought she had hired him for my visit. As we walked, we disturbed a harem's worth of Himalayan cats, all of them trailed by a maelstrom of shed white fur, and finally, at some point, Yasmin took my hand again and tried to talk to me in Dutch, thinking maybe that this was my original language, knowing positively that English was not, knowing perhaps something of my life before we'd met.

I told her that I'd come wanting to know if she'd heard from Franz. If he'd come here. If he'd telephoned her. I knew he did this often. She didn't need to lie to make me happy. I often heard him speaking to her in French from behind a closed door, and while I never could hear her French returning through the line to him, I had no difficulty conjuring the sound. A photograph hung on the hallway wall near Franz's study. Ostensibly this was a picture of the entire orchestra, taken years ago at a summer festival in America, a group of several dozen musicians mugging clumsily for the camera, some of them sunburned, most of them disheveled by the heat. I saw this, however, as a photograph only of Franz and Yasmin. In the group, they stood beside one another. Franz held one end of her flute, and Yasmin the other. Often, when he was talking to her, I imagined that this was the version of them on the line, each of them clutching hold of some common idea I could not share.

I told Yasmin what had happened. Or what I thought had happened. He had come to Vienna, I said. He had left without telling anyone. All of his musicians were fearful for his well-being. He had left his shoes behind, I said. And also his wallet. I worried he was suffering greatly and that he might do something foolish. When I said this, we were standing in yet a fourth large and immaculately white room. Beside us lay a great window that opened to a carefully planted garden of boxwood and creeping phlox and also a small white café table at which Perla sat reading a large book while one of the cats circled her in the grass. I had not articulated my anxieties out loud like this. Not at home to Jonathan, not even to myself. Doing so felt like a shock, but it did not feel like a lie. As I spoke, Yasmin toyed with one of the many scarves wrapped around her neck. I saw that she was wearing a pendant necklace, at the end of which hung a large jade stone, and I remembered an afternoon during which she said to me that many people believed that jade possessed the capacity to cleanse the space around one's self, and I also remembered that I laughed quite loudly in her face and asked what sort of cleansing we were talking about, and Yasmin put a hand up in front of me and made a motion as if she were washing a window that hung between us that only she could see, and she said, like this, Sonja. Like this. Cleansing the space like this. So as to eliminate disturbances, she said, and it was clear, we both knew, that I was the disturbance.

I KNOW he's been unwell, she said. I could tell during our conversations that he was beginning to act unlike himself again.

Exactly, I said.

I thought he was finished with all that silliness and tragedy, she said.

Could you tell me, I asked, when the last time was that you two spoke?

When I asked this she took hold of the jade, which was large and jagged and green in the light, and I thought again how discreditable my jealousy made me, and how unseemly I must have appeared to someone like Yasmin, who cared only for Franz as any decent person would. Beyond her, Perla began to play with her cat, which was very large and very white, like a great but miniature storm cloud transmogrified into animal form, and I could not help but to superimpose this child onto my own child. This sight of Yasmin's daughter standing over her cat while hoisting a beech twig—hoisting it like a conductor's baton, I thought—made me once again wild with jealousy. It was something Yasmin must have noticed. And this noticing, all this noticing of hers, felt heavy on me, and suddenly I felt as if I were the one wrapped in fabric and silver and stone.

Yasmin and I went to sit by the window in a pair of chairs arranged so that she could see out, and see Perla, and so that I did not have to, and could instead look at the house. A kind gesture, I thought. A series of small candles burned beside us on a stone plinth. When she was brand-new, Yasmin said about her daughter, I found the entire experience distressingly terrible, and when I said I thought most of us thought this about early motherhood, Yasmin arched an eyebrow suspiciously, and she said, I have read this, but not heard anyone talk of it aloud, not really, especially the boredom, the painful boredom, which is what hurt me the most, that this child would bore me so badly. Also, she said, it disturbed me how easily I took to commanding my child, and how readily Perla took to such a militantly autocratic form of order. I have tried to stop issuing so many commands, she said, and I wanted to tell Yasmin that she did not have to talk so badly about motherhood for my benefit. Several times during this conversation, I tried to bring the conversation back to Franz, to my reason for being here, and each time I did this, she managed to deftly move the conversation on to other topics, such as cinema or warfare or the American political situation, but when eventually I succeeded in getting her to answer me, Yasmin finally remarked upon the unfairness of our circumstances. You are the first woman in many years who has come to see me all by herself, unattached to a husband, to a man, to a lover, and here you come, asking about him. About Franz. How unfair.

This was true, I said, but then again, unfairness only mattered if one believed the world owed us fairness in return for our suffering.

We spoke last evening, Yasmin said.

Last evening? I asked.

He was here, she said. You've missed him by hours.

Here? In this house?

He did not tell me he was coming beforehand, she said. I doubt very much he'll stay at all in Vienna. You know his feelings on this place.

I do, I told her, although I was not sure I knew what Yasmin was talking about, aside from the very obvious, which seemed ridiculous to mention here of all places.

And you're aware, she said, about his feelings on Europe in general, and I must have appeared confused to her, because this was not something Franz and I ever mentioned, this was not anything that we would have ever thought to discuss, maybe because to do so risked our actually speaking it out loud, or more likely because our histories were the same history, and like all refugees our past lay dead together in the same earth, which meant that there was never any use saying the obvious to one another, to talk of it at all was to summon it, to bring it into the room where we happened to be sitting, however far that room lay from the place where, for instance, my parents lay dead, where Franz's parents lay dead. What Franz had always gotten wrong was this: the dead have no sense of earthly geography. Instead, the dead are magnets. If you move, they move with you. If you look hard enough, they will appear to you in a foreign city, or in a shopwindow, because these are the laws of the world to come: gravity exists between planets, just as it exists between ghosts. To bring any of the dead near to you means feeling the impossibility of their distance. This is why in the movies one always has the impulse to run one's hands through the bodies of ghosts when they appear: we feel we should be able to have everything near us all the time. A great deal of mourning is a version of greed, a refusal to apprehend the present, a desire for more and more and more of what has already moved past us.

Yasmin came closer to me, so close that I could smell her perfume, which was sickeningly lovely, and obviously pricey, and she put her hand on my hand once again, and out behind her in the grass Perla and her cat were dancing together, and Yasmin said in my ear, sweetheart, I really can't imagine he's still here, in this city of all places, even with what that doctor said to you two, which was stupid, she said, he's a stupid man that doctor, filled with stupid thoughts, he was drinking wasn't he, that's what Franz told me, that when you both saw him he had half a glass of gin in his hand, which means you can't trust anything he's saying, not at all. He was always wrong, that man. Always and always. You know that, right?

I'D taken a room at a hotel that Jonathan had chosen for me. This was in the Innere Stadt, in the First District, several dozen steps from the park, a room entangled in greenery both real and imposed: maples arranged against the window banked toward me with a florist's optimism, and beside the window those same maples appeared stenciled on wallpaper the color of pistachio cream, and everywhere else there was this arboreal doubling, real branch, fake branch, real idea, fake idea, real daughter, unreal daughter. Jonathan made sure to tell me that this was the only place Franz would stay when he was here, my idiot husband weakened evidently by the cool sensation of pressed Egyptian linens against his calves, and he lusted after the chocolate dollops dusted with orange blossom water and hazelnut and deposited nightly on his pillow, and apparently he found some genuine purpose in the multiplied layers of maple trees. All these facts were so specific and imbued with such a knowing history that the entire scene made me lonely with confusion.

It was the case that my last name had occasioned pleasant commiseration from the bellhops, the desk clerks, the collection of men in blush-bathed vests whose occupations and responsibilities remained blissfully opaque to me, but who came during the day and night to leave offerings at my door—bergamot wafers of soap the size of a child's hand; Apfelstrudel so sweet and good even a small bite threatened to resurrect the dead; a phonograph that played only Ella Fitzgerald or else the Chopin Ballades that tortured me the most. I understood from this last object that these were the comforts

Franz required when he traveled here and that the hotel staff thought I might need them all as well—marriage, after all, being not only a symbiotic realignment of one's true preferences, but a process of gradual sublimation. All this embarrassed me. Here I am again with all my embarrassments: I warned you, didn't I?

WHAT I thought was this: I thought I was close to the house. By which I mean my childhood house, although writing it out like this feels distasteful; I remembered none of it, it turned out. Sorry, Mother and Father; sorry, Moses. If you want that sort of story, others have written it; their memories might as well be my memories anyhow, this was how little I carried with me when I left. The fact was I thought I was three kilometers away at best. An easy walk if I wanted to make it, which I didn't, no part of me wanted to do this, I would rather have been strung to the hull of a crop duster and suspended over all Vienna for everyone to see, not unlike the woman in the story my mother used to tell me. I say all this even though I did go, of course I went, I walked there my first morning in the city, I felt I had to, although the question of where I was going remained an open question, for I realized very quickly I had retained nothing of the place, no images, no senses, no history, I had no idea where to go or how to get there. In the hotel lobby, I found a tourists' map and when I arrived on the Herminengasse, a half hour after I began, I felt utterly rearranged: the house was on the other side of the street, not on the river side, and the building was four stories high, not three, the front step was shorter than it must have been when it was mine; I thought I had remembered leaping from a set of stairs with the gusto of someone flinging themself off London Bridge, but perhaps that memory belonged to another person and had become mine by way of cinema or a friend's confession; and there were somehow balconies attached to the front of No. 11, where in my memory there was no such thing, I would have spent all my childhood on a balcony had there been one, and maybe then, in that other life with a balcony, I might have remembered some of it, some hint of Mama's real face. I stood for a very long time on this street, which is a short street, a sturdy rung on a stepstool squished into the Danube's east side. And after I stood for an equally long time before a version of No. 11 that matched no part of how I remembered No. 11, during which I felt absolutely nothing, not pain or the urge for vengeance or the grief of loss, I left.

And that was that.

IN the morning, I walked from my hotel in the First District to see my friend Karl Krämer at his house near the Augarten. Karl had been a classmate of ours in London, practically the only other person alive besides Franz who had ever registered that I existed at university, certainly the sole person alive besides Franz who had a memory of me attempting to play the piano. When we were students together, he had loved me, and I had known this, and maybe, in moments, I had loved him in return, in the way in which love exists at that age, which is as an aura one encounters or walks through, the way one imagines walking through a ghost, but then there was always Franz, and because of this, there was always a strangeness among the three of us, one made of jealousy and affection and time, and this, as far as I understood, had never changed.

He had not seen Franz, he told me, but he knew Franz was here in Vienna. Everyone had told him this, and I asked him who exactly he meant by everyone. We had, I said, practically no acquaintances in this city aside from him and Yasmin, and Karl said, oh, that's not true at all. By everyone, he meant Maximillian and Florian and Martin and Anton and Jenny and Sara and Jana and of course Bruno, and I knew none of these people, not one, none of these names, and not for the first time it occurred to me that while we had been building our life together in London, a life that had grown progressively more cloistered and quiet and curtain-shut and rooted in the miserable past of the music Franz made, he had lived another life, another existence filled with noise and people and names I would never recognize.

At one point Karl was a cellist, someone Franz considered one of the better players in London, although I never really saw this in him, he had always appeared to me too vain and too pretty, and as a result, too preoccupied with his own vanity and prettiness. Besides, he had beautiful hands, and for some reason I had never been able to believe that someone with beautiful hands like Karl's could play anything worthwhile. I had always distrusted beauty, whether in people or in art, and I could not be convinced otherwise. Beauty, I understood, was a perfume covering something others did not want you to find. It was no matter: his cello lay unplayed in a spare bedroom. He had come around to my way of thinking, he told me, and for a while now he'd had no wish to make anything beautiful. All of it seemed to him to be a lie, a wallpaper over history, which was something I'd told him when we were young, and when he loved me. Whenever my mother comes to visit, he said, she refuses to stay in there. She says it is the cello's room, as if the cello is the child I did not have, and moreover, a problem child, a child who will not behave properly, a child who has shamed the family and who cannot be reasoned with, who is capable of a terrific disturbance, capable of waking everyone during the night. I think sometimes that my mother is right, and that the instrument is developing its own sense of sentience and might one day begin to try to play itself. Enough with you, Karl! A lifetime of sounding perfect and now it makes no sound and I suspect it misses it, it misses the music, although I do not, he said. I have had enough of that music for many lifetimes. All of it—every note—represents to me the music of death. So I leave the cello here in its own room, just like my mama thinks.

When he said this, I thought of the life I might have had with Karl if Franz had not been my husband, and the daughter we would have had together, and how she would not have been Anya, but would maybe have been alive, and at once it seemed terribly sad to me that he would have stopped playing the cello, and so I asked to see it, could I go take a look, I asked, and he brought me to it reluctantly, it was a gorgeous instrument, he'd had to take out a mortgage to buy it, and here it was, dormant and quiet, and our divergent pasts had reached the same future.

I wanted him to play for me. It was something Franz had refused to do for many years now. Play something, I told him, play something old and lovely, but Karl didn't want to.

I have begun to think, he said, that playing that old music is not unlike turning into one of those costumed actors who work on the campus of a living history museum and pretend for visiting schoolchildren that they are enacting a version of life as one did in the seventeenth century: churning butter and weaving sweaters straight off a lamb's back and stoning sinners with large pieces of granite and fearing witches and whatnot. It cannot be healthy for a man like Franz to surround himself with all this prettiness all the time, he said. How can anyone feel the earth beneath their feet with all this fiction in the air?

Karl wanted me to know that he had involved himself in some new projects involving photography, or involving sound recordings and also photography, or involving both street recordings of people singing versions of the Beethoven pieces he hated now and also photographs of those same people singing these pieces. I wish I had paid better attention so that I could report back to you the absolute truth, but I was very tired by then, and the sight of his dead cello had begun to depress me, and as I may have mentioned, I had begun to drink heavily on this trip, less out of a desire to drink or be drunk than as a way to mitigate what was by then a growing sense of hatred for Franz—hate that he would have me chasing him, hate that he'd do all this with such a painful justification. Karl, meanwhile, was still talking to me about his art projects when he mentioned Franz:

I do not miss the cello, he said, no matter how many times Franz calls me to return to my old life.

And how many times has he called you? I asked.

Oh, many times, he said. He thinks I still have something to offer.

Recently, he's done this? I asked.

As recently as yesterday, he said, although when he called yesterday I could tell his heart wasn't in it. He wanted to come by, but I was busy, and by the end of the conversation I could tell he regretted calling me.

Karl understood that this information wounded me to hear, that Franz would have chosen to contact Karl and not me. We went together into a part of his apartment where he kept a desk. The apartment was one large room, an expanse of unstructured space that Karl had divided and subdivided into more spaces, so that to stand in the center of it all was to see a home made comfortable by its mess, its clutter, its division of itself.

Lately, whenever Franz calls me, Karl explained, I take notes. What he's saying is so troubling to me, and so extraordinarily surprising coming from him, that I felt I needed a record. I've always understood Franz to be such a solid person. A man of concrete ideas. A man who merely reads the notes as they are on the page. To hear him now, Sonja, talking about ghosts, about your child, about her living still, it angers me it is so unhinged. And I've told him this. I've said: Franz, you are an idiot! Franz, listen to yourself yammering like an idiot! Which is why I've kept notes. In case you came. In case the police came. I thought both outcomes were plausible, and now that you're here looking for him, I wholly expect the police will come soon. It's all so distressing, Sonja. I've had to invent another excuse for our friends. To say that he's become a criminal—a thief or a strangler or a swindler. Any of those would be better options than what's happened to him.

Phantoms! cried Karl.

I know, I said. I know, I know, I know.

As if you do not have enough to keep in your head, he said.

His kindness left me momentarily paralyzed, which he noticed. He believed he'd said something wrong, and he tried to correct himself: I just mean, he said, that you've suffered over Anya, and also your parents and brother. This paralyzed me more, if that's possible, and he had to begin to apologize to me for my own life, which is a wretched thing to have to endure—a man in Austria apologizing to me so profusely that of course I had to begin to apologize to him. No, I said, I am sorry for feeling like this, and he said, I am sorry for feeling such a way that it has made you feel such a way, and on and on this went, the two of us in his small apartment, with his cello asleep in the other room, his unborn child, which could have been our child, capable of so much beauty left unattended.

Eventually, this hideousness ended, and Karl said: When you find him, will you smack him for me? Right across the face. You break one of his teeth for me. Or you break two of his teeth. Tell him it's from me. From Karl. His old friend Karl.

And he gave me a kiss on the cheek. Soft and barely there and still I felt the future give way.

WHEN I returned to my room, Jonathan was there waiting. We had spoken by telephone that morning, and he had been in London, in our home on Dunsmure Road, brewing tea, and while we spoke I could hear both the rumble of the water near its boiling point and also the clatter of early October weather, rain and wind and the premature cold, and when I saw him in my room, here in Vienna, I asked about what I thought was an obvious discrepancy, how are you here when you were there, and Jonathan offered a sourpuss frown. Aeroplanes, he said. Aeroplanes! I took an aeroplane, Sonja. You don't need to take a train everywhere anymore! The future has already arrived, and you've missed it, which felt true and cruel and unnecessarily exact.

He had come to Vienna with a stack of posters on which Franz's face beamed out smiling. It was my husband's latest publicity shot: here he was all swan-necked and approachable and distressingly handsome, with his left hand fixed awkwardly in frame while clutching a baton that did not appear to have copied well. It seemed clear that Jonathan had picked the picture of Franz that allowed the best possibility that the two of them were related, father and son.

What do you think? he asked me.

I think you made a wanted poster, I said.

I made a missing person poster, he corrected me.

He's not a lost puppy, I said.

It's not as if he *isn't* a lost puppy, Jonathan said.

And what's the plan? I asked.

We put them up, he said. One by one. People will see it. Someone will call us.

That's all? That's the plan?

He struggled for a more exciting answer: We put them up *quickly*?

And you think this will work?

I don't know what else to do, Sonja. He's not officially missing, after all. He's gone of his own volition.

He's just gone missing from me, I said. That's it, isn't it?

Jonathan went to fetch me a cup of vodka. This was a bad idea for both of us, I knew, but this was also a moment when we'd temporarily forsaken ideas of goodness and badness. The vodka was ice-cold.

His friends here in the city have heard from him, I said. Do you know that?

Who exactly? he asked me. The usual crowd? Maximillian? Florian and Martin and Anton? Or was it Jenny and Sara and Jana and Bruno?

You know these people too? I asked.

At this, Jonathan laughed. Do I *know* these people?

Yes, I said. Do you know them? Because I don't, I said. I know none of them. Not one. I know nothing here. I'm lost in this place, and every day it gets larger and more awful, and apparently you and Franz have been busy building another life here without me, a life with one foot in the false and idiotic and horrific past.

All this sounded good when I said it aloud, but I had already lost him. Jonathan was busy mooning over the picture of Franz. I could have said anything and the boy would have ignored it. Such was his obsession with Franz's cupid face. Here, after all, was his chosen papa.

Anya used to do this. When Franz was away at a performance,

and we could not find him on the television or anywhere on the radio, I sometimes had to give Anya one of his press photographs in order to quell her crying. Here is your papa. Here he is in two dimensions. Here is your father reproduced by light and shadow. He is still there. Just elsewhere. Hold him in your hands, child. Set him to memory. He'll come back to you eventually. And occasionally this worked. Anya stopped, or she softened, she found Papa on the paper beaming back at her, his eyes being the same eyes as her eyes, one's parents being both a mirror and an exhortation, and she would stop and look at me and see me for what I was: not her father, but good enough.

Eventually, Jonathan returned to life in much the same way, with a mild but unmistakable disappointment. The posters are a good start, he said. I think it's our only real option.

Do we offer a reward? I asked. Isn't that what people do for their puppies?

Exactly, he said. I'm glad you mentioned it first. I was afraid you'd find it distasteful.

A woman offering money for a husband who's run off? Who would ever find that distasteful? Even if we did do that, where do you suppose we get the money for this reward? You have it lying around in your rented flat? I do not even know who will pay the bill for this hotel room, I said.

My saying this was apparently so stupid as to make Jonathan laugh again. And his laugh, I registered, was a perfect mimicry of Franz's laugh, a baleful and glassy and vindictive piece of lordliness that deserved a better response than I offered, which was to smile, and to laugh too. At what, I wasn't sure. We really did have no money. Everything of ours was an illusion of wealth, a gift, a set of excellent costumes. Yet Jonathan was not concerned with money. Nor should I be, he said.

The orchestra's benefactors would pay, he told me. The same

people who pay for your house. The same people who pay for all of Franz's suits and his taste for luxurious hotel rooms, for orange-blossom chocolates and Egyptian linen and evenings out in chauffeured limousines with other humans willing to be narcotized by piano and violins. And if these benefactors should refuse to help us with a reward, he was saying, and they very well may—they are admittedly exhausted by Franz's impetuousness and his volcanic mood swings—then we will find someone else to help us. You and me both, Sonja. There are always people who want to help people who make beautiful music, he said, and he believed this when he said it, and this made me sad for him.

He's an internationally renowned conductor, Jonathan reminded me, with no small amount of desperation in his voice. People will want to help.

He's not really internationally renowned, I said. He just flies on aeroplanes a lot.

That is unnecessarily cruel, he said.

And the music is tired, not beautiful. All these things are not the same, I said, which was an indisputable and true fact that devastated Jonathan to hear, I know it did, I think he even said out loud to me after I made this accusation that it devastated him to hear: It devastates me to hear you say this, Sonja.

I know you love him, I said.

I love you both. You're practically my—

And I think that is a very lovely sentiment, although I know your mother does not agree.

My mother agrees with no one. She is the least agreeable person. Which is why I adopted you.

And yet, I said.

And yet, what?

And yet, she is there. Your mother is there. Your real mother is there.

Where? he asked, turning his head. You've brought her here?

There, I said again. You know what I mean. And what are you doing?

I took the posters from him and put them in the room's fireplace. This was my way of saying the obvious: I veto the wanted posters. I veto the lost dog posters. I veto the missing husband posters. Everywhere else in the room lay gifts intended to make Franz more comfortable—his noxious soaps, his preferred brand of terry cloth, his taste in American music, his scalding tureen of coffee, strudel made to conform to a memory of his mother's strudel—but where were the things to make me comfortable? I said this to Jonathan, although what did he know, the poor boy?

While we stood in quiet together in the room he'd reserved for me, he asked the obvious question, which was also the most ridiculous question.

Have you gone to the church yet?

When I feigned ignorance, he put the picture down on the table between us. On it, the other Anya: the new version of my daughter.

I'll ask again, he said: Have you gone to the cathedral yet?

I WENT that night, in darkness, mostly drunk. Once again: I do not want to say much about the part of this that involves drinking, except to say that this part does involve drinking. I did not want to go to the church. The idea of going sickened the part of me most deeply attached to rational thought and emotional clarity and judicious outcomes and the rules of human physics that related to living and dying. Going there in search of Anya meant that I would need to step into a countervailed world, which was the world where the idiots lived. People like my husband. I went alone, leaving Jonathan behind in a state of orphaned gloom. My last image of him that night: clutching Franz's press shot, ensconced in terry cloth like some groom of the stool, while the Raindrop Prelude oozed obscenely from teak-paneled speakers built into every corner. The cathedral lay blocks away, a font of camera-flashed tourist drudgery even in the evening, and also an obvious centerpiece for some vague religious desperation. Inside, the frigid and wet death chill that one finds in cathedrals struck me as terrifying and tedious all at once. Underfoot, I knew, were the graves of emperors and their consorts and also maybe their cats, but again, what do I know about any of these places?

I suppose I should admit here that I was crying. Here I am, sobbing out of panic in the anteroom of Vienna's great cathedral. Crying out of a prolonged fit of mismanaged expectations. Crying out of some combination of revelatory clarity and unplumbed shame. Crying because I was a forty-six-year-old woman looking for a man talking to a photograph. Maybe also crying because I felt some deep, atavistic fear that I might be murdered here, like everyone else had been murdered here, likc all the other Jews. Eleven steps into this place and I felt myself convulse. Any moderately attentive passing stranger would have seen me in my blue raincoat—the same crystalline blue, Franz said once, of the Mediterranean in the moments before Vesuvius made it catch fire—and thought, look at this! Look what we have here! Here is yet another Jew, intent on seeing the collective bloodstains, the pitiful monuments to her own absence, and look what it's done to this poor woman, this woeful Jewess in her fancy raincoat and her baubles and her cropped hair and that obnoxious grief that she wears like another layer of skin. Look! Look! She's weeping in public! Actual Jewish tears landing on the hardened concrete of an actual Austrian church! Who says that history does not run circles around itself!

I looked up at one point amid this crying, which was wretched crying, ugly and awful and disturbing crying, and I saw that a pair of young girls were watching me. I had terrified them, it was clear. It is not an everyday occurrence to see an adult person sobbing like I was. I knew this. I stopped for them. I told the girls everything was fine. This is normal, I said. This is completely normal. Weeping is normal. Weeping in public is fine. I said it in English. I said it in German. Weinen ist normal. Being an adult human weeping in a large cathedral is more normal than you can imagine, I said. The bones of the emperor and his cats are underfoot! Also: I am Jewish! There are reasons! This was, very clearly, the wrong way to handle this situation, because my talking to them terrified them, and eventually they, too, began to cry, likely because a weeping British woman had accosted them in a dark thousand-year-old candlelit church filled with the bones of their ancient rulers. I straightened myself and tried to appear composed, which likely terrified them even more, and eventually they left.

After this, I fixed myself in the exact spot where the other Anya had stood in the picture that started all of this, this picture Franz was very likely discussing somewhere in this city at this moment. By the time I'd arrived in Vienna, I'd destroyed every copy of the picture I could find. There were so many copies in our house, and many more copies in Franz's office. He'd left them behind, I thought, as attestations to his being able to do what I could not do, which was to hear and see and move between the rooms that separate the living and the dead.

I stood for an hour there, in the same place where the woman in the picture had stood, this other daughter of mine, this false Anya. Yes, a small part of me imagined that I'd find Franz here. That it would be this easy. A part of me thought that he'd be sitting here all this time awaiting miracles, just like everyone else was lighting candles, and that I could coax him back to London by pointing out the obvious: The picture is a profanity, this is an execration of our life together, look where we are! When he was not there at first, I decided to wait longer, and when he did not show after an hour, I thought I would give it some more time, another hour, and after that second hour passed, I considered the fact that I had thought I was too old at this point to suffer any more humiliation, but what else to call my stuttering embarrassment when the kindly staffers of this institution—church employees, municipal stewards of the city's tourist economy, volunteers in the service of a vanished history—came to ask whether they could help me. You've been standing here a long while, one of them said to me, in the odd and officious English common to those who learn it in European schools. Are you looking for someone familiar? Have you separated from your traveling companions? Do you require assistance?

This question! Yes, I require assistance! Yes! I've lost every last bit of my mind! It had begun to storm: the autumn rain that explodes from clear skies. I rushed out and immediately turned the wrong way. Outside in the plaza, I recognized nothing. I turned backwards to the church. The weather soaked me. The future had rearranged what I thought I understood as familiar. I rushed out with confidence. And I walked and walked and exhausted myself with walking and hurt my feet with walking and made my toes bleed with walking, and all of it seemed pointless. Before I could get too far from the church, however, a woman stopped me. Miss, she was saying in English, miss, miss. You've dropped something, she said, and when I turned she put in my hand the photograph of the girl, a version of the same photograph I had destroyed in my kitchen in London.

Here, she said, giving me this picture, which was now in perfect shape, uncreased, unbothered, stitched together, revivified. You left this, she said. You dropped your picture.

Two days passed without a sign from Franz. I spent these days in premature mourning on the tenth floor of the hotel in the Innere Stadt, a span of time during which I did not leave the confines of my bed, and instead consumed enough Apfelstrudel to feed a grammar school, while also keeping a team of stewards busy ferrying me lorryfuls of extraordinarily expensive champagne that I would never pay for. At one point, I asked for better music. Please, I begged, anything other than this dead-men parade of ghoulish ivory tickling, anything but this ghastly soundtrack. Please, I told a poor boy from Ottakring, having grabbed his lapels, maybe having complimented him too effusively on the quality of his skin, which was, in truth, otherworldly and envy inducing. Please, I told this little cherub, please bring me some ugly music. What is the ugliest music you know? Please bring this to me! This is what my heart needs: ugliness!

Meanwhile, Jonathan went scouring the city for his papa. Intermittently, he returned having heard a rumour of Franz's presence. This is all one ever hears of a ghost, I knew. From my gloriously pillowed roost, encircled by the clink of discharged Perrier-Jouët, I told him that death had a way of making pilgrims of all of us: chase a whisper long enough and you will find yourself the one whispering at statues. This did not go over very well. He knew, he told me, that Franz was alive in Vienna. When I asked for proof, he merely handed over this same image of the girl in the cathedral. Everywhere Franz had gone, he'd deposited this photograph as a grim calling card, or else as a wish that he might somehow transpose himself into the other world where our daughter had grown and become a stock model for a tourist campaign.

My last night in the hotel, I found him again, once more on the screen. By now, I was very tired and even more drunk (if one mixes extraordinary amounts of champagne and also a great deal of expensive whisky, the result is a form of sense-blindness that begins, however briefly, to obliterate grief) and very angry (cathedrals) and I had singed the skin on my fingers (burning yet again every copy of the picture of the fake Anya) and I was determined to return home as soon as possible. It was the same performance I'd seen days ago, before I left London. I had arrived at the programme at a different point, earlier than I had before, this time during the first movement, with its strings, its sickening sugariness, its grueling prettiness, before the moment the camera would turn to me, or whoever it was I was supposed to be. Jonathan had gone to his own room, and I had the sudden and unfair urge to call him back, to make him bear witness to what I knew was coming on-screen—this other me. But I did not do this.

THE music that night was by Gustav Mahler. *Kindertotenlieder.* Songs on the Death of Children.

Not long after Mahler wrote the music, his own daughter Maria died. She was four years old and had been ill with scarlet fever. Mahler set the songs against a series of poems by Friedrich Rückert, who had himself written the words after the loss of his own two children.

I was pregnant when Franz first wanted to record this. I had disallowed it then. The only time I ever did this, that I ever exercised the privileges of knowing him as I did. Mahler's wife, the great Alma Mahler, had tried to disallow it, too, believing her husband had tempted fate by setting the poems to music. We were living then in a rented flat in Tottenham, a squalid place above a butcher; low ceilings, loud neighbors, blood in the street, beef-stink in the vents, a place of misery for the two of us, a place also where I first began to imagine Anya. Franz liked to hum the most beautiful of the songs, which is, indeed, very beautiful, and also very awful, and I had to ask him to stop, to leave, to hum these songs outside if he needed to, we would not entertain between the two of us any hint of tragedy or darkness. Enough of this, I told him. Enough of you and your addiction to misery and sadness and the grief of others. It was a sentence I repeated years later, after Anya's death, when Franz still registered her dying as a fact and not a myth. This was when he asked me again: I want to make this recording, he said, and again I said no. He had wanted to make our loss everyone's loss, to transfer his grief onto everyone as a way to diffuse it, to lessen its severity, even though I told him that death did not work that way, that to put our loss into the bodies of others would only make that loss stronger, that grief grew in darkness and in strangers and in all the places we would never think to notice or to search. You could shine a light into all the corners of your life and never see it growing. The fact was that I did not think Franz could do it well. His gift was a gift of theater: he was, and had always been, a sentimentalist, a man who performed grief far better than he ever felt it.

At some point, the camera shifted to linger on me, or whoever this other woman was supposed to be. On-screen, I was evidently in the process of being torn apart by the music. Tears had overcome me. The other Sonja cried exactly the way I cried. The other Sonja gripped the skirt of her dress in order to keep from crying, much as I did. The other Sonja very obviously found this music as beautiful as I do now, beautiful and thus reprehensible. Mahler's *Kindertoten-lieder* is written for a singer and an orchestra; either a father or a mother can sing. That night, it was a woman singing, an older woman. The highlight of the *Kindertotenlieder* was for me always a piece called "Wenn dein Mütterlein," or When Your Mama. It's a song narrated by a mother who looks to the space where her dead daughter should be. As the singer approached this song, I got up from the bed and began to try to dislodge the television from the stand the hotel had bolted it to. I grabbed it with both hands and flung all my weight backwards, hoping to kill it, hoping to kill the wall, hoping to reach through time to kill the singer, to kill Gustav Mahler. Maybe I was screaming too. Maybe: I cannot be sure of such things at this late date. What I know to be true is that I did not succeed in ruining the television, of course I didn't, no matter how hard I tried. And I tried quite hard. I was, it turned out, no match for Austrian hardware. The commotion, however, brought Jonathan running headlong into my room, and when I saw him, and saw his obvious terror, I tried to explain. This song, I said, this foolish little pretty song!

Later, he put me to bed like I was child.

Do you know the words to this song? I kept asking him. Do you?

Let's get some sleep, he said. Okay? Sleep, sleep, sleep.

Do you know the words, Jonathan? Do you know the words to this awful little beautiful song? Do you?

SOMETIME the next morning, we decided to drive to Tyrol to see my oldest friend, Annika, at her house in Innsbruck. I decided that this was going to be the last place I'd look. I couldn't take any more of this. After her house, I'd go home, with or without Franz. The trip required a rented car, and two hours' travel, most of which Jonathan and I did in silence, except when he wanted to ask me questions I had no ability to answer. Such as: How does one prepare to make space for loss? It's possible he used other words to ask this, and that I'm doing a poor job of telling you what he said exactly. I spent the drive miserably preoccupied. I had not recovered from the previous night. I would not recover. This seemed unfair: the television seemed fine; Franz was probably fine. And here I was, half-awake, a half dozen espressos into my morning, driving into the sky. Which is probably why I had begun to think that I was searching for Franz only so that I might murder him. I was hunting him, it turned out, the same way he was hunting whoever it was he thought was our dead child.

It had become clear to me that we were not going to find him. Maybe you know this already, whoever you are. Jonathan must have understood this before he asked that question of me. Clearly, he'd known it from the beginning. Maybe he'd known it back in London and was too worried to tell me the obvious truth, which was that Franz did not want to be found. We could look for him until we died and we wouldn't ever find him. Which is what Jonathan wanted to ask about. How does one accommodate such a thing happening? He had invented a father, and now that father was gone, and where on earth does one find another of those?

We'll have to make arrangements to clear out his office, Jonathan said.

Don't leave me in the position of having to be the optimistic one, I told him.

I'll have to write a letter to the orchestra explaining what happened, he said.

Just because I'm going to stop looking doesn't mean you have to, I said. There are so many little mountain towns here where a man like him could go losing his mind.

I don't know what I could possibly write in this letter, he said. Everyone will think I'm the insane one. The sheer facts of this are very weird. I'm embarrassed even thinking them to myself.

Annika will know where he is, I said. Of all people, she will know. He's always loved her.

I can't possibly write the truth, said Jonathan. I can't possibly tell everyone that Franz has lost his mind. That he's been chasing a vision around Vienna, around all of Austria, that he's somehow walked his way through the mountains with no money, no wallet, no shoes. I can't write that, can I?

You're not listening to me, Jonathan.

I am listening, he said. You're not having the right conversation.

And what conversation is that? A question of your own embarrassment? Be embarrassed! Who on earth cares if you are embarrassed or not embarrassed. Facts are often embarrassing.

Such as what?

Such as the fact that Franz is an idiot.

He might be an idiot, but he's an idiot who's left us.

Have a shred of hope, I said, which was the wrong thing to say.

Listen to you! Hope for the impossible!

Hope costs absolutely nothing. It's easy. Which is why everyone does it. People love things that are free.

It costs nothing except for disappointment, Jonathan said. Disappointment seems very expensive to me.

Worrying about expensive things is always a waste of time, I said.

He fell quiet at this. You know, he said, I have no practice at this. No practice at all.

No practice at what? I asked. Practice with people losing track of reality? Practice with people going off without their shoes and talking to a woman in a picture?

You're making jokes, he said, flatly, bloodlessly, so soft I could barely hear him. You're making jokes.

What else should I do?

AROUND us on the road that afternoon was the whole Alpine array, the imposing white peaks, the vertiginous cliff faces that terminated in a quaint but previously hidden village of ten houses and a field church spire and six woolly ewes as adorable as a child's toy, as well as a solitary herder looking skyward at all us fools circumnavigating this small cloud-kingdom of his. It's not an exaggeration to think that, for Jonathan, the fact that I was driving, and that I did not really know how to drive at all, combined with the proximity of the mountain abyss, had him thinking about endings.

It was still early in the day and we were quite sober, both of us. Our coffee cooled in carrying cups. We had attempted to listen to music, but we had decided that we hated music now, all of it, especially the wonderful stuff, Mozart particularly, who we both agreed was the most wonderful, and thus we hated him because of his wonderfulness. And also, we were too high in the sky to get any clear signal, which meant that Mozart came across to us in pieces, cut up by silence, by noise, which is to say that Mozart sounded as if he were coming and going and I had no patience anymore for the sounds of any man who wanted to escape. And this was when he asked this question of me. How was he ever going to continue with his life now that this person had left him? After all, Franz was his father, and if not his actual father, then the father he wanted, and if not that, the father he'd picked out to have, like anyone might pick a jacket off a rack at Selfridges. Because I did not want to answer him, I mainly focused on not killing us.

Please, Sonja, he said, I'm really asking. And I know that you more than anyone will have an answer for me.

And why is that?

What do you mean why is that?

Say it aloud, Jonathan.

Please, Sonja.

Say it with words. Tell me why it is I should know so well about all this dreadful business of death.

Oh, I don't mean it like that. *Dreadful*. It's a genuine thing to say.

The mountain road below us unfurled in a corkscrew, and the cars coming after ours appeared as mice must to hawks. Jonathan waited for me to say something, but what was there to say? He likely knew everything without my telling him. Perhaps an entry bearing my name existed in the student dictionaries that accompanied Jonathan through the British school system: *Sonja Beckman, née Smithson, née Alterman. Hebrew orphan child; see entry for Kindertransport; see entry for the Liquidation of Jewish Vienna; see entry for Lost brothers; see entry for Poltergeist.*

What I might have said if I had the presence of mind or the courage: I had begun lately to think of it all as a form of theft; death was theft and the poverty of mourning was theft and the available literature to help the grieving was aggressively stupid and therefore a theft, and the music for the dead was all very beautiful and sad and also thus a theft; the theft of Mama and Papa and the theft of Anya and the theft of my baby brother and now Franz. The mind cannot endure all this theft, not in any orderly way, not by way of the available explanations, even if the body keeps going. Stay in movement, Jonathan, and your body might trick itself into thinking all this is normal. Keep driving up this mountain highway, higher and higher into the clouds, and you might think this is normal. Or you may believe that you've become the ghost. I could have said this.

It was an embarrassing sentiment, but it might have done him well to hear it, to grow into the truth of being alive, which is that being alive is very frequently embarrassing.

Here is where all the great thinkers of Vienna were wrong: the available language remained lacking. This is why so many of us living like ghosts say nothing. Otherwise, everyone everywhere would stand on street corners and scream for the dead. Jonathan desired a language of death, but I had no language to offer. Yes, I had lost and lost and lost and lost and I had on occasion broken into pieces on account of all this losing, and those pieces of me had broken into other pieces, and in the process I had terrified the neighbors or I had hallucinated the faces of all my great-grandmamas, and I had gone walking in a fit across London at night in the hope of traveling by train back through my life, but none of this altered the silence. And in the silence, the true and deranged senselessness: how else to explain the presence of my daughter some mornings in my house, her voice between walls, her occasionally calling to me; a man on the street in New York the last time I traveled who kept appearing beside me in restaurants, on subway cars, in the elevator at the hotel where I was staying, and who in the end had to apologize to me, and to say, we keep finding one another, don't we, is it possible we know one another, and I, not knowing what to say, burst into tears and said, through my fingers: I hope we do, I hope we do.

I couldn't say any of this, though. Jonathan wanted me to, and I couldn't. Here we were in the Alps, at the very top of the world, practically in heaven, and I said nothing. The words would have sounded ridiculous: maybe I am the ghost and everyone else is still living somewhere else.

ANNIKA opened the door for me before I even knocked.

I knew it would be you, she said.

I did not need to say anything aloud in response, in the same way I hadn't needed to call her beforehand. Franz had done the same thing, she said. He had arrived without forewarning, straight from London without shoes, without money. You would have thought we were children again, she said. Squint and you could have erased the middle-aged man in him and he would have been the same runty, loud, disorganized little genius I knew in Tottenham.

The room was cool and painted gray and she'd scented it with jasmine tea and candles and everywhere windows opened onto mountains striped by snow machines. In a corner, one of Franz's recordings played. She had been listening before we came.

Do you mind? she asked. I would understand if you minded, but it is so lovely. Even if, she said. Even if. The sentence did not need to finish itself. Even if.

It was an early record of his, a record Franz made in Manhattan, at 30th Street Studios, he on the piano, me in the control room behind glass, in a room also scented with candles, our first time in America; I had wanted to stay, he had wanted to stay, for some reason we did not stay. It was always like this—him in the light, me behind thick soundproof glass, our mutual desires set aside in favor of some larger and less happy future.

The view out Annika's window showed the Alpine theater, the tourist throng, the spires of the Altstadt. I was best suited for a place like this, she told me, which is to say a ski town, a tourist spot, a vacation magnet, a place where people came to experience a fleeting moment of happiness apart from their lives. These, she said, were the best places for exiles, especially for exiles whose homes had been erased, and for whom the possibility of return was an actual impossibility, not simply a matter of politics or war, which are permanently temporary. To live in a town like this was to live perpetually in the bliss-wrecked moment of escape. There is no time here. There is weather. And there is setting. And there is the constant substitution of other people in transit. But there is no hope of return. Why do you think I live here? she asked me while we stood looking. You think I'm stupid enough to go skiing?

The facts were these: Franz had indeed come here with the picture of the woman in the church, imploring Annika to accede to his idea that Anya was here, or there, or wherever he thought she was. Our dialogue was predictably brief, and entirely in German, so as to keep the truth from Jonathan, and maybe even to keep the truth from the part of me that spoke and thought and dreamed in English.

You've missed him by days, she said.

You should have called me, I said.

He asked me not to tell you.

Oh, I'm sure he did. All of this is too much.

This is what he said.

What did he say?

That you were chasing him.

*Chasing him?*

That you were disconnected from reality, she said. And that you were chasing him.

This is madness.

This is what he said.

He thinks that Anya is not dead.

Another thing that he said.

And that she has grown and turned into a model for the state bureau of tourism.

Precisely what he said to me.

And I am supposed to think this is acceptable?

This is what *I* said!

There was more: he had not slept. He had not been eating. He had forgotten his hygiene. He was very plainly undone by what his mind had made. I cleaned him up, she told me, and I took him to my doctor, who pleaded with him to stay, to take medicine, we have many great institutions here, the doctor said, we have no great deficit of communal trauma. The entire nation has not processed what has happened here. Also, we have a great number of people who break themselves on the mountains, who leave a part of their brains in the snow, who bloody the aspen trees with themselves, who crash their sports cars on the switchbacks, but he could not be reasoned with. As you must know.

He slept here, she told me. Right there, she said, pointing to the sofa on which Jonathan sat. Only for a single night. He lay awake most of the time, singing to himself, yammering, keeping me up into the night. He had the picture, the picture of the woman in the church, and he showed it to me, and he said, look, here's proof! And I laughed at him. Honestly, I thought he was on bad drugs. Whatever you have in London now: all Sigmund Freud's leftover cocaine; I thought he had eaten all of it, all the drugs all at once, and this was what was going on. I stood over him. I ministered to him like a mother. Look, he kept saying, holding up this foolish photograph. It's her, he said finally, and I said to him, who do you think this is, and he was crying, God he was crying, the crying of an infant!

And maybe it was for the best that Jonathan could not understand precisely the way that Annika referenced this, and the derision with which she said it all. *Weinen*: the German word for what Franz was doing; in Annika's mouth, a long and woeful noise, itself a long double-syllable cry; a flawed bow rung out on a slack gut string.

I took this picture of his, she said, and I told him the truth: This is a fashion model who has been made to stand and look confused in the center of St. Stephen's. This is a woman who has been paid ten schilling to do this. This is a woman probably trying to earn money for her child. This is a stranger, a stranger, a stranger. That's all this is! Now, who do you think it is? I asked. And it took him a very long time to say it out loud, and when he did, I have to say, it was a very difficult moment. All my worst instincts combined into one. I have always worried about him, as you know, Sonja, and in that moment all my worries were confirmed.

What did you do? I asked.

I burned the picture, she said.

I burned the picture too!

But he had more of them. Two more in his back pocket. He made copies. He wouldn't let me burn those.

There are so many more of them! They're turning up everywhere!

By now, Jonathan had lost interest in us and gone to stand at the window facing the back garden. It had begun to storm, which meant we would need to stay the evening. This obviously distressed him.

We need to be out searching for Franz, he said. We need to go. Can you ask her where he went? Can you ask her whether he was carrying anything on him? Did she get him shoes? Does he have his wallet?

Annika lit another row of candles on the table before us. Regarding Jonathan, she made a face at me to let me know how pitiful she found this scene. Jonathan had fixed himself at the window.

They are the same almost, Annika said to me, meaning Jonathan and Franz. It's as if they are father and child.

Out of everything we said that day, this was something he understood. Vater und Kind. He flung his head back to us.

I heard that, he said. And then, frowning, he announced he was going out to search. There are footprints in the snow, he said, more or less to himself. He said it three more times. There are footprints in the snow, and I knew what he was thinking—that if we gathered ourselves and followed the trail we would find him, although we wouldn't, I knew it and he knew it and we all knew it.

WHEN we were alone together, and Jonathan was outside in the weather, Annika explained that the whole time Franz was here at her house she had asked him whether there was anything she could say to change his mind. Nothing I could say would undo his grief logic, which he had built inside himself with the sturdiest concrete. When one has become deranged by grief, one enters a territory built of false astonishment. The slightest sign of disorder can prompt in a person something that feels like revelation. You know this, she told me, and I know it, and we know that this territory can begin to appear just as life appears, with its same markings on our walls, our same gravity, and birds. She told me that she'd asked Franz whether there was anything she could do to change his mind about this picture, about the past itself, about little Anya, and to his credit he said yes: if you can find this woman and prove to me she is not my daughter, then I will be convinced.

You would have been proud of me, Sonja. Three phone calls it took to find her! That is all! First, I called my friends in Vienna who work for the city's advertising bureau, where I was able to find the name of the woman in this picture. It was not hard. Then I called her agency, where I was given a name and a small village near Linz. And then I called the church rector in this village. And here I was: until two months ago, the woman was a seamstress in the north. Livia is her name. It was certainly the strangest conversation of my life. I have a man here, I told her, who thinks you are his daughter, to which, thankfully, she laughed. My papa is here in the room, she said, God bless, God bless. She had been trying to make extra

money, she explained. I want to move far away, she told me, and
when I asked where she wanted to go, she thought for a while and I
thought she would say California or New York, but she said she
would go to Lisbon, where her brother lived by the ocean and where
he wrote poems. This was why she had posed for the picture, so she
could afford the train fare to Portugal. The light that day in the cathedral was very dim, Livia explained, and they had brought in
these very large klieg lights that blinded her, which is why, she said,
I am squinting in the picture, and why it is my papa says I do not
look like me. I did not realize they would put it everywhere, she told
me, and when she said this I could tell she was overwhelmed by the
idea that strangers had seen her, spent time with her face, had even
confused her with someone else, which was her way, I suppose, of
saying that this had happened before, that people were constantly
seeing in her face someone they wanted to see.

Eventually, Annika said, I put them on the telephone with one
another. I was afraid to do this, especially given Franz's state—he
was here, unwashed, without shoes, without identification, humming to a radio I did not have playing, but he was very kind. He
listened to her story about her brother in Lisbon, and he listened to
her story about the klieg lights—as bright as so many suns! my face
became something else!—and he said to her, you know I have a
friend in Lisbon who I'll call and put you in touch with: Gerta. I
should put you in touch with Gerta. She has a big house. She'll send
your train fare and give you a place to stay. I am always happy to
help people, he said to this woman in the picture who was not your
child, Sonja, and I sat across the room, fearful, of course, he would
start acting like a lunatic. But he was kind. I thought, here is all this
fatherly energy and it has no home.

When she was finished, we sat in quiet for a long while. On a
side table was a copy of the picture: the one in which Livia had been
turned into Anya. I took it into my hands. For the first time I saw

what Franz had seen. She did indeed look like him, which meant she looked like Anya.

There is a resemblance, I said.

I suppose, she said.

I see it, I told her. I don't want to see it, but I do. It's possible.

Sonja, she said, do not think that his madness needs to become your madness.

SOMETIME later, hours maybe, many hours of wine later, I realized that Franz's hat lay hanging on a hook on a fence outside in Annika's garden. A brown homburg, faded on the brim, bought for him as a joke when I was pregnant, it clung to a fence post, snow gathered on the lip. I went outside to get it, and when I came back inside, I heard the music. It was faint, but I heard it clearly: a single piano playing. Annika was talking to me—something about the hat or about Livia—but I did not listen. Instead, I focused on the music. I thought it was coming from the stereo, but Annika had not turned the record over. In a corner, the old record still spun. Somewhere on that recording, if you listen with headphones, you can hear me breathing, and in that breath, you can hear Anya somewhere too.

I took leave of Annika then. I went in search of the piano. The house was new—a product of a decade of drafting and work and saving and carving with heavy machinery into the chalky stone on the mountainsides overlooking the Inn River and the city curled around it. Because I often get lost in spaces like this, I got lost, and encountered, as I went, staircases where I thought there should not have been staircases, and then many locked doors, and more staircases, and beyond them, more locked doors, and more staircases, and I thought, how is it that a designer had built a house like this? Why did my old friend Annika need so many staircases and locked doors? Stairs to what? Locked for whom? I hated houses like this. Houses like this left marks on me. I had lived all my life in small spaces, borrowed spaces, far too much of it on trains, yes, an orphan train, yes, a couchette across Europe while my idiot husband entertained the ladies in the dining car with pretty music. This is what I was hearing. All the while the music grew louder and louder.

Did Annika hear this? Did everyone hear this?

I went thundering through this large stupid house, a house in which only she knew how to find her way. Eventually, I came to find myself in a small bedroom at the top of her house. Dormer windows allowed the whole cliff face of a nearby Alpine ridge. Here, the music was at its loudest. I found myself alone. I did not know the music. It was new to me. Very little music like this was ever new. Which is how I thought that it must be Franz playing. A new composition, I thought, a new piece, written for me, written for Anya, written at home in the world into which he'd vanished, where Anya was living still, where she was nineteen and dreaming of a life in Lisbon.

I put my hand against the wall. Here, the music grew even louder, and I could feel the vibrations of every key strike. The music was very lovely. I have to confess this. Even though I had forsworn all lovely sounds, it was very lovely. I think I said this out loud into the wall.

It's very pretty, I said, and when I said it, it appeared that the music responded; it became louder, and also more lovely.

I know, I know: all these protests of mine about prettiness and loveliness and beauty and the cancer they cause. But it was indeed the case.

Are you in there? I asked. A ridiculous thing to say alone in a friend's bedroom, high in the mountains, wearing my husband's old hat. Are you in there?

In the corner, a standing mirror offered a glimpse of the actor on the stage. Here she was, Sonja Beckman, née Sonja Smithson, née Sonja Alterman, somehow in an attic room near Innsbruck and I was in all black, the same all-black gimmick of the past decade or so: graveyard skin, Franz called it. And the hat: when I gave it to him, I had joked that he'd be an old papa yet. This was his fear, that

while I had a child in me, that while I lay awake at night in our flat
in Tottenham and could not sleep from my size and from Anya's
foot wedging itself into the underside of my rib cage, that she would
never know the young version of him, the man with energy and
vigor, but would only know the old man he would become. Or
worse: he worried some nights that he would be killed somehow and
that she would live without ever knowing him. His father had been
killed—shot in the neck—and his father's father had been killed—
shot in the face during the war—and his grandfather's father had
been killed—set upon by thieves on the road between Kremenets
and Rivne and also shot in the neck and the face—and on and on
it went like this, he told me, a series of graves no son could tend,
bullets to the head and neck, the Jews were always chased by bullets,
and I asked him one night not long before Anya was born to describe his father for me, and he told me that he had no image of his
father left, none at all, and I said try please, what is the image you
have of him, and he said, all I have is the color of his suit, brown like
burned chestnuts, almost black, and his hat, a homburg, out of style
for a moment when the fedora was the fashionable choice. That's it:
that's all I remember of Papa. The hat and the color of a jacket.

And here I was alone with my hands against the wall.

Are you in there? Franz, are you in there?

Even as I spoke, the music continued: on and on in a circle of
phrases, new cluster-chords, new tones, I felt undone by this, and I
began to bang on the wall. Are you in there? Franz, are you in there?

Beneath me, I could sense Annika and Jonathan rumbling in
search of me, calling my name, but I had gone up in a way that no
one could follow. Somehow I understood this. My old friend had
built a house with staircases that led nowhere, and this was where I
found myself. Nowhere, nowhere, nowhere. Still, this infernal
music. I began to bang on the wall. This was the good stuff, the
heavy-duty plasterboard, the sort of stuff one needed to pay real

money to install, the kind of walls that did not crumble into dust when one banged the wrong way with a hammer. I couldn't move through this wall. I could only push my ear into it as hard as I could.

Are you in there, Franz? Are you in there, you dunce? Is that you playing this sad, weepy, foolish, gorgeous music? Is that you?

When I asked this, the music quieted for an instant.

Let me in, I pleaded. Let me in.

Still quieter the sound grew.

Tell me how to get inside, I said. Tell me how to get where you are.

Another glance in the mirror: the hat had caught the light from a rooflight above us, a rooflight I hadn't noticed before. The music in the wall quieted to the point where I could hear someone breathing. Maybe you're thinking right now, this is madness, Sonja is describing madness, what else to call a story that ends with a woman in a small room banging to be let into a room that does not exist, so that she might grow closer to music that no one was playing. I began to plead. I dropped to the supplicating and prayerful position.

Tell me, I said. Tell me where the door is.

Somewhere nearby, I could hear Jonathan pleading for me. We can hear you, but we don't know where you've gone!

On one side of the wall music played, and on another my friends called my name. On one side of the wall: a long drive back to Vienna, a longer trip back to London. On the other side: my husband's piano, the grown child, some other less mutable future.

It may have been the case that I stayed there a long while, in this space between where no one came to find me. The music in the wall changed. Here again was the *Kindertotenlieder*, Songs on the Death of Children. Do you want to know how the song goes? What the words are that the singer has to perform? The words that made me—all the various versions of me—come apart?

This is it. Listen, child.

*When your dear mother*
*Comes in through the door*
*And I turn my head*
*To look at her,*
*My eyes light first,*
*Not on her face,*
*But on that place*
*Nearer the threshold*
*Where your*
*Dear little face would be,*
*If you, bright-eyed,*
*Were entering with her,*
*As you used to, my daughter.*

# Hiding Places

MIAMI BEACH, 1979

# FANIA

Aᴛ the beginning of our last week together, Hermann steals me an apartment. What I want to know, seven days before we lose one another, is how he's done it.

"Very simply," he says, and then says nothing more.

"This is not an answer," I say. "I need to know! There were locks," I remind him. "And police officers. How did you get inside, Hermann?"

"What is a lock to someone like me?"

"I think a lock, any lock maybe, is an advertisement *not* to be a burglar."

"A burglar! What have I stolen? The view? Is this theirs now too?"

"They will likely tell you that it is, yes. Since it is not yours, it likely belongs to the person who owns it. Who is not you. This is how it works."

"Who will suspect an older gentleman here in this sun-filled corner of the earth?" he says. "Especially one as handsome as me."

"You're telling me you used your beauty to bypass the locks?" I ask.

"Why is Hermann's beauty so difficult to believe?"

"Your beauty is not difficult to believe, Hermann," I say. "I just did not know it was a factor in breaking locks."

"*My beauty is not difficult to believe.* Perhaps we should say this more often," he says. "Perhaps we should put this on a plaque in our apartment. Perhaps this should be a mantra we begin to collectively utter to one another. What do you say, Fania?"

"I think saying it once a week is good enough," I tell him. "I don't know that we need to be hammering into metal compliments about your appearance. I didn't marry a dictator."

"Nevertheless," he says, "Hermann's beauty can in fact bypass locks. A simple fact. It was true in Vienna. True in the forest. True in Canada. True here also at the beach."

"This is your official answer? That you used your physical beauty to unlock all the locks in this building?"

"What? Is this Nuremberg? Am I on trial?"

"Look who's making the inappropriate jokes now!"

"Hermann's beauty is *considerable*," he says.

"The word *considerable*," I remind him, "involves greatness. A great weight. A great distance. A great effort. Something that occupies a great space."

"In this case, Fania, Hermann's beauty is considerably great. After all, here we are, inside this nice new building. Are we not here? Are we not overlooking the ocean? Were we not, an hour ago, outside this building, wondering about what was inside, wondering about the views?"

This is true. We are, at the moment, the sole two people inside this building, which has over the course of the past few weeks begun to rise story after story into the sky. We have competing wagers on the eventual name. The apartment buildings and hotels on Ocean and Collins are either named in service of imperial aspirations, like the Palace, the National, the Continental, or they are, like ships, or cars, named for women—the Leslie, the Ava, the Janet. Such optimism is either a monument to the future or a headstone marking the death of the past. I have voted for the past and Hermann the future.

When we first arrived in Miami on our motorcycles ten years ago, making loops of the Rickenbacker, mooning at the Biscayne, which was yacht marked, indecently blue, thousands of hand mirrors fused together on the surface of the water, I thought if only I might go up into the sky to look down into the water, only then could I understand what it was I was looking at. When I tell Hermann that this is what I'm thinking—our first impressions of the water—he tells me that this is why he has brought me here.

"You were upset," he says. "And so I wanted to make you less upset."

"I was not so upset that I wanted you to break laws."

"Again: Who will suspect Hermann?"

"You have too much faith in other people. Everyone will suspect you. For one, you often tell strangers very intimate details of your life."

"Only as a way to establish that I have nothing to hide."

"And these details quite frequently involve lawbreaking."

"Law-*flaunting*," he says. "Very different than law*breaking*."

"This will not keep you from being a suspect," I tell him.

"And what will they say? That an older Jewish man broke into this building, which was locked three times on the outside, and then somehow broke into this elevator, which was locked on the inside and the outside, and made it take him to the top floor, to the penthouse unit, and then broke into this very apartment, which was, as you saw, locked another two times? And then what? The police would search for an elderly Jewish man? Every person in Miami Beach would be a suspect."

"What is the alternative to this scenario, Hermann? That you flew here?"

"And who is to say that I did not?"

"This will be your defense when the police come for us? That you flew through the air into this penthouse? They'll take you to the insane asylum. Which, Hermann, is probably a blessing for both of us."

He puts his hands on my waist. "Look around you," he says. "No one is coming for you."

"It is actually very quiet," I say. "This whole place, at night, it's very quiet."

"Because it's empty," he says. "No one knows to look here. That means no one will come."

"In the greater sense, perhaps."

"In all senses. Eyes and ears and organs and dimensions."

"Oh good Lord, Hermann, you read one play in English."

"I was, at one point, need I remind you, Fania, actually employed as a merchant, not exactly in Venice, but close enough. *A Merchant in the Greater Venice Metro Area.* Or *An Occasionally Employed Merchant in the Vicinity Somewhere Near, but Not Exactly in, Venice.* It is not such a wild thought to believe it was about me."

"Yes, Hermann. Shakespeare wrote about you. Three hundred and fifty years before your birth, Shakespeare was struck by an image of you in the future, fixing your hair atop a Harley-Davidson and admiring your own beauty in every one of the world's mirrors."

"My beautiful hair," he says.

"Oh my goodness, Hermann, you are irrepressible."

"Could you imagine the play he would write about me!"

"A tale about a foolish Jewish man circumnavigating the globe for eighteen continuous years, burdening kind strangers with awful tales of grief and tragedy."

"Burdening kind strangers, yes. But in a humorous way!"

"Eventually," I say, "someone will come and find that we have been here. Someone will always come to a place like this."

He tells me that he believes we have many months before this is the case. He has surveyed the state of the construction and has done, he tells me, a good deal of counting. Only two dozen apartments are completed. Some two hundred remain. This includes the units that will eventually render dark our own view of the water, which is visible from the kitchen of our apartment, a building directly beside this new building.

This is why he has done this, why he has gained entry, he tells me.

"You are so upset about the new building," he says. "Upset about the water going away. Upset you can't look out anymore. So what did I do? I told you, didn't I, that I'm going to get you a new place. Hermann will get you a new place. You say that this is impossible. We do not have the money. You say that we are lucky to have had the water for as long as we did, being that we are, in your words, poor and foolish and ill built for the heat. So what does Hermann do? I bring you here. To the top of the world. Easy as that."

"I have very little faith, Hermann, that you understand American real estate laws—"

"What is there to understand, Fania? I have found my way inside. It is mine. I have put the stake into the ground like the astronauts do."

"That was on the moon, Hermann. Astronauts don't just go around putting flags in people's living rooms."

"Are we not closer to the moon, Fania? Tell me this much. Have we ever been closer?"

This apartment is for sale at a price that would require me and Hermann to live a dozen more times, one life for every lock he has outmaneuvered, and to carry with us into those additional lifetimes all our meager savings, and perhaps for both of us, in all these subsequent lives, to conjure some wildly profitable investment scheme so that we may, in the luckiest life, end up here, as owners of this part of the sky. It is an airborne palace—six rooms, all of them positioned in such a way that the curve of the bay is never out of view. Our regular, legally rented apartment lies twenty-one stories below. A distance of lifetimes, the bird's path; on the new earth, the king and queen live in the sky.

I have no real affection for the water. Nor do I have any genuine affection for this place, for Miami, for the heat, the wretchedness of the sweat of my neighbors, for the constant need for sun protection, for the endless kibbitzing and rallying and keening for the dead, for the gathered congress of us mourners. But now I know there are nine things that brought me back to life.

First, the quiet of hiding, our apartment on the Herminengasse, days on end with rotten potatoes, my last hours with Moses, then the opposite of quiet, which is to say the storm-foot of plunder, a gun in my mouth that did not fire, and then my hunger, which existed as an appendage, a third pregnancy, and behind door number four the boy rabbis of America feeding me bread in the forest outside Łódź, as if I were a bird, one bite at a time, and five, the inverse of prayer, a Kaddish read backwards, as if to fold the ancient words inside out might keep my children alive, keep Arnold with me, and leave me afterward heaven-shot, leave my babies in other lives, on separate trains, and then, of course, number six, six being the devil's digit, which is to say the number of murder, so many imagined murders, an infinity of murdering, a continental murdering spree of the mind, then luck—the luck of Canada, the luck of snow, the luck of winter, the endless slow, quiet luck of the cold. At number eight, creation begins again. In my second life, it is the hotel that brings me to life. And Hermann: I will never tell him this, because to tell Hermann anything resembling a compliment is to shuttle him into an orbit from which he will never descend. This is number nine—the water here.

I have gone into the water only once. I had to be taken out of it by the military. We were here a month, having arrived into a profound heat such as I had only experienced in those moments of extreme pain when my nerves suffered a confusion of polarity, when the heat of childbirth, for instance, became so intense that I felt all through my body as if I were being run across an ice sheet by some large and invisible hand. Here I was on Collins Avenue, an imposter in my own life, standing beside a motorcycle, beside Hermann, speaking English with an unfamiliar accent, eating grilled corn from a street vendor, dressed in a loose white dress, like a girl on the advent of Communion, one who had, in that moment, caught sight of herself—in the mirror glaze of shopwindows, in the eyes of passersby, in the glare of Hermann's sunglasses—and saw nothing she understood. This was me at fifty-four, costumed as a Christian child on the outstretched finger of North America, the owner of a motorcycle manufactured in Milwaukee, Wisconsin, marooned into a sun-drunk future, explaining to Hermann that I desperately needed to go into the water, that I was melting, that the constant crash of ocean tides had begun somehow to drive me crazy with longing. And here I was, here she was, rushing, almost running, across the hot sand, which was, she believed in that moment of delirium, the sand on the shore of Elysium, bypassing every iteration of near nakedness, a nakedness that seemed to her to be the inheritance of the victors of war, until she found herself joining them, having flung off her dress, having waded in the nude out into the warm sea, thinking out loud that this surely was the moment she had come unwound into equal parts misery and heartsickness and war-ruin and, yes, elation; if you had seen me that day, as a moment later Hermann did, you would have seen, whoever you are, a woman caught in celebration. Only a moment this lasted. Behind me, the long stripe of the horizon, which is an illusion of endlessness, a cousin of infinity—a feeling almost without end in a place almost without boundary, which was, I thought then, what it had felt like to hold Sonja in my arms on the first day of her life. For an hour in that house in Vienna, which was my mother-in-law's house, I felt exempt from time. I had given birth to Sonja in the room where my husband had been born, in a large room, in a large bed, in winter, where outside the door my husband's father sat at the piano to play the slow movement from "À Thérèse." Did she know this? Is it possible that she knows it now? In this second life of hers, does she hear this music and think of me? Was there ever a moment to tell her this? How does one ever tell a five-year-old anything true, especially a five-year-old who knows nothing but war and hiding? In my dreams she is a musicologist, just as the woman, my Doppelgängerin, told me in Montreal, and it is because she was born into the music. I did not go with her to the train station. I cannot remember why this is so. In the Miami Beach of 1979, where I wear white and speak perfect English and fling off my clothes and run mad into the water, I have begun to lose memories of Europe. A good development, Hermann tells me. Memory is a weight, he says. He is not wrong, but he is not correct. Memory is the skin of existence— layers deep, always leaving us. I watched Sonja go. I was behind the window on Herminengasse and saw her on the sidewalk with her tiny suitcase, her arm extended as far as it could go, lengthened skyward. I had her in my sight until they turned to walk on Franz-Hochedlinger-Gasse, parallel to the Danube. Before they turned, she was caught in sunlight, just her, my daughter at five years old. It was, everywhere else, raining. My daughter walked away from me into death caught in a sunlight that blinded me. This is what I'm thinking about in the water of Miami that day. Why didn't I go with her to the station? What could have possessed me to have done this? The salt of the ocean stunned me. East beyond me lay the Bahamas; south the stone walls of El Malecón in Havana, where gulls launch themselves off the parapets, flaunting their freedom. And beyond that, the dagger in the hand of the sea that is South America. Hermann stands watching me, laughing, a cigar in his mouth. This is my girlfriend, he is telling people, saying it in Yiddish, because here, on the beaches, there is as much Yiddish as there ever was in Vienna. This is my meshugene girlfriend. I'm without my clothing and he thinks this is wonderful and greatly humorous and not at all worthy of concern, even as I begin to walk farther away from him, to a spot where I can no longer stand, and where I am swimming now, oh, that first step when one reaches with her toes and finds nothing to hold on to, here I am being carried out into the tide, when was the last time I was swimming, it must have been before the war, I'm thinking, maybe in Trieste with Arnold before I was a mother, my head is underwater and I am a seventeen-year-old student in Russian literature and beside me is Arnold Alterman, amateur cellist, clerk in the office of Alterman Fertigwaren, and perhaps it's at this point that Hermann realizes that he has to come for me, that I will likely keep swimming until I thread the strait between Las Tumbas and Cancún and reach the mainland. Maybe then I might go in search of Sonja. Later, when I'm brought aboard a coast guard clipper, the exact kind I can see at this moment from the window of this penthouse apartment, carving arrows into the tide break, he'll ask me why—why did I keep swimming, where was I going, and although I'll have an answer, it isn't an answer I can say out loud.

"For now," he says, standing in darkness before the window, "you can see the water."

"Yes, I can," I say.

"And this will make you happy," he says.

"It will?"

"I am telling you, yes, this is what you need. Ever since the building went up, you have been miserable. As if the war has started back up again."

"Not that miserable."

"Nothing Hermann can do makes you happy any longer. Not eating delicious food—"

"Hermann, of all the things to bring up: your cooking is a crime against nature."

"This is not untrue, Fania. Yes, perhaps my cooking violates certain provisions of the Geneva Convention. But nonetheless, I have tried cooking for you, I have tried music—"

"The music is always so sad! And also accompanied by such wretched stories! This piece was composed in a prison camp and then everyone who wrote it was gassed. This other piece was written as its composer wheezed to death from tuberculosis. Beethoven wanted to kill himself; instead he wrote this piece of music. And I'm supposed to feel comfort from this? This is what you're always asking me: Do you want to listen to this soundtrack to misery? Do you want to hear what a man might compose in his last hours on earth? Do you want to listen to this while I read to you letters the composer wrote to his dead children?"

"You are telling me that you dislike Beethoven?"

"Give me something happy!"

"What good is happy music?"

"To make one happy! To create happy feelings! To make one want to dance!"

"But I am, as you've told me, a terrible dancer!"

"Hermann, this is a very lovely crime you have committed on my behalf. We should go home, though."

"I will gladly commit a million crimes for you, Fania."

"You do not need to try so hard," I tell him, taking his hand.

"You are always saying that we have no money, we can't have nice things, only sandwiches from Wolfie's, only those things that are free, like sunlight, like the view of the ocean, like watching other people having vacations on the decks of fancy hotels. Apparently in America these days, one must pay for sunlight and water. So here is a multimillion-dollar-apartment view. Freshly stolen. Just for you. Until someone moves in, you can come here and see it when you want."

When for the next few minutes I say nothing, he grows worried, he is always so worried lately, and asks what I'm thinking, and when I tell him, finally, that I'm thinking that we will, very shortly, find ourselves in the back of a police cruiser, charged with a kind of real trespass that will see us aging in an American prison, he thinks I'm joking, just as he has believed I've been joking all this time. For instance, the key around my neck, which he discovered for the first time only a week after we'd left Montreal ten years ago, after we'd reached the lip of the shore in Vancouver, where the yawning maw of the Lions Gate lay before us. There, the twin mountain peaks exploded from the earth around us, peaks that the Squamish, who had lived on that land for twenty thousand years before the Europeans claimed it as their own, called the Twin Sisters. I kissed him later that day for the first time in a hotel room that had, on its wall, a photograph of an owl's eye, as if to remind us that we were in proximity to a certain wildness here at the edge of the continent, but which I understood differently, as a message to tell us that we were, all of us, under the constant witness of someone, all were under the eyes of the Twin Sisters and those who named them, even if they were long gone, even if the only things on earth that remembered them were the birds, like this owl, that were born with the memories of their ancestors. I had, I thought, fallen in love with Hermann. I told him he was the first man I had kissed in thirty years, and he said, smiling, that he wished it were true for him that he had not kissed anyone else, but he had, in fact, kissed many women across many countries, after all, he had driven two motorcycles around the world for eighteen years, one for him, and one for God, and he had, all that time, worn many gorgeous leather jackets, and was, as everyone knew, a great, world-famous beauty. I knew this to be a lie. Anyone in my situation, this close to his lips, would have known it to be so. More importantly, he knew, when he said it, that I understood it to be a lie. And what were we to do then? When he found the key sometime later, slung around my neck, resting against my chest, having been hidden beneath my coats and sweaters, I told him that it was the key to my house in Vienna, which was true, as true as anything in my life had been true, and that I had come to have it in a way I would never admit to, he did not believe me. And when he sees me, standing against the window of this apartment in Miami, toying with this key, he does not believe it is the key to anything real.

"Maybe you would like us to go back to Vienna, so you can use your key," he says.

"Would you take me?" I ask.

LATE evening, in our small apartment on Collins Avenue, the radio plays a piece of music his daughter loved. He has said this tonight very casually, without emotion, and it is the first I have heard of this daughter, whose name is Vera—forever after always this, always the present tense, *her name is Vera*, what is the harm in the belief of the ever-presence of love, in the ever-presence of daughters, of earthly creatures, of Vera, he asks, even if the dominant memory he has is not of her birth—in the bedroom of a house in the Leopoldstadt; hours of agony; hours of his torturous commiserations with an unfamiliar and hostile God; hours in which he seemed capable of communicating with all the fathers before his father, and during which all the voices of these dead fathers came to him, one following the next, buried as they were in every corner of Europe, in graveyards turned over by tank tread and vandals, and where he has driven his motorcycle, a fact he will never tell anyone but me, especially because the message of these fathers was quite simple, run, run, run, they told him—but the memory that returns and returns is of the day police came to the house to remove the family piano, which Vera, nine-year-old Vera, watched from the sidewalk with a mixture of confusion and childish impatience as the instrument swayed limply above the Wipplingerstraße. They are taking it away to tune it, he tells her. This is a very funny way to tune a piano, Papa, she says to him. Up until her death, he explains, I lied to her. In the dark at the very end, I told her we were being made into stars, that this way, our dark train car, was the way to the building where this was going to happen. This is the worst lie a father can tell, a lie about history, a lie about life, a romancing of treachery and violence.

The record player is between us on a wood stand. Lately, we have done this in the evenings—gather around this small machine, as if it were both piano and pianist, inert machine and alighted incarnation of his ever-present Vera. Some nights, the connection between the receiver and the speaker begins to fail, and the music is interrupted by interference, a crossing of signals—the phantom noise of night, the sound of a room somewhere very far away in which a man is walking with wooden shoes; once, a woman's voice called out *Antonio! Antonio!* Tonight, while it plays, Hermann watches me, and I assume the part, which is to say I understand what is expected as the one listening—an expression of being moved, of being taken up by the shoulders by the pianist's hands, by Vera's hands, and lifted up out of this apartment and into the sky above Miami.

We listen in darkness, on opposite sides of the room, on twin leather couches that adhere to our skin, in sweltering heat, amid the palm chitter. It used to be that I could sit here and see the bay, large and peaceful. Now, instead of the water, there is the dark skeleton of the Collins Condominium Complex, a dark slab that obscures my view. Beneath us, high-pile carpet the color of sea-foam, which is the unofficial color of this city, this place we have come to by way of wind or momentum or accident or some other force I have yet to understand.

When we left Montreal, he asked me where I wanted to go, and I told him only that I wanted, if I could, to be warm. Give me the sun, I said. Please take the cold out of me, I said, take Montreal from my blood. Get me out of this hotel basement, I told him. Get me out of this frozen cafeteria. Put me in the heat, I said to him. I believed then that the sun would burn away the past. A foolish and childish and insipid thought, yes. A wonderful thought, also.

What I really wanted I could not say. Not even to Hermann. Because what I wanted was to exist in four futures at once—one for Moses, one for Sonja, one for Arnold, and one, also, for Hermann. It was the case now that I had known Hermann for longer than I had known my husband and my children. Eight years of the old life, ten years and counting in this new life, in Miami Beach, in the ever-present sea-foam.

Here, we are immediately understood. We are standing at the terminus of a migration, and like all migratory species, like song-birds, lemon sharks, like antelope, we find ourselves in a state of torpid longing. My first few days in the city I am stopped on the street by people my age, born in the bracket of darkness, thinking I am someone they have lost. I do not yet have the costume for the weather, or the skin for the heat, and I am, very clearly, the person to stop and ask, the new person.

From the back you remind me of, from the side you are the spit-ting image of, the mirror image of, I saw just your arm and I had to ask, I heard your voice through the noise of the crowd. I am told my walk is the same walk as, my mouth takes the same sad shape as, my expressions of boredom and worry and hunger are the same as those of the people I am searching for. All of which is to say that there are others. Everywhere, we are told this. We are told this in German, in Russian, in a Yiddish that schmilzt in the heat, we are told this in the bad and beautiful English we all share, that there are others. At a back table at Pumpernik's, a man comes to our side, looks dra-matically at Hermann, and then tells me, in a voice I have not heard since girlhood, not to stick my head in a wolf's mouth, shtek nit dem kop tsum volf in moyl arayn. Meaning: beware of this town, this momentary wave-dream of sunlight, the optimism of sea-foam. Or, having taken one look at Hermann: beware of men playing you pretty music in rented rooms late at night while telling you tragic stories of their lost daughters.

When Hermann is finished playing me the music, he asks what I think. The music is by Chopin, who he tells me was apparently known to have harbored poor feelings about the Jews. *So? Chopin? What do you think? More? Anything? Did Chopin kill you? Did Chopin kill your heart with his icy Polish beauty?* And when I tell him the truth, which is that I would rather have an alligator consume me whole than listen to any more music like this, that I consider this music to be the music of betrayal, a dispatch from a dead-letter office rescinding an invitation to all possible futures, he tells me in response that I am missing the point, that there is beauty inside this, that to deny the music is to give purchase to the treachery. Yes, he is telling me, Chopin did not like the Jews, and yes, there are some very bad details about us in his letters, and a great many slurs against us, that we are in control of all the money and thus that we are the source of all his miseries et cetera, et cetera, but we are to understand this, he says, as a product of the times, not as the seed of something that might grow to strangle us, something that might grow one day to send the worst of Germany into my house to spit on my infant and stick a gun into my mouth. No one is going to come and arrest you for thinking the music is pretty, he wants me to know, as if this is something I am worried about.

What he really wants to tell me is how, when Chopin died, his sister took his heart from his body, his actual heart, preserved it in cognac, and brought it with her by horseback some sixteen hundred kilometers to Poland, where it was installed in the Church of the Holy Cross.

"It is still there," he says.

"What is still there? His heart?"

"His heart is in Poland, yes."

"You're speaking of this metaphorically? Or actually."

"His actual heart is interred inside an actual church in the actual nation of Poland."

I think about this awhile. "Does it play the piano?" I want to know.

"Ah, Fania, you are always making jokes out of the most severely inappropriate material."

"An organ playing the piano," I say. "The Europeans have thought of everything."

"Again with the bad joking," he says.

"I suppose that would be worth a visit back to Europe," I say.

"If only I knew how to pretend to laugh," he says, "you would feel like a famous comedian."

"I suppose one would need a very good piano stool, though, to get his heart so that it could reach the keys."

"Fania, you are drawing out this joke to its death."

"Do you think if you talked sweetly to the heart, Hermann, it would play you 'Heart and Soul'?"

"If you must know, this particular nocturne is one my mother played for me, and my wife played for my daughter, and which now, I play for you. It is special and very gorgeous and speaks of the heart."

"A heart," I say, "it appears, which was cut out of the composer's body and delivered by horseback into Poland. Ah! I love European fairy tales!"

I have exasperated him. A rare occurrence. Perhaps it is because I know this already. Perhaps it is because I lived once with a man who often did exactly what Hermann is doing now, who played me records, probably this record, who held me hostage with European treasure and watched with expectation for the effect, for my face riven with emotion, for me to cry out in heart pain, in premature mourning, at the beauty, which, even now, evades me. Not the superficial beauty, which is easy to hear, it is obviously lovely, all the tinkling piano notes, the redolence of certain aristocratic staterooms, the periodic detour into three-quarter time that we all understand as being the soundtrack of romance, it is so lovely even elephants at the circus are known to become overwhelmed while dancing to this. I know better. I know, for instance, that during the war, the Polish were so worried that the Germans would steal Chopin's heart for themselves, it was secreted away into the forest, only to reappear again after the war, having lived outside the body for ninety years, imbued because of this with new power, the power of being hidden, of hiding, of continuing to supply blood.

Which is not, I think, unlike what the young people in this city believe about us. We are invited to talk to children in schools, to lift our shirtsleeves in order to show our having been marked, to pass our bodies around as if we are a piece of the cloth on the coat of Napoléon on the day he disembarked at Trafalgar to survey the ruin of his men, we are moon rock, shuttled to the surface, singed on the edges by reentry. The metaphors nauseate. Show me, I want to say, tell me where the power is, explain to me how to use the power! These people are all the ages my children would have been. Moses in 1979: forty-one years old, gray at the temple; when I dream about my son, whom I cannot remember any longer, he appears to me as sound and only sound, but it is a sound that makes a noise only in Vienna. Where else on earth but Vienna? Sonja in 1979: forty-six years old in the Stadtpark before the statue of Schubert, explaining to her children the art of dying young. This is what I see. This is the power.

Chopin had been afraid of being buried alive, Hermann tells me. One needed to test for death, to stitch the heart, to determine what was life and what was its opposite, what was coma and hibernation, Winterschlaf, winter sleep, and what requires the tombstone. His was a widespread fear, says Hermann. I don't think it was the burial that scared him, but the possibility of waking after the burial. Maybe these are the same ideas. Because of this, it was required of those who saw him to his death that they open his body after he passed to make sure he was gone.

I do not believe this, I tell Hermann. It is more likely, I say, that Chopin was batty, a word that Hermann is only beginning to disentangle from the word for the animal, Fledermaus in German, which in English translates literally to a fluttering mouse. He cannot see it any other way—that to be crazy is to be a fluttering mouse. On occasion we see bats from our motorcycle at night, casing sycamore groves, alighting in formation, in biblical curtain-clouds swarming swamp waters. To see this is to see a great beauty, even if up close, yes, I agree with you, whoever you are, they are terrifying, tiny monsters with human faces—the human face after it is possessed by demons. To see them all at once, however: miracles! Even if it is a convocation of demons. Anyone who has seen a parade of enemy soldiers toting their rifles knows that menace can on occasion assume beauty, which is why, I want to tell Hermann, one cannot trust music this beautiful. My choice of words is no accident. He is especially fearful of bats. I have only seen him scared twice in ten years. Once at the border to America, when it became clear to me either that he was carrying false papers, or that he, like anyone having crossed so many borders, was worried the Americans would think his papers were false and decide he could not come with me, that we would be separated. The only other time I saw fear in him was in the presence of bats—thousands of them exploding from the limpid murk of Lake Okeechobee. At the sight of this, he screeched into the air—the sound of a man at the verge of death, the sword looming above the neck—but it was also the sound the bats made back at him. I understood what he did not, that it wasn't the animal that scared him, but of what exactly the animal reminded him.

He begins the nocturne again despite my protest.

"Would you like such a thing?" he asks me.

"Would I like, in the moments right in between life and death, to be disemboweled, as a matter of ending debate on whether I am alive or not?"

"When you put it this way, Fania—"

"Oh yes, Hermann. Please. Let's go out tomorrow and find an attorney so that we can add this to my will."

"Since when does Fania have a will?"

"Of course I don't have a will, Hermann. What do I have to leave to anyone?"

"You have an apartment. You have a library of books. A collection of fancy European skin creams you have secreted from the hotel," he says. "You have a wonderful and powerful American motorcycle capable of very high speeds and capable of inspiring both jealousy and fear. And you have me, of course."

"Am I allowed by law to bequeath you to someone? To the grandmothers at Pumpernik's, maybe? They would adore you. And your powerful beauty."

"Thank you, finally, for acknowledging the truth."

"You are an impossible man," I tell him.

"Of course," he says, "you have a key that you say opens a lock in a door in Vienna."

"Not this again," I say.

"Delirium," he says. "Dreams!"

"It is not a dream!"

"This is not the world to come! You cannot go waltzing back to the old Vienna and expect your key to open every door."

"I'm not an idiot," I say. "I'm not talking about the world to come. This is a phrase for little children."

"This key is a key to nothing."

"It does open the door," I say. "I don't know why this is so confusing to you. It is a key. Its purpose is to turn the lock."

"It used to open the door," he says. "This is a matter of grammar. A conjugation of possibilities."

These are the notes to the real music of our life: this argument, these rehearsed parts, this inanity about the conjugation of possibilities, which is a phrase he is very proud of, his greatest accomplishment in the English language, the title perhaps of his American memoirs. This is an argument I can play without any sheet music.

"Believe me," I tell him. "This key works."

"The locks have been changed. I promise you."

"I told her that she was not, under any circumstance, allowed to change the locks."

"And she agreed," he says.

"She did agree."

"Because you had her locked inside a massage room in the basement of a hotel in a foreign nation."

"For some reason, you make this sound terrible, Hermann."

"This is what rogue nation-states do to extract false confessions."

"The woman agreed. She agreed readily when I told her she could not change the lock."

"Did you have a weapon?"

"No!"

"No warm stones to soothe the spine?"

"Of course I had warm stones."

"No weapons, then, aside from the rocks in your hands."

"Are you asking me if I murdered her?"

"You are the one who has brought up murder," he says.

"Did I murder the woman? Is this what you're asking?"

"I would not have thought of it, Fania. But now that you've raised the subject, it must be on your mind. You can tell me," he says. "If it is true, I will want to know."

"That I am a murderer?"

"Is it such a terrible question to ask?"

"Yes, Hermann! It is a terrible question to ask!"

"Listen," he says. "If you murdered her, sweet Fania, if you murdered this terrible little Nazi woman, and you are in need of hiding out in some very beautiful forest hideaway, or escaping very rapidly to a country where you will not be found, like New Zealand, or South Dakota, if you are in need of someone to dig a deeper grave for you—"

"Then what? You'll help, Hermann?"

"I was going to say that if this is true, I will go outside and get help for you."

He has made me smile.

"Everyone is the villain of someone's story," he says.

"What is that supposed to mean?"

"It means that if it happens to be the case that you murdered this woman in your hotel massage suite with hot stones, then you are, for her, a villain, and that to me, Fania, you can continue to be the same wonderful person."

"I didn't murder her, Hermann. Of course I didn't murder her. I am a good person. I am a good person who does not murder people. I just spoke very sternly to her and she happened to give me the key to her house."

He is smiling. Behind him, the music has continued to play. It has moved into a new part of the piece, one I have not heard before, or a part, more likely, I have decided not to remember, and this has begun to color the room blue, this new section has put me on the sidewalk outside Hermann's house on the Wipplingerstraße, where the piano on which this piece is being played hangs overhead, not swaying exactly, but dangling, as dictators do at the end. Beside me is Vera, small Vera, a child forever with her head held aloft to see this piano at the end of a noose, while shrikes circle. If I crouch, so that we are eye to eye, perhaps we might be able to speak. She is talking to me, saying a hundred times the same words, wo ist mein Papa, wo ist mein Papa, wo ist mein Papa, where is my father? It is morning in Vienna. If I walk east until I reach the opera house, and then north along the edge of the Stadtpark, past the beautiful homes, and the hotels where I would likely work if I were to live there again, and then west again along the river, I could go home. The music has done it. The house is empty. The key does not in fact work. Hermann has been right the whole time. I am banging and banging on the door, and perhaps this is the end of this godforsaken piece of music, the end of Chopin forever, this endless capture of night, my furious banging, or maybe I have, after all this time, figured out how to split myself into four places at once—the impossibility of life before, the immeasurable misery of life during, the darkness of the life after, and this blue, blue life of the present.

No more of this, I tell Hermann. He has his eyes closed. The music has paralyzed him. Oh, the beauty. Oh, the poisonous beauty. What to do with Jewish boys and the deathly venom of pretty music? You look like a prisoner, I tell him. But he hears me wrong.

"I look like a prince? Ah, Fania. You are a doll. How did I ever live without you?"

Wo ist mein Papa? Well, he is here, Vera, on the edge of the continent, in an elevator shooting skyward above the Miami Beach of 1979.

Hermann wants a party, and so Hermann throws a party. This is nights later, in the empty apartment above Collins Avenue. Ten couples have joined us. We gather first in the darkened belly of the construction site, in what will eventually become the parking garage, a space we have descended into by way of ladders, all twenty of us climbing our way into the darkness. We have come in bright polyester, in Chanel perfume, in the coconut scent of Miami sun protection creams. We have come in various states of misgiving and anticipation, which is, in America, the only way that one is ever truly affiliated with Hermann Pressler. He smuggles us up in pairs, twenty-two stories in the dark inside a rigged box that tonight he calls his space shuttle. "Go back in time to Vienna," he tells our friends during this trip to the penthouse, "go back in time and tell my father at his sewing machine that I have become a spaceman! Tell my mother at the steam iron that her son has gone into orbit! Look at me," he cries in the elevator, "look at me, look at me!"

A shock of the new world: here, there are friends. It seems impossible that they would have appeared at all in our lives, that they would have chosen us, but here they are, my first genuine friends since childhood, clutching my elbow, laughing in my ear as we rocket upward. We have come from work. We are professors of literature, department store clerks, a hotel masseuse, we are radio announcers, retirees, inveterate correspondents into the void, translators from the original languages into English, we are women and men begging consulates for information.

Beside me, my friend Rahel cups her hands around her eyes and pushes her face to the new window facing south, where outside there is nothing but the black of the water and the periodic mess of tides.

"This is the first truly illegal act I've made as an American," she says. "Despite what I have been accused of in the past, this is my first really illegal act ever, in fact."

"If you like," I tell her, "we can go back down to the street. This is Hermann's idea of fun, not mine."

"Oh no," she says, turning to me. "This is thrilling. Positively thrilling. After all the accusations, it is a relief finally to know what it feels like. Do you think they will come for us?"

"The police?" I ask.

"Anyone. Do you think anyone will come for us? Or do you think up here we are all finally invisible?"

Until not long ago Rahel worked as a pediatrician in an office not far from this apartment. When I met her, years ago in Lummus Park, she explained that she had begun to enter the grandmotherly period of the pediatrician's life, which meant, she told me, that her current patients were the children of her original patients. "Certainly, this is a blessing," she said. "I recognize this, of course. The cycle of life, the miracle of birth, et cetera, dayenu, et cetera. In some way it is a function of my good work that these patients feel so comfortable with me that they might bring back their children. It is also the case," said Rahel, "that I only see these patients at their worst—full of infection and misery and wailing for God and bleeding on my waiting room carpet and cursing me for their illness. My America," she said, "is an America of illness, an America of fever and crying, an America of whining in fear against the impending needle. Which is understandable, of course," she told me. "Who is not afraid of the needle? But then, my little patients, they see me in the aisle of the

Winn-Dixie while I am trying to shop for cantaloupe, and do they say, oh, hello, Dr. Rahel, it is so good to see you, thank you so much for giving me my inoculations, thank you for curing my throat infection, my ear infection, thank you for bandaging up my hand? Do they do this? Of course not! At the sight of me they scream in terror! Here I am with an American cantaloupe—luxury of luxuries!—and I am scaring off the children! They think I have followed them to the grocery to poke at them with my needles. In America, I am somehow the little butcher lady. I survived for this? To be the lead actress in the nightmares of Miami's children?"

Three years ago, she retired. "I had grown too old to wrestle young children into health," she told me, "but too young to sit out in the sun waiting for death." With her free time, she had intended to travel. "Isn't this what one waits to do in retirement? To fly off to the far corners, to have my husband take a photograph of me in front of the pyramids of Giza? Except I discovered, Fania, that if one is too old to work, then one is really too old to travel properly."

She has made, to this point, only one trip, which was a trip to a place she refused to name, but which, I understood, was the place where she lived when she was young. She is from the east. This much is clear from her accent. To name the exact city, to say it aloud, to say Vilnius or Warsaw or Katowice, or to say Minsk or Kraków or Odessa, to say any of the names of these places aloud, is to fashion a weapon out of the past, and we have agreed, all of us, not to do this.

Instead, there are books. She found them for sale on a street in the center of the city where she was raised. Fifty volumes in the original binding, with nameplates on the flaps, all written in German, none of which any of us will touch. They are books by Jewish writers, some of whom I recognize, most of whom I do not. For two years she has tried to get us to take these from her, to claim what she says is rightfully ours. At every social function, every gathering in

Lummus Park, every dance in the community center, every holiday, every weekend day, Rahel pushes her library cart full of books. She is no longer Dr. Rahel; everywhere she is the Book Woman. Tonight she has pushed her cart to the top of the city, taken her books through each of these twelve locked gates, and then lined them volume by volume against the window and told each of us to take one for ourselves. "Please," she implores us. "I brought these for you. Who else in this city would enjoy them? Who else in this city would even be able to read them?" We do not accept the offer. Or maybe it is more accurate to say that we will not. Some of us get close, merely to look at the books lined up in front of us. Some of us even get close enough to get a scent of the glue wafting from the pages, and with it, the smell of those certain rooms of our childhoods. For instance, the reading room of the national library on the Josefplatz, with its frescoed winged seraphs stalled in flight above me, its Jacob's ladders reaching into the painted clouds. I went here as a girl to read with my mother. Or I went here as a mother to read with my girl. I do not know, any longer, which is true: all of it, some of it, or none of it at all.

Our continued unwillingness upsets Rahel. "You do not know what I had to do to bring these back," she tells us. "Do you know how difficult it is to wheel all these books through an airport? How hard it is to wheel these books through Miami Beach day after day? Please take one! I brought them for you!"

"You should not have done this," Rahel's husband says to her. "I told you."

"His favorite three words in English," says Rahel. "Many years of marriage and love, and this is what has become of us."

"Who brings books to a party?" says Rahel's husband. "Who brings *German* books to a party like this? I told you," he says again. "Lugging this meshugene trunk across Europe."

"Have you met my American husband?" asks Rahel. "Peppering

his sentences with words from the old country, even though his family has been in America now for five generations. His family is as American as the Morgans."

"I find Americans speaking Yiddish very adorable," says Hermann. "It's like when people train their parakeets to speak. Have you seen this on television? The bird just wants to make you happy. It doesn't really know what is coming out of its mouth. It's just a series of noises. This is all he is doing, Rahel. Making noises to please you."

"What did I do?" Rahel's husband asks. "Did I use the wrong word? Did I say something wrong?"

"No," I say. "It is all quite meshugene. You are right. All of it. All of this," I say, pointing to the apartment that is not ours, to the view that we cannot afford, to this group of improbable refugees, to this city that is ours only temporarily and will within a decade see all of us leave one by one, "all of this is sadly quite meshugene."

At home that night, I will wonder whether we were waiting to see if these books might begin to open on their own, and to start to read to us as we read to our children.

"I could not resist buying them," Rahel says later, while we are sitting in an open window above Biscayne Bay. "Here I was, walking in my old neighborhood, which looks for the most part unchanged from my memory, a fact that both comforted and horrified me. Comfort, because it is the same. Horror, because it had been destroyed and then built as a mirror of the past, except with one crucial difference—that we are all gone. The books were for sale at a cart on the road by the river. A hundred books, all in German, for sale in a city where no one has spoken German for three decades. Where did you get these books? I asked the man selling them. We could not communicate, though. He had just come to the city because of the war in his own country, thousands of miles away. He could tell me how much the books cost, but very little else, no matter how hard I tried. In Polish and Russian and German and yes, even in Yiddish, God help me, in English, in my terrible French, in my very terrible Italian. I needed to know. How did these books come to rest here, these Jewish books, written by Jewish hands, how did they come to live on this table, in this language, in this city without Jews? All the man could tell me was how much it cost. This many for one, this many for two. If I had a larger suitcase, I would have bought all of them. What can I say, Fania? It was a stupid impulse, perhaps. They are all very boring books. For instance, there is one here on the history of the horse cart in Düsseldorf. My husband, he says to me, who on earth wants to read this book? Even the horses of Düsseldorf, if you taught them to read, would not be interested in this book."

What happened, she says, is that she found herself walking home from work one night before her retirement and saw an advertisement in the window of a travel agency. "Even now I don't know if it was real," she says, "or if I imagined it as some kind of elaborate pretext to bring me back home. Maybe it was a message sent from the next world by my mother, haranguing me for not visiting her grave site. What I saw in the window was a poster of a castle near the city where I was a child. The picture on the poster was clearly shot from a helicopter, so that the city lay beneath the castle in miniature, with the river curving away west in a perfect loop, as if someone had drawn it with a pen. It fills me with a terrific shame to say this," she says to me, "to say that it was the poster in the window of this travel agency that made me do this. Or that, as I stood out front of the window, I believed that the curve in the river was bending toward me. Oh! I am embarrassed even to think these words to myself," she says, covering her face. "In the picture, there was a small group of people standing to wave at the helicopter. They were blurry, of course. The camera was very far away. Nevertheless, I stood at the window of this shop on Collins Avenue staring for so long. If there was someone inside they must have thought I was an insane person. It was a very hot night, very humid, and I was standing there in the heat sweating through my clothing. I thought to myself, quite embarrassingly, surely I must know someone in this picture. This is the foolish thought that came to me, a thought I am ashamed to say out loud. That surely someone in this picture would know me. For some reason, it seemed a matter of immense importance to me that I might find someone who maintained a memory of me and my family. Is this foolish?"

"Not at all," I say.

"Eventually, I buy these tickets. It turns out that one can procure airfare and hotel to Soviet-occupied Eastern Europe for a very fair price. Once I arrive, I find that I'm unable to speak the language with any conviction. Everyone assumes me to be a tourist, which, in some fashion, I am. To hear me order bread in a bakery, Fania, it was as if I had studied the language in a book. Soon, I find myself consumed with pain. Not psychic pain, mind you, although it does not come without pain to see the faces of all these people in my city who regard me with disgust for having the temerity to come back and remind them what has happened. Everyone wants to know why Europe struggles so much, and the answer is that Europe killed its most vibrant hope, that it gassed every last possible light away! Yet I felt actual pain, a hot, dislocating pain, which radiated up from my limbs toward my heart.

"On my fourth day in this city, I woke late, which was a problem, Fania. I had an important meeting with an important person in the claims office, or in the Office of Hopelessly Vanished Refugees, or in the Department of the Impossible, or in the Ministry of Erased Babies, or whatever they're calling it these days. I wanted to know, as you can imagine, was there anyone, anywhere, left in any place on earth, who might know me. I did not plan on explaining why it was that I'd come—that I'd seen a blurry photograph in a

shopwindow in Miami, and that I had, on the spot practically, purchased a ticket from there to here, something I had known in theory
I could have done all this time, the quick magic of air travel: get on
board in one place, in one piece, and travel in a matter of hours back
into the landscape of nightmares. I'd fallen asleep very late the night
before because I could not for the life of me get comfortable in this
horrible city, in this horrible place, even though I'd bought myself
the nicest room, in the nicest hotel, the room where the American
president would stay if the American president were for some unholy
and tragic reason marooned in my old city. Because of all this I'd
woken very late, and as I rushed to the building where I was to have
this meeting, where I was bound to get terrible news, I saw a great
crowd gathering on the main avenue, an enormous surging crowd,
filled with screaming men and women. I needed to get on the other
side of the square, but when I tried to cross, I was stopped by a
young man. Wait, he said, in English. Maybe it was then that I saw
everyone was dressed in suits and overcoats, and that everyone was
waving the old flag. To see this here, I felt cold, suddenly, even
though it was July. It became clear to me that I was asleep still, that I
was at home also, here on Collins Avenue in Miami, and that the
scene I was living in was a particularly vivid delusion, a nightmare. I
began to say this to myself. You are asleep, you are asleep, you are
asleep, and at some point a man beside me turned and said, you are
very awake, ma'am, I'm looking at you and you're definitely not
asleep. He was young, very obviously American, and I did not know
exactly what to say to him in this moment, except that he was
wrong, that he did not exist, that he and everyone here had been
vanished a long time before. There is a darkness coming, I believe I
said, also. He found this very funny. There is a certain young person
who finds anything from a woman my age humorous. The screaming came again. On the street, a series of cars were driving by, cars
I had not seen since I was a young woman, and in those cars, people

I understood finally to be actors were standing in them, ramrodding out the old Hitler salute, which I remember first seeing not far from this spot, in a small park where my first husband and I used to walk our family dog, Alger. It was this I thought of then, when it all became clear to me: a facsimile of the past, done in the exact spot of history, with all the best costumes. Sweet Alger, who frightened at car engines, at fireworks, and who dreamed such vivid dreams that I loved to watch the emotion fill his face. What happened to sweet Alger? It occurred to me then, standing here, that I both felt his presence beside me for the first time since I was a young woman, a girl practically, and also I felt his absence from me. I believe I began to cry. We had all been taken, but not Alger. He was left inside. He could not be separated from us, I recalled, especially from my husband at the time, who carried treats for him in the pocket of his raincoat. He would moan incessantly. Oh, Alger, what did they do with you?

"Stop me," she says, "if I am making you miserable with these sad stories."

"Rahel," I say, "my husband has suddenly decided to become a burglar late in his life. After this, who knows what my life will look like? Will he suddenly decide he wants to live in the White House? The Hearst Castle? The Louvre? Who knows where my life is taking me. So tell me your stories. I can handle it."

Here, she sees the key around my neck. In the midst of trying to cool myself, I have made it so that anyone can see that I have this still. That I am, among all of us, the fool who still believes she has a place back where this key might work. It emerges, rests against my shirt, which rests against my heart, which is rushing away from me, which has been rushing ever since I crossed the border into America. Rahel, however, says nothing. She knows what it is, just as I would know what it is, just as anyone in this room, or anyone in a room like this, would know.

"It turns out," Rahel says, "that what I'd stumbled into was a movie. These people were filming a movie about the extermination of the Jews. As if this might be a substitute for actual entertainment. As if one would very readily pay money to see such a thing. Of course, the movie was not about any Jewish person, per se. The Jewish people in the movie are nothing but a large group of weeping people in dirty clothing slowly shuffling into train cars, into gas chambers. Occasionally, there is a solitary Jewish boy playing the violin, or playing the piano, or singing—always something very tragic and also very musical. The movie instead is about the Germans, a small group of very good Germans. The three good Germans who are very upset about what is happening, and who want to give help to the poor, bedraggled Jews, who are, even in the ghetto, managing their own economies, selling and hawking and buying everything, and of course, playing wonderful music on their violins and their pianos.

"The filmmakers had put out word that they were looking for people to come to stand on the street and to make a ruckus and to dress up in the armbands and to cry out in joy for Hitler until their voices went raw."

"I'm guessing it was not very difficult to get people to come."

"No!" she cries. "Not at all! Thousands of people came. They needed to turn people away. This American man told me this. Evidently, it was a chance for national unity, he told me. An opportunity to feel whole again. Extras, the American called these people. What I wanted to say was that these are not extras—we are the extras. We are the ones who they called extras, I wanted to say.

"The other day, Fania, I saw that this movie was playing at the Cameo Theater here. It stars a very glamorous American movie actress affecting a terrible version of my own accent. Against my better judgment, I bought a ticket. I go in the middle of the day, thinking that I will be alone, that no one will want to see this, who here would want to relive this. Most importantly, no one will see me, no one will say, oh there is Rahel the doctor, there is Rahel the lunatic book woman who is always trying to get me to take her boring books about German horses and such. Of course, the theater is full. All our neighbors are there. Even though the movie is terrible, and does not show us as humans, the theater is full. This is how home-sick we are living in the constant sun, Fania. Halfway into the movie, I find myself. I know exactly where to look. There I am, standing in the crowd, amid the cheering masses, behind flags. Ev-eryone is saluting, and there I am. Of course, I am a bit blurry," she says. "Just like in the picture I saw in the window of the tourist shop here, I am blurry. It was me, though. I stood up in the theater full of our neighbors and friends and I went to the screen and began to tell everyone. This is me! This is me! I am in this picture! It's me! Certainly, this will not dispel any of the rumors about me and my mental state, but I was caught up in the impossibility that I had lived a life about which a movie might be made, and which I had somehow wandered into. I am certain it was me. I would know my-self anywhere."

I AM not so sure," says Hermann later that night.

We are alone in our stolen apartment. Between us on the floor, we have set up sleeping bags. The windows are open to the sea. Hermann has lit candles, which he has put on the floor around us in a half circle, and for which he has said a long and silent prayer. It is late, very late, an hour of night when, from sea level, the shade of water beyond Lummus Park and the shade of sky above it exist indistinguishably from one another. From this height, however, the difference is clear.

"What are you not so sure of?" I ask.

"Whether I would know a version of myself from that far away," he says.

"Half of your life you've been admiring yourself in the mirror—practically in every reflective surface in nearly every country on earth—and you think you would not recognize yourself on the big screen?"

"This is actually a very funny joke you've made, Fania."

"I am occasionally capable," I say.

"Rahel the Book Woman believes that she sees herself everywhere. I've heard her tell me this on many occasions. Oh, Hermann, I saw myself out in the ocean the other day, except that it was not me as I am, but me as a child, in a yellow bathing suit, diving for clamshells with my mother in Trieste. Or, in synagogue two days ago the man beside me, Hermann, saying mincha was in fact me, also, but in a beard and tzitzit and knitted yarmulke, and it was something both he knew and I knew, but which we were powerless to do anything about. Did I tell you, Hermann, I saw myself in the grocery store buying cantaloupe—it's always cantaloupe with Rahel—and I saw myself walking with all my sisters, just as we did in Warsaw or L'vov or wherever it is she comes from? All the time with this woman, Fania. She has made golems of herself in her mind and every person in South Florida is a version of her risen from some other world. This is a sign of a serious problem, Fania, a sign of darkness, a sign of a person in need of a white room and many colorful pills, not the sign of someone from whom you should take advice regarding the key to your old house."

"But I didn't tell her about the key," I say.

"She told *me* about the key," he says.

"What did she say?" I ask.

"That she saw you had it around your neck. That the fact you were wearing it after all this time indicated that you had romanticized your eventual return—a matter of childish emotions that will only disappoint you. She told me what I have told you: that such keys are very dangerous. Only babies believe in the possibility of homecoming. And she said that if you decide to go back to Vienna you will surely end up in a movie about Nazis, standing in a crowd saluting Hitler, and that your history will have become corrupted by the ideals of American entertainment. And that somehow this is how you will be remembered, as an extraneous woman in the background of a movie about three good Germans."

"I somehow think this is very unlikely," I say.

"Which part?" he says. "The disappointment? Or your ending up in a movie dressed like a murderer?"

"With every passing day, Hermann, you become more impossible."

"I think, for the record, that you would make a very great movie star, Fania."

"Thank you, Hermann."

"Although I would prefer it was not the case that you became a movie star playing a Nazi. Or standing behind one, or being menaced by one, or dispossessed by one, or frightened by one."

"I would prefer that as well, Hermann."

"If you like, we can go to Hollywood in the morning and knock on the doors of all the famous producers and demand they put you on-screen."

"It's that easy, is it?"

"With Hermann, yes," he says.

"You just knock on some doors?"

"Not anyone, mind you. If *Hermann* knocks on the door, yes. It's that easy. But it has to be done with the right sort of panache," he says. "This is the secret to most everything."

"I'm happy where I am," I say.

"You're happy here, in this stolen apartment?" he asks.

"I didn't necessarily say that," I say.

"But you're happy here?"

"I am," I say.

"In Florida," he says. "You're happy in Florida?"

"You say the word as if it's another planet."

"But this is another planet. Look around you. Do you see where we are? All of us, and all the Cubans: it's a planet of the lost."

"I'm happy here," I say.

"You never say that you are happy," he says. "In fact, in all the time I've known you, which is a number of days approaching four thousand seven hundred, I have heard you, at best, express mild satisfaction, or even more than mild amusement. Once or twice on our motorcycles, you appeared happy, but wouldn't admit to anything more than feeling excited. But never happiness."

"You've counted the days?" I ask.

"If you were me, and got the chance to spend time with you the way I do, you would count the days as well," he says.

From where we're sitting it seems wholly possible that we might be able to get a glimpse of the window of our old lives in Canada. Or even if we look long enough, a picture of the two of us arriving in Miami ten years ago on our motorcycles. What I would not do for some snow, for a sheen of ice on the sidewalk, for the cloud of my breath exploding out of my lungs in such a way as to remind me that I am living. The past, suddenly, feels within reach. When I say this, having stood to gather the view from the edge of the apartment window, with all of Collins Avenue below me and lit like a carnival attraction, Hermann says that this is a matter of age, a narrowing of certain critical neural pathways that control emotion and our vision of our own history. "Childhood can come rushing up," he says. "Not that I know what I'm talking about. After all, I am not a doctor, like your friend Rahel the Book Woman. Nevertheless, I have ideas. Or at the least, I have read certain newspaper articles in which ideas are discussed."

"I don't think anyone has ever accused you of not having ideas, Hermann. It's that you don't stop talking long enough for anyone to consider your ideas."

"First, you make a completely respectable joke about the mirrors and my own vanity. Not the most incredible joke ever heard, Fania, not something that will land you on the television, but a wholly decent joke."

"Your flattery is oppressive," I say.

"And then you tell me you are happy. Happy with our life together."

"I am *quite* happy," I say. "You're forgetting the important part."

"Then you levy insults against me. As if I deserve this."

"I apologize, Hermann."

"What I wanted to say is that I suspect that this will keep happening," Hermann says, and by *this* he means the surprise of memory. "This feeling is a way to make death feel less terrifying, just as one does not fear the imperative to sleep simply because there is a chance one might not wake," he says. To think that we all must have gone to sleep for millions of years before anyone began to think about the terror of such a thing—to vanish from wakefulness for so long, to die with the night.

"Here is where ideas of the afterlife emerge in human thought," he says. "This combination of our bodies readying themselves for the end, and our minds continuing to make stories out of the pictures left. Soon," he tells me, "you will think your mother is in the room with you, reading you stories to make you fall asleep."

"You sound like you are on the marijuana," I say.

"I am on no such thing," he says.

"Which one of our friends did this to your brain? Who gave you these ideas? Who gave you these drugs that put these ideas into your brain?"

"You think I am not capable of important thinking?"

"Important *thoughts*," I say.

"What?"

"The grammar," I say. "You made a mistake. What you want to accuse me of doing is thinking you are incapable of important *thoughts*, not that you are incapable of important *thinking*."

"Oh, Fania, you are the wisest and most lovely teacher. You are the real tzaddik among us. What would I do without you?"

"Likely, you would not have stolen this apartment. And you would have not taken whatever drug that is making you think like this. And talk like this. My God! I should record you."

"If one, hypothetically, drives a motorcycle around the earth many times, for eighteen consecutive years, and then at the beginning of year nineteen, meets the very best woman ever to have been born in Vienna, one will develop many important and beautiful ideas."

"I am far from the best woman Vienna ever produced," I say.

"You are absolutely this woman," he says. "It is not a contest. Find me a better woman. Go out and do it. I challenge you."

"So you're saying that eventually the voice in my head will turn into my mother's voice?" I ask. I am trying, as always with Hermann, to make a joke, but in the dark, he has turned serious.

"I would do anything to hear this," he says. "Short of giving my own life, I would do anything to hear my mother's voice."

"If we were to go back together to Vienna," I begin to say.

"If we were to go back to Vienna, I would have to be in the presence of the Viennese," he says.

"This is true," I say. "But it is also true that you might get a chance to, say, visit the restaurant in the Stadtpark where you had your bar mitzvah lunch."

"And you think this restaurant would jog the voice of my mother from me?"

"I think, at the least, you would enjoy a somewhat decent lunch with me."

"Which I do every day of my life in this sun-filled paradise. Why do I need to do it in Vienna?" he asks.

"This is not a suitable lunch. Delicatessens will kill more Jews than Hitler ever did," I say.

"This is a horrifying joke, Fania! The worst, most offensive joke you have ever made!"

"All I'm saying is that while it may be painful, we will come back," I say. "I don't want to stay there. I just want to visit."

"If you go back," he says, "someone will recognize you perhaps. And this person will say preposterous lies to your face. For instance, that they did not know what was happening. That they were not aware. Oh, we were not aware! We had no idea! We knew nothing at all! What crimes, what camps, what murders, what bullets in the brains of your aunties, what children gone missing, what temples gone missing, what houses gone up in flames? All of which perhaps could be true in a world without brains, which, yes, it appears, at times, is the world in which all of us are living. In the odd event, Fania, that you meet some old school acquaintance whose brain is still alive, and she or he says this to you, and maybe, while this happens, you're sitting outside the Tiergarten, or the Albertina, or St. Stephen's, and you are perhaps trying to eat a piece of overpriced Viennese strudel, then what are you supposed to do? Are you supposed to believe this? Are you supposed to argue about facts? Are you supposed to roll up your shirtsleeve and begin to enumerate moment by moment the way in which the world has ended, a process that somehow has left both you and me and the city of Vienna in relative good health? Is that what you want?"

"I think what I want is my house," I say. "My bedroom. My windows. My floorboards."

"This again," he says. "These are romantic ideas. And romantic ideas are for children."

"I'm not one of those people asking for a painting back. Take the paintings. I don't want a tiny little sculpture that my granny loved. Keep the art. Give me the house instead."

"What about this particular house?" he asks. "This house here, with all these beautiful views, and all the wonderful sounds of the sea. How about this house?"

"This house, which you've stolen? And which we're almost definitely going to be arrested for stealing? You mean this house?"

"No one is coming to arrest me," he says.

"Ah," I say. "Famous words!"

"You were happy," he says quietly. "Two minutes ago, let it be known, you said out loud that you were happy."

RAHEL has left us with two books. One, a book of poems by a young Czech dissident killed by the Soviets in Wenceslas Square, translated into German by a woman whose face peers out at me from the back flap with a certain degree of shrewdness, as if to tell me that, if only we were in the same room together, she might have something more important to tell me about these pages. The second book is a collection of photographs of European pedestrian spaces destroyed by war. It is an architectural treatise, a compendium of contrasting arguments on whether these spaces should be rebuilt as they were, or whether they should be replaced by a version of the future. The arguments, which Hermann reads out loud, are impenetrably dull, and written by men ensconced quite safely in large American cities, in American university departments, in well-lit offices where no one threatens to evacuate the building, where no team of former garbage collectors will arrive in trucks to line all the professors on an auditorium stage and murder them in full view of their students, as happened at the last school I ever attended. They are, these men, very far away from the real life about which they are writing so confidently. Implicit in their arguments in favor of the future is the claim that the grandeur of the past has always been a fiction, that the character of old Europe, of Austria and Germany especially, the sunlight on the dome on the Albertina, the shadow on the roof of St. Peter's Cathedral in Cologne, requires a new vocabulary now that such a great evil has come. It is, by this point, a question that has largely been answered, but in the dark of our stolen apartment, with the windows open and with candlelight upon us, the question does not interest Hermann as much as the pictures do.

For twenty minutes, Hermann says nothing. This is the longest I have ever heard him silent. Even in his sleep, the noise of life leaves him. Beside me in bed, he narrates his way into dreams, first in English, then in a whispered Yiddish I have always understood as the language he used to speak with his children. I am right here, he is saying, Papa loves you, tomorrow is a new future. He hunches over Rahel's book. She saw my key and put this book in my hand. A key does not always unlock what you suppose it will. This is, I suspect, what she wanted me to understand. Hermann brings his eyes close to the page, his nose to the photograph, as if this proximity, here in the dark above the ocean, might allow a bridge to form to take him from here to there. All this time you have been mocking Rahel the Book Woman, I want to say, and look at you now, Hermann, look at how interested you find her gift, look at how Rahel's book has captured you.

What captures him is this: a photograph of the Tiergarten—the Vienna Zoo—in the aftermath of its being bombed by the Allies in the spring of 1945, at the end of the war.

"To bomb a zoo," he is saying very quietly to himself, first in English, and then, for the first time since we have been with one another, the first time since his initial letter to me in Montreal, he begins to talk to me in German.

"I did not know that this happened." Ich wuste das nicht.

In his lap, Rahel's book shows the aftermath of the bombing, and in it, the body of an elephant, and it is this picture of the elephant on its side that causes Hermann to begin to weep. It is not so much, I understand, the elephant, but the combination of himself and this elephant, the combination in his mind of him and his children and this elephant, the combination of him and his children and the Tiergarten itself, lush in summer with chestnut trees and the

smell of frying dough and grilled sausages, and of course this elephant, who was, I don't need to ask, an elephant Viktor and Vera
had mooned before, had begged him on Sunday mornings to go see.

What I would like to tell him is that if he had gone back to
Vienna, as I had, in the immediate aftermath of the end of the war,
and had lived, as I did, in a shelter for displaced persons, in a home
in proximity to all our homes, in a basement room hidden from
view of those aboveground, filled almost entirely with Jewish men,
in a cold basement of the walking Muselmens of Austria, he would
have known that the state opera had been bombed as well, just as
the Albertina was, and that fires set amid the eventual Soviet occupation caused the roof of St. Stephen's to collapse. If you had come,
I want to tell him, if you had not been on your motorcycle, you
would have known all this had happened in your home. Yes, the zoo
was bombed, and yes, not only were our children taken, but the animals our children loved were taken too.

"It has been rebuilt," I tell him. "The zoo has been rebuilt. There
are new animals."

But he is beyond my reaching him. Maybe this is the reason I
begin to work on Hermann. Sit upright, I tell him, and because he
has done all that I've asked all this time, he does what I say. Close
your eyes, I tell him, and he closes his eyes. For a long while he holds
in his hands the picture of the murdered elephant. The picture
shows that the elephant died with her eyes open, a fact that says a
good deal about her courage. In my purse, I have a small bottle of
birch root cream—something to calm the nerves, to induce good
memories, to ease swelling of the muscles. I mix the birch root
cream with two drops of arnica and rub it together in my palms and
place these palms beneath his nose. Breathe deeply, I tell him. Three
inhalations, I say. And he breathes deeply three times. On the page
opposite the elephant is a photograph of the exterior of the aviary,
everything on fire—the cage house, the carousel, the carousel

horses, the concessioner's stand, the flags of the doomed regime, the stands of children's toys. He has his hand on the picture, and although I don't ask, I understand what he is doing: a hand on the picture of the past is as close as he can get.

This is the first time I've done this for Hermann. In Montreal, before we left, he asked if he could make an appointment at the hotel, if he could come and see me the way all these wealthy men had, and I refused. He would pay full price, he told me, a sum of money that equaled a good deal more than his monthly allowance check, far more than what it cost for his room at the YMHA. Here in Miami, he has asked the same question, and I have told him the truth, which is that if I were to see him as a patient, he might come apart in my hands, and that if this were to happen, I would not be able to bear to see it. And, more importantly, that I would not be able to reassemble him.

I crack him. It is not difficult to do. His body has been waiting. Beneath me, it sounds as if I have split wood. Only now does he tell me. "I have pain," he says, and he points to his back, to his neck, to his shoulders.

"One might think from the looks of me that I am a picture not only of great and profound and serious beauty, but that I am a model of perfect health. Apparently, though, eighteen years continuously driving a motorcycle is not good for the body."

"Stop joking, Hermann. For once, no jokes."

He reaches for me as he begins to come apart. As if he is falling. And maybe this is why: that life seldom provides ropes to hold. This is what I'm thinking as he disassembles in my hand. Beneath the surface, he is made entirely of scar tissue. There are no creams for this, no salves, there is no essence to breathe. When I push against him, I come up against rocks, and when I push against rocks, the dust comes away on my hands, and when I push into the dust, I understand at once that he has not survived in the way that our friends have. He has not passed through. He has not dived into the water and emerged reborn. He has not prayed alone and found solace in the idea of the temple being rebuilt. Instead, Hermann has lived inside the ruin. There is, for him, no reconstruction of the elephant enclosure, only life in the immediate moment of the rifle shot. This is what he has done on his motorcycle—revivification, not resurrection. He has held close the fire of his childhood and has never left the heat. He is, at once, the Hermann I have known all this time, with his hair slicked back, his Green Water cologne on his neck, his sunglasses folded into the front pocket of his floral shirt, his zinc-stained nose, his hunger for Automat sandwiches, his irrepressible mouth, his quick talent for friendship, his great and profound and serious beauty, his hidden and heavy sadness, and also, in pieces, he is a young groom outside the Stadttempel standing for a photograph beside Elma, who is young, and who dreams of the sea, and who has in her already the beginning of Viktor, who will take with him to the end of the world a conch that has in it the sound his mother loves most, and also she has in her the beginning of Vera, who knows, into eternity, the opening dozen measures of Chopin's Nocturne No. 7, which she will play in her head in the cattle cars through the bloodlands, and like her father and mother, will always live in the old Europe, the Europe where the Jews are alive.

This is why he refuses to stop talking, why he drove for so long. To do so, to stop, would leave him as he is now. Beneath me, he comes apart in pieces on the floor, first his hands, which have always been large for his wrists, and which when he was young easily captured an octave on the keyboard, these hands that grabbed hold of Viktor at the end, and that overturned every large shell on the beaches of Sharm el-Sheikh, of Antalya, of Eilat, of Salalah, of Mykonos, searching for what it was Viktor heard, these hands that held on to him before he vanished, and then his feet, which at the end were pocked with sand from a corner of the earth he likely never imagined as a boy, and then, just before the knocking came, his legs, his hips, his flat stomach, his polyester shirt that has on it a fury of birds, his long neck, his mouth, his small nose, and then, one by one, the rest of him, eyes, ears, organs, dimensions, and in the moments before the police come to the door, having made easy work of the twelve locked gates that separated us from the ground, which separated us from the life stolen from us and the life we in turn stole from them, all these pieces of Hermann lift up off the ground in such a way that I can see him flying off.

Three policemen come for us. They are, as they always are, very young. They wear leather gloves. They draw their weapons. Later, I will understand this as a matter of their own fear. What else can one think about a man in pieces? Hermann's mother's voice comes back to him just before his arrest. Is it true that in these last moments together I heard it as he heard it? She had been hidden from him all this time beneath the strata of his body, the layers of gathered earth in his skin, in much the way that God is both hidden to the world and glimpsed only in revelations. This is what I find beneath the dust of him: mother.

Here they are, in the Stadtpark, alone for a half hour. What can I tell you that you don't already know, she says to him. His grandfather is in the other room, his grandfather who was a bar mitzvah in Vienna, and whose grandfather's grandfather was a bar mitzvah in Vienna, and who was exiled and received again and exiled once more and carried to death under cover of darkness because it was not only illegal to live in the capital as a Jew but also illegal to die in the capital as a Jew. Look at you, his mother says, on your big day, this day you will remember forever. Look how serious and profound and beautiful you look. Look at my son. Look at you. Look at how much I love you. Do not ever forget your mother loves you.

This is it. This is what he struggled to remember.

WE are separated on Collins Avenue, where we linger for moments before each of us is put in our own car, lights whirling, and then we are broken apart. In the moments just prior, Hermann has charmed the police officers into giving him a cigarette, which, because he is cuffed, he smokes without his hands. This is the image I carry with me. My Hermann, in his sixty-fifth year, in handcuffs, in bird print, in conversation, always in conversation, his hands behind him as if he is hiding something from me, which he is. My Hermann, with a cloud of smoke between us that hangs as shrouds hang. "Don't be upset," he says, "you were right, you knew it would happen, don't cry, Fania, don't worry, I will see you back home," he says to me, "do not spend a moment of time being upset, Fania."

Before he is driven away, he kisses my cheek. Tobacco, Green Water, ocean wind, my Hermann's hair. This is the last time.

Last words. Last words.

I AM kept in a crowded room lit as bright as two suns combined, and then, without words, I am released within hours. It's the middle of the night. Or the beginning of morning. I want information about Hermann and stand for a very long time at a series of intake counters, a lieutenant's desk. "He is my husband," I say. "He is an old man, we are always together, we do not sleep apart, we have been through the actual gates of the underworld." No one here, however, will tell me anything, no one very much notices that I am there. I walk home along the beach, where even though it is dark and an hour of night in which everyone else in this city ought to be asleep, my neighbors are out in the park, in lawn chairs, on sea walls, looking out, hours and hours of this. I understand, I want to tell them, of course I understand. Sleep brings dreams, and dreams bring visits from old faces.

At some point as I'm walking, Hermann is taken from his cell, photographed against a wall that marks his height in inches, a unit of measurement he has never understood entirely, a word he understands only as a verb—to inch closer; I am inching toward you; my memories are inching away from me. From here, he is moved. First to a holding cell in a part of the building reserved for those awaiting a judge, and then, some hours later, when it is discovered not only that he had found his way inside the apartment where we entertained our friends, and where we had aligned our sleeping bags, and where, in our final moments, he wept over the body of an elephant his children adored, but that he'd also found his way inside other apartments across Miami, hundreds of them, it turns out, searching for one that I might enjoy, and that while I had carried my key around my neck for thirteen years in the hope I might somehow find the opportunity to turn its lock, he had gone for years without keys—after all of this, he is moved to a larger prison at the edge of the county. From here he is arraigned. I am not told when this happens, and because of this I miss the chance to see him in court. He is assigned a number for the second time. Also, he is given a worth. For a fee I can have him back with me at home. The fee is not enormous, but it is enormous to me. I would have to work in the hotels of Miami Beach every night for decades to afford my husband back in my house. For weeks I try to raise money. I go with Rahel and her book cart and try to interest my neighbors in books about the horses of Düsseldorf. It is a good book, I tell my neighbors. The horses have many thoughts about us. Don't you want to know what the animals think of the humans?

When he dies, he does so at night, in a cell sixty miles from our home, two days before I would have visited him for the first time. He had been unwell, apparently, long before this, in ways that were invisible to me, but must have been apparent to him. This is what the message says when it comes to my house via certified mail: Heart issues, the message says, but then again, who does not suffer this way?

Sometime long after all this—long after this very long night, long after I drive on Hermann's motorcycle to collect the clothing he wore when we were last together, and his wristwatch, and his wallet, in which I will find ink drawings of everyone he loved, drawings of Viktor and Vera and Elma and me—I will read through his criminal file and find, in a detective's longhand, a note wondering as to Hermann's state of mind. *It appears that nothing is missing, and that he has taken nothing away.* Which is, of course, incorrect, in every way. In the file was a map of the buildings. It is, as we had long joked, a list of names: the Eileen, the Paulette, the Rebecca.

IN each, the building looked to the water.
What else is there to know?

IN Judaism, a body after death is never to be left alone. I say this on the telephone to the people at the prison responsible for Hermann's body. "Do you understand?" I ask. "The dead require company, require the hands of the living. Do you understand?" Nobody ever understands. What I'm asking can't be given—for me to stay with him until burial. He's a prisoner, I'm told, a criminal. "Do you know," I tell these people, "that I have no idea where my children or my husband are buried, if they were buried, if they were not, if they were burned, or evaporated, where any part of any of them rests. My baby boy was never alone in his entire life. Now, in death, he is forever alone, somewhere else, somewhere I am disallowed. This is how it feels," I say into the phone in the middle of the night my husband dies. To die as a prisoner is to die invisibly, I know. The authorities say as much, although they say it in words that purport to mean the opposite of this. I know, I want to say, because I was, long before this night, both invisible and dying at the same time, and it is clear after a certain amount of time that I've been speaking with a series of officials just out of high school, who cannot help me, and whom I have likely harmed just by telling them the truth of life.

After all this, I take Hermann's motorcycle and drive. Can you see me on the road? Can you see me on the night Hermann dies? Can you find me, whoever you are, wherever you are holding this, in the weeks after, on his motorcycle? Here is South Florida, two hours after midnight, where the air is heavier than water, and there are flamingos gathered in the shallow canal water off Highway 41. The city vanishes and the dark is a series of automobiles rushing.

Can you see me here, America? After an hour I find myself alone in the national preserve, where there are, signs tell me, cougars in the trees. Words that thrill me. On the map, one only finds the enormous expanse of green—someone jutting two fingers into the air. The right finger is the Everglades, where I have seen alligators on the cusp of waterways in various states of delirium and engorged exhaustion, having recently swallowed some medium-sized beast or interloper. They are, in this way, not unlike my neighbors on Collins Avenue, my friends at the good end of very bad lives, aligned on the sand beneath a cloth canopy, half-human, half-SPF, watching the ocean for the sign of a pirate's sail, for the Princess cruise liner to take them across the Lethe, or for the hull of the boat that brought their parents to America breaking across the horizon, Mama and Papa hanging over the starboard railings waving a white cloth. Tonight I have come to the western edge of my map's green, parked at the edge of a preserve where signs tell me that humans are not allowed, where deep in the forest a park ranger has jammed a placard into the earth warning me that if I go any farther—which I do, of course I do, what could possibly happen to me now—I will find a wild state, true dark, pythons readying their jaws. We cannot protect you if you cross, the sign says, in hasty paint, the work, I'm sure, of a man whose only experience with terror is in the movies. As I go, I drop twine behind me, as Theseus did in the cave on Crete. I have been dropping twine behind me all my life, I think. The only difference is that tonight the twine can be moved by wind, found by others, tracked by police should they wish, once again, to put me in prison, to take my husband. All this is to say is that I know my way back.

At the mouth of the trailhead, a mangrove root grows aboveground, a spider born with fifty legs frozen before death and fossilized. The earth falls away in this state. The sea swallows the ground; the sea demands the river's water; it's always one or the other. One needs to be buried aboveground here, entombed in mausoleums, a fact that Hermann liked: Make everyone a king, he'd told me once. Bury me this way, he said, as Ramses was buried. And because I am delirious, and in mourning, and wandering foolishly in the swamps of Florida far past midnight, and because I will not be here when Hermann in buried in a pauper's grave, this is where I lay the first stone to his memory, in the arms of this big tree.

Let it be known that I tried Hermann's method. I drove my motorcycle, my beautiful and foolish and thrilling and idiotic blue motorcycle, alone from the southeast corner of the continent to Vancouver, and I found I was incapable of memory. I could not place myself into the past the way he could. I could not stand in an American forest in order to remember a Ukrainian forest, or a Russian forest, or a Polish forest, and I could not find in that American forest any hint of my mother at her stove on Grodski Street on the edge of the forest where she and all her neighbors are buried. I did not wade in the shallow seawater of Miami and feel against my thighs the shallow seawater of Trieste, nor could I retrace my steps in the hope of retracing Hermann or Arnold or Sonja or Moses out of the air. I tried, though. Oh, I tried, Hermann. I did.

Instead, try this: measure the noise of a woman's blood, a woman who has lost her children to murder and war, and see how loud the sound is. Try as you might, Harley-Davidson, you will not beat me. No matter where I drive, I can still hear the racket of my pulse over the colossal quake of the engine.

In this way, I drive backwards through 1980, from Miami to Vancouver, where at the border I feel myself coming apart as my passport is stamped, just as Hermann did at the end, in the apartment that was not ours. What was the purpose of your trip, the Canadians ask me when I come back, as if this is what I've been doing with Hermann, taking a long trip. I drive through Canada alone, through winter, where the cold hits as a relief, and where, as

I begin to freeze along the shore of the St. Lawrence River, I have the idea that every part of Hermann I saw come apart in the sun might find me and reassemble itself as I'm driving. Where else would he come for me but here, I think. But this does not happen, not here, not as I drive his motorcycle around Montreal for days, not as I park outside the Automat where I met Hermann first, not as I eat his favorite hard bread. And when I leave for good I feel what I suppose everyone else feels when leaving a good home, which is that there is very rarely enough time to close all the doors one needs to close.

I drive east to the edge of the country, to Halifax, where I come on board a ship crossing the Atlantic, and where, in my small wave-tossed cabin, I have the gray slate of the water available to me for days, and where, even here, I do not feel his eyes on me. When we reach Liverpool, I do not stop. Can you see me, here? Do you see me, Hermann, on these narrow roads, cutting through heath, rushing through Birmingham and London? Do you see me on the boat between Dover and Calais? Do you see me on a gangway, on the sundeck, holding stamped papers, wadded up and creased, do you see me in the cold on my way back into the old country?

I make it to the outside of Brussels before the bike breaks. It is March and midafternoon and I am sixty-five years old and I have no idea how to repair a broken motorcycle and so I walk some fifteen kilometers into the city to buy a ticket on a train. At the counter I wonder if he can see me, if he is judging this foolish burst of grief—whether he knows, as I lean against the window, where I am headed, or whether, on the street outside our stolen apartment in Miami, when he was cuffed by police with his cigarette dangling from his mouth, whether he understood what would happen. I wonder whether he knows that some hours after this the key around my neck will indeed work, and that, for thirty minutes, I will wander my old house at an hour of day when the front room is flooded by sunlight, this room where my family was last together, and where, I come to understand, the woman who took this house from me is no longer alive, and where I find in the room in which my children slept the sound of someone learning to play the piano, the halting, the stopping, the circling back, this brief glimpse of magic, and although there is no such child anywhere in this house playing this music, although I am hearing this music from some other life, from some other earth, I wonder whether he knows all this, whether he knew that when I left for good that I would put the key in the lock and head back home to our place at the sun-filled corner of the earth.

# Blue Cities

PRAGUE, 2002

# MOSES

IN all the rooms of my mother's house the walls are vanishing. They began to come apart, she tells me, just as the roof did, in layers, as if someone were peeling fruit. We are together, she and I, for the first time since I left Prague, some twelve thousand days have passed between us, and she is telling this to me, that the walls of her house have begun to fall away, even though I can see it for myself. Overhead, there is the afternoon, bare, not unbeautiful, the afternoon of childhood. She wants me to know that she has not yet found the right language for what has happened. Not to her house, not to her. When the walls go, she says, it's as if she is losing skin, and that any passerby can see the interior of her, which is more complicated than the neighbors understand, because, she says, she is made entirely of grief, every bone and every joint, and grief, as you know, is both invisible and also the heaviest substance on earth. Or this process is not unlike someone who has entered the house while she is asleep and found the letters sent to her by various governmental refugee organizations in response to her inquiries about the location of her family. Wo sind mein Kinder, wo sind mein Kinder? Instead of taking the letters themselves, she says, it's as if these intruders have taken only the vowels, so that nothing makes sense for them, as nothing made sense for her. All year this has happened, she wants me to know, this collapse of her house, this gradual invisibility, this theft of vowels, this disfiguring of the names of her children, this wholesale blotting out of her husband's identity, his bones, his gravestone, blessed is the true judge, and as a result, she says, she has felt as if anyone could see not just what this has done to the out-side of her, but as if they could see instead the worst parts of her memory.

As she says this to me, she puts her hand through the wall into the open air and lets the late-day rain fill a porcelain cup, which she uses to douse the fire in her woodstove. Amid smoke, she says, "I keep losing centimeters, Moses, I keep losing thickness, I lose weight, I lose my protection, I lose the color in my hair, I lose the floor be-neath my feet," and then, "here I am, in bed, in winter, in my nine-tieth winter, and I don't know where I am in all this, where the real border of me starts and where the end of me might eventually begin if it hasn't already." Through the roof, which is no longer a roof, there are birds, murmurations of birds, and "maybe it is because I am stubborn," she says, "maybe I tell myself, for once, Dina, imag-ine this is a good omen and not an omen from the dybbuks, not an omen from your wicked mother who never appreciated you, pretend this is Moses, pretend he is coming for you, pretend he is trying so hard to find you from wherever it is he is living, back from the Yen-isei, back from Magadan, imagine that he has made it so your house is becoming invisible and that you will become visible within it. And so what did I do?"

"What did you do?" I ask her.

"I did this. I went to sleep saying your name, Moses, Moses, Moses, and maybe it is the case that my wretched neighbors could not only hear me doing this, and likely thought to themselves, look at the Jew in her awful house calling out the name of the prophet in hope of some eventual exodus, not only could my idiot neighbors hear this, Moses, but they could see me as well. When the roof began to open, I told myself that if you were to fly overhead, Moses, you might eventually find my little head. Just as the birds do. Every one that passes over me makes me think for a moment that it is you peering down at me. Then I remind myself that I am only making stories so that the time may pass easily.

"And look what has happened," she says. "Here you are. Here you are."

Kadosh, kadosh, kadosh.

HER vision of it is not entirely wrong. I have indeed flown here. Over seas, over her house, down through the roof, and here I am, here I am. What happened was this: a man in New York who claimed to know my mother found me outside my apartment, after what he said was a painfully long search, mostly because he was searching in the wrong nation entirely, he was scouring the Russian countryside instead of this corner of Manhattan. To make matters worse, he told me, for days he had been buzzing my apartment hoping to get me, to find me, but all this time he'd had the wrong place, the wrong place. The wrong continent, the wrong country, the wrong home, he said. Except, the person who had the wrong address was not him but my mother. She had somehow found me here, after all this: absences upon absences. And he had letters. An entire folder of them, each of them imploring me to come find her, telling me that she was unwell, explaining that she was not dead, she was sure I had heard that she was dead, which I had, but instead she was living in a house that was flying away bit by bit, that was being stolen from her by the Czech weather, which is a weather consumed by a thousand invisible hands—these were my mother's words—that she had spent all her remaining money to hire him to come and track me down.

Is your name Moses, he asked me, is your mother, by any chance, a woman from Terezín, a woman named Dina Adler, Dina Adler of Terezín, Dina Adler of the Czech Republic, Dina Adler of Europe, Dina Adler of the past, Dina Adler of your childhood. Words from a second life. My initial impulse was to say, no, this is not my mother, my mother is someone else, she is elsewhere, or she is nowhere by now, there is no way this is my mother, my real mother, but he had two photographs to prove it. One was a picture of the two of us when we were both young, outside our house, her house, the house of childhood. In the other, she is older, and in front of the same house. Beyond her, the river low and slow and occluded by clouds.

And so I flew. I flew right away. Mother calls.

SOMETIME later my mother tells me that the neighbors have been wishing ill on her account. "All the time I see them passing and they glower at me with their wretched faces. How do I know this is the case? For one, they have always done this. If not them, then their mothers, if not their mothers, then their grandmothers. Every generation of this village has been a wicked generation. Also: I have no walls! I can see them as clearly as I can see the daylight! Perhaps they think because I am in my house, I cannot see them, even though all my thousands of bad wishes against them have come back to cost me, for my house is losing itself just as I am losing myself."

As a result, this is what happens: gust by gust, pieces fly away as she is trying to sleep. At first, she believed it was part of an elaborate dream. "My own mother," she says, "when she was nearing death, she felt the earth coming apart in slices, like a cake being tended to by a large and invisible knife, something both tempting and revolting at once, Moses, and so I told myself, Dina Dina Dina, this is death, this is the ultimate darkness, this is the hallway of God, prepare yourself, you will die without ever seeing your son again."

We move into her kitchen. This process involves walking through a dining space and also through a thicket of tall grass, for the outside has now become her inside. She puts her large stockpot on the open fire of her stove, and it is the case that what has very likely happened is that her house has come apart in the face of her inability to fix it. The home is near the Elbe, and the ground here has always been susceptible to sinking and vanishing. There has been a fire, I can see. The ceilings are singed. Just as it did in my boyhood, the river has flooded, and waterlines have left runes on the bedroom walls.

I offer to fix this. Let me call a carpenter, I tell her. Let me put up walls in your house. Let me bring you to America, where at least you will have something warm around you. I tell her about my apartment, about Žofie's apartment, where the curtains work on electricity, where her voice alone makes the water boil. At this, she bursts into laughter.

"America!" she cries. "America! As if my problems are not large enough! As if I should live this long to be shot in a grocery store parking lot!"

In the corner, amid all this, Ambrož sits smiling, as if to say, I know a thing or two about what she's going through, be easy on your mother, Moses, this is why you came. Buy her a new house, his smile says. Buy her new walls, a new roof, a new collection of good sweaters, what sort of son are you?

In the near future, if my grandson reads this, I suspect he might worry over these details. Was his grandfather constantly talking to a ghost at the end of his life? Eli, I don't want to say it was the case, but I also don't want to say it was not. What good would lying do at this point?

LATER that night she wants to talk about the distance.

"For a very long time," says my mother, "I suspected you were taken, I thought they'd got you, because you never came home, you never returned." It is late when she says this, and we have moved into the living room, and also out into the garden, where the fire in the chimney warms us but where the birds also come and go, passing through windows that are not windows. "You should know that I waited," she tells me. "Also, you should know that I disbelieved the radio every time the news was bad, and the news on the radio then was always bad, for many hundred days on end, and for many years after those hundred days. You should know as well that I put glass into the door so that if you came back I would not have to wait a moment to know it was you. Then someone came to tell me one day that the Soviets had seized you, that they put you in a truck, and that the truck drove east into Warsaw, then Kiev, then Moscow, and then farther east until they put you on a train and brought you to Siberia, to the Yenisei to break ice. This is what I was told. Either a neighbor told me this, or it was told to me in my sleep. My Moses, breaking ice. I told myself I would never imagine it. In my dreaming, however, you are there, night after night, the child you, swinging an axe into the frost. Year after year it never changes."

She takes me by the hand. We climb a staircase that passes between the rain-soaked evening of a small town at the crook of the Elbe, and also through the rooms of this house where I spent my boyhood. My mother asks me to move her mattress, which I do, and then she asks me to lift the wood beneath the mattress frame, which

I do as well, and she says that while the neighbors' curses have stolen her walls, and also the roof, they have not found her hiding places, and once I have done all this, once I have lifted the mattress and lifted the wood off the floor, she takes a small white box from the place where she has kept her most important documents, and from it, she takes the newspaper from the day on which we were shot. What she has secreted away is the official photograph of all of us before the protest at the train station, but instead of finding myself vanished against the wall of the train station, as I always have, I find that not only is Žofie there, running forward in the moment just before she is shot in the leg, and not only is Ambrož already dead on the concourse ground, but I am there as well, running after them, where before I had not been, and where—this is clear if I hold the picture close to my eyes—a bullet is about to explode into my shoulder.

From across the room Ambrož tells me not to worry.

"If I did not know better," he says, "I would say that someone in the propaganda office took it upon himself to inform your mother of what you could not tell her yourself. In a way, he did you a favor, this man. How else could you have fled the country if you had to stop and tell your mother why?"

A serious question: What do you call a joke that a ghost makes?

Ambrož tells me all this with a version of his smile that I understand as a silent form of pleading. What he is saying is this: Do not make more of this than you need to, Moses. Do not misconstrue this small derangement of history as anything more than a single picture. Remember where you are, his smile says, remember what city you are in, and what city you are not in. What he is saying is that if this was in New York, then your shoulder would already be bleeding, but since this is Prague, you will simply live forever now with the nightmare of having both been shot and not shot, and this is a fine substitute for the real thing. This country birthed the Golem, he is saying to me, and in a country that births the Golem, all manner of the unbelievable should be believed. He closes his eyes and puts the flat of his palm against his stomach, and in this way I understand that he is right, that years ago I searched this entire city for a picture like this, and that now I have it. "Stop asking for so much," he says. "Look around you and accept what you have."

At this, my mother turns to me. "Are you going to introduce me to your friend?" she asks. "Or are you going to just allow him to follow us from room to room?"

Ambrož responds in wordless confusion, as if to ask my mother if she is really talking about him. My mother sees this as well.

"Yes," she says, "I'm talking to you, young man. Announce yourself! Announce yourself or begone!"

WHEN I call Žofie in New York that first night from my hotel to tell her all this—about my mother, the walls and roof of her house that are coming apart piece by piece, and about Ambrož, who I tell her is beside me in the room from where I'm calling, as if this were thirty-five years ago—she tells me that she's been expecting my call.

"I knew that when you arrived you would need to talk to me. For good reasons, Moses, and for bad reasons too." She says this calmly, as if I were one of her students and I've answered some important question incorrectly. I can see her in her apartment, against her large windows with their automatic curtains and their views of the enormous American bridges that I love. "I was tracking your flight on my computer. My Lord," she says, "the abilities we possess now. I saw you aloft first over Newfoundland and over the Cliffs of Moher and over Calais and over Silesia and naturally I thought of my mother, who traveled in a donkey cart from Novograd-Volhynia to Prague on top of a basket of turnips to sell, a journey that took weeks, Moses, and required, at the end, on some far edge of the Vltava, that she and her family leave their donkey, who had served them for many years, wandering alone in the brush. It was a very sad story. For my mother and the donkey."

"This is not helping me," I tell her.

"You do not want to know about my mother's donkey?"

"No one will ever say yes to this sentence," I say.

"It was a very good donkey," she says. "And it lingered, like any good member of the family, on the outskirts of their life for many years."

"For some reason I have come back to Prague," I say. "Either to see my mother. Or to bring my ghost home. Not to listen to this story."

"Do you hear the words coming out of your mouth, Moses? You've been back in Europe, what, five hours? And already you have turned into a crazy person. Taking your ghost home? Is that what you just said? You think you're being kind to your illness, but you are instead just being ill."

"I do hear the words," I say. "I know I sound ridiculous. But here you are, talking about donkeys. As if this will help me."

"Why couldn't you fly your mother to America?"

"She wouldn't take the ticket. This was the only way."

"When I met you," she says, "you were so smart and so serious. The young version of you would never have done this."

"I remember," I say.

"You memorized poems."

"I did no such thing."

"All day you were memorizing poems. You believed this would assist our cause. You said this to me on so many occasions. If the Soviets hadn't confiscated my diary in advance of their attempting to execute me, I could read to you from all the entries I made in which you said this. You were always saying, the way out of this terrible mess is to convince our neighbors of the truth. All we need is to recite them the best poetry. This will convince them of the errors of subscribing to an idiotic political ideology. As if they ever had a choice. As if I was about to get out of bed and recite Russian poetry to a bunch of drunk and violent communists."

"This version of me sounds quite dreadful, Žofie."

"You were very stupid, yes, but you were also very adorable," she says. "You had this ridiculous haircut. You looked like someone whose mother had kept cutting their hair far past the point where it was acceptable."

"This is not the reason I've called you long-distance."

"Another thing about my mother," she says.

"I don't know that I have the time," I say, "or the currency."

"My mother used to go every month by train to the outskirts of the city to try to find her donkey," she says. "Far into adulthood she used to do this."

"Žofie, I feel quite badly for your family's donkey, but I don't see how this is related."

"My mother used to tell me, Moses, that she saw this donkey everywhere in the city. For instance, she saw this donkey once on a school trip to Karlštejn Castle, just wandering alone on the hill by itself. She tried to scale the walls and flee off into the woods to try to find him. Here she was, my small Russian mother, still in her shtetl coat, telling her firm old Czech teachers, in her bad tongue, that there was a donkey wandering in the country."

"Žofie, I am protesting this story. In the name of my telephone bill, I protest."

"I am trying to tell you, Moses, that just because you see it or hear it does not mean it is there. This goes for ghosts, or sad stories from one's mother, or a house that may or may not be coming apart piece by piece."

"I was in the house," I say. "It's not an illusion."

"But, Ambrož? Are you still talking to him? How long has this been going on now, Moses? You may not be intelligent, or very well educated, or even halfway decent at a dinner party, but you were, at one point, a respectable man."

"I'm so glad I called you," I say, "for this burst of confidence."

What I don't say to Žofie is that my mother saw him, that she saw Ambrož, and that she spoke to him, and that while he did not speak back to her, it would be, going forward, nearly impossible to pretend that he did not exist—as Žofie has. Nor do I tell her that the reason I've come is not purely out of generosity, but because my mother spent all her remaining money to hire a man to find me.

What I do tell her about, however, is the newspaper photograph.

"This is not possible," she says.

"I saw it with my own eyes, Žofie."

"Then your eyes have become confused. Which is not surprising," she says, "because you have become clinically unwell, my friend. It is not unusual in these cases to see people, things, donkeys even, that are not there."

"I thought the same thing at first. It's not the case, however."

"Someone in the ŠtB has very likely spiked your drink and you've gone mad, Moses."

"The ŠtB is gone, Žofie."

"Now you're really talking nonsense, Moses. The spies are never gone," she says. "You, of all people, should know this."

"Ambrož saw it too," I say. "He will tell you."

"I am not going to get on the telephone with your ghost, Moses. I am not cosigning to your hallucinations."

"The bullet was right against my shoulder."

"And how does your shoulder feel now?" she asks.

When I lift my shirtsleeve, I find it for the first time. I have, all at once, a small tattoo made by the Soviet Union in the form of a scar.

"Oh my Lord," I say.

"Come on, Moses! You are smarter than this! Don't lose it! Especially not in Prague! Remember your life! Your real life! Remind yourself of your sanity!"

"What happens if I lose it in Prague?" I ask. "Does the Golem come up and take me with him to his clay underkingdom?"

"No, you idiot," she says. "It means, Moses, that I have to come and get you."

My mother's grocery cart is gone. Someone has stolen it. The neighborhood boys, she says, who are venal and wicked and who, she is positive, will meet a vicious and ugly end in one of the worst circles of eternal damnation—the neighborhood boys have taken it. She draws a diagram of hell with her fingernails in the hardwood of her dinner table, and it is a corkscrewed vision, a Yiddish-speaking version of Dante's afterworld. "Here," she says, pointing at the dead center, the heart of the whorl, "here is where they will live. Put all the boys of this awful village in the middle of the end of the world. In the dead center of hell, one is lashed by the fire of every outer ring of lesser hells, which makes eternity ever the worse. Some of this is the presence of fire, which is unpleasant, of course, but also because of the proximity to a place that is not hell. If one is always circling heaven but cannot get inside, what other kind of torture could you imagine? This is what life has been like here."

Or maybe it is the neighborhood girls who have taken the cart. My mother cannot say. "The girls are also dishonest and cruel," she says, "and they sing songs about me on Friday nights when they think I am in synagogue, as if there is a shadow of a synagogue left anywhere near here, as if I cannot hear them, as if I do not understand their language, as if I have not spoken this language since before their mothers were born, as if in school I was not given a medal of commendation for my elocution, for what my teachers called a profound mastery of the Czech language. In their songs I am a toad, this is what they call me, a toad, ropucha, because I am hopping from room to room. Yes, I hop. Not because I am a toad, but because there are holes in my floor! What do they want? They want an old lady to fall through the floorboards? Is that what their life has turned into? Another group of blond women waiting in vain for the hilarious death of an elderly Jewish woman? It is one of them, I am sure. All of them will fry in the underworld. I am sure of it. Hell to all of it!"

"Maybe," I say, "we should leave the eternal damnation to God."

At this, Ambrož laughs.

"Your stupid ghost friend is laughing," my mother says. "Don't waste your breath," she says to Ambrož. "Everyone knows that ghosts only have so many breaths left. Eventually you will die too. Don't think I don't understand you. I see you," she says, "I see you, I see you, I see you."

"But there is nothing to see, Mama. There is no ghost here," I say.

I have come to think that this is the best way forward—to pretend for my mother that he is not here, and to tell Ambrož to keep quiet, which, apparently, he is having trouble doing.

"Is that what we are telling ourselves today?" she asks me. "That there is no ghost here, Moses? That there is no man sitting in the corner of my house wearing a black leather jacket, smelling of cigarettes half a century old? Is this the fiction we are serving this afternoon—that you are not attended to by the dead?"

"There is no such thing as a ghost," I say.

My mother walks to the corner where Ambrož is sitting and runs her hand around the outline of him.

"You think I have lived all this life, Moses, without having a friend or two, or a lover or two, or a child or two, or a rabbi or two or three or four, following me around as this man is following you around? You think one lives a long life in this village, which is a village of mass murder and torture and eternal curses, without some trace of death lingering?"

"Why don't we go get you a new grocery cart," I say.

"Why don't you go next door to the neighbor's house and light the roof on fire," she says.

"I won't do that," I say.

"Why don't you stop trying to calm your mother's very legitimate concerns and do something useful: go desecrate the neighbor's vehicles for me. Do it for your mama."

"Mama, there will be no desecration."

"Ah, I see: the neighbors get to desecrate my house, my grocery cart, but my son can't do this simple thing. Is that what you are telling me?"

"Mama, I'm here to see you, not to desecrate anything."

"In my dreams, I waited for you, Moses, and when you came back, you were always the young man with the long hair who left me here, and in those dreams, you did whatever I wanted: you enacted all my ideas of vengeance. If I wanted you to light a little roof on fire, one measly little roof, on one tiny little house in a corner of a country no one cares about, you always said yes. Whatever you want, Mama."

"In real life," I say, "you get something better."

"And what is that, Moses?"

"You get me. A reunion of impossible dimensions. You get the real version of me—someone who will not light a stranger's house on fire. Or desecrate their car."

"Explain to me, son, how is this something better?"

My mother walks to the space where there used to be a window, and where there is now half a window, half a pane of glass, half a spider's web, and all of the afternoon. She puts her head through the open space and yells at the passing schoolchildren, first in Yiddish, the old curses—may you have a hundred houses, and in every house a hundred rooms, and in every room twenty beds, and may you contract a furious fever that drives you from bed to bed. Then she says it in German, which is her language, then finally, in Czech, where it sounds positively wicked, this levying of a death wish against small children.

When I tell her this, she looks above her for help—at the ceiling, at the firmament through the ceiling, at the day shadow of Sagittarius.

"Every week since the day you were taken, Moses, I pushed this cart to the market for food. Now you are back, miracle of my life, and these immensely stupid creatures next door have taken my cart. I am not the best human being who ever lived," she says, "but I do think it is not unreasonable for me to ask for more than one good thing to happen at once, without having bad things also visit me. Would it kill God to allow these two basic ingredients of life— a child *and* a grocery cart? Could I have some joy without suffering some misery?"

"I will get you a better grocery cart. I'll buy you one that moves on its own. You won't even have to push it."

"No robots, Moses. You trust a robot to push your groceries, eventually the robot pushes you."

"I will get you a replacement, then," I say. "You tell me which one you want, and I'll get it for you. I have money," I say, showing her my wallet, which is, for foolish reasons, for reasons of doubt and insecurity, overloaded with American currency.

"Look at you, a rich man," she says. "All this time, you were accumulating American money, and did you ever think to check whether I was really dead? Or to maybe send me back any of your American money? Did you ever think to send someone for your mother, Moses, to see if, perhaps, she needed a house, a freezer box full of food, a radio dispatch telling her that her son had survived? Oh, Moses, Moses, Moses. Wasn't I a decent mother to you?"

I DECIDE to accost the neighbors. There is a version of this town tattooed in me, but it is not this version, which is whisper quiet, manicured with winter cabbage, which is ready for its tourist post-card, which does not feel populated by death, and where, in the chestnut trees, there are starlings in song. I remember no birds in my childhood. I think it is the case that the war killed them too. I tell this to Ambrož, who is behind me, always behind me, and who tells me that he does not feel well, which is something I have never heard from him. I am not under the impression that ghosts fall ill, I tell him, to which he responds that he was under no such impression either. Every few steps, he winces, and it is like, he says, the bullet in him is trying to wake up. He is holding his stomach. It must know where we are, he says.

"Your bullet knows where you are?" I ask this out loud, just as we cross a line of high school students running out from an alley. My talking like this to Ambrož, which is to say, to nothing at all, is not something the teenagers miss.

"Look!" one of them says. "The old man is talking to the air!"

He is small, a redheaded boy in Nike sweatpants, in Air Jordan sneakers the color of coal. He is maybe sixteen or seventeen, and he is carrying a silver mobile phone. When he stops to tell me that I am crazy for talking into the thin air, he takes my picture, and when I ask why he does this, he tells me that he is doing a project in school about the twentieth century, and that he was going around trying to find the Jewish graveyard and that I am the first Jewish person he has ever seen in this town. "We see Jews nearby, in Terezín," he says, "because Jews like to take vacations to the location of their own deaths. But not here. Not in our town." When I ask how he knows I am Jewish, he laughs, and his friends, who have emerged from the alley to surround him, laugh as well, and now all of us are laughing, me included, I am laughing somehow, for some reason, and there are now maybe fifteen young men who have formed a circle around me, and I am, not for the first time in this town, the center of a circle of this sort of laughter, and the one with the camera, who has not stopped photographing me, begins to explain that he knew right away. "First of all, you look like a Jew. This is obvious. Second, there is a smell in the air, it smells like brine, and this is the hallmark smell of the Jew: like salt," he says, "vinegar and onion and mustard seed and herring. All of us know this is the case. Our fathers have told us, and it is in our schoolbooks. It is the smell of the ocean. This is what the Jew smells like—they are always coming and going, slipping past boundaries, moving diamonds, and because of it, they are always bringing with them the smell of the sea. This," he says, "and of course the smell of money!" This makes everyone laugh again. The main boy goes on. "One can always tell when our koruna is handled by Jews, because the smell is there. All you have to do is smell the coin, and if it has on it this brine, we know it is a Jewish coin. And this is lucky," he says. "We collect these coins."

"Ask them," says Ambrož from behind me, "whether they believe in ghosts, ask them," he says, "I will make their hats fly off their heads." But I don't do as he says. Instead, I ask about the grocery cart.

"The woman over there," I say. "In that house. The one that is falling apart. Her grocery cart is missing."

"What woman?" asks the boy.

"The woman in that house," I say.

"The house with no walls?"

"Yes, that house."

"The house with no roof?"

"Yes," I say, "that house exactly."

"The pile of stones that used to be a house?"

"Yes," I say, "that one."

"There is no woman in that house," says the boy. "No one lives in the house without walls or a roof."

"Yes, there is," I say. "She is my mother. My mother lives in that house."

This is the funniest thing said all day. The laughter rebounds across the main street of the village. The laughter is so raucous it very well may travel up and force the church bells to ring.

"Your mother is living in that house? Ah, the Jew is crazy! The Jew is crazy!" Soon, all the young men are singing and dancing around me, as if it is both my bar mitzvah day and the day of my death: *The Jew is crazy!*

"Understand this," says the young man, who is still photographing me: "There is no woman in that house. There *was* a woman in that house. But she has been gone for a long time. Her son appeared one day from nowhere, and he took her back with him wherever he lived. He was very rich, just like you. On the day she left, we were made to go in black suits with torn ribbons pinned to our lapel and stand on the road as if it was a funeral. It was the case that she had no family but this very small rich American man, and we were made to feel guilty about this: we had killed her children before we were even embryos. Her grocery cart has sat outside that house ever since I was born. It rusted into the earth. When we were young we tried to move it, and no one in this village could do it. The cart glued itself to the ground like a tree root. So if someone succeeded in moving it, then that person needs to be made king. And if there's a woman in there who's talking to you," he says as he takes my picture one last time, "then you're seeing things, and that means you're crazy, the Jew is crazy, the Jew is crazy. Does everyone hear me? The Jew is crazy!"

W<small>HEN</small> Žofie comes on the line, she says right away, "I'm going to need to come save you, aren't I?"

"Stay where you are," I say. "I'm fine."

"You sound as fine as I sound when I try to exercise, Moses."

"Žofie, I'm fine. Prague is fine. The newborn Czech Republic is fine. Europe is fine. The future is fine. The European currency experiment is fine. I mean it. Really, I mean it. I'm fine."

"That's precisely what I told the first doctor I had in Morocco," she says, "who saw the bullet in my knee and explained that because of the way it had landed inside me that it might, at any moment, decide either to explode or travel north to my heart. Which was, of course, not exactly sound medical advice. Or at least I don't think it was. The doctor may or may not have been pretending to be a doctor," she says. "I did not have very much money to pay for medical care. This is not the point, though. Let me ask you a question," Žofie says. "Is Ambrož there with you?"

"As a matter of fact—"

"Your ghost," she says, "has he been by your side this whole trip?"

"Of course he has. He goes with me everywhere."

"He goes with you *everywhere*?"

"Everywhere he goes, I go."

"You can leave him, you know. I did this. Years ago, when I saw him, I refused him. This is the proper way to handle being haunted."

"He is not haunting me," I say. "He's my friend."

"And your invisible friend," she says, "have the two of you been carrying on conversations?"

"It would be rude not to," I say. "Especially since he's traveled here with me. Especially since he, too, has thoughts and feelings about this place."

"Thoughts and feelings," she repeats. "Thoughts and feelings. Like a real boy."

"Oh, I see. You want to make fun of me also? Being accosted on the street by a gang of preadolescent fascists was not enough for one day?"

"I keep wondering whether you are Geppetto, or whether you are Geppetto's toy."

"He is very real," I say.

"And also very dead. I know this because I watched him die right next to me."

"I thought you were dead," I tell her. "After all, I saw you shot. I saw you die. Then you knocked on my door in New York, very much alive. And here we are talking to one another."

"Oh, Moses. What has happened to your brain?"

"My brain is the same brain you have known all this time."

"Here is some advice," she says. "Maybe until you are back in New York, resist talking out loud to your friend. Especially in the presence of children. Also, especially in the presence of adults. Basically, what I am saying, Moses, is not to do this in the presence of anyone. Not in Prague. Not in your mother's village."

"He is your friend also."

"The man who died thirty-four years ago? That friend?"

"Yes, exactly."

"At least in New York there is a great tradition of talking to oneself. People won't assume too much of you if they see you on Columbus Avenue carrying on conversations with nothing. In your mother's small village, this is a bad idea.

"Tell me," she says, "what is he doing at the moment, what is Ambrož doing?"

He is, I tell her, asleep on the daybed in my hotel room. What I do not tell her is that I have never seen him sleep. Nor do I tell her that I don't think that he has ever slept, not since the moment he woke in the station square with a bullet having run through his stomach. When we arrived back at our hotel, however, he told me that he felt quite tired, that it must have been the shock of being back here, or the jet lag, because he had an overwhelming desire to sleep, a desire, he said, to be put into bed with a blanket pulled up to his neck, a desire for the comfort of a childhood that was only returning to him now. This was something Ivan would do when he was sick, to cocoon himself, something Ambrož thought was as childish as it was adorable, but now he felt this same pressing urge.

The initial idea was that I would help him find Ivan. This was only an idea, however. I knew nothing about how to make this happen. Nor, it was clear, did he. I have no map of the geography of ghosts. Whatever map Ambrož thought he had turned out to be false. He had thought that once he arrived in Prague, he would vanish. Or that when he arrived, Ivan would find him, and that he and Ivan would vanish together. On the airplane, he had told me as much, and all across the Atlantic, he paced the aisles of the jet in preparation for what he had described as his eventual disappearance. He had imagined it, he said, not unlike paint being stripped from a brush. "I used to love to watch Ivan clean his brushes," he told me on the jet, where we were somewhere aloft over the Atlantic, which out the window was nothing, something we could not see, also something that occupied all that we could see, the convergence of everywhere and nowhere. "We were always awake deep into the night," he said. "Mostly on account of his job, his father's company, his father's onerous idea of the future, which was a future where Ivan would rise to chairman, where he would marry the daughter of one of his father's colleagues, or one of the party officials, Veronika K., for example, who had modeled fur stoles in her youth, and who, at the age Ivan would have been expected to marry, suddenly immigrated to Montreal, in order, she wrote sometime later, to escape a life in which she turned day by day into wallpaper—inert, unfeeling, unnoticed."

On the plane, in the aisles, it was clear Ambrož did not want to go. "I do not like the world of the dead as much as I liked the world of life, but, Moses, what other future is there?"

He is dressed, I could have told Žofie, as he is every day of his death, as he was on the evening before he was killed: in a black leather jacket and his black pants, inside of which, I know, are all his poems, stitched to the lining.

What I tell Žofie instead is this: "He is happily asleep. He has been quite tired. After all, he has been dead a very long time, and death is exhausting."

And what Žofie tells me is this: "You say you're not seeing things, Moses. Listen to yourself! He is not there! You are all alone! You are all alone! Tell yourself this: you are all alone!"

I T'S not as if I am not guilty of this myself," says Žofie. "Everywhere I go," she says, "even now, I see the face of the soldier who came into my apartment house when I was a child. It is my first memory, this horrible, violent, viciously ugly face, and then, as if excised from the filmstrip, merely a pair of hands, which are gloved, which are always gloved. They take my mother by the back of the head. This image appears in isolation, disconnected from any setting or background. How does one ever forget this? Every day I see that heinous nose, those immense and vile eyes. What he did to my mother's head—how does one ever forget this? It is the case that all through history we have been ridiculed for our noses, our beautiful Jewish noses, but it is also the case that the man who came to slay my mother had the ugliest nose ever put on any human being. The nose was so large, Moses, it could have supported a family of noses. This nose, which was the capital of a nation of smaller and no less heinous noses, it likely required special care, this was how especially terrifying this nose was. This nose was so ugly it ought to have had monuments built in its honor. What I'm trying to say is that his nose needed its own passport, it was so large and ugly. She knew him all her life, my mother did. This man who came to take her, this man with the nose, she had known him as a child, they had studied in school together. In the last minutes, she said this to him repeatedly. 'Gregor, I know you, I know your mother, we played together as children, please don't do this!'

"Imagine," Žofie told me, "remembering this so often that it becomes visible enough to seem real. When I am not seeing the face of pure evil, I find instead that terrified moron who shot me outside the train station. I had seen him training his rifle on me, Moses. A redheaded man. Does he imagine me still the way I imagine him? In his death, which I am positive is a wretched and endless death filled with torment, filled with ugliness, can he still find me? And I encounter the faces of the boys who came later and put the white sheet of death over me, and who left me in the concourse of the train station so that I might frighten anyone who would think to challenge their muscle. I frequently see the faces of the boys who put me in the back of the hearse, and of course, I will forever see the face of the man in the morgue who, when he took the sheet off me, lunged for the hand of God when I got up off the table and told him that he had never seen what he was seeing, 'do not trust your vision, Citizen,' that I would be leaving now, that I wished him and the whole country a terrible future. This is just my life in *Prague*," she said. "I've told you nothing about my life in Spain, the boat I took across the strait, the men on the ferry who understood that I was traveling in costume, who saw underneath my layers of clothing that I was an imposter, that I was traveling this way because I was running. And I have told you nothing of Amado, who comes and goes in all the rooms of my life as weather, who brings with him music, which is sometimes real, and which others can see and hear, and which is more often not real, not in the room with me, but which is as loud as anything on earth—this is how I know he has come. The question, Moses, is not whether you are being followed by death, it is how often you realize you are being followed, and how you choose to coexist with this."

This business of my being haunted, she says, requires me to find something solid to hold on to, and when I ask what she means, she says that I need a stone or a lover or the rampart of a bridge or perhaps some blindingly powerful alcohol that might cause me to grab hold of the world. Or else I need to visit someone who can push deep into my body and excise the derangement. Years ago, she knew of such a woman, working in the basement of a hotel in Montreal, who did this for her. "This woman, she was a pain artist. A genius at pain. She took me by the limbs and undid me. This is what you need. Someone like the woman I met in Canada, in the snow."

"The last thing I need," I say, "is a pain artist."

"When I was in Prague last," she says, "and Ambrož began to appear everywhere around me—I refused him, as I told you. I understood that it was not so much that he was surrounding me, that it was my memory of this place that had decided to upturn itself and appear where I could see it. I thought this was obvious. For you, apparently, it is not. This is a process," she says, "which replaces one's idea of life and in its place builds a false model of the world, a world in which there are no boundaries, where my voice, for instance, might appear in your ear out of nowhere. Your voice came to me in this way when I was alone in Tangier. For instance, this might happen to you while you're walking alone on a street in a city where no one from your past ever had the opportunity to visit, say, Miami Beach, or Montreal, and you might see your mother in the sun, or your sister in a train car, and all this might drive you to the brink of your own sanity.

"It is likely what is happening to your mother. She thinks her house is coming apart and that airplanes and birds can pass overhead and see straight down onto her small head? It is more likely that she is, in her very old age, being picked apart by memory.

"This happened to me," Žofie says, "when Amado was disappeared. He had gone from Tangier to Zaragoza for a concert. This is where I spoke to him last. A very brief and lovely conversation. It was snowing in Zaragoza. He had opened the windows of his hotel room. 'It's inside on the carpet,' he was telling me. 'I have snow in my house, Žofie!' He had seen snow only four times in his life before this, and they were, each time, memories of great happiness, so much so that he understood the appearance of snow as an auspice. Which is a beautiful word, the word *auspice*—it comes from the Latin and refers to someone who observes the migration of birds. Which is what he wanted to tell me that day. When he saw snow first, he was on a train in the center of France, and he had just woken from sleep to see the weather in front of the great cathedral in Auxerre, and he believed the snow to be pieces of something terrific, like an airship, or a flock of waterbirds having been blown out of the sky. His mother had clasped his hands at the sight. This was how he knew what it was. They were traveling all of Western Europe in the hope of finding a teacher to train him to sing. Later on that trip, he would sing by himself for the dean of a musical academy in Vienna, the end of the Lacrimosa, accompanied only by his guitar, a performance that made the dean cry quietly to himself, for it reminded him of his father, who sang this on his own deathbed, just as Mozart did. It makes me glad, Moses, to think that Amado had this very happy memory, alone in his hotel, before he was taken from me.

"To think: snow on the carpet of a room in the shadow of the Alps.

"Amado wanted me to put Felix on the telephone," she says, "which I did, and I could hear, from across the room, my husband singing to my child. After this, Amado was to come to Tunis, to sing again in another concert, but at some point, somewhere, he was gone. On the day he was to return, I stood at the doorway of our small home near the medina, where if I stacked three large books, I could see the water. While he was gone, while I waited for word of him or sight of him, the crown of his head on the narrow street, the high reed of his voice, I continued to stack books outside the doorway—his favorite books—so that I could be raised higher and higher, and so that I might find him.

"It was the case that Felix knew before I knew. He was three years old then, and he told me, in the plainest speech, that his father was dead. We were in the doorway, he and I, and I had piled so many books up on the steps, a tower as tall as ten of me, from the top of which I could see all of our city, waking and dying, and where I could meet the eyes of the muezzin, and if I opened my arms I had in front of me the whole of the sea to Spain, which was clear of everything but the moon pull of waves. And he was gone. I knew it was so because I saw dozens of him below me on the street. Here was Amado on the morning he left me, on the morning before the morning he left, Amado on our wedding night dressed in a purple robe, here was Amado in his childhood chasing the great singers of the medina, here was Amado in the old age he would never reach, here was Amado in the window of the hotel room in Zaragoza calling his wife for the last time to report something I see ten times a season now, and here, too, was Amado in the underworld clinging to a picture of his son made of smoke.

"How had my son known? I wanted to know. A year later, we buried an empty coffin in the ground in back of the synagogue where he'd been named, and there, surrounded by lemon trees, I asked Felix, and he told me that he knew because his father had begun to appear to him on the edge of the water to tell him it was so.

"'Tell your mother to climb down from her tower of words,' Amado said to Felix.

"When I asked Felix if he believed this or not—my Felix who was only a child—he shrugged, as if to say, does it really matter what I believe, Mama?

"What I'm trying to tell you, Moses, is that this Ambrož is not real, not as real as you are real, and that this newspaper of your mother is not as real as you worry it is, the injury to your arm is not real, and that just because you found yourself erased once does not mean that you can exist in two places at once. Do you understand what I mean?"

And when I ask which two places she means, she laughs quietly and says to me that I cannot be both dead and alive at the same time. "Only great geniuses have that ability," she says, "or great monsters, and I am both sad and delighted to tell you that you are neither dead nor by any stretch of the imagination a genius. And you are far too sweet and simple, Moses, to be a monster."

This, I know, is a joke, or at least half a joke, and because I don't laugh, she grows worried. She tells me that I sound very tired, which I am, and that the first thing I ought to do is to sleep. "Ambrož had the right idea," she says, "even though he is not real."

"I've been trying to sleep," I tell her, "but it's impossible here. Either I am left awake or I am run over by nightmares. In my dreams, I am the one who is shot, the one in whose body the bullet is left, and you are all the ones left wondering whether I am real or not.

"What do I do?" I ask her.

"Are you going to bring your mother back home to New York?"

"I think I will try."

"Did you tell her about Eli?"

"Not yet."

"Did you bring pictures of him?" she asks.

"Of course," I say.

"Then show her the beautiful pictures," she says. "When you do, she will come. People always go where the fruit is."

I must wait too long to respond, or I must let loose some awful and involuntary noise into the receiver, because she tells me she is worried.

"Oh, Moses," she says, "you do not sound very good."

"I'm here," I told her, "and I thought it would feel okay to come back."

"I know," she says, "that there is no good comparison. You are home, and also not home, and you have the map of this place memorized but also cannot find your way. It is a terrific shot to the soul to feel this."

"I keep waiting for you to come around the corner," I say.

"I am quite far away," she says.

"Will you come?" I ask.

"Not for every dollar in New York, or crown in Prague," she says.

"I will pay your fare," I say.

"You would have to send the secret police," she says.

"Do you have the number for the secret police? I can call them for you and see if they are free for the job."

"Moses, I am afraid if I came back I would either get myself arrested or somehow I would turn into a secret police agent myself—and root out all the people who would not help me when I needed it."

"You would make a very good secret police agent," I say. "With all the languages you speak—they could dispatch you anywhere."

"They would never take me," she says. "I am far too forgiving. And far too easy to convince. If I got a spy in my grip, it would not take much for them to talk their way out of arrest."

I'm quiet for a long while, and in the intervening minute or two of silence that grows between us, a city bus arrives outside my open window and it honks twice with its Soviet-era horn in such a way as to scare the mass of pigeons flocked on the road, which in turn causes a great mass of wing chatter, so many thousands of pages of a great book being flipped backwards in search of the perfect passage, and beyond that, a woman across Vězeňská begins to play on her bagpipe the melody of a folk song I have not heard since I was young, and beyond the grief-yawp of the bagpipe, a tour guide is leading a group of Germans around the small bend at Dušní past the hidden front of the Spanish Synagogue, which is a museum now that there are no Jews left, and which is flanked by police officers, because even though there are no Jews left, not really, there is still a desire to ransack and torch and defile buildings like this, and what the tour guide is saying to the group of Germans through a bullhorn loud enough for Žofie to make out clearly is that this is a beautiful street, a famously beautiful street, don't you think so, can't you imagine, she is saying, walking here with your parents in the fine weather?

My mother is packing her belongings. When I ask her where she is going, she tells me she is going off to find me. She has waited far too long, she says, to be waylaid by imposters.

"But I am here," I say.

"Not the real you," she says.

"I am the real me," I say.

"No," she says. "You are mistaken."

"I am quite sure I am not mistaken, Mama."

"You seem to me to be a very nice boy," she says, "a very kind and sweet person, but you are not Moses. I paid the man to find Moses, but he brought back the wrong person. Or perhaps you are *a* Moses, or someone's Moses, but you are not mine. That is clear now."

Above us the afternoon has carved another hole in the roof, and from here the sky over the village has turned gray and wind-bothered and marked by beech leaves.

On the floor in front of us is a large steamer trunk into which she has put a pile of sweaters, and also a photograph album. "Here," she says, showing me a picture of a child I have never seen before. "This is Moses," she says. "This is the real Moses."

"No," I say. "This is not the real Moses. That is not me. I don't know who this is."

"He's Moses," she says.

"There are pictures of me in this book," I say, which there are, hundreds of them, pictures of me at every age, in the costume of the small Czech boy I tried to be, in painted smiles. "Look," I say, "this is me. This is Moses."

"You are a close facsimile, but you are not the real thing," she says.

She buries her hand deeper into the trunk and puts in front of me the newspaper photograph in which I am about to be shot, and the moment I see this, I feel my arm begin to throb, and beside me, where Ambrož had been standing, he begins to groan audibly, and to say in English that he is not feeling well, and my mother hears all this, she very clearly feels in her arm that my arm is hurting, and experiences all this as a further proof that she must leave.

Before she does, she takes my arm, lifts the cuff of my shirt to my elbow, then up to my shoulder, to see if there is a bullet in my arm, or if there is any marking, which there is not. What had been there only the day before—the circular scar, an imprint not unlike a kiss—had vanished.

"You were shot," she says, "they told me you were shot, they delivered me the newspaper that showed you being shot, the radio told me you had been shot, and yet you show no sign of any injury. Which is how I know you are not who you say you are. My Moses was shot. My Moses was taken by the Soviets by bus to break ice. My Moses languishes still in the Yenisei. My Moses was not living as an American in New York.

"See him," she says, "swinging the axe. See him frozen in the ice."

She points at the picture. "Everyone wants to tell me that what I am seeing I am not seeing. First the townspeople tell me my house is fine, that the walls are not coming apart in layers. Then the children tell me that I am not even here, that I am already a ghost, that all my life in this village I have been dead. Then you—you tell me I am not allowed to see what I can very clearly see."

I attempt an explanation, although I know there is no explanation that will prove sufficient for my mother, who has begun to haul boxes down the staircase. I follow her through the house, up one story and down another story, in and out of the rain, through reed grass, beneath alder limbs that have begun to grow overnight through the dining room, through puddles in the kitchen where lily pads have begun to sprout, and I tell her that the real version of this picture has no sign of me. "In that picture, Mama, I was erased. I did not run. I was a coward. I saw my friends murdered and I did not run after them. I searched everywhere for evidence that this was not so. Censors in an office near Wenceslaus Square likely spent an entire evening removing me limb by limb and replacing me with bricks. If one cannot expel the saboteurs of revolution with politics alone, with the theater of oratory, with the paintings of the Great Men, with Stalin's imperial mustache, with the suit of the dead Lenin replaced once a year, then one sends tanks, and conscripted redheaded boys with Kalashnikovs that resemble exactly the toys they played with in the apartment blocks of Leningrad, and if that does not take, Mama, one sends the problem to the art students, the gaunt paint-flecked graduates of the imperial academy holed up in the censor's office, in the Ministry of Invisibility, the Ministry of Erasure, the Department of Spiritual Evacuation, the College of Lost Recognition. This is what happened to me. Since the Soviets tried to kill us and did not succeed, they erased any evidence that anyone had lived, that the army had failed."

She is already upstairs again when I tell her that I searched the entire city for proof that I had not imagined what I'm telling her, and that for months after we were shot and not shot I lived not far from here, and yes, I ought to have come home to her, but I knew they would be here waiting to arrest me, and that instead I went every afternoon through the train station in a borrowed suit and a new haircut laying stones on the graves of my friends. I tell her about the Soviet soldier who asked why I was doing this, why the rocks, why the rocks, why place rocks at all if the whole world itself is a grave, everywhere it is a grave.

"I need to leave," she says. There is a train to catch. And when I ask where it is she's going, she says Siberia, so that she can walk the entire length of the Yenisei, from the Kara Sea to Mongolia. "Or maybe I will go to Moscow and ask to be let into the state archives so that I can see your file. Maybe I will walk every block of every city I cross, searching for my son. I did it once, when I was young. Before you, before whoever you are pretending to be, I did this once. I can do it again. Or maybe I will find on the train some person to explain to me where I might find my child."

"Mama," I say, "let me take you back to New York."

"New York? What do I need New York for? So that I can trade my feelings for money? So that I can feel even smaller in the world? I want the opposite, fake Moses: I want to feel enormous. I want everyone on earth to see my face. Don't I deserve this? Shouldn't everyone have to see me? Stare into this face, world!"

"Mama, your great-grandchild is there," I say.

"I have no such person," she says.

"Here," I say, trying to show her photographs of Eli. "Here, meet your great-grandson. Elijah. Meet Elijah. Born two years ago. Born in a hospital on Central Park. Born in a beautiful room, surrounded by your family. Born already full of wisdom."

"If this were true I would feel it in all of my cells," she says.

"You don't feel it?"

"I feel nothing."

"He's real. I'm real."

"Explain to me how you are both here in the picture, Moses, about to be killed, and also that you are here, in this house, which is being made invisible day by day, and you are very clearly not dead, not killed. Yet you come to my house day after day after all this time with an actual ghost, who you pretend is not really there, as if I am a fool."

What is there to say to my mother about this? It has become

inexplicably cold in her house, and she is shivering in her sweater. The skin on her neck shows bird shadow. Above her, the daylight drops a momentary sheath of brightness so that she glows.

"Your friend," she says, "he is very clearly this man." She points on the picture to Ambrož's body, laid out on the concourse stones. Blood beneath him in the shape of the sickle, like every protestor killed by Soviet bullets. "And here he is," she says, pointing to the corner where Ambrož is standing, holding a cigarette that he will never light. "Your friend has not aged. Nor is he dead. Which means that it is time for me to leave. You must think I am a lunatic, or that I am blind, when the truth is that I have been in this terrible place far too long. Maybe you understand this, whoever you are, maybe you don't. I never even intended to stay here. I had other ideas. Everyone always has other ideas. Never forget this, Moses. If your life has worked out according to plan, then you had very bad plans. And if you think this is not so, and that your plans have worked out fine, then you have had a very bad life. I was supposed to go to Vienna. Or maybe to London. I was never supposed to stay in this village. Can you imagine? A life spent here, becoming less of a person every day, less and less, staying in this one house waiting for my son to return, day into day into day, until finally all the walls begin to disappear, and the roof disappears and my grocery cart disappears. As if it is not enough that God takes my family—my husband, my children. Then there is this: one last test. A version of my son, but one who is not my son."

She goes upstairs and then downstairs. We follow her, me first, then Ambrož, who is whispering in English that he is becoming sick, that he feels as if he is sweating. "Is it possible, Moses," he asks me, "that I might be sweating, or that I might actually be sick, is that possible?" In the remainder of her fireplace, she lights a bundle of sticks on fire. She has a box on the floor, into which she has stuffed all the important artifacts of her life—correspondence, photographs, her undeposited reparation checks from the German government. "This way," she explains, "no one will follow me. If you burn a letter from someone who is dead, then the sender cannot come for you." When I ask how she knows this, she shows me her arm. "If you were to cut me right now, and count the inside of me as if one counts the inside of an oak tree, you would lose count, Moses. That is how I know."

We watch this, Ambrož and I, for some time. My mother burns everything. She burns everything in the box. The fire is steady, and remarkably undiscerning: whatever my mother wants to vanish, it vanishes for her. Then she burns the box itself. She smashes her dining chairs against the wall and burns the legs and the cushions. She shakes loose all her tea into the fire. She takes her radio, from which nothing but bad news has ever played, and burns it. She burns the curtains on her windows, and when she does this, we see that the village's teenagers are peering in. *The Jew is lighting the world on fire!* they cry. For hours this happens. When a piece of the roof comes loose, she is happy to light it on fire.

In the end, she drags her trunk to the fire. "Now I can finally go," she says, putting into the fire the newspaper that shows me being shot. When she does, Ambrož grabs hold of my arm. It takes a moment to understand that this is the first time I have felt him since he was alive. And when I turn to see him, he has split in two.

IN room 412 of the InterContinental Prague, Ambrož speaks from opposite corners of the room. It is midnight, a drunken hour, when the lights in our old life are on bright. "I need help," Ambrož says, on the left side of me, on the right side of me, in Czech, in French, in German, in Russian, in English, as if I have also split, and that along the way I have forgotten how to hear him, and as a result, I hear him in every way. At first, the words arrive at the same moment, both versions of him rebounding in synchronicity, until they do not. "I need help, which one of me is the real me, Moses, what do I do, what do I do now?

"Perhaps all these pieces of me," he says, "will be lucky to meet a minister somewhere in this other-heaven over Prague, someone who is also splitting infinitely, splitting, splitting, into pieces of himself, and maybe this priest will help me, Moses. Perhaps there is a single benediction one must receive to stop this. Some powerful prayer. Holy Father, full of grace, please grant my soul, both of my souls, all my souls, all my future souls, peace from division, peace in the underkingdom, in the after-heaven. Amen," he says, and he says it out loud, with all the volume a ghost can muster.

The two of him are, for a brief moment, mirrors of one another, until they are not. The Ambrož on my right, who is, I think, the original Ambrož, stands up while the other Ambrož, who is no less a version of my friend than the part of him standing on the side of me, continues to sit. "Isn't that the way it always is?" this second Ambrož asks. "In American movies, isn't this the way it always is, Moses? When one becomes distressed, all one needs is the kindness

of a single Christian prayer to become repaired. Do you know one
for me? Have you learned one living in your big Christian country?
Or maybe it is the case that I will find myself a good rabbi, Moses.
Maybe I will come across any number of the thousands of rabbis
who are also somewhere on the earth's edge of this city, these rabbis
who we burned and drowned and shot in the brain and stabbed
through the breast and flung from the roofs of our buildings while
they were holding their children, whom we wrapped into the scroll
of their holy text and buried alive with the words of God—maybe
one of these men will help me."

"I can help if you tell me," I say. "Just tell me. Whatever it is."

"Oh please," says the second Ambrož, reclining in my bed, his
head on my pillow. "What could you possibly do?"

"I don't know," I tell him. "I can try to help. Just tell me what
to do."

"You don't know because the answer is that you can't help! Look
at me," says this second Ambrož. "Look at all of me! This part of
death is not advertised, Moses! This is quite obviously the punishment I get for all I did in my life! The Soviet Union has died, and
now it is quite obvious that all the old Soviets are running the world
of the dead! It makes sense, doesn't it: What other more perfect
Marxist utopia exists than the world of the dead, where all of us are
equal? Who else but the Soviets would devise a hell like this? Why
would you ever send a man to Siberia if you could just wait until
death and then split his soul into pieces and make him watch his
own ghost coming apart? I would not be surprised if Brezhnev himself was in charge of Prague's afterlife! Or if the KGB had a branch
of their service that oversaw all the souls of the dead. They are coming after me again! This is the truth. All the ghosts of every secret
policeman are after me. Look what they've done to me!"

"This is not what's happening," I say. "Don't be foolish."

"I am a ghost, Moses. I have been a ghost far longer than I ever was a man. Has there ever been a more foolish thing than this? All I ever wanted to do was to walk with my boyfriend in public and now I am a ghost! Or better yet: I am two ghosts! The fact that I am in the position even to say this ridiculous sentence aloud is punishment enough."

"Tell me what to do," I say.

"Moses, you could barely do the easiest thing for me. You couldn't even buy an airplane ticket. I told you to do this and you did not. For two years you did nothing. Two years! You couldn't even go on a simple vacation for me. Look around you. Prague is no longer forgotten by time. We are no longer some benighted medieval backwater. We have commerce and visitors and souvenir shops! Look how modern we've become! Everybody wants to come to Prague now! The Communists are gone, and look what's happening. Can you even count all the tourist shops? Have you seen what is inside for sale? What our money-hungry friends and brothers are selling? Toy Orloj clocks to put on one's shelf in one's library in Milwaukee! A coffee mug with the castle painted on it! T-shirts with Kafka's face spread across the belly! What more Kafkaesque thing could ever be imagined than this! In Kafka's afterlife, he appears on T-shirts on the stomachs of fat Belgian tourists! This is what he spent all his time up in his bedroom for? All his labor over his manuscripts and this is what he gets? This is what I was shot for?

"Everyone is coming here for fun!" he says. "Imagine that: fun! Never in the history of this city has this word been uttered more intently, more frequently than now. Can you believe this, Moses: Fun? It's fun these days to live in Prague! The castle is fun! The medieval gloom is fun! Not for you, however! Not for Moses! All you needed to do was to buy a ticket for me and come and have some fun," he says, and he is about to ask why this was so hard for me, which is a question he knows the answer to, a question he knows both dead and alive, and it is the case, I understand, that even the dead can become so consumed with anger that they lose track of the truth, and the words linger on his tongue, his dead tongue, and these words accumulate so much weight that he exhales—an impatient exhale—and it is the first time, I realize, that I have seen him breathe, actually breathe, and when he does, the weather changes. Suddenly, the room grows cold. Outside, the others in the city must feel it too. Perhaps everyone thinks it's nothing but an errant gust of wind, strong enough to extinguish a cigarette.

At the window, the first Ambrož offers a different explanation.

"You want to know the truth, old friend? Here it is. Ivan is gone. That is what has happened. In your mother's house, Moses, I understood the truth. She was burning her belongings, and it came to me in the same way that all the rules of the dead have come to me. He is not here any longer. How this happened, I don't know. The Americans were afraid he was contagious, and so they burned him, cremated him into a million pieces of himself. What can anyone do about the perpetual stupidity of your country, this enormous, flagrant, ballooning, endless, hideous, poisonous stupidity? His illness was such that even his corpse worried your government. In your mother's house, I saw all this. I saw, for instance, how he was brought back home in an urn, a metal box inside a sealed coffin, this is how terrified of his death your country was, how terrified of his body your people were. While your mother burned her letters, her dresses, her roof tiles, her dining room chairs, her bedsheets, I saw all of Ivan's friends scattering him everywhere in the city—on the river, in the Modřany Gully, inside the empty statue of Kafka's suit. There are pieces of him everywhere. Two years' worth of pieces. And because of this, I will eventually be everywhere. Someone must have put a piece of him in the earth near this room. And here I am. Here we are.

"Maybe this is why I've split," Ambrož says. "Maybe this is what you are seeing when you see two versions of me. And it is the case that I would rather all of me disappear at once. If you want to help, try to help me disappear. Try to help me disappear for good. You will want the same thing when the time comes. No one wants to die piece by piece."

THE next day my mother's house is empty. I enter through the front door, which is half a door, and find only the vanished front hallway, through which reed grass grows, and where there are marsh frogs dreaming in the daylight. The neighborhood teenagers have been here. Their names are carved on the wall, along with painted taunts that tell me that they are the real owners of this place, they always have been, and moreover, they own this village, this nation, our language, which I cannot speak without haunting it, without it haunting me. Up the stairs, in my childhood bedroom, the windows onto the river are gone, and in their place there is only the air of the afternoon settling in vapor above a bend of the water gone mostly dry in the summer, and beside which the neighborhood girls lie on their backs in the sun with their T-shirts hiked to warm their stomachs.

When I was young, my mother told me that a window onto a river is a window onto everything that river touches: this town, the town beyond this town, eventually the great sea, the boats on that sea, the men and women in good fabric inside ship cabins decorated too loudly listening to someone play the piano with too much feeling, and also the stevedores on the opposite shore working amid snowfall, New York it always was, winter on the brim of their caps, fire in barrels along the shore arranged in the shape of a moon that very well might match the moon above this window.

As I write this, my grandson is asleep beside a window high above the shoreline my mother imagined nightly. He wears pajamas the color of tangerines. This evening, I drew for him on the back

page of the newspaper a map of the Hudson so that he could understand where the ships go when he lost track of them. This is something that interests him, the movement of boats, which he takes care
to measure with his finger pressed against the glass, the imperma-
nence of perpetually impermanent objects. The prospect of the current freezing in such a way that the lapping waves might somehow
end up captured for a season—this obsesses him. I asked him where
he thought the boats went and he thought for a moment and then
pointed up into the sky. "There," he said. His mother and father
laughed, but it was not such a terrible answer.

From my childhood window, my mother's footprints are visible
in the mud until they are not. Outside, I trace her to the village bus
depot, where the neighborhood children greet me with their
cameras—*The crazy Jew returns! Watch the crazy Jew try to purchase
the remainder of his memory! Smell the ocean on the coat of the crazy
Jew!*—and where I find myself back again at the river, where, beneath the clear glass of the water, there are guppies exploding into
life, and where, steps from the town cemetery, where her mother is
buried, and where her mother's mother is buried, and onward like
that just as in Genesis, I find my mother's shoes and her heavy
sweater and her hair clips arranged on a makeshift fisherman's dock.
It is unlike her to have left a note, and so I don't look. I am to understand she has gone into the water.

Ambrož confirms my suspicion. Both versions of him, in fact,
do this. He trails me in pairs, and then, by the river, he becomes ill
once again, complains of fever in a voice that is two voices, a synco-
pated stereo, sits in the grass, where his feet—four of them—linger
amid the high reeds, and while I watch, he becomes four, and very
quickly, he doubles again, and within the hour the entire riverside is
filled with him, so many that I cannot count.

"My friend," I say, "what is happening to you, what did I do,
how can I help?"

I have lost my ability, however, to talk to him. Even though he has swarmed me, can meet my eyes, he has no voice.

Then I say, "Can you tell me where my mother has gone?" I point at the Elbe, which runs like an arrow through Bohemia until it dumps into the North Sea. "Where is she?" I ask. "Where did she go? Where is my mother? Where is my mother?"

There is, however, no answer. Instead, one by one, these versions of Ambrož fly away from me. The whole flock of him moves skyward, as if on account of some great noise beyond the reach of my ears. It's something Eli would have drawn for me if he could.

At some point, the village children see me talking into nothing, shouting after him, yelling for my friend, yelling for my mother, and once again, the village is full of song: *What did I tell you, the Jew is crazy, the Jew is crazy, what did I tell you!*

Ž OFIE arrives the following afternoon. At the airport, she takes me by the hand, like a child, directly to the ticket counter so that we can fly back to New York. "I am not spending one more moment in this city," she says, both to me and to the confused man to whom she has given her passport and her credit card and to whom she has given instructions to put us both on the earliest flight back to America—"any city will do, it does not matter, Columbus, Des Moines, Fort Worth, any place, any airplane, at any time, but make it America, please, any inch of America, give us any odd inch of the USA, any place, any place."

"Being here this long," she says to me in German, "I can already feel my skin burning hot."

"This isn't something one normally associates with bad memories," I say, also in German, but she is, as always, unmoved by my attempts at reason, or merely at the way my German has slackened after all this time, the way I sound as if I am from nowhere, as if I am imitating a young version of myself. She grips my hands like a pair of handcuffs, as if to tell me, you have gone quite obviously insane, Moses, as if to say, I warned you about this place, this museum of morbidity masquerading as a city, I warned you about your obsession with ghosts, your optimistic conviction in European progress, your deliriously misguided idea in the eventual safety of the Jewish people, as if to say, here I am, old friend, taking you back home, as promised.

When I ask about the children and Eli, she says that she told everyone that I broke my leg. "Felix and Martha—they wanted to know what devil had possessed me that I would willingly buy a ticket to return here, and so I told them that you had fallen while drunk and broken your leg and that I was the emergency contact on file with the State Department, and thus the only person legally allowed to collect you. I suppose it is our fault that we raised children stupid enough to believe this."

"You told them I broke my leg?"

"Yes," she says. "I told everyone you got very drunk and hurt yourself. The drunkenness is important. It confers some critical spiritual collapse and emergency. Which is not entirely inaccurate, if you ask me."

She continues. "I needed to give them some excuse as to why I was coming. After all, Moses, I'd told my son a hundred times that I would not come back here under any circumstances, that I would not return to Europe at all unless I was driven there against my will, and that I would not return to this country unless I had been rendered unconscious while being driven against my will, and that I would not ever come back to this city unless I was slowly being burned alive while rendered unconscious while also being driven against my will, and that if I was, somehow, discovered in this city, it was because the ghost of Brezhnev himself had wormed its way through the thin sheet that separates the world of the dead and the world of the not-yet-dead to arrest me and finally finish me off. The only other reason I would ever go back, I had told Felix, was if I had suffered some rather unfortunate but legitimate psychological event, in which, for instance, I was seeing the ghost of my mother and the ghosts of my dead friends. Given what I am doing, and where I am standing at this moment, and given the air I am breathing, this is quite possibly true.

"Also," she says, "one broken leg is a nuisance. Two broken legs is a real problem. Which is why I told everyone you had broken both of your legs."

"Both of my legs?"

"Anyone can limp their way onto an airplane. Try doing that with two broken legs."

She then slams down on my foot with the heel of her boot.

"You may have actually just broken my foot," I say.

"Not badly enough," she says. "We'll need to break it before we get back home. Maybe your hotel has a hammer I can borrow. Also, we'll need to do something about your other leg. I told the children you fell from a tram car."

The man behind the counter seems appropriately alarmed by this conversation.

"Not to worry," I tell him. "We are very old lovers."

"On a different planet," Žofie says, "we were lovers. But we have long since left that planet."

I had called her the night before from room 412 of the Inter-Continental, standing at the window where the Jewish Quarter lay beneath me crowned in light and glass and silence and where there were no Jewish people. I had lost both my mother and Ambrož, and I told Žofie, in the plainest way I could describe: "I've lost my mother to the river, and I've lost my ghosts, each one of them." When I was finished, she told me to stay in one place. "Do not even make a telephone call, Moses. Do not go outside for one moment, Moses. I will pack a bag and come to get you," she said.

"I didn't mean to alarm you," I tell her now.

She does not let go of my hand, not in this moment, not while the man behind the counter explains that he cannot get us out of Prague for two days, some forty-nine hours from now, there is bad weather, there is a volcano erupting, there are twin cyclones circling over the Atlantic, there is widespread mechanical trouble on all transcontinental jets heading to America, there is a global strike of baggage handlers, the Jewish-controlled aerospace commission has made it so that this story of ours needs continuing, there is a

mandated waiting period for Czechs who fled the nation under aus-
picious circumstances, for people with bullets in their knees the cost
is extra, for people separated by gunfire it is the case that you cannot
board, not today. She holds me as we walk slowly, so slowly, to the
pair of electric doors opening and closing on the afternoon.

I worry that this is not enough time to do all I need. Forty-nine
hours is nothing. I try to say this to her without saying it to her, and
she understands.

"The dead will do fine on their own, Moses," she says. "They
always have. Either they keep living in the world of the dead or they
will ruin us trying to make us hear them."

SHE holds my hand until we are at my hotel. "This is not necessary," I tell her in English, this hand-holding, which is, of course, wonderful, even amid the circumstances of my potentially having lost my mind. "I speak very little English," she says loudly, too loudly, a way of mocking her own accent. "Deutsche vielleicht? Čeština? Française?" This terrible joking is her reaction to the city she must not recognize, and which, at the same time, she must not have been able to lose from her memory. When our car takes the eastern edge of the Royal Garden, where Chotkova rises to reveal the spires of the castle complex, I hear her breath catch and collapse—celebration and chastisement: a reveling in the beauty, or a reveling in the reaction to a memory of the beauty, or perhaps, a passing experience of breathlessness in the presence of her mother having for an instant come alive again. Then the chastisement: to feel any of this, to see any hint of her dead mother, to believe at all in the fictional and poisonous idea of beauty, which is an idea that ultimately disappoints everyone.

So there is this: her hand-holding. A job to do.

"Here is what will happen," she says as our car approaches the hotel. She speaks in Yiddish, which is the only language guaranteed to evade eavesdropping. An old trick from when our life was filled with microphones. "When we arrive," she says, still holding my hand, "you will eat something. You will eat, preferably enough for two people, then you will bathe. You smell horrid, Moses. It degrades me to have to say this sentence aloud. Our good driver here will have to fumigate his car, the poor man. In your unraveling, you

have forgotten hygiene. So, you will bathe. Then I will give you a
sleeping pill. A good sleeping pill, manufactured by the great scien-
tists of America, guaranteed to bring you into tomorrow. When you
wake, we will repeat these steps: eat, bathe, sleeping pill. Two days
from now, I will deliver you to the airport, to your seat, to your
apartment on the West Side, where our children will complain
about your broken legs, which, do not forget, will need ultimately
to be broken.

"What you will not do, Moses: tell anyone about what has happened here. Nothing about Ambrož, nothing about your supposed
mother. Ghost stories only eventuate one outcome in America, my
friend: the institution. Your daughter still thinks you are a good
man full of sound judgment. A dutiful member of your synagogue,
a doting father, a man who for Christ's sake plays racquetball! You
don't want them to have to visit you in a hospital in some far-flung
American suburb, some old man in a rocking chair, murmuring in
German about invisible men splitting into thousands of other invisible men. Nobody wants to see that happen to you."

When I begin to protest, she quiets me. "You have lost your
mind. Absolutely lost it. Probably years ago. Probably in small
pieces. Thought by thought. But it is lost. This is not anything to be
embarrassed over. You held on, all things considered, remarkably
well for a long time. You had a hard time. Nobody would say otherwise. I should have interfered long ago—when you first told me
that you had made friends with Ambrož's ghost. I should have involved myself then."

"Maybe you are right," I say. "Maybe I am already gone."

"Forty-eight hours," she says. "That's all. Can you last forty-
eight more hours in this city without cracking, without running
away?"

We are crossing the Vltava when she says this, on our way into
the old city, which is, at dusk, lit from the ground up, so that the

shadows of the people in the narrow causeways emerge in gigantic forms onto the old stone walls, projections of projections, and where on the sidewalks we pass university students bundled against the quickly cooling evening, one of whom, I think, very well may be her, very well may always have been her, or always is her, I do not understand how time functions, or what remains of us when we leave, or how cities remember us if they do at all.

"While we're here," I say, "don't you want to go out into the city? After all, you've come all this way. You don't have any place you want to see?"

"No, Moses."

"You may hate this place as much as I hate this place, but we can go see anything you'd like. There's no shame in being a tourist for a day. Would you want to do that?" I ask.

As we drive in silence, she seems to consider it.

"There's no shame in saying yes," I say.

From a restaurant atop the Golden Well Hotel, Žofie traces St. Vitus onto a cocktail napkin. "I used to do this drawing exercise in Tangier, over and over," she says. "Mostly, for entirely sentimental reasons. You know: to keep the city with me, as if I would forget, et cetera, et cetera. It's terrible to admit this, but I would draw all of Prague on top of a newspaper. Or onto a receipt from the cleaners. It's not as if I didn't have photographs to look at. I could very easily have gone to a bookstore or a library and found travel manuals for Prague, the sort they sell to potential tourists, everything glossy, every corner filled with latent adventure and undiscovered culinary gems, but I liked my drawings better, because my drawings were bad, or they were warped by the pain I was feeling, the physical pain in my knee, and in this way the city looked real to me. Maybe even more real than it does right now," she says.

We had come to the restaurant after visiting the castle, where she had wandered slowly out onto a part of the concourse that overlooked the hillside and the Vltava and where, I hoped, she had whistled for her mother's lost donkey. As she returned, I tried to see her the way others might see her, as a rich tourist, a woman with a cropped bob of immaculately white hair, a woman with a periwinkle-colored cashmere coat, someone with a pronounced limp, someone decamped from one of the hundreds of buses that clogged the access roads. It is not unreasonable to say that I had always been in love with her.

She stopped to take a picture with her phone, then walked a few steps, then took the same picture from a closer vantage. It was, I would come to understand later, a version of the picture everyone took of this city: the layering of bridges curving around the bend in the river in such a way as to imply that they were in fact not bridges at all but bandages keeping the two halves of the city from drifting off without one another.

At the restaurant, she orders for us—smoked salmon sandwiches, chilled Sancerre that arrives in a gilded bucket, a dessert tart with glazed boysenberries that looks as if has taken three people to construct, and which, I am sure, cost more than two months of our rent the year we were killed and not killed. We are onto the dessert when she tells me about the police.

"I've called the local dispatch about your mother," she says.

"Oh," I say.

"I've told them that there is a chance that your mother has thrown herself into the river."

"I see."

"I told them also that the business with the river was potentially untrue. That I was traveling from America with this woman's son, who was suffering—this was the word I used, Moses, I hope you're not offended."

"I understand," I say.

"I told the police that if she were found, in any way, that we were wondering if we could see her."

"That would be good."

"I told them about you," she says. "You know, the terrible stuff."

"My personality, you mean?"

This makes her smile. "If only it were that easy," she says. "Your childhood, I meant to say. Don't make me spell it out."

"You don't think that she's real," I say. "You think what the schoolchildren said is true. That she's been long gone."

Žofie will not answer. There is food to stab at, cathedrals to draw onto napkins.

"I didn't have a picture to supply them with," she says. "In the case of missing persons, they like to have photographs. Do you have a picture?"

"No," I say. "I don't have a picture."

"You were with her in her house all these days and you didn't take a picture?"

"I should have, shouldn't I?"

"Yes, Moses. Obviously."

"I was happy to see her. It had been such a very long time. And also, I was concerned that she was in such a state."

"Well," she says, "let's hope we find her."

"What did the police say?"

"My conversation did not exactly engender confidence."

"This happens whenever you start telling people about my personality," I say.

"They have boats," she says.

"I see. Because of the river?"

"They mentioned that sometimes it takes several days for bodies to come to the surface, or for bodies to come to a crook in the river where they get caught on trees or some other impediment. As I was describing the situation to them, it became clear to me that this was not the first time they had faced such a situation."

"I understand," I say.

"I'm sorry to be so graphic."

"It's a graphic arrangement."

"I had to tell them the facts, and I feel I should tell you what they told me."

"I hope it does not come to that," I say.

"Also, I've called a car to take us to Ivan's memorial."

I do not look up at her when she says this.

"I worried overnight about indulging this fantasy of yours, this mental abyss you've found yourself flung into, but in a few hours we'll be on a plane, and then you'll be back home in New York, in your real life, with your daughter, with your grandson who is marvelous, and who is real, real, real, and I don't want you wondering about this place any longer, or anything you might have done, or wondering about the emotional state of Ambrož's various ghosts. Or about your mother's location, God help her soul."

For a long while we say nothing more, and I watch while Žofie finishes the tart and the wine, and while birds circle the castle spires in clockwise convolutions, until some subsonic signal commands each of them to shoot upward, dozens of them at once, in immaculate synchronicity, where they hover for a moment aloft on a current we cannot feel, then begin to fly in the opposite direction.

IVAN is buried in a small cemetery near his parents' house in Střešovice. We arrive by way of taxi, and by way of a short drive through suburbs transformed by time and communist ideas of urban renewal, alongside Line C, with its red trolley cars gliding unevenly along tracks laid into the mowed grass.

His headstone is small—only his name, the dates of his birth and death. Around him are members of his family, aunts with lovely names: Britta, Lara, Gabi. It is afternoon on my last day in Prague. Žofie stands off to the side, amid the looming ornaments of other graves. The wind is bothering her hair. This is how I will remember her: at sixty, mildly irritated by the atmosphere, against a row of ivied crosses, resting her bad leg on the tomb of a stranger. I will tell her this, some years later, as she lies dying in a hospital bed overlooking Manhattan, from which she will tell me, in a language that is a combination of all our languages, that she has always imagined the moment of death as an explosion. Look for me, she will say; look for me everywhere.

I crouch beside Ivan's grave, which has been mowed recently, and which gives off the hot and rancid scent of hay. I had met him only once, at a Christmas party in his father's very large house, where he told me he was planning to defect, to jump out the window, he had said, which I understood to be code. One hopes, he said, that the landing is not entirely awful. He told me to take care of Ambrož once he was gone. "Can you do that for me, Moses? Will you? He is younger in his soul than he looks." Ivan had been wearing a leather jacket that was a twin of Ambrož's jacket, and I remember that he had the habit of smiling very widely when our conversation fell silent, as if he found his own mild discomfort, or my own discomfort, over our silences to be enormously amusing. "Once I'm gone, check in on him every once in a while. Will you?"

The idea comes to me before I have an opportunity to consider its futility. I take the poem Ambrož gave me in New York, which I have had in my wallet for two years, and unfold it to the air, turn it so that the words are facing down, and bury it in the earth. Or, more accurately, I make an attempt to bury it in the earth. The ground has other ideas. The soil here is too hard to move with my hands. I try nevertheless, thinking if I move faster, if I claw at the ground with more speed, then I will have better success.

When Žofie asks what I'm doing, I tell her that I'm leaving something for him, and she asks incredulously if I mean Ivan, and when I say yes, of course Ivan, who else, this is where he lives now, Žofie says that I ought to just leave a pebble on his headstone like a good Jew. But there are no pebbles on the ledges of any of the headstones in this cemetery, just as there are no Jews left to put pebbles on the ledges of any headstones.

It seems impossible to admit exactly what I am doing, that in burying this poem, I hope to bury Ambrož as well.

"The ground is hard," I tell Žofie. "I can't get into it."

Žofie stands over me. "What are you doing, exactly?" she asks.

"I'm burying him."

"Burying him how?"

"I think this will work."

As I try fruitlessly to get my hands into the earth where Ivan is buried, all the various fractions of Ambrož's ghosts return to me. One of Ambrož's ghosts, or all of them maybe, implore me to get it over with. Do it quickly. Have mercy on the dead. It is the case that he has split at this point into many hundreds of thousands of versions of himself, and that each version has contained less and less of him, so that he appears around me more as vapor than as a version of a human. Ambrož is saying something to me, but I cannot hear it, he is too faint, too loosely built around me.

Behind me, Žofie has her hands on my shoulder and is begging me to stand up. As she tries to console me, shield herself from the embarrassment of me, as she tries to get me back into the taxi that is idling in the parking area, I remember a conversation we had when we were very young, possibly a night during which we had contemplated defecting ourselves, a night when we'd wheeled suitcases into our living room and took turns attempting to fold ourselves inside them, or a night during which we had stayed awake writing our biographies so that when we were ultimately captured or executed or driven at great speed to Lubyanka in the trunk of a charcoal-colored Volga, where we were sure to have our names affixed to false confessions, that some part of us would remain—it was very likely on one of these nights when we had the idea to build a golem.

We were not far from the Old-New Synagogue, where is it said the Golem still sleeps in the hayloft above the street, just as he was left by his maker, Rabbi Loew, the Maharal of Prague, who first made the Golem, so says the story, to protect the Jews of Prague. Maybe we could see the windows from our windows, light the color of a holiday etrog. "He's asleep still, waiting to protect you and me," Žofie had said that night. "From whom?" I had asked, and she answered, "Oh, Moses, we have many enemies," and I remembered that she tapped her hand on the wall and made the hand signal we used then to convey that there were microphones in the architecture: our pointer finger drawing the letter $M$ in the air. Of course, she knew how to do it, how to build a golem, that is. "It is quite easy," she said, "but also quite dangerous: once we make life, we become the protector of the protector." We went sometime later to the banks of the river, and she stepped into the water so that it lapped at her calves and she plunged her hand in until she had a fistful of mud, it has to be this mud, which, in our living room, she used to mold a man, just as Rabbi Loew had done, and she told us how to bring it to life, how we were to inscribe in Hebrew the word for truth onto his forehead—emet—which, if we were to remove the first letter, the aleph, would give us the word for death, and thus take away his powers.

Ambrož was the one who wrote the letters onto the man's forehead. We waited, I remember, many hours. The microphones were listening. Somewhere in Wenceslas Square, in Moscow, in Lubyanka itself, men sat beneath Prima smoke transcribing our conversations about making life out of clay. Žofie was the one who said that it is possible we had done it wrong, although I knew we had not. If she had given the instructions, the instructions were correct. The truth was something all of us understood: no one would come to rescue us.

I'm thinking of this now, our failed and inept protector made of clay, whose body sat on our windowsill until we abandoned our apartment, who was very likely collected by Soviet inspectors, by Czech collaborators, by an army of plainclothes spies and informants, and who eventually was put into a landfill where he sleeps still, or who was, better yet, delivered as a child's affection to rest on the desk of the son or daughter of the man who took it, who upturned our home, and who waits still for it to be woken, who puzzles over the letters for truth, which are also the letters for God's favorite name.

The ground is too hard to bury the poem. Instead, I burn it. The idea strikes me and within moments the paper is lit. Ambrož is everywhere around me by this point, my golem made of poetry, who has been so sick in death, evaporating into versions of himself—and although I could have read the words in this poem he'd given me years ago in New York, and although I could have taken one letter from the word for truth so as to hasten the arrival of death, I do not.

HE goes, he goes, he goes.

THERE is one last thing:

My mother is waiting in our hotel room when we return. She wears a blue floral dress, a headscarf wrapped twice around her temples, fur-lined leather gloves on her hands in spite of the overwhelming heat of the room, and a necklace that she drapes on the outside of her sweater, onto which a pendant rests against her chest—a piece of wood fashioned into a small mezuzah. "If one has no house, one wears the house around in life," she says to me when she sees I have noticed. She says this in German—a language I have never heard her speak. She has with her a man about my age, who has come pushing her wheelchair, and who stands in the hallway beside a member of the municipal police. The officer speaks to me in English, which my mother does not speak, nor does the man. "I'm very glad your friend called us," the officer says. "We have a fairly large database into which we have entered the names of those who have registered the disappearance of their families. The registry exists in the hope that two entries will match—someone is looking for someone else who is searching for that same person. Does this make sense?" he asks me, and as he does, my mother begins to wheel herself closer to me, unbeknownst to her helper, and while I am watching her, she is watching me. "When your friend here called us," the officer says, "we put your name into the registry and saw that she was still with us." He lifts his chin toward my mother and says that she is physically fine, it seems, although she has not been back to our village in some years, and it is plainly evident that her memory is not solid. She is quite tired from the short trip from her apartment, which is only two kilometers from here, and where she is tended to by nurses. "Please do not startle her," he says. "Do not talk about the river. She quite obviously did not go into the river. We're not even sure who it was you were talking to in that village. It is possible you were dealing with an imposter—some impoverished person determined to exploit your generosity. Or someone cunning enough to have understood that there is always someone eager enough to believe in a story like yours."

When we are left alone, she and I, she pulls herself close to me and asks who I am supposed to be, and when I say that I am Moses, her son, she closes her eyes, as if to receive the news in darkness, and it is clear that she is a different person than the woman who I saw burning every item of her life in our living room, the woman who packaged letters into the satchel of a private investigator, and who called me home from New York. Either I have, as Žofie thinks, lost my mind or I have lived twice, lost her twice, and have now found her twice on different earths. I think of the Golem, asleep not far from here, and understand this to be its work: this is protection. Here is my mother, alive, cared for, without any memory of me.

"Let me see your hand," she says, and I give her my hand. "The doctors think I am unwell, but I am only unwell because of them. No matter what they say, I have still, for instance, all of my mind, every centimeter of it is intact, every one of its windows, every one of its telephone calls, its news dispatches, its airplanes, its murals, its bomb shelters, its sheet music for lullabies I played for my babies from my mother's piano. What else is a mind but all this?"

"I am very happy to see that you're well," I say.

"You say that you are Moses?"

"Yes," I say.

"I knew a Moses once," she says. "He was very young when I knew him."

"I know that," I say.

"But you do not look like him."

"It's been a long time," I say, "since I've felt or looked like myself."

"For one, you are an old man," she says. And then she laughs.

"That is true," I say. "Somehow that is true."

"Do you think we know each other?" she asks.

"Perhaps," I say.

"Wouldn't that be funny," she says. "To see one another again after such a long time."

"It would be," I say.

"Can you make yourself young for me so I might remember you better?"

"I am afraid I don't know how to do that."

"Oh, it is very easy."

"Will you show me?"

"You need to close your eyes," she says.

When I do this, she says that all she needs to do is to hold on to her fingers and that she will get a vision of me from childhood. "I have been able to do this since girlhood—to see people as children. It is not the sort of thing one can talk about in open company, but nonetheless," she says, "what is one supposed to do with the articles of life that do not fit cleanly into society?"

I have opened my eyes at this point and am watching her. Her eyes are closed still, and she opens her palms, one beside the other, as if anticipating my giving her a prayer book.

After a long time, she opens her eyes, which are dark brown, the color of battlefield mud, and says that I possess a passing resemblance to one of her sons.

"Yes," I say. "That's good to hear."

"A miserable story," she says.

"I've heard something about this," I say.

"Even now I cannot imagine it was ever true. It seems, day by day, to have been a rumor that I believed, rather than my own life."

"I have had this very same experience," I tell her.

"I am told that you were looking for me," she says. "You called the police on me! What excitement."

"We knew each other very well."

"Of course we did," she says.

"I was gone for a long time," I say.

"And now you have come back," she says.

"Exactly," I say.

"Your mother will be very happy to hear this," she says. "Very happy, indeed."

I take her hands when she says this.

"My son," she says, "he was taken from me. Did you know this?"

"I did know this."

"I waited for a very long time for him to come back. I bargained with God, using all his names, hoping for some trace of him. All I ever got, though, was my son's face coming to me in dreams. Or appearing to me in disguise. You have had this experience, I am sure: your mother's face in the tea leaves, et cetera, et cetera."

"Once or twice," I say.

"I used to work at the museum," she says. "Did you know this?"

"I did," I say. "I did know."

"I was very studious when I was young. People do not believe this. Mostly because I spent my adult life working with my hands, and there is always a bit of noise in the air when people who use their hands claim also to have a mind. As if it should be so surprising. All this was an inconvenience to my mother, who had arranged for my marriage to an older man, someone who would have made life unpleasant. *That* was someone I could never see as a child. All that man's life he had been old and terrible and malodorous. In the months before my wedding, I raced to submit my dissertation to university, hoping it would save me from a life I did not want. Apparently, my luck ran high that year. It was not unimpressive, my writing, that is, and then I got a job at the museum. It was the happiest day of my life. Because it meant I was free. You should have seen me, the way I ran back to tell my mother that I was on my own. I worked for the first year to buy my own dowry. This was my childhood: one foot in the old world, one foot in the city.

"Then I couldn't work in the museum any longer. A rule was passed."

"Yes," I say.

"I had babies by this point. Three of them."

"Three?" I ask. "Are you sure? Not just one?"

"Am I sure?" she asks, laughing. "Am I sure?

"When they wanted us dead," she says, "the Jews of my village, we did not have far to go. We could, if it were necessary, walk ourselves to the gates at Theresienstadt without very much difficulty. It was like a walk to the market. The Germans did not even need trucks to deport us—they just pointed. Near the end of the war, when the Danish Red Cross came to inspect the camp, I was hired to plant flowers on the roadside leading to the gates. Until this point, neighbors had hid me and my babies and my husband rather successfully. Then they were called away—these were their words to me, my friend's words, they were called away, as if friends had arrived with something better to do than to shelter me. After this, I was put to work in preparation for my eventual deportation. First, I was to make the road leading to the camp as beautiful as possible. A movie was being made, I understood, in which the camp would seem harmless, in which the imprisoned Jews of Austria played Verdi's Requiem for the cameras, a choice that evaded the idiot men making the movie, but which says everything it needs to now that they are all dead."

She pauses here to look at me, as if trying to place me.

"Are you all right?" I ask.

"Did I tell you," she says, "that my mind is still a perfect mirror, or what? I haven't lost anything. Don't you see?"

"I do, yes."

"Can I tell you the very bad part?"

"Of course."

"It is very bad."

"I know."

"But you seem familiar to me."

"And you are to me," I say.

"Also, no one wants me to talk about it. Especially now. No one ever wants to hear it."

"Tell me," I say.

"One of the men who worked beside me—very young, freshly volunteered, happy with the outfits, with the free liquor, the leather gloves—he came to my house not long after the visit from the Red Cross, and he climbed the stairs, and took my husband and my babies out into the street, and shot all of them one by one with a pistol his father had given him for his ninth birthday. He shot even my baby boy. His name was Rafael. The man was very drunk obviously, the boys were always drunk when they did this. My mother had told me this, and her mother had told her this, and eight hundred years of Jewish mothers had told their daughters this, and he was yelling, this boy was, he was yelling this fact about the pistol out into the street. His father had been bankrupted, his butchery had gone under, he'd had to dispose of hundreds of kilograms of pork, and this, of course, was the fault of the Jews, who had very obviously cursed the meat, and after this, he had purchased a small crop of land to grow grapes but the weather was dry that year and the grapes did not grow, and surely this unexplained trouble with the weather was the fault of the Jews as well, everyone understood that various international cabals were able to bargain with the weather makers, and after this the boy's father took his sewing machine and opened a small shop but his customers told him that he was quite bad at being a tailor, that the Jewish men could do what he did better and faster and cheaper, and this, of course, aroused his anger, and he tried to raise chickens but the chickens did not survive, all of them died at once, slaughtered at the necks, surely the work of a blood ritual, and now, look, Papa, he was yelling, look, Papa. You gave me a great gift, he was yelling, and now I have given you a great gift!

"I had been made to watch. Rafael had only been nine months old. After the murder, the boy had taken Rafael's body with him. For days, I searched for him," she says. "Maybe you have had children, maybe you know what I am speaking about, I went to every house, bribed the men in the graveyard, I was unafraid of consequences, I went to the gates of the concentration camp, I begged in my prayers for a bullet in my skull so that even my spirit could not remember the horror of the life I was given.

"A truck arrived in the middle of the night," she says. "Maybe this was months later. I had not yet been taken away to be killed. For some reason, they were leaving me to rot in my misery. It was always the case that when a car came near the house the building shook. I understood," she tells me, "that I was finally going to be murdered, either right there, or that I was about to be led to my murder, and so I submitted, I remember, I lay on the ground in Rafael's bedroom, and I prepared, I buried my face in the small rug on which Rafael had crawled to me, and where, I believed, if I pressed my ear deep enough into the hardwood, I could still hear his breathing in the underworld, and I waited, I waited, I waited for the end. There was a very long silence, a silence in which I was not killed, but during which I was not sure I did not die. The quiet grew to such an extent that I could not only hear the sound of this soldier breathing, but I could hear the blood in this boy's arms, the whole machinery of his young, idiotic body.

"What the soldier told me was that the boy who had killed Rafael was his brother—his bad, and foolish, and violent brother. 'He has been a problem ever since he was a child,' he said. 'He had always been a problem, always been a shame on the family, had never found stability until the war.' These were the words. 'We are all sorry,' this soldier said, 'me and my mother and my father, we are all terribly sorry for what our brother did to you and your children.' He could not stop thinking about this fact, that his brother had put a gun to the head of an infant, and because of this, the soldier had done what he thought he needed to do, which was that he'd brought me a child. He'd brought me a replacement boy.

"He had me stand up," she says, "and he brushed the dirt from the hem of my dress. He had a buttered roll for me to eat. 'Here,' the man said, helping me to stand. 'We are your friends,' the soldier said, 'do not fear. If you are still hungry,' he said, 'we will get you more food.'

"You need to understand," she says, "I had not eaten butter or fresh bread in over a year. He was smiling. This soldier was smiling and he was, I understood, very drunk, and when I sensed this I knew I was going to die, but then he lifted me up with his hands, which were clad in very dark leather gloves which stank of vodka, and he brought me down to the steps of my building, where there was a woman—I will never forget this woman—dressed entirely in white, and she was holding a basket. Both of them thought they had done so well.

"'Here he is,' the soldier said. 'Here is your new son. Delivered to you in straw and cotton, just as the holy book demands. Now you have a child again. Please forgive us. Don't say we didn't try to help you. Don't say all of us are evil men. I thought of you tonight when I saw this child. And now he is yours. So, good night, good night.'

"I kept thinking," says my mother, "who are these monsters, who plays this joke? What madness! What hideous madness? And then I was alone with this child. It was very late, very dark, almost morning, the streets were empty, empty, empty, except for me and this infant, who smelled of powder, whose cheeks were buttered with cream. On the back of the baby's jumper there was a tag, onto which his mother, his poor mother, his poor lost mother, had written his name. Of all the names in the world! They brought me a Moses in a basket. Do you believe this? Could you ever, ever believe this story? His name was Moses!"

# Separate Rooms,
# Separate Rooms

VIENNA, 2016

# ARNOLD

I WILL keep this short: you knew before I knew, whoever you are: she is not there. Or maybe it is better to say, I learned again what I knew before: she is not there. I am always learning this. They are not anywhere, any of them, which I knew already, and which I am forgetting and forgetting. Sonja, no small child, no grown woman, no person stepping off onto the railway platform at Vienna Central Station wearing blue and writing me letters from her life to my life, no shadow clinging to a doll calling my name as she does occasionally while I am sleeping, calling after me, Papa? Papa? What are we doing today? Have you heard from Moses? Have you heard from Mama?

TWO days in London I lasted. It is not worth a story. Better to say, I went on the train and I came back on the train and now I am home again, where it seems to be the fate of my being alive to learn constantly what I knew before. The newspaper here issues a corrective update: SURVIVOR IS FOUND SURVIVING ONCE AGAIN! At home once more, I keep my attic study warm. I play the music of my childhood. Above me, through the skylight, all of Vienna passes by: its airplanes and its greenfinches and its children's balloons. I like it best, however, at night. This is when the city makes its odd noises, its humming, its occasional howls of danger.

Maybe someone else might tell you, as they tell me, that this is what I can expect of the world to come, a changing vision of the sky, and out of darkness, a rush of gorgeous sound and all the important stories I missed. Maybe after this comes the great recollection of souls. For instance, the reappearance of the children taken from me. Or an ending to this story of ours, in which we find one another alive. My family: knocking at a door that does not exist and coming back into a life that has felt unreal for some time. Or maybe, the sound of everyone moving from one room to another. Maybe: I am still saying maybe.

On the way back to Vienna, my train stalled near Paris. An engine had given way. Smoke surfaced in a ribbon over all the train cars, and we were put on the edge of the tracks while snow fell and while engineers gathered near the smokestack. For an hour we were made to wait outside in a line near a row of chestnut trees. Soon, we were told, we would be picked up and put on a different train and taken on a different track and we would, they promised us, arrive home only moderately later than the scheduled time. Do not worry, the announcements told us, there is no reason for concern. For a time, we were separated from our luggage, about which we were told that we would be reunited soon or afterward or when we were moving again, on the new train, or at the end of our journey. Night grew close. I struggled to keep warm. Elsewhere, the sky betrayed the city glow of homes nearby, people in their comforts. At the end of the line of us passengers, I found a young boy playing the violin while his sister sang. Around them a small crowd of us gathered to listen. They were, the two of them, genuinely wonderful. At a certain point while they played, I realized that the people standing beside the tracks had begun to cling to one another.

How often this happens, I thought, when the goodness of life collides with the fear of life passing: we need so often to grab hold of one another, whether anyone is there or not.

WHEN we were put onto the train home, I found a book someone had left on my seat. It was an empty book, a journal left behind in error by someone I hoped had great plans for it. A whole life, I knew, could fit into a book like that, even mine. I held it for a long time while we moved east, first through Brussels, then across the Rhine, which at night in the snow had turned lilac, the color of electricity in a child's story.

I used to know a man who collected empty books like this. In fact, he filled a room of his house with these books in such a way that eventually he had a small library filled with nothing. I remember going once to see this room, which was on a high floor of a modern building with distant views. He wanted to show me some of what he'd collected, all these books that were different from one another, except that each of them was entirely blank. I asked him why so many of them, what does it all mean, exactly? His past was the same as my past, and we had been friends as younger men, although we never spoke of this, not the past or our being younger men: it did not feel useful to speak it, and as we aged, it did not feel particularly real to us either.

He told me what I have just told you, which is that a whole life could fit into a book like this. He took one of them from the shelf and he said, let me show you, and he flipped the pages near my ear. The sound of an empty book is wonderful, isn't it? One hundred pages, two hundred pages, everything empty, everything possible. He said he thought of the empty book sometimes as a prayer against the impossible. If you put your ear to it, sometimes you can hear it aloud, he said, because a prayer to the impossible is one of the loudest sounds on earth.

That's how it started for him, with this idea, although after a while, he told me, the sound of the prayer changed and he began to feel consumed with the idea that in one of these books someone had written the story of his family, and that he had missed it somehow, overlooked it, he had not paid good enough attention to the world in front of him. The idea came to him during sleep, he said. Or it overwhelmed him in an otherwise quiet moment, very frequently on airplanes, when he was traveling a long distance, almost always on transoceanic flights. He knew it was a false idea, he said, but the idea was that someone else, someone with a better vision of the world, had written everything he had no ability to write. And this story was here. Nowhere else in the world, but here in this house, in this room. I had been building this room without knowing why and, one day, on the airplane over the Indian Ocean, I arrived at the reason, he said. Somewhere in one of these books was a dispatch from the world of the dead. Occasionally, he was so consumed with this idea that he felt this was all he should be doing, looking for this book that very obviously did not exist, stories that were not real stories, a voice calling to him even though he knew there was no such voice, even though it was a loud voice sometimes, a voice calling out to him specifically, saying you, you, you. A voice sometimes he answered to. And this feeling, it was a truthful feeling, he wanted me to know, also it was a feeling very close to madness, a place where the world of reason came apart in pieces in his hands.

Maybe, he said, this is why on occasion he disassembled the books by the staples. This ashamed him to admit. All of what he told me, in fact, ashamed him to admit. He did it so that he could have all the pages spread across the room, a thousand pages in a scatter, ten thousand pages, a hundred thousand pages, all of them around him in this room where we were standing, with views over

Vienna, which is a view of the way history overlies the future. He took a book apart to show me. It's easier to see this way, he said, and when I asked him to clarify what he was trying to see exactly, all the pages were obviously and glaringly empty, he grew quiet, or better to say that he filled with quiet shame at the truth, which I know is a noise more deafening than prayer. He was a serious man, my friend was, and this was the most unserious he had ever allowed himself in my presence.

He began to spread the pages across the floor, across the armchair and the two green sofas and the bed where his dog slept and on the windowsill. Within a few moments, our bodies were the only space in the room not covered with paper.

Sometimes, when I do this, it is very quiet in here, he said.

And other times? I asked.

We were standing far from each other at this point.

If you put your ear to it, he said, sometimes you can hear it all calling.

Do you hear anything? he asked.

THE morning I return home from London, the newspaper is filled with stories of doctors transplanting organs. A man with a new set of kidneys beams the smile of resurrection. A woman with a new heart runs along the Ringstraße. I am new all over again, she tells the reporter, I can go on forever and ever. This is, I think, a better explanation for the lines in Isaiah:

> But your dead will live, Lord;
> their bodies will rise—
> let those who dwell in the dust
> wake up and shout for joy.

Lines that have obsessed me all my life. Lines the Talmud says I am not to take as proof of reincarnation. Yet the Talmud assumes I am smart enough to read the Talmud. What I need, I say aloud into my apartment, is a transplant. Find me a doctor to transplant my past. Undo the blockages, the occlusions, the collections of nightmare and injury and this great theft.

But I know the truth. Alone at night, with my empty book, I allow it into the room where I sleep. Slowly, I undo the binding. My friend is right and yet he is wrong also. Yes, they are loud, these pages, they keep me awake sometimes. Although the sound is not anything but the old noise, the others growing closer and closer but never appearing.

AT home again, a memory arrives.

Sonja has put up a show in our parlor, an opera of her making, in which we are all the stars, forced to sing in our awful voices, me and her mother and her. She has sold tickets along the Herminengasse while holding a sign that reads: MY SINGING FAMILY, COME WITNESS THEIR GENIUS! This must be very close to the end, for Moses is there, in the bassinet my father has bought for him, onto which Sonja has affixed a sheet of paper explaining that in the event of an emergency, he will perform as her understudy. DO NOT UNDERESTIMATE MY BROTHER'S VOICE OR HIS MUSICAL TALENT. To our surprise, the neighbors come. Fania sees them into our parlor, onto our sofa, where Sonja's stuffed bears occupy the good seats. It is the only time our neighbors have come to our house. It is in some cases the first time in many years that our neighbors have willingly engaged us in conversation. A man whom I knew in school claps me on the shoulders to ask how I have been managing, what with the news, he said, the news, the news, can you even believe the news? In the kitchen, behind the closed door, Sonja hands out the libretto. Did you write this yourself? Fania asks, to which Sonja offers a wicked smile. In the story, our characters are granted the choice of seeing the future, any future we want. If we are to choose different futures, she explains, we can never find our way back to one another. You've a written a tragedy, Fania says. We are in our kitchen when Fania says this, and Sonja regards this blankly, or she regards it with an expression of mischief. In my memory, both this blankness and this mischief; both versions of the past. Keep reading, Sonja says to her mother. To represent the entity granting our choice of futures, she has made two puppets out of her winter mittens and affixed to these mittens a pair of our reading glasses by way of a thumbtack. The resemblance is unmistakable. You've made new versions of us, I tell her. Look at that!

WHEN the opera is over, and I am putting Sonja to bed, she looks up to me, half-captured by sleep, to ask what I thought. It was terrific, Papa, wasn't it? You sang and people laughed and Mama sang and people laughed and we pretended to have Moses sing and all the people laughed, and it was terrific. The sheets on her bed have been made especially for her in my father's factory. She has them pulled to her chin. A border of golden-leaf thread lines the edges. This was my mother's idea, so that when one shined a light onto it, such as a candlelight, or a child's night lamp, the edges of the bed would appear to glimmer. When I showed this to Sonja for the first time, she understood immediately that she was on a ship, that in fact all beds were ships, that sleep was a way of moving one's body from day to day. Didn't you know this, Papa, didn't you?

Look, she says that night after her opera, can't you see the water moving? Can't you see it, Papa? Stand over there, she tells me, stand as far from me as possible and squint, she says, and it'll appear as if I'm asleep on top of the ocean, and you are far away on the shore looking for me. Look, she says, look. Can you see me? Can you?

## ACKNOWLEDGMENTS

While writing this book, I have been blessed to have been surrounded and lifted up and helped by so many people. Thank you to PJ Mark for your wisdom and good counsel, for your friendship, and for all these years together. Thank you to Pilar Garcia-Brown for your brilliance and for making this book real. Thank you to Sophie Jonathan for your great insight and for untangling what I'd tangled. Thank you to Mona Lang; thank you to Francis Geffard; thank you to my early readers, Megan Mayhew Bergman and Andrew Malan Milward; thank you to Kerry-Ann Bentley; thank you to Madeline Ticknor; thank you to everyone at Janklow & Nesbit, in New York and in London; thank you to Ella Kurki; thank you to Vi-An Nguyen for this glorious cover; thank you to Stuart Wilson for the wonderful cover in the UK; thank you to Stephanie Power for years of lucidity; thank you to Alice Dalrymple; thank you to everyone at Dutton and PRH; thank you to Camilla Elworthy and everyone in London at Picador; thank you to everyone in Köln at Kiwi Verlag and to everyone in Paris at Albin Michel for these years of support; and for the great gift of community, thank you to all my friends and colleagues and students at Bennington College.

And to Shamis, first reader, queen of queens, all-time baddest girl in the game; together on this earth, the next earth, and every other earth to come.

## ABOUT THE AUTHOR

**Stuart Nadler** is a recipient of the 5 Under 35 Award from the National Book Foundation and the author of two novels, *Wise Men* and *The Inseparables*, as well as a short story collection, *The Book of Life*. His work has been named a *Kirkus Reviews* Best Book of the Year, a Barnes & Noble Discover Great New Writers selection, and an Amazon Best Book of the Year. He is a graduate of the Iowa Writers' Workshop. He teaches in the MFA program at Bennington College.